Award-winni... avid reader h... managed to train as a nurse, marry her doctor hero and have two sons. Now she writes chapters of her own in the medical romance, contemporary romance and women's fiction genres. Louisa's books have variously been nominated for the coveted *RITA®* Award, and the NZ Koru Award and have been translated into twelve languages. She lives in Auckland, New Zealand.

Emily Forbes is an award-winning medical romance author for Mills & Boon. She has written twenty-eight books and in 2013 won the Australian Romantic Book of the Year for her novel *Sydney Harbor Hospital: Bella's Wishlist*. Get in touch with Emily at emilyforbes@internode.on.net, via her website emily-forbesauthor.com, her Author Page on Facebook or chat with Mills & Boon Medical Romance authors at loveisthebestmedicine.wordpress.com

Marion Lennox is a country girl, born on an Australian dairy farm. She moved on because the cows just weren't interested in her stories! Married to a 'very special doctor', she has also written under the name Trisha David. She's now stepped back from her 'other' career teaching statistics. Finally, she's figured what's important and discovered the joys of baths, romance and chocolate. Preferably all at the same time! Marion is an international award-winning author.

Second
Chance
Christmas

LOUISA GEORGE

EMILY FORBES

MARION LENNOX

MILLS & BOON

First Published in Great Britain 2021
By Mills & Boon, an imprint of HarperCollins*Publishers* Ltd
1 London Bridge Street, London, SE1 9GF
www.harpercollins.co.uk

HarperCollins*Publishers*
1st Floor, Watermarque Building,
Ringsend Road, Dublin 4, Ireland

SECOND CHANCE CHRISTMAS © 2021 Harlequin Books S.A.

Her Doctor's Christmas Proposal © 2015 Harlequin Books S.A.
His Little Christmas Miracle © 2015 Emily Forbes
From Christmas to Forever? © 2015 Marion Lennox

Special thanks and acknowledgement are given to Louisa George for her contribution to the *Midwives On-Call at Christmas* series

ISBN: 978-0-26-330276-9

MIX
Paper from
responsible sources
FSC™ C007454

This book is produced from independently certified FSC™ paper to ensure responsible forest management.

For more information visit: www.harpercollins.co.uk/green

Printed and bound in Spain
by CPI, Barcelona

HER DOCTOR'S CHRISTMAS PROPOSAL

LOUISA GEORGE

CHAPTER ONE

'ODDS ON IT'LL be the Pattersons. She was telling me the other day that she missed out on winning it a couple of years ago, so she's going to cross her legs until the twenty-fifth. No hot curries, or hot baths and definitely no hot sex for her.'

You and me both, girlfriend. Obstetrician Isabel Delamere tried to remember the last time she'd had anything like hot sex and came up with a blank. It was all by design, of course…working in a maternity unit was enough reminder of what hot sex could lead to—that and her own experiences. But every now and then she wondered…what the hell was she missing out on?

Plus, how could she possibly be lonely when she spent all of her waking hours surrounded by colleagues, clients and lots and lots of wriggling, screaming, gorgeous babies?

Sighing, she wrote *Patterson* down on the First Baby of Christmas sweepstake form and added her five-pound note to the pot. 'If mum has her way there's no way that baby's coming until Christmas Day. She's set her heart on the hamper, and between you and me they don't have a lot of money. I think she needs it.'

'I admire your optimism…' Bonnie Reid, one of

Isabel's favourite midwives—and new friend—at the Cambridge Royal Maternity Unit, added her contribution of a large box of chocolates and a bumper pack of newborn nappies to the crate of donations that threatened to overshadow the huge department Christmas tree and wooden Nativity scene. With a heavy bias on baby items, some gorgeous hand-knitted booties and shawls, and heaps of food staples, whoever won would be set up for the next year. 'But when I saw her yesterday that baby was fully engaged and she was having pretty regular Braxton Hicks contractions, so my bet is that baby Patterson will make a show well before Christmas Day.' Bonnie stepped back and surveyed the decorations, her lilting Scottish accent infused with wistfulness. 'Oh, I do love Christmas.'

Me too. Isabel dug deep and found a smile. Well, in reality, she loved being with her sister at Christmas; they shared a very special bond. This last year here in the UK had been the longest they'd spent apart, and the prospect of Isla doing all the traditional celebrations without her bit deep. Especially…she sighed to herself…especially when Christmas had always been so full of memories.

Isabel slammed back the sadness and tried to immerse herself in the here and now rather than thinking of her sister back in Melbourne on the other side of the world, all ripe and ready to have her first baby. She wondered whether the Melbourne Maternity Unit was taking similar bets. Maybe Isla would win the Aussie sweepstake? Now that would give the rest of the department something to giggle about: the head midwife winning with a Christmas Day baby! 'So, go on, then, who will it be?'

'Who will what be?' A deep male voice, redolent with her beloved Aussie tones. The sound of home.

The sound of heartbreak.

Isabel inhaled sharply.

Sean.

And even if the man had been mute she'd have known he was behind her simply because of the full-on reaction her body had any time he was in the vicinity. Every tiny hair stood to attention. Her heart rate escalated. Palms became sweaty. Seventeen years on and she'd managed to deal with it...when she didn't have to face him every day. She'd almost erased him from her heart.

Almost. She'd come to the other side of the world to forget him. And she'd managed quite well for close to nine months until he'd turned up, out of the blue, and those feelings had come tumbling back. The memories...and his questions... Questions she couldn't bear to answer.

Somewhere a phone rang. Somewhere voices, raised and harried, called to her. 'Dr Delamere. Please. There's been an accident...'

Oh, God. She was shaken from her reverie but her heart rate stayed too high for comfort. 'Isla?'

'Isla? No,' Bonnie called over from the nurses' station. 'Susan Patterson. Motor vehicle accident. They're bringing her in to ER. Heavy vaginal bleeding. Mum shocked. Foetal distress. ETA five minutes.'

'What? No! We were just talking about her.' Without even looking at Sean, Isabel jumped straight into doctor mode. 'Right, Bonnie, sounds like a possible abruption. Get Theatre on alert. I'll meet the ambulance down in the ER.'

'I'm coming with you.' Sean was heading towards the door.

Only when hell freezes over. 'No. Sean, absolutely not.'

Silence.

She realised that all the eyes of the staff were on her. No one knew about their history, and for as long as there was breath in her body no one was going to. 'I mean... thank you very much for your offer, Dr Anderson, but I'll be fine.'

He shrugged, following her into the corridor, into more quiet. 'I'm in a lull here. Everyone's discharged or doing well, I don't have a clinic until two o'clock. Are you really saying you couldn't use an extra pair of hands? I have done this before, you know.'

'Yes, I know.' She also knew what a talented and empathetic obstetrician he was, she just didn't relish the prospect of spending any time with him. But she had to give this mum everything she had and an extra pair of confident hands would definitely help. 'Okay. But this is my case, my theatre, my rules.'

'Of course. If I remember rightly, it was always your rules, Isabel. Right down to the bitter end. In fact, I don't remember having any say in that at all.' He gave a wry lift of his eyebrow as they hurried towards the emergency room. 'This one time I'll abide by them. But once we're out of there then...'

She stopped short. 'Then, what?'

'Then I change the rules to suit me.'

She shrugged, hoping upon hope that he couldn't see through her recalcitrant façade to the shaking, smitten teenager she still felt like when she was around him. 'Do what you want. It won't affect me. At all.' *Liar.* It seemed as if everything he did affected her. Just being here. Breathing. In Cambridge. Goddamn him.

Isabel threw him a look that she hoped told him where exactly to shove his rules, and strode straight in to Resus. She would deal with Sean Anderson...later... never, if she had her way. 'Now, Susan? Crikey, love, what on earth has been happening?' She took hold of her patient's hand.

Mrs Patterson was lying on a trolley, tears streaming down her cheeks. Pale. Terrified. Her voice was barely audible through the oxygen mask over her nose and mouth. 'Thank God you're here, Isabel. I'm so scared. I don't want to lose this baby. Please. Do something.'

'I will. I just need some details then we'll make some decisions. And we'll be quick, I promise.' She'd have to be. If it was a placental abruption, as she suspected, both mum and bub were at serious risk. Outcomes weren't always positive. And well she knew. Too well. Isabel examined Susan's belly for the baby's position and well-being. Then she tightened an electro foetal monitor belt over the baby bump. 'Has anyone called Tony?'

'I did.' Jenny, the paramedic, filled her in on further details. 'He's on his way. Grandma's looking after the toddler. They were in the car at the time of impact. Hit from behind. Susan felt a tight pull in her belly. Possibly from an ill-fitting seat belt, but there's no visible marking or bruising on the abdomen. I have normal saline through a wide-bore IV in situ. Moderate vaginal bleeding. Blood pressure ninety over fifty and dropping. Baby's heart rate jittery and at times...' She pointed to her notes and let Isabel read. The baby's heart rate was dipping, a sign of foetal distress. Mum was clearly shocked. Judging by the blood staining her clothes the baby needed to be out. Now.

'Okay. Thanks.' Isabel turned to the ER nurse that had appeared. 'I need you to cross-match four units of packed cells. I need clotting times, usual bloods and that portable ultrasound over here as quick as you can.'

Susan's hand squeezed in Isabel's. 'But I wanted... I wanted to hang on...two more weeks....'

'I know, but these things happen and we just have to deal with them as best we can.' Isabel gave Susan a quick smile, positioned the ultrasound machine in front of her, squeezed jelly onto the probe and placed it over Susan's tummy. 'I'm just going to take a quick look.' Baby was okay—distressed, but alive. Isabel exhaled deeply. Thank God.

She looked over at Sean and saw his reassuring smile. She gave him a small one back. They both knew that at least some of the immediate anxiety was over.

But the placenta was, indeed, partially separated. The baby was at serious risk and mum's blood loss was not stopping. Despite the desperate urgency Isabel needed to be calm so as not to frighten mum too much. 'Okay, Susan, we do have a problem here, but—'

'Oh, my God. I knew it...'

'Sweetheart, we'll do our best. It'll be okay.' Isabel prayed silently that it would. 'Your placenta is failing, I think the car impact may have given it a nasty jolt or tear and there's a real risk to the baby if we don't do something soon. As you know the placenta is what keeps baby alive, so we have to take you to the operating theatre and do a Caesarean section. I need your consent—'

'Where's Susan? Susan? Where's Susan?' A burly-looking stocky man covered in dust pushed his way in, steel-capped boots leaving grubby imprints across the floor. 'What the hell's happening?'

Isabel scanned the room for Sean. But he was there already, his hand on Tony's forearm, gently slowing him down. 'Are you Tony? Here, let me bring you over. It's a lot to take in, I know, mate. There's a few tubes and lines and she looks a little pale. But she's good.'

'She is not good. Look at her.' The room filled with the smell of beer and a voice that was rough round the edges, and getting louder. 'Is that...? Is that blood? What's happened? What about my boy? The baby! Susan! Are you all right?' Then his tone turned darker, he shoved out of Sean's grip and marched up to Isabel. In her face. Angry and foul-mouthed. 'You. Do something. Why are you just standing there? Do something, damn it.'

Isabel's hand began to shake. But she would not let him intimidate her. 'I'm doing the best I can. We all are. Now, please—'

'No need for that, mate. Come away.' Sean's voice was calm but firm. At six foot one he was by far the bigger man. Broader too. And while Tony was rough and menacing, Sean was authoritative. There was no aggression, but a quietly commanded respect and attention. 'We're going to take her to Theatre right now, but first we need to know what we're dealing with. Yes? Have a few words with Susan, but then we need to get moving. I'll show you where you can wait.'

'Get your hands off me.' Tony pushed his way to the trolley. 'Susie.'

'I'll be fine, Tony. Just do as he says.' Susan started to shake. 'I love you.'

'If they don't—'

Sean stepped forward. 'As I said. Come with me. *Now.* Let's have a quiet word. Outside.' He bustled Tony out of the room.

'He's not a bad man.' Isabel's patient's voice was fading. Alarms began to blare.

'I know, I know, he's scared, is all.' Thank God Sean was able to contain him because the last thing Isabel needed was a drunk father getting in the way of saving a mother and baby. 'Now we need to get you sorted, quickly.' Isabel nodded to the porter. 'Let's go.'

She all but ran to the OR, scrubbed up and was in the operating theatre in record time. Sean, somehow, was there before her. 'So we have a crash C-section scenario. Your call, Izzy. Whatever happens, I've got your back.'

'Thank you.' And she meant it. Well drilled in dealing with emergencies, she felt competent and confident, but having someone there she knew she could rely on gave her a lift. Even if that lift involved her heart as well as her head.

Within minutes she'd tugged out a live baby boy. Floppy. Apgar of six. But, with oxygen and a little rub, the Apgar score increased to ten. As occurred with every delivery Isabel felt a familiar sting of sadness, and hope. But she didn't have time for any kind of sentimentality. One life saved wouldn't be enough for her. Placental abruption was harrowing and scary for the mother but it was high risk too. That amount of blood loss, coupled with the potential for complications, meant they were perilously close to losing her.

'Blood pressure's dropping...' The anaesthetist gave them a warning frown.

'Hang on in there... I just need to find the tear.' Isabel

breathed a sigh of relief as she reached the placenta and started to remove it. 'Attagirl.'

Within an hour they'd managed to save Susan's life too, although she had hung close to the edge. Too close.

And now…well, now that dad was with baby, her patient was in recovery and the rest of the staff had scarpered, Isabel was alone. Alone, that was, with the one person she never wanted to be alone with again. Rather than look at him she stared at the words she was writing. 'Well, Sean, I don't want to keep you while I finish writing up these notes. Thanks, you were a great help. Things could have turned nasty with Tony.'

'He just needed me to explain a few things. Like how to behave in an emergency department. But I get it. The bloke was worried. I would have been too if I was losing my wife and my baby.'

Guilt crawled down her spine. How would he have been? At seventeen? Quick-mouthed and aggressive? Or the self-assured, confident man he was now? She stole a quick glance in his direction. 'You wouldn't have acted like that. So thanks for dealing with him. And for your help in here.'

'It wasn't just me. We almost lost them both, but your quick thinking and nifty work saved both their lives. Well done.' He threw his face mask into the bin, snapped his gloves off and faced her. 'You look exhausted.'

'Gee, thanks. I'm fine.' She didn't feel fine. Her legs were like jelly and her stupid heart was still pounding with its fight-or-flight response. She looked away from the notes and towards the door. Flight. Good idea. Easier to write them up in the safety of her office, which was a Sean-free zone. Snapping the folder closed, she looked up at him. 'Actually, I've got to go.'

'Wait, please.'

She stepped towards the door and tried hard to look natural instead of panicked. 'No. I have a million things to do.'

'They can wait.' His tone was urgent, determined. He was striding towards the exit now too.

'No. They can't.'

'Isabel. Stop avoiding me, goddamn it!'

He was going to ask.

He was going to ask and she was going to lie. Because lying had been the only way to forge enough distance between her and the one thing she had promised herself she could never do again: feel something.

She calculated that it would take precisely five seconds to get out of the chilly delivery room and away from his piercing blue-eyed gaze. For the last two months she'd managed to steer clear from any direct one-to-ones with him, shielding herself with colleagues or friends. But now, the things unsaid between them for almost seventeen years weighed heavily in the silence.

He was going to ask and she was going to lie. Again.

The lies were exhausting. Running was exhausting. Just as getting over Sean and that traumatic time had been. She didn't want to have to face that again. Face him again.

His scent filled the room. Sunshine. Spice. His heat, so familiar and yet not so.

Seventeen years.

God, how he'd matured into the sophisticated, beautiful man he was destined to be. But wanting answers to questions that would break her heart all over again... and his.

She made direct eye contact with the door handle and started to move towards it again.

'Izzy?'

She would not turn round. Would. Not. 'Don't call me that here. It's Isabel or Dr Delamere.'

'Hello? It's not as if anyone can hear. There's only you and me in here. It's so empty there's an echo.'

'*I* can hear.' *And I don't want to be reminded.* Although she was, every day. Every single day. Every mother, every baby. Every birth. Every stillborn. Every death.

She made it to the door. The handle was cold and smooth. Sculpted steel, just like the way she'd fashioned her heart and her backbone. Beyond the clouded glass she could make out a bustling corridor of co-workers and clients. Safety. She squeezed the handle downwards and a whoosh of air breathed over her. 'I'm sorry, Dr Anderson, I have a ward round to get to. I'm already late. Like I said, thanks for your help back there.'

'Any time. You know that.' His hand covered hers and a shot of electricity jolted through her. He was warm. And solid. And here; of all the maternity units he could have chosen... This time it wasn't a coincidence. His voice was thick and deep and reached into her soul. 'I just want one minute, Isabel. That's all. One.'

One minute. One lifetime. It would never be enough to bridge that time gap. Certainly not if she ever told him the answer to his question.

'No, Sean, please don't ask me again.' She jabbed her foot into the doorway and pulled the door further open.

Then she made fatal error number one. She turned her head and looked up at him.

His chestnut hair was tousled from removing his

surgical cap, sticking up in parts, flattened in others. Someone needed to sink their fingers in and fluff it. So not her job. Not when she was too busy trying not to look at those searching eyes. That sculptured jawline. The mouth that had given her so much pleasure almost a year ago, with one stupid, ill-thought-out stolen kiss, and…a lifetime ago. A boy turned into a man. A girl become a woman, although in truth that had happened in one night all those years ago.

Onwards went her gaze, re-familiarising herself with lines and grooves, and learning new ones. Wide solid shoulders, the only tanned guy in a fifty-mile radius, God bless the sparse Aussie ozone layer. Toned arms that clearly did more working out than lifting three-kilogram newborns.

His voice was close to her ear. 'Izzy, if it was over between us… If everything was completely finished, why the hell did you kiss me?'

Good question. Damn good question. She'd been brooding over the answer to that particular issue for the better part of the last year, ever since he'd crushed her against him in a delivery suite very similar to this one, but half a world away. It had been a feral response to a need she hadn't ever known before. A shock, seeing him again after so long, turning up at the Melbourne hospital where she'd worked. He'd been as surprised as she had, she was sure.

Then he'd kissed her. A snatched frenzied embrace that had told her his feelings for her had been rekindled after such a long time apart. And, oh, how she'd responded. Because, in all honesty, her feelings for him had never really waned.

Heat prickled through her at the mere memory. Heat

and guilt. But they had to put it behind them and move forward. 'Really, Sean? Do you chase most of the women you kiss across the world? It must cost an awful lot in airfares. Still, I guess you must do well on the loyalty schemes. What do you have now, elite platinum status? Does that entitle you to fly the damn planes as well?'

His smile was slow to come, but when it did it was devastating. 'Most women aren't Isabel Delamere. And none of them kiss like you do.'

'I'm busy.'

'You're avoiding the issue.'

She held his too blue, too intense gaze. She could do this. Distract him with other issues, deflect the real one. Get him off her back once and for all. She was going away tomorrow for a few days. Hopefully everything would have blown over by the time she got back. *Like hell it would.* She could pretend that it had. She just needed some space from him. 'So let me get this straight. You turn up out of the blue at the same place I'm working in Melbourne—'

'Pure coincidence. I was as shocked as you. Pleasantly, though. Unlike your reaction.' The pressure of his thumb against the back of her hand increased a little, like a stroke, a caress.

She did not want him to caress her.

Actually she did. But that would have been fatal error number two. 'Then after I leave there you turn up here. Also out of the blue? I don't think so.'

'Aww, you missed a whole lot out....where I didn't see you or have any contact with you for many, many years. As far as I was concerned you were the one that got away. But also the one I got over.' At her glare he shrugged shoulders that were broader, stronger than she remembered. 'I put you out of my mind and did exactly what I had planned to do with my life and became a damned fine obstetrician. Then one day I turn up at my cushy new locum job at Melbourne Maternity Unit and bump into my old…flame. I never dreamt for a minute you'd be there after hearing you'd studied medicine in Sydney. I assumed you'd moved on. Like I had. But then, Delamere blood runs thick with the Yarra so I should have realized you'd be there in the bosom of your… delightful family.' He gave a sarcastic smile. Sean had never got on with her hugely successful neurosurgeon daddy and socialite mother who ran with the It crowd in Melbourne. 'Well, in that sumptuous penthouse apartment anyway. Cut to the chase—the first chance you get: wham, bam. You kiss me.'

'What?' She dragged her hand from under his and jabbed a finger at him. 'You kissed me first. It took me by surprise—it didn't mean anything.'

'No one kisses like that and doesn't mean it.'

He'd pulled her to him and she'd felt the hard outline of his body, had a crazy melting of her mind and she'd wanted to kiss him right back. Hard. Hot. And it had been the most stupid thing she'd done in a long time. Not least because it had reignited an ache she'd purged from her system. She'd purged *him* from her system. 'And now you're here to what? Taunt me? Tell me, Sean, why are you here?'

'Ask your sister.'

'Isla? Why? And how can I?' There was no way Isla would ever have told Sean what had happened. She'd promised to keep that secret for ever and Isabel trusted her implicitly. Even though over the years she had caught Isla looking at her with a sad, pitiful expression. And sure, Isabel knew she'd been badly scarred by her experiences, they both had, but she was over it. She was. She'd moved on. 'Isla is back home in Australia and I'm here. I'm hardly going to phone a heavily pregnant woman in the middle of the night just to ask why an old boyfriend is in town, am I? What did she say?'

'It was more what she didn't say that set alarm bells ringing. I asked her outright why you had suddenly gone so cold on our relationship, she said she couldn't tell me but that I should ask you myself. Between her garbled answers and your sizzling kiss, I'm guessing that there's a lot more to this than you're letting on. Something important. Something so big that you're both running scared. My brain's working overtime and I'm baffled. So tell me the truth, Isabel. Tell me the truth, then I'll go. I'll leave. Out of your life.'

Which would be a blessing and a curse. She was so conflicted she didn't know if she never wanted to set eyes on him again or…wake up every morning in his arms. But if he ever found out why they'd split up option two would never, ever happen. He'd make sure of it. 'It doesn't matter any more, Sean. It was such a long time ago.'

'It matters to me. It clearly still matters to Isla, so I'm sure it matters to you.' He leaned closer and her senses slammed into overdrive. Memories, dark, painful memories, rampaged through her brain. Her body felt as if it were reliving the whole tragedy again. Her heart rate jittered into a stupid over-compensatory tachycardia, and she squeezed the door handle.

It was all too much.

In her scrubs pocket her phone vibrated and chimed 'Charge of The Light Brigade'. She grabbed it, grateful of the reprieve. The labour ward. 'Look, seriously, I've got to run.'

'Doing what you do best.' He flicked his thumb up the corridor, his voice raised. 'Go on, Izzy. Go ahead and run. But remember this—you walked away with no explanation, you just cut me adrift. Whatever happened back then wasn't just about you. And while I've thought about it over the years it's hardly kept me awake at night, until Isla hinted at some momentous mystery that she's sworn not to talk about, and if it involves me then I deserve to know why.'

Isabel glanced at the phone display, then up the corridor, where she saw a few heads popping out from rooms, then darting back in again.

She looked back at Sean. She thought about the dads in the delivery suites, so proud, so emotional, so raw. How they wept when holding their newborns. She thought about Tony, who'd have fought tooth and nail for his son, even if it had riled every member of hospital staff. She thought about the babies born sleeping and the need for both parents to know so much, to be involved. They cared. They loved. They broke. They grieved. Both of them, not just the mums.

So damn right Sean deserved to know. She'd hidden this information for so long, and yet he had every right to know what had happened. And once he knew then surely he'd leave? If not because it was so desperately sad, but because she had kept this from him. He'd hate her.

But the relief would be final. She'd be free from the guilt of not telling him. Just never, *never* of the hurt.

She opened her mouth to say the words, but her courage failed. 'Please, just forget it. Put it behind you. Forget I ever existed. Forget it all.'

'Really? When I see you every day? Forget this?' He stepped closer, pinning her against the doorway, and for a moment she thought—hoped—he was going to kiss her again. His mouth was so close, his scent overpowering her. And the old feelings, the want, the desire came tumbling back. They had never had problems with the attraction; it had been all-consuming, feral, intense even then. It was the truth that she'd struggled with. Laying bare how she felt, because she was a Delamere girl after all, and she wasn't allowed to show her emotions. Ever. She had standards, expectations to fulfil. And dating Sean Anderson hadn't been one of them. Certainly carrying his child never was.

His breath whispered over the nape of her neck. Hot. Hungry. Sending shivers of need spiralling down her back. He was so close. Too close. Not close enough. 'What's the matter, Izzy? Having trouble forgetting that I exist?'

And what was the use in wanting him now? One whiff of the truth and he'd be gone.

But, it was time to tell him anyway.

'Okay. Okay.' She shoved him back, gave herself some air. She made sure she had full eye contact with him, looked into those ocean-blue eyes. She was struggling with her own emotions, trying to keep her voice steady and level, but failing; she could hear it rise. 'We had to finish, Sean. I didn't know what to do. I was sixteen and frightened and I panicked. I had to cut you out of my life once and for all. A clean break for my own sanity if not for anything else.' She took a deep breath. 'I was pregnant.'

He staggered back a step. Two. 'What?'

'Yes, Sean. With your baby.'

CHAPTER TWO

'WHAT?' THIS WASN'T what he'd expected at all. Truthfully, he'd thought she'd been embarrassed about being seen with him. A lad from the wrong side of the Delamere social circle with two very ordinary and dull parents of no use to the Delamere clan. Or perhaps a bit of angsty teenage intrigue. Or possibly some pubertal mental health issues. But this…?

He was a…father?

Sean's first instinct was to walk and keep on walking. But he fixed his feet to the floor, because he had to hear this. All of it. 'Pregnant? My baby? So where is it? What happened?' Two possibilities ran through his head: one, he had a child somewhere that he had never seen. And for that he could never forgive her.

Or two, she'd had an abortion without talking it through with him. *His child*. Neither option was palatable.

She followed him back in to the OR and looked up at him, her startling dark green eyes glittering with tears that she righteously blinked away. With her long blonde hair pulled back into a tight ponytail she looked younger than her thirty-three years. Not the sweet delicate creature she'd been at school, but she was so much more, somehow. More beautiful. More real. Just…more. That came with confidence, he supposed, a successful career, Daddy's backing, everyone doing Miss Delamere's bidding her whole life.

But her cheeks seemed to hollow out as she spoke. 'I lost it. The baby.'

'Oh, God. I'm sorry.' He was an obstetrician, for God's sake, he knew it happened. But to her? To him? His gut twisted into a tight knot; so not everything had gone Isabel's way after all.

She gave a slight nod of her head. Sadness rolled off her. 'I had a miscarriage at eighteen weeks—'

'Eighteen weeks? You were pregnant for over four months and didn't tell me? Why the hell not?'

So this was why she'd become so withdrawn over those last few weeks together, refusing intimacy, finding excuses, being unavailable. This was why she'd eventually cut him off with no explanation.

She started to pace around the room, Susan's notes still tight in her fist. 'I didn't know I was pregnant, not for sure. Oh, of course I suspected I was, I just hadn't done a test—I was too scared even to pee on a stick and see my life change irrevocably in front of my eyes. I was sixteen. I didn't want to face reality. I…well, I suppose I'd hoped that the problem would go away. I thought, hoped, that my missing periods were just irregular cycles, or due to stress, exams, trying to live up to Daddy's expectations. Being continually on show. Having to snatch moments with you. So I didn't want to believe—couldn't believe…a baby? I was too young to deal with that. We both were.'

He made sure to stand stock-still, his eyes following her round the room. 'You didn't think to mention it? We thought you'd be safe—God knows...the naivety. You were pregnant for eighteen weeks? I don't understand... I thought we talked about everything.' Clearly he'd been mistaken. Back then he'd thought she was the love of his life. He'd held a candle up to her for the next five years. No woman had come close to the rose-tinted memory he'd had of how things had been between them. Clearly he'd been wrong. Very wrong. 'You should have talked to me. Maybe I could have helped. I could have... I don't know...maybe I could have saved it.' Even as he said the words he knew he couldn't have done a thing. Eighteen weeks was far too young, too fragile, too under-developed, even now, all these years later and with all the new technology, eighteen weeks was still too little.

The light in her eyes had dimmed. It had been hard on her, he thought. A burden, living with the memory. 'I spent many years thinking the same thing, berating myself for maybe doing something wrong. I pored over books, looked at research, but no one could have saved him, Sean. He was too premature. You, of all people, know how it is. We see it. In our jobs.'

'He?' His gut lurched. 'I had a son?'

She finally stopped pacing, wrapped her arms around her thin frame, like a hug. Like a barrier. But her gaze clashed with his. 'Yes. A son. He was beautiful, Sean. Perfect. So tiny. Isla said—'

'So Isla was there?' Her sister was allowed to be there, but he wasn't?

'Yes. It all happened so fast. I was in my bathroom at my parents' house and suddenly there was so much blood, and I must have screamed. Then Isla was there, she delivered him...' Her head shook at the memory. 'God love her, at twelve years of age she delivered my child onto our bathroom floor, got help and made sure I was okay. No wonder she ended up being a midwife—it's what she was born to do.'

He wasn't sure he wanted any more details. He had enough to get his head around, but he couldn't help asking the questions. 'So who else helped you? There must have been someone else? An adult? Surely?'

'Evie, our housekeeper.'

'The one who turned me away when I came round that time? Not your parents?' He could see from Isabel's closed-off reaction that she hadn't involved them, just as she hadn't involved him. He didn't know whether that made him feel any better or just…just lost. Cut off from her life. After everything he'd believed, he really hadn't known her at all. 'They still don't know? Even now?'

'No. Evie took me to a hospital across town and they sorted me out. Because I was sixteen the doctors didn't have to tell my parents. I never did. They were away at the time, they wouldn't have understood. It would have distressed them. The scandal—'

'Of course. We always have to be careful about what our Melbourne royalty think.' He didn't care a jot about them now and he hadn't back then. They'd cosseted their daughters and he'd struggled to get much time alone with her despite his best efforts; over-protective, she'd called them. Of course, he knew better now. But even so, Isabel had been nothing more than a pawn in their celebrity status paraded at every available opportunity, the golden girl. The darling Delamere daughter who couldn't do any wrong.

No…that wasn't what he'd believed at the time, only the intervening years had made him rethink his young and foolish impression of her. When they were together

he'd come to love a deep, sensitive girl, not a material-
istic, shallow Delamere. But then she'd cut him off and
he'd been gutted to find out she was the same as her parents after all. But this news...and to keep it to herself all
that time. Who the hell was she? 'And that's why you
broke off our relationship? That's why you sent my ring
back to me? No explanation.'

She fiddled with her left ring finger as if that ring
were still there. 'I didn't know what else to do, to be
honest, I was stressed out, grieving. I'd lost my baby. It
felt like a punishment, you see. I hadn't wanted him, but
then, when I lost him I wanted him so badly. And seeing
you, telling you, would have brought back all that pain.
I wasn't strong enough to relive it again.' She'd walked
towards him, her hand now on his arm. 'I'm sorry, Sean.
I should have told you.'

'Yes, you should have.' He shook his arm free from
her touch. He couldn't bear to feel her, to smell her intoxicating scent. To see those beautiful, sad eyes. And
to know that she'd let him live all those years without
telling him the truth.

He forced himself to look at her. To imagine what
must have been going through her head at that time.
The fear, the pain, the confusion. The grief. It must have
been so terrifying for a young girl. But still he couldn't
fathom why all of that had been a reason to shut herself
off from him. To keep all this from him.

She looked right back at him, not a young girl any
longer. She was a beautiful, successful woman with tears
swimming in her eyes—tears that did not fall. She wiped
them away. It was the first time he'd seen any emotion
from her in the months that he'd been here. Now, and
when she'd kissed him back in Melbourne. There had

been a few emotions skittering across her face back then: fear mainly, and a raw need. 'Please, Sean. Please say something.'

He didn't know what to say. How to feel. Right now, he was just angry. Empty. No...just angry. It was as if a huge chunk of his past had been a lie. He should have known about this. He should have been allowed to know this. 'I've spent all these years wondering what turned you from being such a happy, loving girlfriend to a cold and distant one literally overnight. I thought it was something I'd done and I went over and over everything until I was lost. Or that you'd had a nervous breakdown. Or that I wasn't good enough for you. I tried to see you but had the door closed in my face so many times I gave up. You refused to answer my calls. I tried hard to understand what was happening. In the end I just presumed your parents had somehow found out and banned you from seeing me.'

'They wouldn't have done that.'

'Wouldn't they? You weren't exactly thrilled at the prospect of telling them we were an item. *Let's keep it a secret,* you said. *Our secret love.* It seems you had a lot of secrets back then, Isabel.'

She flinched, so she must have remembered saying words he'd believed at the time were heartfelt. 'I didn't want to cause you any pain. There wasn't anything you could do. I thought it would be for the best, for both of us. Just put it all behind us.'

'I could have grieved, Isabel, I could have helped you with that.' He held her gaze. 'So was it? For the best?'

She shook her head. 'No. Not for me, anyway.'

'And not for me, either. I'm sorry, Isabel. I'm sorry you had to go through that, I know how hard it must have been. But...' And it was a hell of a big *but*...what was he supposed to do now? Why hadn't she told him? Even though she'd lost their baby, did that mean she'd had to throw their love aside too? He couldn't think straight. Just looking at her brought back hurt, and more, stacked alongside the fact that he'd been a dad. He'd had a son. And he hadn't even known.

Words failed him. 'I can't imagine your state of mind, you're right. But one thing is for sure. If I'd known something like that that deeply involved someone else, someone I'd professed to care about—to love, even—I'd have mentioned it.'

She hung her head. 'It was a long time ago. We have to move on, Sean.'

'Easy for you to say, Isabel.' He was loud now, he knew his anger was spilling into his voice, his face, but he didn't much care. 'You've had many years to get over this. It's in your past. But this, this is my present right now. So you'll excuse me if I take a little time to come to terms with it all. I had a son? Wow. It would have been nice to know that.'

'Oh, yes? Well, it was horrible. I was distraught, traumatised. I was a young girl, for God's sake.' Her voice was shaky now, like her hands. 'You know what makes it all so much worse? *You.* Seeing you brings it all back, and I don't want to think about it any more. It hurts. Okay? It hurts, so I wish you'd never found me.'

You have no idea what she's been through, Isla had said when she'd encouraged him to come all this way to confront Isabel. *Don't hurt her.* No? He didn't want to do that. He didn't want to make her relive that pain.

But he didn't want to be with her either. Right now

he didn't even want to breathe the same air as her. Not after this.

A difficult silence wrapped around them like the foggy December day outside.

Her hand covered his. 'I didn't mean to hurt you, Sean. I'm sorry for leaving you to wonder all those years.'

'Yeah. Well, so you should be. Keep out of my way, Isabel. I mean it. Keep out of my way.' And without so much as looking at her again he stalked out of the room.

'You've had a major operation and a big shock to your body. Three units of blood. That's an awful lot to get over.' Isabel gave Susan Patterson what she hoped was a reassuring smile. Twenty-four hours post-op many patients felt as if they'd been hit by a truck. But because they always, always put their babies first they tried to recover far too quickly. 'The good news is, you're making an excellent recovery. Your blood pressure is stable and your blood results are fine. We're going to move you from High Dependency back to the ward so you can be in with the other mums, and we'll bring baby up to be with you. He's ready to leave SCBU now. Between you both you've kept us on our toes, but things are definitely on the way up. He's a little fighter, that one.'

'He's got a good set of lungs, I'll give him that.' Susan gave a weak smile back. Kicking back the covers, she tried to climb out of bed. But when her feet hit the floor she grabbed onto the bed table for stability. She was still a little pale, and Isabel made a note to keep an eye on that. It wasn't just haemoglobin she needed to watch, it was Susan's desire to do too much too soon.

'Hey, there's no hurry. Rest easy. I'll ask a nurse to

come help you have a shower. That scar's in a tricky place, so you need to support it when you move. And remember, Caesareans do take longer to recover from, so don't expect too much from yourself.' Glancing at the chart, she realised Susan's baby was still listed as Baby Patterson. 'Have you thought of a name for that gorgeous wee boy yet?'

Doing as she was told, Susan sat down on the side of the bed; a little more colour crept into her cheeks. 'We had thought about something Christmassy like Joseph or Noel, but as he was early we had to change all that. If he'd been a girl I'd have called him Isabel.' Her cheeks pinked more. 'After you, because you did such a great job of saving us both. But instead we thought we'd choose Isaac. It has the *Is* in it—and that'll remind us of you. I guess you get that all the time?'

Isabel felt her smile blossom from the inside. 'Actually, not very often at all. It's very nice of you. Thank you. I'm honoured.'

'Oh, and Sean as a middle name. After Dr Anderson.'

Sean. Of course. Why not? She forced the smile to stay in place. 'Oh. Lovely. I'm sure he'll be thrilled.'

And she'd got through ten whole minutes without thinking about him, just to be reminded all over again.

Last night had been filled with internal recriminations that had intensified in direct proportion to her wine consumption. From: she should have told him years ago, to…she was glad she'd kept that pain from him, to…how dared he be so angry? She'd been the one going through the miscarriage. She could choose who she disclosed that information to.

But the way he'd looked at her had hurt the most. He'd shut down. Shut her out. The light and the vibrancy that she'd always seen in him had been extinguished. He hadn't even been able to look at her. And that had been her fault.

And now…now that she thought about it, she realised that he had a very disturbing effect on her. Even after all the intervening years she still found just looking at him made her mouth water, made her heart ache for more. Thinking about that kiss made her…

'Isabel? Dr Delamere?'

'Oh, sorry. I was miles away.' Now she couldn't even focus on her job properly. First and last time she'd let that happen. It was Maggie, one of the ward clerks. 'I have a message from Jacob. He wants to see you in his office, as soon as you can.'

'Oh, fine, thank you.' Isabel turned to excuse herself from her patient. 'I'm sorry, Susan, but Jacob's the boss around here, so I'd better get going. I'm off to Paris tomorrow for a conference with him. But I'm so glad we managed to get you on the road to recovery before I go.'

'Paris? Lucky you.' The new mum looked almost wistful.

'No. You have a husband and a lovely family. I'd say you are the luckier woman right now.' Isabel tried to put all thoughts of Sean out of her mind. Once upon a faraway innocent time she'd dreamt of having what Susan had: a husband and family. But the thought of risking her heart again left her more than cold. Terrified, in fact. She just knew she couldn't survive that kind of loss again.

So seven days away from Sean would be the perfect antidote. She could lose herself in the bright lights and the Christmas markets and the lovely amazingness that she'd heard Paris was—oh, yes, and she had work to do, at least, for the first few days. 'I'll pop in this evening,

Susan, to make sure you're okay before I head off. In the meantime, be good and rest up.'

Thinking about which boots to take with her to Paris...and deciding, oh, what the hell, she'd take all three pairs...she sauntered along the corridor to Jacob Layton's office. She was just about to tap under the Head Obstetrician sign on his door when she heard voices. Two men. Not happy.

What should she do? Knock and enter? Wait?

Ah, whatever, she'd been summoned, so she knocked.

'Isabel.' Jacob opened the door with a frown. He seemed flustered. Not his more recent relaxed self, but more a throwback to the days when he used to have the nurses quaking in their boots. Maybe things hadn't been going so smoothly with him and Bonnie. But they seemed fine, beyond happy even. Or...worst-case scenario, maybe he was sick again? The man had a habit of keeping too much to himself and not allowing others to share the load.

'Hi, Jacob.' Instinctively she put her hand out to his arm. 'Are you okay?'

'Yes. Fine.' He stepped back from her hand, looking a little alarmed. No, embarrassed.

'Are you sure? You look—'

'I'm absolutely fine. In all respects.' Not one to expand on anything personal, he gestured her to come into the office. 'But I need to talk to you...both.' He nodded towards Sean, who was standing at the far side of the office, looking out of the window, hands thrust into his trouser pockets. Everything about Sean's manner screamed irritation. Anger.

He turned. 'Isabel.'

'Sean.' So they were down to monosyllables. Okay,

she could live with that for the next five minutes. But, dang it, her heart had another idea altogether and tripped along merrily at the sight of him standing here in a dark-collared shirt and asset-enhancing charcoal trousers, all grumpy and angry and so very, very gorgeous. Why did he have to look so damned delicious?

He always looked delicious to her, she realised, with a sudden pang in her tummy. Even when he was angry. But that wasn't important, couldn't be important.

'Look. You're not going to like what I'm going to say. So…' Jacob beckoned them both to sit down '…I'm just going to cut to the chase, here.'

'Why? What's the problem?' Something inside Isabel's gut tumbled and tumbled. She looked from Jacob to Sean and back again.

Sean shrugged. 'We are. Apparently.'

Jacob shook his head. 'I'm sorry to say, I need to talk to you about an incident yesterday. An argument, between the two of you.'

Blood rushed to her cheeks. Isabel couldn't believe it. She'd never had so much as a frown about her behaviour, never mind being involved in an 'incident', as if she'd been rude or unprofessional or worse. It had been a private conversation, opening her very shattered heart. 'Someone complained about it? A patient?'

'No, not a patient.' Her boss looked a little red-faced. 'This meeting is unofficial and won't go down on your records, unless…well, let's just say, if you can resolve this situation amicably…'

'What situation?' Uh-huh. Of course. Sean hadn't been happy about what she'd told him yesterday, he felt betrayed and now he wanted to get his own back by getting her fired? Surely that was too underhanded even for him? That would be callous and bullying and very unlike the Sean she'd known. But she didn't know him now, really, did she? They'd been apart too long. He wouldn't…would he? She turned to look at him. 'Did you make a complaint, Sean?'

His blue eyes fired black. 'Don't be ridiculous. Of course not.'

Jacob's hands rose in a calming gesture. 'No, no, it wasn't Sean. It wasn't a complaint. *I* overheard a lot of arguing yesterday in the OR. Raised voices. Personal things were said. It made for unpleasant listening— which, I might add, was unavoidable and a few other people overheard too. The staff now think they're going to have to work in world war three, dodging bullets flying between you two.' Jacob leaned towards Isabel. 'I know I've been difficult, I know I can be a grouch, but I hope I never had cause to raise my voice or make everyone feel as if they couldn't work with me.'

He'd been sick, poor man, and had wanted to keep that to himself. He'd told no one and borne the weight of the department's needs along with his illness. He deserved a bloody medal. And yes, he'd been grumpy too, but things had changed—in his love life, mainly—and he was a lot happier now. And well again. The atmosphere in the department had become much more relaxed, until…

'So are you saying that people don't want to work with me? That it will be awkward?' Because of Sean? This was ridiculous. Never, ever, had her private life interfered with her work. Never. She was a professional. Her work was her life and she would not let anything get in the way of that. Damn Sean Anderson. Damn him for making her life hell all over again.

'No,' Jacob continued. 'I'm saying that I can't have my top obstetricians in such discord. You need to be able to assist each other, to work together at times. I want a harmonious atmosphere when I come to work. Not Armageddon. My staff deserve that, the patients certainly deserve that and so do you if you're going to do the job well.'

Sean nodded, and his reaction was surprising. 'Things got a little heated, I admit. It won't happen again.' She'd expected him to level the blame at her, but instead he wore it. He continued, 'We will be back to situation normal as soon as we leave this room. You have my word on it.' But Sean didn't look at her and she knew from the tightness in his shoulders and the taut way he held his body that he was livid, and only just about managing to keep it together in front of the boss.

And he was right, of course. They had to be normal and civil with each other, for the sake of their colleagues and their jobs. Their patients deserved the utmost professional conduct, not two senior doctors fighting over something that happened years ago.

But still…she didn't know if she could face him and be normal. Not after the way he'd looked at her. And definitely not after the kiss that still haunted her.

She needed time away from him, that was the answer. Although, she ignored the nagging voice in her head that told her that seventeen years apart from him hadn't made a huge difference to her attraction to him. This time she'd make it work. She'd erase him from her life. She'd go to Paris and teach herself all things Zen and meditate or something, she'd learn the huffy aloofness of Parisian women, she'd become sophisticated…

and she'd come back immune to his generally annoying attractiveness.

'Yes, you're both right. Things got out of hand and it won't happen again. You and I are off to Paris tomorrow, Jacob, so we can all put this episode behind us. When I get back things will very definitely be back to normal.' She felt better already.

Jacob scraped his chair back and stood, signalling the conversation was coming to an end and that he now wanted them to act on their word. 'Actually, Isabel, I need to talk to you about Paris. Unfortunately, something's come up and I can't go. I'm going to have to leave you to do the presentation on your own. I'm sorry.'

'Oh. Okay.' Not so bad. Paris on her own would be wonderful. Perhaps she could play hooky a little and do some sightseeing? Have a makeover?

Her boss scrutinised her reaction. 'You'll be fine, don't worry.'

'I'm not worried at all. It'll be great. But I thought you wanted to schmooze the SCBU ventilator manufacturers for some discounted prices?'

'I'm sure you can manage that just fine.' He started to walk them both to the door. 'And Sean will be on hand to help.'

Isabel screeched to a halt. 'What? Sean? What?'

Sean looked as incredulous as she did. 'What the hell…? Absolutely not. No way.'

Jacob shook his head to silence them. 'I need two representatives over there to handle the schmoozing requirements and networking meetings. You're both rostered on over Christmas when we're short-staffed, and currently we're a little top heavy—no one tends to take leave just before Christmas, it's a vacation dead zone.

So, it makes sense to send you together. I'll have the documentation transferred into your name by the end of today, Sean, and a synopsis of who you need to speak with and when. Who knows? A little *entente cordiale* might do you both some good.' Like hell it would. 'Really, I don't care. I just need two reps there and a harmonious atmosphere here. Got it?'

'No.' Isabel's mouth worked before her brain got into gear.

'No?' Jacob stared at her.

'I mean, yes.' No. She couldn't go with Sean. Four nights in Paris with her ex-lover who could heat her up with one look and freeze her bones with another. She needed space from him, not to be banished to a damned conference hotel with him. 'This is—'

Ridiculous. Painful. Harmful.

So, so stupid.

But if they couldn't sort it out amicably it would go down on their employment records—and who knew what else, a warning? No way. She wasn't going to let this ruin her, so yes, they needed to sort it out once and for all. But that meant she was going to be stuck with him in the famous city of love with harsh memories and increasing desires and a whole lot of tension, trying to sort out a situation that was far from normal.

'That is, if you don't kill each other first. Now, I'm running late for another meeting, so if you'll excuse me.' Jacob's word was final. 'Play nicely, children. I'll see you when you get back.'

CHAPTER THREE

'WHO THE HELL has a symposium just before Christmas?' Sean lugged his duffle bag onto the train, threw it onto the overhead rack and sat down opposite Isabel.

Angry as he was with the whole situation, he couldn't help but note that she looked as pulled together as any self-respecting Delamere girl would be. A dark fur-trimmed hat sat on her head, her straight golden hair flowing over her shoulders. A smattering of mascara made her green eyes look huge and innocent, and her cheeks had pinked up from the bitter north-easterly that had whipped around them as they stood on the Eurostar platform. A red coat covered her from neck to knee. At her throat was a chain of what looked like diamonds. They weren't fake. He knew her well enough to be sure of that. She looked like an Eastern European princess rather than a doctor.

And, despite himself and the rage still swirling round his gut, he felt a pull to wrap her in his arms and warm her up. *Damn it*.

She barely took her eyes away from the glossy magazine she was reading. 'It was originally planned for September, but had to be postponed because of a norovirus outbreak at the hotel the day before it was due to start.

That's smack in the middle of conference season so all the other appropriately sized venues were already full. This was the only time they could rebook it. So we're stuck with it.' Now she lifted her head and glared at him. 'Like I'm stuck with you. But I won't let that spoil my time in Paris.'

She was angry with him? 'Whoa. Wait a minute. Let's backtrack a little...you're pissed with me because of what exactly? Because I don't remember me keeping any secrets from you for the last seventeen years.' The train was beginning to fill. People were taking seats further down the carriage, squealing about Christmas shopping, so yes, he knew this wasn't the time or the place.

But she answered him anyway, her voice quiet but firm. 'Sean, I apologised for that and I cannot do anything about it. You want to keep going over and over it, feel free but it won't change a thing.'

Her eyes clashed with his in a haughty, assertive glare. She was not going to move on this, he could see. But he could see more than that too. He could see how tired she was. How much she was hurting. How the proud stance was a show. And he felt like a jerk. She'd been through a traumatic time and had achieved so much despite it.

And how she had him feeling bad about this whole scenario he couldn't fathom.

Dragging a book from his backpack, he settled down. It would get easier, he asserted to himself, being with her. He'd get over the swing of emotions from anger to lust. He'd get bored of looking at her. Surely? He would stop being entranced by that gentle neckline, the dip at her throat where the diamonds graced the collarbone. He'd get tired of the scent...expensive perfume, he guessed, but it was intoxicating nonetheless, sort of exotic and flowers and something else. *Her...*

Now, where was he...? Ah, yes...neonatal emergencies...distraction therapy.

As the train jerked to depart she closed her magazine and gazed out of the window. Luckily the seats beside them were free; they had the four-berth area to themselves. 'I've never been to Paris before.'

For a minute he thought she was talking to herself, then he realised it was actually an attempt at a civil conversation. Fine, they were in a public place. He could do civil just to get through the two-and-a-half-hour journey. But that would be as far as it went. 'It's a great place. I went a few years ago, when I did my gap year. I travelled around Europe for a bit.'

An eyebrow rose. 'I didn't know you did a gap year?'

'There are lots of things you don't know about me, Isabel. There are years and years of my life you know nothing about, and you've spent the last couple of months that I've been here running in the opposite direction whenever I'm around too. Hardly surprising you know nothing at all.'

'I know.' Tugging off her coat and hat, she plumped up her hair and looked at him. 'I'm sorry. After what I told you yesterday you'll understand that I just couldn't deal with you being back in my life again.'

Guilt could do that to you, he mused. 'And now?'

She shrugged a delicate shoulder. 'Now I don't have a choice. Thanks to Jacob.'

'Indeed. So let's make a deal, shall we?'

'Depends what it is?'

'We'll attend this conference as a team to represent the department. But after that, in our downtime, you don't get in my way and I won't get in yours.' That should do it. No cosy dinners, no shared intimacies. He could revisit some old haunts, discover new ones. On his own. He stuck out a hand.

'Fine by me.' She took it, her eyes widening at the shot of something that zipped between them as their palms touched. Heat burnt her cheeks as, with equal force, it seared through him, wild and unbidden, shocking in its intensity. For a moment she locked eyes again with him; this time he saw fire there. Then she let go and wiped her palm down her trousers as if trying to erase any trace of him from her skin. 'So, what are you going to do? In Paris? Do you have plans?'

'Oh, we're doing polite chit-chat? The ever-so-charming Delamere dialogue?'

All heat extinguished in a second, her glare intensified. 'Gosh, you really do hate me and my family, don't you?'

'Isla's sweet.' He let the insult by omission sit with her for a moment. What was that line between love and hate? He knew he was straddling something of equal measure. He wanted her, and he didn't want her. Too much either way, it was disturbing. 'I was actually referring to the way you smooth over any difficult social encounter. How easy it is for you to glide seamlessly from one meaningless subject to the next.'

'Then you don't know me at all either, Sean. You think you do, but whatever misapprehensions you have about me, they're wrong. I'm not like my mum and dad. I never was. I used to hate being paraded in front of the cameras and the elite with a begging bowl for whichever charity they favoured that month. Don't get me wrong,

I loved the causes they were fighting for, but I always felt awkward and embarrassed to be there.'

He kept his face passive. 'I thought I knew you. I always believed you were polar opposites to your parents.' And even though he'd consoled himself over the years that she had just resorted to Delamere type and turned her back on him, here she was challenging him. Because he'd seen her in action, the compassion and the dedication. Truth was, he didn't know her at all now, not really. He knew what she'd once been, but the young, bright Isabel Delamere didn't exist any more—he was learning that very quickly.

And the other unpalatable truth was that he was intrigued by her. He'd found out her secret and should have packed his bags—job done, history exposed—and put her and Cambridge behind him. But now he was in forced proximity with her and, well...she was a whole new fully realised version of the girl he'd known—a more professional, more intense, more dedicated version. It wouldn't hurt to learn just a little bit more. For old times' sake. 'I guess the Delamere name would have helped your job prospects no end, though.'

They were interrupted briefly by a waiter bringing the Chablis and cheese platter Sean had ordered on boarding.

Even though they were at loggerheads she still accepted a glass of wine from him. Took a sip. Then answered, 'Just like you I got where I am by sheer hard work. My name didn't open any doors for me. Once out of the State of Victoria no one's heard of Daddy—well, a few have but no one cares. He's a neurosurgeon too, which isn't very helpful to someone who wants a job in obstetrics.'

'It can't have hindered you, though.'

She shook her head. 'Whatever you want to believe, you clearly have it all worked out. But in reality I'm just bloody good at my job. I certainly don't have to prove myself to you; my competence is between me, and my patients. Who, I might say, have ranged from a pre-eclampsic mum in Kiwirrkurra, to a too-posh-to-push minor British royal and everything in between. So get off your high horse, Anderson, and give me a break.'

'You worked in Kiwirrkurra? I didn't know that. Impressive.' Kiwirrkurra had to be one of the most remote areas in the country so up-to-date technology and equipment would have been lacking, not to mention the barren, dry heat that shrouded the place. Not many would have been able to cope with the workload and unpredictability of outback medicine. It was the desert, for God's sake; somehow he just couldn't imagine Isabel there. 'How the hell did you keep your diamonds free from all that red dust? Must have been a nightmare.'

'Well, I didn't take—' She paused…looked at him… shook her head again, eyes rolling. 'You're pulling my chain. Ha-bloody-ha. Well, let me tell you, it was so-o-o hard, the dust got everywhere, and I mean, everywhere. I had to polish my diamonds every night before I went to bed.'

'Yeah?'

'Nah.' But there was a smile there. It glittered, lit up her face. And for the first time since he'd been in this hemisphere it felt as if there was a breakthrough between them. Tiny, compared to what they'd had years ago—or at least what he'd thought they'd had—but it was something they could hang the next week on instead of all this anger-fuelled bile. She laughed then. 'Well, you still know how to wind me up, I'll give you that.'

'Too easy, mate. Too easy.'

She had some more wine. 'Tell me about your gap year.'

How to capture the wealth of experiences in one conversation? 'It wasn't much different from a lot of people's to be honest. I took the year off between university and internship. Went to India to do some volunteer work at a community hospital—went for a month, stayed ten. Then took two months to see some of Europe.'

Her eyebrows rose. 'Must have been interesting, India?'

He laughed. 'Interesting is definitely one way to describe it. It was hard, harrowing, enlightening and liberating too. Maternal death rates are diabolical. Infant mortality's the same…all for the sake of a little bit of knowledge and some simple resources. Running water would be a good start.'

'You always were altruistically minded. You wanted to save the world. You wanted to achieve so much. And clearly you have. Do you remember when we—?'

'Anyway, when I was in Paris…' He cut her off, not wanting to do any of that Memory Lane stuff. He didn't want to remember that all-consuming passion they'd shared—for life, for their futures, for each other. The soft way she'd curled around him, the kisses. She might have let her guard down a little but he needed to make sure that his was firmly in place.

She'd already shattered his heart once—offered no explanation at the time and expected him to accept the new status quo, her rules: no questions asked. What were the chances she'd changed? Very little. And maybe she was right, maybe he didn't know her now, but he knew she was all but married to her job. He knew she could be single-minded when she wanted. And, if her actions at sixteen were anything to go by, she didn't allow anyone into that private part of herself. Not really.

So yes, while he could be convivial and keep the peace and put up a decent social front, he was better to be always on guard when it came to Isabel Delamere.

'Best thing about these conferences is the extra-curriculars, right?' Phil, the man sitting on her left, a portly GP from Hastings, nudged Isabel's side with a conspiratorial wink and clinked his glass against hers. All around the long wooden table people swirled and sipped and laughed and chatted in a dozen different languages trying to identify flavours that Isabel was sure shouldn't be in wine. *Petrol? Asparagus?*

'Yes. Well, I guess so. This is particularly fun. Any excuse for drink.' Although, she'd probably had quite enough on the train. Any more and she might lose her good-sense filter. Thankfully they'd had check-in at the hotel and registration for the conference before coming out on this delegates' do, so she hoped the lunchtime wine had cleared her system. The only downside to the trip so far—apart from Sean's presence—had been finding out that his room was next door to hers, so any downtime activities he'd be having in the City of Love had better not take place in their hotel. She did not want to hear that through the walls.

'Ah…' The man next to her laughed. 'I detect a funny accent. Aussie, are you? Or Kiwi? I can never tell the difference.'

She gave her new friend a smile. 'No one ever can outside of the southern hemisphere, apparently, but we are very proud of our differences. And our wines. I'm Australian.'

'It's a bit like the league of nations here—that guy over there, Manuel, he's from Spain and Natalie's from Belgium.'

'Nice to meet you.' It was lovely to be surrounded by such a diverse group of people. Phil seemed pleasant enough, but even though Sean thought she was the queen of small talk Isabel just didn't feel in the mood tonight, which kind of went against the whole conference spirit. Thank goodness Phil wasn't one of the people she needed to schmooze, because schmoozing was the furthest thing from tonight's wish list.

Before she got embroiled in any more conversation she looked down the table to the woman standing at the end leading the wine-tasting, and noticed things were getting started again. 'Oh, she's talking. All this swilling and sniffing… I'm never going to get the hang of this.' Isabel listened intently and tried to think about the taste of biscuits and did Madame really say pomegranate? Isabel wasn't sure she could taste anything other than, well…wine. But she wasn't going to admit that.

It was lovely. It was. The wine was delicious, pomegranate or not. The atmosphere in the ancient stone wine cellar—*le cave*—was cosy and lighthearted. She was in Paris! She'd had a glimpse of the Eiffel Tower, and the amazing old buildings and the Seine River and it all looked breathtakingly beautiful, like a film set. She should have felt on top of the world to be here. Drinking wine. Lots and lots of different kinds of wine, with clever, articulate people. But something was niggling her.

And he was sitting to her right.

All six feet one inch of dark and distracting niggle.

By some cruel twist of fate the organisers had placed him next to her. Which did not adhere to the *keep out of my way* game plan. The seating had been arranged so they were all squashed in along narrow benches that meant that she couldn't forget him. She could feel him. Couldn't keep out of his angry gaze. Couldn't ignore him chatting up the beautiful French midwife on his right.

Brunette. Stacked. Young. Hanging, open-mouthed, on his every word. The dashing, antipodean doctor with stories of daring deliveries in deepest Rajasthan. Damn him. It was hard not to listen, as Isabel, too, was mesmerised by a history she knew nothing of.

'"*Rabies!*" my colleague was shouting. "This camel has rabies, get me off, I want a different one!"' Sean was entertaining their half of the table now. His smile engaging, his drawl lilting and captivating. 'He was half sliding, half scrambling round this poor animal's neck in his hurry to get off it. I told him not to be such an idiot. It wasn't rabies—male camels foam at the mouth to attract mates. "He's not sick," I said. "He just fancies you, mate." You should have seen his face…'

I could have been there, Isabel thought to herself. They'd planned volunteer work abroad. They'd planned a future. And instead of listening to his adventures she would have been the one retelling them. Oh, damn…this wine was going to her head and making her maudlin.

Paris, she reminded herself. *I am a Parisian woman. I care not for ze ex.*

The very beautiful Frenchwoman at his side seemed to have forgotten her haughty Gallic woman-warrior roots and was flicking her long bouncy curls in a very flirty way as she tilted her head back and laughed at Sean's story.

'Very good. Very funny.' Isabel patted Sean's arm and gave the brunette a hard stare before flicking her own hair and snagging her fingers in it. 'Ouch. I...mean... Can you please pass the crackers?'

Flicking and flirting were way out of her comfort zone. She made a mental note to practise in the comfort of her hotel bedroom.

'Of course.' Sean turned around and gave her a weird look as she dragged her fingers through a knot and grimaced, before he flashed her a lovely wide smile. And she was the only one in the room who knew it didn't have an ounce of authenticity to it. 'What do you think of the wine, Isabel? As good as back home?'

'Oh, I don't know...' She looked at her surroundings, breathing in the age-old aroma of fermenting grapes and oak barrels, and sighed. 'There's something about Paris... Sacrilege, I know, but everything seems better here.'

'Even me?' This time his grin was real. And her gut tightened in response. He was joking with her, and she was aware that she'd drunk more than her fair share of wine, so yes...he did seem a teensy bit better. Not that she was about to admit to that.

The newly adopted Frenchwoman in her wanted to throw him a disdainful shrug as if he were but crumbs on ze floor, but the Aussie in her came out fighting. 'Ah, Seany Boy, I don't want to burst your bubble, but there's only so much that grog goggles can enhance.' And so that had been a little over-loud and rather more matey than she intended.

His voice again, close to her ear. Too close. Was it hot

in here? 'Are you okay, Isabel? It's been a long day. You look a bit flushed. You sound a little…tense.'

Hardly surprising under the circumstances. 'I'm fine, thank you for asking.' The wine-tasting woman was handing out small glasses of something that looked like cough syrup. That made how many glasses they'd each consumed? Isabel didn't dare to think. 'Too much of this, I guess. I'd better be careful.'

'Spoilsport. We're in France—you need to chill a little.' He swirled the stem of his glass before he looked at her again. 'Vivienne and a few of the others are thinking of going to a club after this…'

'Vivienne?'

His confused frown deepened as he flicked his thumb to the woman on his right. 'Yes, Vivienne. She's from Aix-en-Provence.'

'Lucky her. She's very pretty.'

He shrugged. 'Yes, she is.'

A pang of something Isabel didn't want to acknowledge, but knew damned well was jealousy, arrowed through her tummy. He wasn't hers to pine after. She'd made sure of that years ago, and to hammer that message home she'd spilled her secret to him and watched any kind of hope shrivel. 'Well, have fun. At the club. With Vivienne.'

He grinned, eyes darting to the long dark tresses, the flicking. 'I intend to.'

I bet you do. Irritation rising from her stomach in a tight, hard ball of acid, Isabel tried to wriggle her feet out from under the table, which was easier said than done. 'Really? You can't wait until I've gone?'

'What the hell…' he growled, his voice hard and low, '…has it got to do with you?'

'Because…' *It hurts. Because*—she realised with a sharp sting in her chest—*I want you to look at me like that, as if you're anticipating a delicious treat.*

Definitely too much wine.

The best idea would be to leave him to it. Really, the best idea would have been not to allow him to come in the first place. No, the best idea… She sighed. Why was it that the best ideas always happened after the event? She finally managed to get her feet out from the bench and tried to stand up, wobbling a little, then losing her balance in her new high-heeled suede boots. 'Oops.'

Quick as a flash he caught her by the arm and steadied her. 'Are you okay?'

'Oh, for goodness' sake, I just wobbled. I'm fine.' But she wasn't, not now. At the touch of his hand on her bare skin, desire fired through her. It had been so long since she'd felt it, so alien to her, it was a shock. All at once her body craved more touching. More touching him. More everything.

Oh, God. She looked at his broad chest covered in a crisp white collared shirt. At the model-worthy jawline. At that smiling mouth that seemed to mock and tease and was still so damned kissable. At those dark eyes boring into her. But most of all she felt his heat against hers. And she realised, with even more disbelief, that she wanted Sean Anderson in her bed.

Which was…well, it was surprising. Ever since she'd lost the baby her sexual experience had been marred by a deep-seated fear of getting pregnant; she'd been uptight and never really enjoyed herself. And she'd always felt, strangely, as if she was betraying Sean. So she hadn't really explored that side of herself.

Of all the idiotic things. Of all the pointless wanting… She could not want him. After all, he'd made it very clear that he didn't want her at all. And who could blame him?

But it was happening. And not only that, his breath was whispering across her neck sending more and more shivers across her body. 'Do you need a hand getting home, Izzy?'

She edged away from the heat. 'Not at all. I'm a big girl now. Besides, don't you have *la belle* Vivienne from Aix-en-Provence to consider? I don't want to cramp your style.'

He blew out an irritated breath. 'Really?'

'Yes. Really.' She could hear her voice rising and struggled to keep it low and steady so the others couldn't hear, particularly the hair-flicking lady. 'I'm just saying what I see. It's clear as day that you have plans for later. And we all love extra-curriculars, right?'

Sean's hand dropped from Isabel's arm and she could sense the rage rippling through him. His eyes darkened beyond black. His voice was hushed but angry. 'You made it very clear a long time ago that there was nothing you wanted from me. What the hell do you expect me to do? Keep hanging on? Because I will not do that, Isabel, I have my own life to live. I won't wait around for you to decide what you want.'

'I'm not asking you to.'

'Funny, because that's not how it seems to me. You don't want me to go with Vivienne? You don't want me to have fun, that's for sure.'

'Never in your wildest dreams, Sean Anderson, would I ever want anything from you. It's too late for that, way too late.'

'And whose fault is that?'

As if she didn't know already.

His words were like daggers in her heart. And he was so close, too close. His mouth in kissing distance—which was such an inappropriate thought right now, but there it was. Her heart thumped in a traitorous dance.

'Whatever. Go, do what you like. I'm leaving now anyway.' Biting back her anger as much as she could, Isabel looked from Sean to Vivienne to the rest of the table, who were grinning in the candlelight and had no idea of the shared history and the huge amount of balls it was taking just to be here with him at all.

She needed to get away from him. To put their past life far behind her. To put this new attraction back where it couldn't hurt her. Who'd have thought it, but after seventeen years of fighting she needed to get over Sean Anderson all over again. And fast.

CHAPTER FOUR

TWENTY MINUTES AND a decent dose of fresh cold Parisian air later, Isabel was feeling much more in control. The walk—or rather, the angry stamp—back to the hotel allowed a good view of the Eiffel Tower down the Champs de Mars, and oh, what a spectacular light show as it changed colours; red and green like a Christmas tree, then the tricolour and then so many different colours it was enchanting...or it probably was to anyone else, but everything was tainted with their stupid argument and the feelings of jealousy and hopelessness raging through her.

Added to the glorious sight of the Eiffel Tower there were strings and strings of twinkling Christmas lights draped along the street lampposts and trees, giving the whole place a really magical atmosphere. She'd never been anywhere cold at Christmas so this year was going to be a first. It was already breathtaking—or might have been if she hadn't been struggling for a calming breath anyway. If she wasn't mistaken there was a hint of snow, too, in the cool breeze that whipped around her cheeks and blasted Sean from her skin.

Just about.

She decided not to think about him any more. She

was in France to enjoy herself, so that was what she would do.

Except...she couldn't get him out of her head. Annoying man! Annoying hormones that made her want him and want to run from him at the same time.

The claw-foot bathtub in her en-suite was just about overflowing with lavender-scented bubbles, a small nightcap of red wine was sitting on the window ledge, and if she craned her neck to the left she could see the street Christmas lights from the bathroom window.

A quick bath. A peruse of her presentation, then bed. If she could sleep at all with her emotions still coating everything she did. She slipped the white fluffy bathrobe off and stepped one foot into the warm water, stiffening quickly at the sharp rap on her door.

Probably housekeeping. Or room service—not that she'd asked for anything. But who else would it have been at this time of night?

Sean?

And there was a mind meld of thought process. Unlikely—Sean was out with a beautiful woman.

Another knock.

Ignoring the mysterious tachycardia and excitement roaring through her, she told herself not to be so stupid; it was probably someone knocking on the wrong door. She wrapped the bathrobe around herself again, and pattered one dry, one wet foot to the door. Through the little eyeglass she could see a man. *Sean.*

No. Not when she'd managed to flush him to the darkest corner of her brain. Not when she was pretty much naked. Not when she'd realised that these lurching feelings about him were a heady combination of guilt and lust. Which had to be the worst kind of concoction of hormones, surely? Especially when the lust was not re-ciprocated and the guilt just made him glare at her with anger in his eyes. What did he want now? To gloat? What to do?

Pretend she was asleep? Yes. Good idea. She turned her back to the door and held her breath. He would go away. She would sleep. She would be fine tomorrow.

'Izzy?' The knocking recommenced. 'Isabel, for God's sake, woman, open the door.'

Starting to feel a bit light-headed from holding her breath, she very slowly let the air from her lungs and said nothing.

'Isabel... You are the worst liar in the world.'

'What?' Man, he really did know how to wind her up. Irritation now skittering down her spine, she threw open the door. 'What the hell are you talking about?'

'You. You were pretending not to be here.'

'I was not. And please be quiet, you'll wake the neigh-bours.'

'I am the neighbours.' Shaking his head, he gave her a sort of smirk that made her heart patter and her breath hitch. 'You were standing at the door, you saw who it was and you pretended not to be here. Don't deny it. I saw the shadows changing under the door frame.'

Busted. 'So, why are you here? Seeing as you hate the air I breathe.'

'You know why. You don't get to talk to me like that. To make me think...' He scuffed a hand through his hair and shook his head. Exasperated.

'What?'

'That there's unfinished business here.'

She swallowed through a dry throat. 'What do you mean? Unfinished business?'

'For God's sake, Isabel, you know exactly what I mean. We have to deal with this.'

She shook her head. She was so confused, her head muddled with the unending ache and so many conflicting thoughts. 'I remember that we agreed to stay out of each other's way. I remember you were going to go and have fun. Why aren't you out at a club? Vivienne seemed very interested in going, and particularly with you, if all that hair flicking was anything to go by.'

'I don't care about Vivienne.' Without seeming to give any thought to how this looked, or what she thought about it, he stepped into the room, his presence filling the space. *God,* he looked amazing, all wrapped up in a scarf and heavy coat, his cheeks flushed with cold and his hair peaky. Eyes glittering with emotions, ones that she couldn't quite read but she was pretty sure were rage. And desire. Oh, yes, she could see that. Maybe he was still thinking about Vivienne?

'She'll be very upset.'

'I doubt that very much.' He looked at her, his impassioned gaze running from her hair—all shoved up into a messy clip on top of her head—to her throat, then to her white bathrobe, and lower.

Heat prickled all over her like a rash. How could a man make her feel so...so turned on with just a look? He reached for the top of her robe and ran his fingertips across the fabric, touching, ever so minutely, her skin. Pulled the robe tighter across her body.

Standing here, almost naked but for one very precarious item of clothing, she felt set alight. Swallowing was hard. Speaking, finding words, even harder. He was so close and all she could smell was him and the lavender and Paris. He was so close she could have...might have…kissed him, invited him into her bath. To her bed. Her heart. Then she remembered.

Stepping away she snarled, because it was the only thing she could manage, 'You're drunk.'

'Don't be ridiculous.' And, truth be told, he looked about as sober as she'd ever seen him. He pulled the robe tighter across her chest, covering up her exposed skin. 'Do you think I'd only come here if I was drunk?'

'I can't see any reason why you'd come here at all. You hate me, Sean, you've made that very clear.'

He frowned, stalked to the console, poured a glass of red wine and sank half of it in one gulp. 'I don't hate you, Isabel. I just hate what happened—there's a big difference.'

'You said you couldn't bear to look at me.' She hauled in a breath, two; every moment she spent with him had her fired up one way or another. 'As far as you're concerned I lied to you, betrayed you, and that is unforgivable, no matter what I went through.'

He slammed the glass down. 'You think betrayal is excusable?'

'Yes, given the circumstances.'

'The circumstances were that I loved you, Isabel. You meant everything to me. And you said the same to me, over and over. *We* created that baby.' His jaw set. 'I guess that counted for nothing? You just cast me aside.'

She felt his dismissal keenly in her chest, ricocheting over her heart, remorseless. She'd known he loved her; that knowledge had carried her for a long time. It had allowed her to excuse what she'd done in the name of protection, of love. It had allowed her to function. To grieve, and to heal. 'Your love was everything to me and, God knows, I loved you too, Sean. More than you could imagine.'

'So, that's why you kept the truth from me? Why you refused to even speak to me?'

'Yes, actually it was.' She stepped closer to him, her hand on his chest. Because she wanted to touch him one last time, because she knew there was no coming back from this. How could there be? There was too much looming between them. Too much past, too much hurt. Too much for them ever to surmount. Too much lost love. 'What was the point in ruining two lives?'

'Knowing what you were going through, what we'd lost, wouldn't have ruined my life—don't you get it? It could have made us stronger. You just didn't give us a chance. You didn't give me a chance. You shut down, hibernated your life, ran away from any contact.'

'I was protecting myself.'

'That was my job,' he growled. The rest of the wine went down his throat. 'For the first time in your life you did exactly what your parents taught you to do, Isabel, you put on a mask and pretended all the pain had gone, that you were just fine. And by doing that you closed yourself off from anyone who might help you.' He moved away from her hand as if it were a dagger, a threat. 'What a waste. What a bloody shame.'

'Yes. Yes, it is. Because you're right, what we had was special and I regret not letting you in, more than anything. Happy now?'

'You think hearing that makes me happy?'

She waved towards the door, trying not to show how much his rejection hurt on the back of so much need. She just ached to feel his arms around her, to taste him again, to make everything right between them. And it would never happen. Not now. 'There isn't any more to say. Go. Please. Just leave me alone.'

'Fine.' He stalked to the door. As he pressed down the handle he rested his forehead against the wood, took a minute to regulate his breathing. Then he turned dark eyes on her. He held her gaze for longer than anyone had ever looked at her. She saw flashes of gold in there, anger. Pain. Desire. A struggle with all three. 'What did you mean, earlier, when you asked me to wait until you'd left before I went to the club?'

Her heart hammered against her breastbone in a panicked beat. 'Nothing. I didn't mean anything by it. I'd had too much wine.' But he knew exactly what she'd meant. That she still had feelings for him. That she wanted to be the woman he took home tonight, not Vivienne.

'And now?'

'Now what?' Dangerous. Heat skittered through her abdomen. Lower.

He stepped closer and grabbed her wrist, pulling her to him, his eyes wild now, his breath quick, his growing hardness apparent. Despite everything, he wanted her.

Her ragged breathing stalled. All the tension and emotion bundled into her fists and she grabbed his coat lapels, her mouth inches from his.

For God's sake, leave.

It made no sense to Sean that he wanted to hate Isabel Delamere, but couldn't. She peered up at him with questions in her eyes. And he didn't know the answers. Couldn't tell her any more than that he was crazy with the seesawing of his head, the push-pull of attraction.

As she reached for his coat her robe fell open a little and he looked away, not willing to glimpse something so intimate. He did not want to be intimate with her; he knew what price that came with. And it was way too high for him—long, long years of getting over her. But too late, he'd caught sight of creamy skin, a tight nipple bud. And a riot of fresh male hormones arrowed to his groin.

He needed to get out.

That was about as far as his thoughts went as he lowered his mouth. She gasped once she realised what he was offering. Then her lips were on his and his brain shut down.

The kiss was slow at first, testing. A guttural mewl as his tongue pressed against her closed mouth. But when she opened to him the groan was very definitely his. The push of her tongue against his caused a rush of blood and heat away from his brain and very fast headed south. She tasted divine. She tasted of wine and sophistication. Of anger and heat. She did not taste like he remembered, a sixteen-year-old girl fresh from school. She was different, hot, hungry, and very definitely all grown woman. And he wanted to feast on her.

'Oh, God, Isabel...' Dragging his mouth from hers, he kissed a trail down to the nape of her neck, his fingers grazed the edge of the robe and he slid his hand onto the bare skin of her waist and drew her closer. She softened against him with a moan and everything finally made sense. This was what he needed. *She* was what he needed. The chaos swirling in his chest cemented into a stark hunger as he slid fingers over silken skin.

She pulled back with a smile. 'Wait a minute... I'm here wearing relatively nothing, and you're dressed for an igloo. Too. Many. Clothes.' She unwound his scarf and threw it to the floor, pushed his coat from his shoulders and let it fall. Her hands stalled at his shoulders; she stroked the thick fabric of his shirt, down his arms to his hands, which she clasped into hers. 'I can't believe…after all this time…is it what you want? Am I, what you want?'

'Do you even need to ask?' He pulled her back to him, felt her melt against his body as he plundered her sweet mouth. The smell of her drove him wild, but the taste of her pushed him close to a place he'd never been before. God, yes, he wanted her, wanted to be inside her, to hear her moan his name, to feel her around him.

She wound her hands around his neck and pulled him closer, grinding her hips against his. He had no doubt that she wanted him as much as he wanted her, and that stoked even more heat in his belly.

Unable to resist any longer, he dragged the bathrobe from her shoulders and lay her down on the bed as she fumbled with his shirt, dragging it over his head. He kicked off shoes and socks, dragged down his jeans and then they were naked. Like all those years ago. But this was not the same. She was not the same. And he had so much more experience now—no clumsy fumblings, no teenage angst. He knew how to please a woman and he intended to please Isabel.

Taking a moment, he gazed at her face, at the kiss-swollen lips, and misted eyes. At the soft, sexy smile that spurred him on, that made him weak-kneed. Then he looked lower, wanting to feast his gaze on a body that he hadn't seen in seventeen years. And to learn about her. To relearn what she liked. To acquaint himself with the new dips and curves, with the smooth, silky feel of her skin. The perfect breasts, a tight belly that belied a miscarriage, that a baby had been inside her.

His baby.

At once he was filled with profound and gut-wrenching emotion—she'd been through too much on her own. He should have been there with her. He should have done something. He should have known—somewhere deep within himself he should have intuitively known that she was suffering, that a part of him was inside her and broken. That she'd carried that guilt around with her for all these years, too afraid to speak of it, too scarred to share it. Until he'd pushed her...that secret was theirs, only theirs.

The emotion had a name—he didn't want to think about it.

Pushing a curl of hair behind her ear, he gave her a gentle kiss on her mouth. 'Izzy, we can't do this.'

CHAPTER FIVE

'YOU'RE FREAKING KIDDING ME, right?' Isabel drew away from the best kiss of her entire life and took a deep breath. 'What do you mean? You just said you wanted to…'

'I do want to. I just don't think we should. It's late. We're probably drunk. We have to work tomorrow. And there's too much baggage and history that sits right here.' He pointed to the space between them. 'Getting in the way.'

Instead of feeling frustrated, she felt a rush of affection. God love him, he was trying to do right by her. And okay, well, she had to admit there was a teeny hint of frustration there. Wriggling closer to him, she smiled, relishing the touch of hot bare skin against hers. 'Oops, that baggage and history just got squashed under my gargantuan ar—'

'Whoa, Izzy.' His eyes lit up, the darkness she'd seen momentarily before now gone, replaced with humour and heat. 'I've never seen you like this before.'

'I've never felt like this before.' It was true. Suddenly so hot, so alive and fired up, Isabel stroked down his naked chest. Abs that she'd never seen before, honed to perfection. Arms so muscled and strong that she felt featherlight and ethereal in his embrace. A sun-kissed chest she wanted to shelter against, to kiss, to lick… She'd never wanted a man so much in her whole life. Truth was, she'd never stopped wanting him.

He was right. What a waste of all those years. Of running and hiding and trying to cover up real deep-down feelings. Of being so, so frightened of falling in love and risking her heart all over again. 'Don't stop. We *can* do this. We can do what we want. Don't wrap me up in cotton wool, Sean. Don't treat me any differently to any of your other—'

'There are no others.'

'Liar.' She knew he was attractive to every damned woman he gave five minutes' attention to and knew, too, through the MMU grapevine, that he had a history of breaking hearts. Couldn't commit. Never gave a reason why.

'No. Not any more.' He frowned but his hand stroked the underside of her breast, sending shivers of desire rippling through her. How could she have lived her whole life never having him again? How could she have survived? Being in his gaze felt as if she'd come home to a warm cocoon after being out in a freezing wilderness. Sure, there were things to work out. A lot of things. But right now, in this room at this moment, it felt so right to be with him.

'And Vivienne?'

'For goodness' sake. She is nothing to me.'

'In that case…' she pressed a kiss onto his creased forehead '…forget the past.'

Then, she pressed a finger to his mouth to prevent him from speaking as she kissed each of his eyelids. 'You don't know me. Not really. You don't know who I am, what I want, what I need.' Her finger ran along the top of his lip; she laughed as he tried to nip it with his teeth. 'Or what I like, Sean.'

'Izzy…' There was a warning in his voice.

'This. Is. New. Everything starts from now.' A kiss onto the tip of his nose. 'Hi, my name is Isabel. *Isabel*, not Izzy. I am an obstetrician and I live in Cambridge, England. I'm here in Paris at a conference and I want to have some extracurricular fun.'

Then she licked across his lips, hungry, greedy for his mouth. 'I'm very, very pleased to meet you.' Her hand stroked down his stomach towards a very-pleased-to-see-her erection. She touched the tip and enjoyed the sound his throat made as he growled her name in warning.

'Isabel, you want to watch what you do with that. It's got a mind of its own.'

'How very convenient.' She bent and licked the tip, then took him full into her mouth ignoring his protestations, and pushing him back against the duvet. She could feel he was holding back a thrust so she sucked down his length again and again, his throaty groans spurring her on. She loved the taste of him, the hard length. She loved that she could make him feel so good.

'Izzy.' His hand grasped her hair and she stopped. 'Isabel. You'd better stop.'

As she paused he shifted position, edging away from her grasp and sucking a nipple into his mouth. Heat shimmied through her. She arched her back, greedy for more, for his mouth on her body, on every part. Hot and wet. His fingers now on her thigh, higher, deeper, sinking into her core. And she was kissing him again, exploring this new taste that was laced with an old memory.

His smell that was different yet familiar. His touch...
my God, his touch was expert now. He knew just how
to take her to the edge and tease. His erection was dangerously, enticingly close, nudging against her opening.

'You still like this?' He pressed a fingertip into her
rib and she screamed.

'Stop that! No tickling. Kiss me.' She didn't want to
relive anything; she wanted to create new experiences,
to build fresh memories. She didn't want to look backwards. She wanted...she wanted him inside her. For a
second she was serious, the most serious she'd been in
a long time. Made sure she looked deep into his eyes
and told him the truth. There had been too many lies
between them. 'I want you, Sean. I want you so much.'

'Back at ya, kiddo.' This new kiss was slow and hard,
Sean taking his time as he stoked a fire that had smoul-
dered over the last year, burst into roaring flames over
the last week and was now burning out of control. She
moved against him, feeling the pressure of him, hot and
hard, against her thigh.

'Condom?' he groaned, his forehead against hers.
Eyes gazing down at her, startling in their honesty.

'Yes.' She held his gaze. The last time they'd done
this had ended in such heartbreak. Was it so stupid to be
doing it again? To risk everything once more?

He touched her cheek as if he could read her thoughts,
his smile genuine, so loving and tender it almost cracked
her heart. When had he become so thoughtful? So sexy
and so within reach? When had he become so expert at
knowing what a woman needed? When had he changed?
Her throat filled because she knew the answer: in those
wilderness years, without her.

His voice was soft yet filled with affection that went

deeper than sex. 'It's okay, Isabel, it won't happen again. I won't let it happen again.'

Neither would she. 'Of course.' And if a baby did happen again she would tell him, she wouldn't hide anything from him. This time she'd be honest. 'In my...in my bag.'

'In my wallet.' He reached down, took out a foil, and slipped on the condom. Then he was pushing into her, slow and gentle, and she felt him fill her. So perfect. So complete. She wrapped her legs around his backside to feel him deeper. Harder.

'Oh, my God, Isabel. You are so perfect. So beautiful.' He began slow thrusts, his fists holding her wrists above her head, snatching greedy, playful bites at her nipples and her breasts. She felt captured, captivated, possessed by him. This man. This wondrous man whom she had broken as much as she was broken. And yet he put her back together again with this act.

The moves changed and the air charged. He stopped the playfulness as he kissed her hot and hard and wet. Sensation after sensation pulsed through her. She was hanging on by a thin thread. His body tensed; she could feel pressure rising as she met him thrust for thrust, joining the rhythm as he picked up pace.

His eyes didn't leave hers. His hands didn't release hers. And as they both shuddered to climax—releasing the tension coiled so deep between them for so long—she wished, *God* how she wished, she had never let him go.

'Well, wow.' Sean shifted to Isabel's side and stroked her cheek. It was the first time he'd seen her looking so bone-deep relaxed. 'I wasn't expecting that.'

'Me neither.' She shuffled into the crook of his arm,

blonde hair splayed out over the pillow. 'That was very lovely, thank you.'

'Your manners are impeccable. Daddy would be proud. You sound very English all of a sudden.' He pretended to look under the duvet. 'Where's my Aussie girl gone?'

'I'm still here.' She stroked fingertips gently down his chest, her voice a whisper. 'I'm here.'

'So you are.' Something he'd never believed possible had been possible. He tipped her chin and kissed her again. She returned the kiss eagerly. It had been amazing and surprising that intensity went so deep. A dream. Something he'd imagined for years. Making love into the night, no reason to leave. Hours and hours stretched ahead of them. Days, years. A lifetime. He'd never had the chance to do this before. Time together had been so limited, snatched moments that had ended in disaster.

He felt frustration begin to roll through him. But tried to push it back.

He wondered when he'd be able to stop thinking about the baby. The lie. He wondered if he'd ever be able to truly move on now that he knew, and he realised that moving on was something Isabel had been trying to do when she'd moved to Cambridge. It wasn't to get away from him; it was to restart her life.

So lying in bed with him probably wasn't what she'd had planned. Or him, either. In fact, this whole sex thing had pushed them across a line now and made things even less clear than they were before. And even though he'd lain awake in many other women's beds over the years trying to work out just how to leave, he'd never felt so conflicted about his next step.

Everything he'd said was true. She was perfect. She

was beautiful. She was so much more than he'd imagined. And he'd wanted her so badly, for so long. All those years of wondering, of dating other women, of trying to put her behind him. But it had been pointless because the attraction was still there. The need. The visceral tug towards her—even though there was danger with every step.

He wanted to think there could be a future, but he couldn't get past the fact that she'd treated his heart with so little respect before—would she do the same again? Did he even want to give her the chance? Had it, in the end, just been sex for old times' sake?

Like he was even going to ask that dumb question. He didn't want to contemplate what her answer might be.

'What are you thinking?' Her voice brought him back to the now.

'That you, missy, have a very important presentation in a few hours and you need to get rested up before it.' He started to pull the sheet back ready to make his leave. They both needed time to get their heads around this whole new complication. Well, he did, that was for sure. What did he actually want now? Other than a rerun of ten minutes ago.

But before he could stand up her fingers slowly tiptoed across his thigh. She spoke, her words punctuated by soft kisses down his chest. 'For some reason...I'm just not...sleepy.' Her fingers connected with his now growing erection. Because he was, after all, just a red-blooded man with the most beautiful woman in the entire universe lying naked next to him. Oh, and a whole host of emotions swimming across his chest. Yeah, his body still wanted her, regardless of the past. It was his head that was causing trouble.

Her voice was a warm breeze over his skin, tender yet filled with a promise. 'Don't know about you, Seany Boy, but exercise always makes me sleep so much better. And short of going downstairs to the hotel gym, I can only think of one kind of exercise we could do at this time of night. You?'

'Isabel—' He turned, then, with gargantuan effort, to tell her. To put some distance between his feelings and his needs. But the trill of her mobile phone jolted her upright.

'Oh. Who could that be at this time?' Wrapping a sheet round her, she grabbed her bag from the floor next to the bed and pulled out her phone. 'It's Isla. What would she—? Oh? The baby? D'you think?' Throwing Sean an apologetic look, she pointed to the phone. 'I'm so sorry…but I've just got to get this. I won't be long.'

And so he was surplus to requirement. It was a decent enough excuse to regroup and rethink. To get the hell out, and work out what to do next.

Isabel watched the door close behind Sean and blew out a deep breath. Getting her head around whatever the hell had just happened would have to be banked until after she'd spoken to Isla. But she got the feeling he hadn't been able to get away quickly enough. Maybe he was having second thoughts, too? 'Isla? Isla, are you okay?'

'Isabel. Oh, my God, Isabel.' The line was crackly but she could still hear her sister's voice filled with wonder. 'He's beautiful. Perfect. I can't believe. Oh…'

'You've had the baby?' Isabel's heart swelled and she fought back tears. Her sister was a mother. She hadn't been there for her. Her mouth crumpled as she forced words out. 'Oh, sweetie. How was it? Are you okay? Is he okay? A name? What happened—aren't you early? Was Alessi there?'

Clearly having a better handle on things than Isabel, her sister drew a sharp intake of breath and began, 'Okay, I can't remember which question was first. You have a nephew. A gorgeous, gorgeous nephew, all fingers and toes accounted for and lots of dark hair like his daddy. Born three hours ago.'

'Oh, wow. Three hours? You were going to phone me when you went into labour.' Isabel stopped short. Three hours ago she was busy. With Sean. Speaking to her sister wouldn't have been the best thing to happen. But maybe if they had been interrupted she wouldn't now have these weird mixed emotions whirling through her chest. What they'd done had made things more complicated, not less. 'Oh, wow, I'm so happy for you. Mega congratulations, little sis.'

'It was all so quick, and I couldn't remember the time difference with my scrambled mummy brain—and the labour drugs—and your last email said you were going to Paris? So I wasn't sure—'

'Yes. I am. *Je suis ici*—in Paris.' *Having sex with my ex. And now I want to talk about it, but I can't.* Bad timing. All round. 'So, what was your labour like? Textbook? Knowing you it was probably textbook.'

'Quit schmoozing. It was okay. No, actually it hurt like hell…' There was a pause. 'Iz, are you okay with me talking to you about this? I mean…you know…because of before?'

Because of her own baby boy? Because he'd been too frail, too tiny to live, because she hadn't been able to protect him the way other mothers could. Hadn't been able to grow him to his full potential the way Isla had.

An arrow of pain seared her heart. He would have been a teenager now, getting ready to fly the nest. She would have had all those memories, sleepless nights, first days at school...so many firsts; long hot summers, a house full of primary-coloured plastic and arguments over too loud music. Instead she had heartache and an extremely unwise choice of sexual partner. She couldn't even blame that on mummy brain.

She had to let it all go. She had to move on. Her baby was gone. Gone, but in her heart for ever. *Do not spoil your sister's day.* 'Of course, I'm fine, Isla. Talk away. I want to hear about everything...absolutely everything. I'm so happy for you. I'm just sorry I couldn't be there to hold your hand. I'm sending hugs, heaps and heaps of hugs.'

'Oh, you know I'd have liked you to be here, Iz. I would have, but you need to be away from here... I totally get it. I love you.'

Emotion constricted Isabel's throat; she had to force words out. 'I love you too.' Ever since Isla had waved Isabel off onto the flight to London she had been nothing but supportive of Isabel's need to get away from Melbourne, to put her life there behind her. To forget Sean. Yeah, that plan had worked really well. 'So come on, a name? What did you go with in the end?'

'Geo, after Alessi's brother, the triplet who died. I told you about him, didn't I?'

'Yes, yes. The baby who didn't make it...' Another one. *Breathe. Breathe.* 'That's a lovely gesture, Isla. Alessi must be so proud.' Isabel had chosen a name for her boy too but had never properly given it to him. She hadn't been able to think straight after she'd given birth, after they took his little body away. There'd been no burial. Nothing to remember him by. But she did have a name for him.

'Alessi? Proud?' Her sister laughed down the line and it was so good to hear her so happy. 'Oh, yes, and then some. He's acting like he's the only man who's ever fathered a child. Still, if it means he continues to treat me like a princess then I'm happy. I'm not allowed to move a single muscle without him making sure I'm okay.'

'Lucky you, enjoy it while you can. Give baby Geo lots of kisses from his very happy auntie and email me some photos, now! Oh…who delivered you? Don't tell me it was Alessi?'

There was a kerfuffle in the background, familiar hospital noises—bleeps, voices. The sweet, soft snuffle of a contented newborn. 'No, he was too busy up the top end dealing with me, trying to keep me calm. Darcie was the attending, she was amazing. Very patient, all things considered. I think I may have been a bit rude to everyone, but at least it made them give me more pain relief. Talking of Darcie, did I tell you…? It's all hearts and roses over here. You'll never guess who she's dating. True love and everything.'

Sometimes Isabel really missed the gossip of her home town. The familiar. 'No? Who? Spill.'

'Only Lucas bloody Elliot!'

The heartthrob of the MMU. 'Mr Playboy himself? No way! I thought you said they hated the sight of each other.' But Isabel knew that there was a thin line between love and hate—that passion came in many forms and was fuelled by many different emotions.

Isla sighed. 'It's really cute to watch actually. There were fireworks all along the way—neither of them wanted to admit they were falling in love. Little Cora's thrilled too. Now she has an auntie as well as an uncle to watch her. Quite a unit, they are.'

Hearing all the news she'd missed out on made Isabel realise just how far away from them she was. Darcie had only been in Melbourne less than a year herself, having been part of the same exchange as Isabel. In fact, Darcie would be scheduled to return to Isabel's job in a few weeks, when the year's exchange was over. 'Well, that'll cause Darcie a few sleepless nights if she's fallen for Lucas, because he's firmly committed to staying in Melbourne with his brother and niece.'

'I know. He's been such a rock for them both since his sister-in-law died. There's no way he'd leave all that behind. But I hope it won't mean you're not coming home? Your job will still be open if she decides to stay here, right?'

Isabel had a brief image of her and Sean arriving off the same flight hand in hand stepping onto Aussie soil. Then she shook away such a fantasy. But whatever happened, she was definitely going home. And soon. 'Absolutely. Try and stop me. Oh, I do miss you all.'

'We miss you too. They all say hi.' It seemed the labour drugs were still in Isla's system as she chatted on oblivious to the fact it was five o'clock in the morning for her. 'Come home soon. I want you to meet Geo. Oh... and talking of babies...more goss hot off the press. Oliver and Emily are looking to adopt another baby. So sweet. Toby's growing into such a lovely boy and they want to add to their family.'

Another MMU romance—seemed there had been quite a few recently. Something in the water. Obstetrician Oliver and midwife Emily had been having marriage problems back when Isabel had been there; it was good to hear that they'd managed to put their rough past behind them. It was good to hear that at least some re-kindled relationships could work.

She'd bet that Oliver hadn't hot-footed out of the bed-room at the first opportunity. 'I'm glad things worked out for them in the end. Their marriage was put under so much pressure struggling with IVF. It was hard for them to see beyond that. Time makes such a difference.' Geez, she could have been talking about her and Sean. But there wouldn't be any happy endings for them. Not with the way he'd looked as he'd left. She couldn't help the yearning in her voice. 'But now everyone sounds so settled and happy.'

'They all want to know what you've been up to. Have you met anyone?' There was a pause, then Isla cleared her throat. 'How's Sean?'

What to say? *Hot sex is epic. It's the aftermath that's the problem. How to move on from here?* 'He's...he's okay. Actually, he's here in Paris with me.'

'What the hell? What do you mean? Here's me rab-biting on... Have you told him?' For a woman who'd recently given birth, Isla was very animated. Those pregnancy hormones were amazing. Isabel had seen some women act as if nothing earth-shattering had hap-pened—popped out a baby and gone straight back to normal life, thank you very much. 'Are you...? You know...?'

We just did. 'It's just a conference.'

'Nothing's *just* a conference if Sean's there. You're away with him? Isabel? In Paris?' A loud squawking zinged down the phone line. Voices. A lot of loud gar-bled language. Greek? Cries, a loud hullabaloo. Then Isla was back. 'Sorry, hon. I've got to go. Geo's hungry,

I think. Alessi's parents have just arrived. It's chaos. I'll call you. Call me. Talk soon. I love you.'

And she was gone. Isabel's head was spinning. There was never enough time to chat properly and the long-distance hum always interfered. She wanted to sit down and talk to her sister, to hold her precious nephew. She wanted to go home. A few more weeks and she would... only a few more weeks until the end of this contract. And then what?

She scrunched up the Egyptian cotton sheet in her hand and looked down at where Sean had been lying a few moments ago. Remembered how good he had made her feel. And how easily he'd slipped away. So instead of *then what*, it was, *now* what? Now how to face the elusive Dr Anderson?

Isabel had absolutely no idea.

CHAPTER SIX

ISABEL NEEDN'T HAVE WORRIED. There was no time for chatting at breakfast with Mr Incubator doing all the talking. No chance to catch up over lunch as she'd been cordially invited to the speaker's special VIP luncheon. Then after her presentation she'd been whisked away on a tour of the Sacré-Coeur followed by dinner and a show in Montmartre, which, it appeared, Sean, or rather Jacob when he'd registered, hadn't signed up for. And after all that French flavour she was good and ready for bed. To sleep on her own.

And no late-night visits. She didn't know whether to be relieved or disappointed.

Turned out there was rather more of the latter than she expected.

The next day flew by with more meetings—one a real success with the promise of a hefty discount on some new high-tech monitors—and interesting talks all round. She only had one more day to dodge Sean's questioning eyes, then he'd be heading back home and she'd have a couple of free days to shop. The French baby clothes were so gorgeous and chic, she just knew Isla would adore them; Isabel had no problem hanging on to spend time perusing and indulging her new nephew.

Right now, though, she was spruced up ready for the gala dinner and surveying the majestic ballroom for someone to hide behind. And yup, no Sean as yet. Thank goodness. She still had no idea what to say to him. But if she zipped towards the medical-rep crowd she might be able to get stuck in a conversation before he arrive—

'Wow, Isabel. You look amazing.'

Too late. His hand was on her waist as he drew in close and pecked French *un-deux-trois* kisses on her cheeks. She closed her eyes briefly at the sensation of his touch on her cheek, his aftershave mingling with his sunshine and sex scent. Goddamn, the man was irresistible.

But she was measured in her response. He couldn't hike out of her room after sex without an explanation. She needed to know what was going on in his head.

Hers was a lost cause.

'Oh, this old thing? Just something I threw on at the last minute.' She looked down at the midnight-blue silk shift dress that had cost the best part of a week's salary but, hell, it had been too beautiful to resist with its teeny shimmery jewels round the halter neckline and the cutaway back. She eyed her favourite sparkly silver sandals, then her gaze strayed onto him and she almost lost her balance. The man was drop-dead hot in a black tuxedo.

Worse, she knew how hot he was out of it too. And so that wasn't helping her equilibrium, not at all.

'Well, you're just too damned beautiful. Drink? Because I need one if I'm going to spend all evening looking at you, not allowed to touch you.' He took her elbow and steered her towards the bar. 'And I get the feeling you're avoiding me because every time I turn around you've disappeared.'

She drew her arm away. 'Oh, trust me, I know that feeling. Wham, bam and suddenly you're gone.'

'What are you talking about?' He leaned over the bar and gave the barman his order, then turned back to Isabel, his eyes widening as the penny dropped. 'Oh. You're cross because I left you to talk to your sister in private? Really? Or are you cross because I didn't come to your room last night?'

'Shh…people will hear.' Not that there were many people in earshot, but…well, really.

'I don't care who hears. *Did* you want me to come to you last night? Should I have?'

She looked down at the mahogany bar because that was safer than looking into those dark eyes and saying one thing but thinking the opposite. Yes, she'd wanted to sleep with him again. Had lain awake for hours imagining him naked in bed, the wall between them a barrier she hadn't been able to bring herself to cross.

Because she didn't want to want him so much, and put her world into free fall again. She didn't want to hand over that part of herself that she'd kept safe for so long, the memories and emotions locked away. She didn't want to feel anything. And right now she was feeling a lot of things. Mainly hot and bothered and very turned on. But more, complicated things she didn't want. 'Mmm.' That should do it. Nonchalant and undefined.

'Mmm? What the hell does that mean? Listen, Izzy, the truth is, I thought, seeing as we hadn't spent any time together talking, that it would be… I don't know, to use an old-fashioned word, unchivalrous to expect a booty call. But that was what you wanted? Yes? You wanted me to be unchivalrous?' His mouth tipped up, the grin widening as his hand smoothed round from her waist to the back of her neck, sending ripples of desire through her. His mouth was close to her throat. 'Go on, admit it. You wanted me.'

'No.' *Yes.* She couldn't help the smile. How had it gone from complicated to sex? From difficult to downright easy? Was it that straightforward? To stop thinking and start doing? She made sure she looked right at him. 'No.'

'Next time, say it and mean it. You wanted a booty call?' He nodded and smirked. 'Noted, naughty girl.' Then he handed her a glass of bubbles. French. Yummy. 'So, we're celebrating?'

'Sorry? Why?'

'Isla's baby? Boy? Girl? All's well?'

'Sorry. Yes, a boy. Called Geo, apparently…both doing fine. She's emailed me some photos and he's desperately cute.' She took out her phone and flicked through the photos, trying to stop tearing up, because Geo was so, so gorgeous and Isla looked as deliciously happy as she deserved to be. Alessi, indeed, so proud. And far from feeling jealous, Isabel just felt her heart filled with happiness for them.

Sean tilted her chin and looked at her. 'You miss them.'

She looked away because he saw the truth inside her as if he knew her too well. 'Yes. Of course. They're my family. It's my home. My place. Coming here was only ever temporary.'

He took a drink of the champagne. 'You're not enjoying it?'

'Oh, yes. The people are really friendly, I've had some fabulous work opportunities, like this conference. Job satisfaction is high.'

He smiled. 'The sex is pretty good too.'

'Exceptional, yes.' Her cheeks bloomed hot. She was still so new to this, she didn't know the art of flirting, but Sean made it easy today. Maybe she'd misunderstood his frown the other night or the reason he'd left. Maybe he had just been giving her space. Maybe he'd forgiven her?

Forgiving was one thing, but forgetting? She imagined that would take him a whole lot longer. It would always be there between them. Wouldn't it? God, if only she could thrash this out with Isla, the only person who knew everything.

Apart from Sean now, of course.

They walked towards a table, so beautifully decorated with silver tableware on a crisp white linen cloth and a small silver and white Christmas tree centrepiece. He nodded to the other guests sitting there, pulled out an empty chair and indicated for her to sit. 'So tell me, Isabel, why did you really come to the other side of the world? All this way away from your family?'

She sat. 'To develop my skills and knowledge. To take part in an international study and hopefully open a new Australian strand of it when I go back to MMU.' That was what she'd told them over the video interview anyway. There'd been no mention of running away from her ex because his questions made her uncomfortable. Made her remember things she'd prefer to keep under lock and key.

'So you'll be going back when your exchange has finished?'

'If my job's still there—I get the feeling that Darcie might want to stay in Melbourne. Apparently she's hooked up with Lucas.'

He grinned. 'Really? Now that's something I'd never

have predicted. They'll keep your job open for you too, though, surely?'

Isabel sighed. 'Yes, I hope so. That was one of the conditions of the exchange. I'm ready to go back, to be honest. I've had my year of living dangerously.'

'Not nearly dangerously enough.' His eyebrows peaked and his smile was as dirty as could be mustered at a dinner shared with two hundred delegates. 'There are a few things I have in mind that you could do. Only takes a bedroom. Well...not even that really. A willing mind.'

Her body was willing, it was her closed-off mind that she was having trouble with. To stop herself from slapping a kiss on that smirking mouth she desperately tried to keep the conversation on a civil track. 'And you? Will you stay here or move on somewhere?'

He shrugged. 'I haven't decided yet. My contract runs for a couple more months...then I'll make some decisions. I'm registered with a locum agency in London, so I may just stay in the UK for a while, perhaps see what Edinburgh's like. I'm happy moving around for now but I guess at some point that'll grow old. I like the challenge of new places, meeting new people. I like not having to commit to one place. There's a lot more to the world than Melbourne.'

Her heart began to hammer a little uncomfortably. 'You'll want to settle down at some point, surely? Family?'

And she didn't even know why she was asking him such a question...it wasn't as if that kind of life was anything she'd been working towards. She was happy being on her own, making her own decisions, living the single life. Wasn't she? At least she had been. A bit lonely, perhaps, but nothing serious.

Maybe that tiny ache in her gut that she'd tried to ignore was a reaction to Isla having a baby. Yes, that was it. Isabel decided she was a little unsettled by that, that was all.

The food arrived, and even though it might have seemed a little rude to ignore the other diners Isabel just wanted to sit and listen to Sean; his voice was lyrical and smooth. 'My parents have hinted about grandchildren. No, make that, my parents ask about potential wives and babies every time I phone or email. It's like something out of the eighteenth century. Neither of my brothers look like they're settling down either, so I'm in the firing line.'

'Your parents are lovely. How are they these days?'

'Same as ever, working hard on the business. Dad's still in accounting and Mum's still doing his paperwork, but she craves grandkids and won't leave me alone.'

Isabel laughed, remembering the not so subtle hints her father had been dropping about continuing the Delamere line. 'Mine too. So hopefully they'll be appeased by Isla's bub and leave me alone now.'

Sean looked surprised. 'You don't want that for yourself?'

And risk the chance of losing everything again? 'No.'

He paused to eat some of the amazing chicken pâté and bread, then continued with a frown, 'But you always used to talk about having kids—a whole mess of them, I think you said. You wanted to be a different parent from yours, you were looking forward to chaos.'

'You remember things I don't remember saying. And anyway, people can change, can't they?'

He put his knife down and turned kind eyes towards her. 'Not that much, Izzy. You can't give up on a dream because of one knockback. You help women achieve that dream every day—you can't tell me that things have changed so irrevocably for you?'

The food was tasteless now, a lump in her throat. 'A knockback? Is that what you call it?'

'No. That's not what I meant.' His voice grew darker. 'I could call it a lot of things. And I'm trying to deal with it…but damn it—'

'I'm sorry, Sean.'

'I know you are and so am I.' He shook his head, his fists tightening around his crystal wineglass stem. 'I promised I wouldn't hark back to it because just thinking about it makes me angry.'

He probably would never get over it—she hadn't, not really. But he had to deal with her lies as well as the loss. 'I've given you my reasons.'

'I'm trying hard not to be angry with you. I understand why you kept it from me. I'm angry about the whole sad scenario, Izzy. But you can't let it scar you for ever.'

'I've told you, I'm not Izzy, not any more.'

'And I don't know who you're trying to kid, but I'm not buying it. Older, yes. Wiser, definitely. More confident in lots of ways…apart from intimacy, which is a shame. Because that would be cool—you deserve to have that in your life. I'm betting that inside you're still the same girl who desperately wanted a family. A husband. The things everyone wants. And I bet that it's worse now that Isla has it. You're Izzy the girl, in here where it matters.' Touching just above her heart, he seemed to resettle himself, shake the demons away, and she envied him that. Or maybe he was just better at sorting his head out? 'Don't think for one moment that I'm belittling anything. I'm not. I know what you went through. I can't imagine what it was like to have it happen so young...so alone.' His hand covered hers now and the feel of him there... just there...made everything seem so much better. 'You said yourself, it happens. You have to look forward.'

She didn't want to be that frightened girl any more; she'd worked hard to be someone else. But yes, he was right about the intimacy—she didn't know how to let herself go, not on many levels. She hadn't dared. As far as she was concerned intimacy led to heartbreak. She knew it because she'd lived it. 'As it happens, I am trying to move forward and let go...that's the real deep-down reason I came to England in the first place. I needed to get out and breathe a little. Get away from you.' She nudged him playfully. 'But then you keep turning up like a bad penny and bringing me right back to the beginning.' Creating the same wild feelings she'd had when she was a teenager. Only this time they were more intense, more enduring. More potentially painful.

'You think? A beginning?' He frowned. 'Is that what you want to do? Start again?'

She rubbed her fingers across strong, skilled hands that had brought so much life into the world. 'I have no idea. I haven't dared want anything. It's too painful to risk going through all that again,' But he almost made her feel as if she could take a chance. She looked up into eyes that seemed so understanding and she felt as if she could pour her heart out to him. But that would surely send him running to the hills. So she deflected. 'What do you want?'

She didn't know what she wanted him to answer.

She just hoped it was somehow in sync with what her heart was telling her. That maybe, just maybe, she could work things out with Sean. Start afresh. If they both had enough courage. At least for a little while, they could have some fun and then she'd be gone and so would he.

He laughed. 'Hell, Isabel, it's messed up. I'll be honest with you and say I've gone round in circles. I've worked back and forth across the world, travelling thousands of miles just to get you out of my head and each time I end up back with you. I can't tell you straight up that I'm one hundred per cent okay with any of this. But I do know what I want right now, right this second. That's the best I can do.'

'Oh, yes? What do you want?' But she had a feeling she knew already. Just one look at the gleam in his eyes...

He paused as a gentleman stepped up to the stage and said something in French. The room hushed. There was applause while another man walked up to the microphone, all big smiles and wide arms as if giving the room a warm hug. She looked across to the woman opposite her and laughed when she laughed. Hopefully at some point there'd be a translation. But all Isabel was aware of was Sean next to her. The heat. And her unanswered question.

There was a break in proceedings as the microphone screeched, a brief technical hitch, and an embarrassed smile from the compère. Suddenly Sean's voice was in her ear, warm and deep. 'I want to peel that dress off you...very slowly. I want you and me naked.'

'Huh?' She swallowed, with difficulty. Her mouth was suddenly very dry. If she turned her head she'd be mouth-to-mouth with him and the temptation to kiss him was overwhelming. Where Sean was concerned there were no half measures, no light feelings; it was intense and deep and raw.

'I want to be inside you again. I want you, Isabel Delamere, with every ounce of my being. I want to kiss every inch of your stunning body.' He withdrew his hand from hers and placed it on her thigh. The heat and tingles arrowed in waves straight to her belly as he circled his fingertips towards her core. 'I don't understand what that bloke's talking about on stage. I don't understand much of the stuff that's in my head because it's like a washing machine all churned up. But I do know that I want you. Now. And I don't think that feeling's going to go anywhere for a while.'

She turned and whispered back, barely able to form words. 'It's bad, isn't it?'

Suddenly her heart began to thump in anticipation. Adrenalin surged through her veins and fired her nerves. Two people. That was what they were, just two people taking what they needed. No one was going to get hurt. She'd built that protective barrier around her heart over the last years; it was strong and sturdy; she knew what she was doing just fine. He was thinking of going travelling, she was thinking of going home. It was just two people taking what they wanted while they had the chance. They'd missed out on so much already. She dared to reach out and put her hand on his thigh too and felt the contraction of muscle at her touch. Heard his sharp intake of breath.

He growled. 'It's very, very bad. And yet somehow we keep ending up here. Maybe it's time to stop pretending and accept reality. This isn't stopping any time soon. There's nothing either of us can do.' He wrapped her hand in his and pushed it further up to his groin. Her fingers made contact with his growing erection. 'Hell, Izzy, it's bigger than both of us.'

'Good lord, it's very big indeed.' She knew he was fooling around, but she didn't want this to end. It was like a dream, a fantasy. 'Maybe when you go back to Cambridge and I stay here for a few days things will get back to normal again.'

'What exactly is normal? At each other's throats? Not speaking? Shouting? Not seeing you for too many years? Not sure I want to go back to any of that. I do, however, want to go back to bed, with you. Or, not bed… I have an idea.' He leaned in close and whispered, 'How about now? A night together. Then, what say we play hooky tomorrow? Have some fun in Paris?'

'We're supposed to be working.' Okay, so she said it out loud just for the record, but she didn't mean it. The last thing she wanted was to be sitting in a stuffy conference room when she could be playing with Sean.

'Who will know? You always were such a goody-two-shoes.'

He slid his hand up inside her dress, stepped fingers towards the inside of her thigh. Here in the middle of a gala. What the hell? Daddy would freak. 'And you always were such a tearaway.'

'No wonder your father didn't like me. Miss Dela-mere, this is not how you behave at dinner.'

'I was thinking the exact same thing.' He was hot and hard for her. 'Besides, I don't care what he thinks.'

'I wish you'd said that seventeen years ago.'

'Okay… I'm not apologising any more for stuff that happened a long time ago. Let's plan forward.' Her rag-ing heart was thumping so hard she wasn't sure she could breathe properly. Or make much sense past *take me now.* But for the benefit of others on the table—if they could hear—she tried to sound normal. 'I'd really like to go on the field trip to the homeless perinatal clinic in the morning…but then? Maybe we could duck out after?'

He nodded. 'I'd like to take you on a boat ride down the Seine—we could have lunch. Then visit the Louvre… Dinner in the ninth arrondissement, I know a place…' As her hand wrapped around him he tensed, eyes fluttering closed. 'Okay. I can't take any more. Let's duck.'

'Now?' His hand was still over hers as she stroked him.

He looked as if he was in pain, or at great pains not to show any reaction at all. 'You want to spend the next two hours listening to a man droning on about maternal care in Limoges, that's fine. But I'd like to get some hot sex. *S'il vous plaît.*'

She almost choked on her champagne. '*Mais oui.* Since you asked so nicely.'

'Okay, so stay close, no one needs to see this.' He pulled her up and held her in front of him as they sneaked out the back way, then half walked, half ran to the lift. As he hit the down arrow he turned to her. His hand was on her thigh, warm through the thin layer of silk as he dragged the old-fashioned outer metal lift door to a close. Then the inner one. It jerked, then started to descend. 'You have any preference in venue?'

'None whatsoever.' She threw her head back and laughed, feeling the rasp of his stubbled jaw on her neck. The lift smelt of old leather and Paris. Of daring and adventure. Of the exotic and sophistication. 'How about here?' So she wanted to get dirty with him in the lift. That was new.

'Great minds think alike.' He jabbed the lower-floor-car-park button then pushed her against the mirrored glass, kissing her deep and hard. She pressed against him, feeling his hardness between her thighs. His hands skimmed her body, palming her breasts, thumbs flicking gently against her nipples. Next thing, he'd untied her dress at the neck, it fell to her sides and his mouth took over from his hands, slanting over her hardened nipples.

When they hit the empty dark cavern he reached out and grabbed the metal car park sign and jammed it in between the lift doors so they wouldn't shut. The lift wasn't going anywhere. Neither were they. Pulling him towards her by his now unravelled black tie, she breathed, 'Smooth move, Dr Anderson. Very smooth indeed.'

'I like to think so.'

Then, feeling the most turned on she'd ever been in her life, she wrapped a leg round his waist. 'So, come put that clever mouth to good use.'

CHAPTER SEVEN

'THIS WASN'T QUITE what I had in mind as a date,' Sean whispered to Isabel as he handed over the steaming plate of beef bourguignon to the eighteenth homeless man of the morning. But working side by side with her gave him a punch to his gut that was filled with warmth as thick as the heated cabin they were in. After the tour of the homeless shelter and perinatal outreach clinic she'd accepted the request to help out at the soup kitchen with grace and humility. Every day she surprised him just a little bit more. Not least last night with the lift escapade. He couldn't help grin at the thought. 'Still, this stuff smells delicious, if there's any left...'

'It's for them, not us.' She kicked him gently but smiled at the dark-haired, olive-skinned young woman in front of her, wrapped in layers and layers of tatty grey cloth and a dark red headscarf. She had a full round belly and was breathing heavily. Pre-eclampsia, probably, Sean surmised—*needs assessment*. A small boy dressed in clothes more suitable for summer perched on her hip, grubby, pale and with a drippy nose. *'Pour vous, madame. Merci.'* Isabel turned. 'Actually, no, wait...oh, never mind. I want to ask about the boy, I wish I could speak the language a bit better.'

'Don't worry, the smile says it all. She understands.'

'And I want to take the tray over to the table for her, but she won't let go of it. I think she's so glad to get some food she won't take a chance on losing it.'

'Then let her manage if that's what she needs to do.' The kid looked feverish. 'He's not looking too great. When they're done I'm taking them both over to the clinic.'

Isabel let the tray go. 'It's zero degrees out there and look at the poor state of them both. It's Christmas in a week or so—what's the bet he's not going to have the best day?'

The boy coughed. Wheezed. And as he breathed out he made a short grunting sound. He didn't smile. Or cry. Thick black rings circled sunken brown eyes. Mum didn't look much better. Pregnant. Homeless. Sean pointed to the boy and made a sad face. Mum shook her head and jabbered in a language that didn't sound French. Then she handed the child towards him.

Sean took him, noted his flaring nostrils as he struggled to breathe, and felt his forehead. 'He's burning up. He needs a good look over. I'll take him through to the clinic now.' He gesticulated to the mum to follow him, but she clearly didn't understand. He tried again. Made another dramatic sad face and pointed to the boy. Mum shook her head again and tried to grab the tray of food and her son back.

'Okay, okay.' Sean held his palms up in surrender and let her take the boy. She clearly wasn't going to let the kid out of her sight, regardless of where she was and the minimised risk. And she was determined to get that hot food in both their bellies before they went anywhere.

Not such a bad idea, all things considered. But the child needed help and soon. 'Eat first.'

She squeezed into a chair at a small melamine table and in between greedy gulps tried to feed the boy some of the meaty gravy, but he slumped down and shook his head. She tried again, jabbering in a smoky voice, cajoling him. Pleading with him. And still the boy didn't open his mouth.

Eat. Sean felt an ache gnawing in his gut. *Eat, kid. For God's sake, eat something.* He watched fat tears slide down the mum's cheeks and wondered just how awful it would feel not to be able to provide for your child. To not be able to make him better. To not be able to feed him. That ache in his gut intensified. How helpless must Isabel have felt to not be able to grow her baby, to lose their son? And he hadn't been there for either of them.

Sean had never been helpless and he wasn't about to start now. He was three steps towards them before mum looked up and shook her head.

He turned to Isabel. 'His breathing's laboured. Bluish lips. Exhausted. Won't eat. He's going next door, now.'

'I'll come with you.' Obviously seeing the danger too, Isabel nodded, handed the plates over to some of the other volunteers from conference and between them they managed to get mum to follow them into the outreach clinic. As they tried to lay the boy onto a trolley he had a severe coughing fit, then went limp.

'Quick. Oxygen. Come on, kiddo. Don't give up on us.' Sean checked the boy's airway and grabbed a mask and Ambu bag, wishing, like Isabel, that he could speak the mum's language. Or even the language of the healthcare workers. But luckily they all spoke the language of emergency and in a flurry of activity anticipated what he needed, drew up blood, cleared secretions, put in an IV line—eventually. The boy was so dehydrated that finding a vein was almost impossible. 'Come on, buddy. Come on, breathe for me.'

As he watched the kid's chest rise and fall Sean blew out a huff of relief.

He caught Isabel's eye as she stood waiting with an intubation tube. 'I think we're good. He's settling a little. Pulse rate down from two twenty to one sixty. But we need blood gases and a blue light to the nearest hospital. Probably a bolus of antibiotics to be on the safe side. Who knows what the French is for that?'

Dr Henry, whom Sean and Isabel had met earlier on the clinic tour, appeared from the kitchen and explained in his very decent English that the paramedics had been called. The boy would be given the best care available at the public hospital and he thanked them very much for the help.

Mum, meanwhile, was another issue. As she stood and watched them working on her son a keening cry came from deep in her throat as if he were being ripped from her body. She refused to let go of the boy's hand, getting in the way of the staff. They tried to encourage her to take a step back. She pushed forward. In her confusion and distress she became more and more distressed. In her world, control was key. One wrong foot and you lost what precious little you had.

'It's going to be okay. It's going to be okay. Come with me, love. Let's sit down, shall we?' Isabel took her hand and gently pulled her away, wrapping an arm round her dirty clothes and walking her to a quiet corner of the room. The clinic was a prefabricated building with curtains delineating cubicles—the little fella's crisis had stopped any other consultations from happening and all eyes were on the emergency. A perinatal care centre they might have been, but an emergency care facility they definitely weren't. 'They're doing good. He's sick, but he'll be okay.'

Mum clung to Isabel and jabbed a finger towards the trolley. 'Teo. Teo.'

'The boy?' Izzy smiled and pointed towards the child. Her calm demeanour seemed to have an effect on the woman as she stopped gesticulating quite so frantically. 'His name is Teo? He's beautiful. And he's going to be okay. He's with Sean, and Sean won't let anything bad happen.'

Now that belief in him was another hard punch to his gut. She believed in him? She believed in him.

'*Oui.* Teo.' This was getting surreal. The woman was speaking French now to Isabel.

Isabel nodded, smiling, and pointed to the woman's belly. 'Another baby there?'

Mum rubbed her stomach and sighed, dejectedly. '*Copil mic.*'

Taking her hand, Isabel monitored the lady's pulse. 'Hey, Sean, hand me that sphyg, will you? I'll take her blood pressure while I'm here. I have no idea where she's from. Are there any translators?'

'I'll grab Dr Henry when he's finished. Oh, wait... he's just there.' They waited until the doctor sauntered over.

Isabel took it from there. 'I'm a bit worried about her, blood pressure's skyrocketing—I think she's pre-eclampsic; swollen feet... I need a urine sample but I don't know how to ask. Kid's sick and she's scared for him—it's not helping. And I have no idea where she's from. What do you do about language barriers?'

The doctor shrugged. 'It happens all the time, we have a good network of translators. I'll call one in.' He turned to the mum. 'Romania?'

'*Oui.*'

'She's from Romania? Wow. That's a long way from home. Who's looking after you? Where do you live? Will she have to pay for her medical treatment? Because I don't think she'll be able to. I'm sorry, I have too many questions and none of them in French or Romanian. Pretty useless, really. I don't even know her name.'

Dr Henry gave her a big smile, because, really, who wouldn't? 'That's okay, Dr Delamere, you care, it is enough. We have about twelve thousand homeless people in Paris and many of them are immigrants. But we also have good medical facilities to look after them, if we can reach them. Many are illegal aliens and don't want to be caught, so they get lost. Or worse. She may have friends around outside—they often meet people from their home country and hang out with them. Or she may have no one. I didn't see her come in with anyone. You?'

Isabel shook her head. 'No. She was on her own, and, in this state, that's a very scary place to be.'

Sean looked over at the kid and thought about Isabel all those years ago, on her own, dealing with the worst thing possible. That would be how this mum felt right now—even worse, she didn't understand what was happening and couldn't communicate. But she'd quietened down since Isabel had befriended her, so he wasn't going anywhere. 'So we'll stay with them until we get her and the boy into a stable state.'

'Are you sure? You don't mind?' Isabel was still holding the woman's hand, which she stroked as mum gave a small sheepish smile. 'We'll stay with you. It's okay. It's okay.' Then she turned to Sean. 'Thank you. I know you had things planned.'

Nah. Other than give her the best doctor award? The boat cruise would have to wait. 'I'm not going anywhere apart from to check on Teo. I'll be right here with you.' His heart swelled just watching her compassion. So much for guarding his heart; where Isabel was concerned it seemed she was determined to blast it wide open.

Two hours later as they stepped out of the maternal and paediatric hospital onto the Rue de Sèvres, Isabel inhaled deeply and tried to stop the hurt in her heart. 'Wow, that was an eye-opener. But thank you for staying. I don't know how I'd have felt if we'd just left them all alone. By the sounds of it Marina lost contact with her friends when she got evicted.' Thank God for Sean, too, because his quick thinking had stopped that boy deteriorating. 'I'm going to go back to the hospital tomorrow to see how they're doing.'

'You know, you don't have to. They're quite safe now. *In good hands*, as we always roll out to our patients. And they are, so cheer up.' He slipped his hand into hers, and she still didn't know how to deal with this rapid turn of events. She was holding Sean Anderson's hand, discussing patients, looking forward to spending a date… in Paris. She felt a surge in her heart that quickly evaporated. They'd done good, but she felt… She couldn't put her finger on it. He must have sensed it because suddenly he asked, 'You okay?'

'No. No, I'm not okay. I mean, I should be, I know

this stuff happens. But it's still distressing to see. That poor woman, what kind of a future does she have? She lives on the streets of a city where she doesn't even know the language. She's going to be the mother of two kids under four. She has no easy access to medical care… Aaargh, it's so unfair.'

His warm hand squeezed hers. 'You can't make everyone better.'

'I know. But I can help this one. I can make one difference today and that's enough for me. But it still makes me so cross.' Not least because there were so many little lives out there that needed saving.

He bent and pressed his lips to hers, pulling up her collar around her ears to protect her from the icy wind. 'There she is. That's my girl. She's back.'

'What do you mean?'

He ran a thumb down her cheek, making her shudder with warm fuzzies. Didn't seem to matter what scenario they were in, he made her shiver with desire. No, more than that. She liked watching him work, liked his cool calmness and the way he put others first. Not many did that in the precious little downtime they had. Not many offered to spend a few hours in a soup kitchen instead of sitting in a plush hotel eating dainty finger food from silver platters. 'There's the old Izzy…the spunky girl who wants to save the world. She's here. Don't tell me that you've changed, that all your dreams are different, because they're not.'

Isabel didn't want to admit anything, because right now she didn't know what she wanted—from him. From this. From anything. 'She was on her own and frightened. I've been there and I don't recommend it. One thing I promised myself back then was that if I ever saw someone else going through a hard time I'd try to help.' She looked up and down the busy street. 'Er... where are we?'

He shrugged. 'Damned if I know. I was thinking we could go to the Louvre, but I fancy some fresh air after that little adventure. You? Fancy a walk down by the river? We can grab a taxi—look, there's one.' He stuck his hand out, told the driver where to head to then bundled her inside the warm car. The journey through the Parisian streets was halted a little by congestion. Snow had started to fall and the roads became chaotic.

'Look! It's snowing. My goodness, just look.'

'Isabel Delamere, you've seen snow before.'

'I know, plenty of times. But it's just so perfect to be snowing while we're here. It makes everything seem like a fairy tale.' But then she thought about Teo and his flimsy cotton shirt and sandals and decided that whatever else she did in Paris she'd find him something decent to wear. A Christmas present. Because he wasn't exactly living any kind of fairy tale at all.

She looked out of the window and dragged a huge breath in. There was one thing she'd never confessed to anyone, one reason why she'd always hated and loved Christmas at the same time. Why she wanted to keep busy, why she'd offered to work, why she always tried to surround herself with people at this festive time and not dwell on what-might-have-beens and what-ifs.

She brushed a threatening tear away from the corner of her eye and hoped Sean hadn't noticed. She was getting too soft in her old age. Maybe it was seeing the little that Teo had and the fight in his mother. Or maybe it was being with Sean and feeling all these new emotions rattle through her that made her a little off balance.

They were let out by Notre Dame cathedral. Isabel looked up at the grand façade of the famous building. 'Amazing. I always wanted to come here. I've seen so many pictures of it, brochures in the hotel, I feel like I'm looking at something so familiar, it's almost like I've been here before. Look—' She pointed up at the huge rose window and the majestic arches. 'It's breathtaking.'

'Do you want to go inside?'

'No. Well…' There was a small part of her that wanted, for some reason, to make a special commemoration of their newfound friendship. And of the child they'd both lost. Perhaps a candle? But she didn't want to add something so solemn to the day. Didn't want to dwell on how she felt about Sean, given that things were so uncertain between them. Another day, maybe, when they were on a more even footing. She gave him a bright smile. 'No, let's walk. I want to tramp along the riverside in the snow, and, if you're not careful, hit you in the face with a snowball.'

'I'd like to see you try.'

She reached out and caught the falling snow in her hand, watched the snow melt on contact. 'It's not snowball kind of snow.'

'Never mind—I'm sure we can find something else for you to play with.' Then he picked her up and twirled her round, pressing cold lips against hers. 'You want to go straight back to the hotel? I know a good way we can get warm…'

Oh, it was tempting. 'Yes…but I'd like to spend some time out here. It's like a wonderland. Look at that cathedral, all lit up. It's amazing.'

'In that case…' He put his hand into one of her deep

coat pockets. Didn't find what he was looking for. So shoved his hand into the other one.

'What are you doing?'

'Gloves.' He pulled out her woolly gloves and shrugged them onto her hands. 'Now you're appropriately dressed, which, I might add, is a shame. I liked you a lot better with your dress round your waist.' He gave her a wink that started an ache down low in her belly and spread to a tingle across her breasts. 'But I wouldn't encourage that here—you'll get frostbite. Later...definitely.'

'Is that a promise?' Suddenly she found herself looking forward to later.

As they trudged across the square in snow that had started to stick the street lights flickered into life. Looking up, Isabel watched the swirl of the flakes as they danced around her. Sean wrapped an arm round her shoulder and she hugged into him as if it was the most natural thing in the world to do. They walked in silence for a few minutes, crossed through the souvenir stalls, round the side of the cathedral to a garden. 'If you want we can walk through the Latin Quarter...the Left Bank. We can cross over there.' Sean pointed to the left, past a large fountain and through the gardens. 'Or over there.' To the right.

'It's prettier through the gardens.' And it was; snow tickled the tree branches, coating each leaf like ice frosting.

As they walked Sean began to talk, his voice surprisingly serious. 'Isabel, is it hard for you to do your job after what you went through?'

'It's hard when I see a young frightened kid having a baby, hard when I see a difficult birth, but it's made me more resolved to help, to strive for a happier outcome.' It was actually quite a relief that they were side by side as they talked, so he couldn't see the pain she knew was in her face. Couldn't see the need for him to hold her. *And yes, it hurts like hell when things don't work.* She still shed a tear for the young mums; she felt the righteous anger when a baby didn't make it. She still felt the kind of pain that Marina had voiced earlier. Would it be different if she'd never been pregnant, never had that chance? She didn't know. 'Why do you ask?'

'I'll be honest with you—I had a different feeling in there with Teo and Marina. Watching her trying to feed him and failing gave me a gut ache like I've never had before. I felt her pain. Viscerally. I needed him to eat. I was willing the kid on. Sure, I'm driven to help them all, but this was different.'

'Empathy? You've always had empathy, Sean.'

'It was more than that. This was like a weird force in me.' He turned to her. 'You know I'd have done anything to help you, don't you? I'd have fought for that baby with everything I had.'

'I know.'

He was speaking so quietly now she had to strain to hear him. 'I wish I'd been there.'

'I know. Me too.' Her heart twisted. She tiptoed up and kissed him, hoping that whatever he felt could somehow be kissed away. She doubted it, but he pressed his lips to hers and held her close, his eyes closed, reverent. And he pulled her closer, wrapping his arms tightly around her as if she were a lifeline. An intense kiss that shook her to her soul, had her falling, tumbling into warmth. And even when there was no breath left they stood and held each other, listened to the distant traffic, to people laughing. People living their lives. People sharing, kissing, loving—taking a chance. When she eventually stepped away she felt as if a small part of her heart had been pieced back together again.

And shaken a little by the ferocity of it all.

It comforted her to have him close, but it scared her too. It was happening so quickly—they'd fallen so fast. She could lose herself in him, she thought, in *us*. She could let herself go. But what would that be like, in the end? Would it last? Or would she have to piece herself back together all over again?

That was something she couldn't contemplate. But, for now, he was here and she wanted him to know how she felt. 'I'm sorry, Sean, for the way I treated you. You're a decent, smart and sexy guy. I did bad by you, I should have been honest instead of selfishly hiding myself away.'

'You did what you had to do to cope. I understand.' They walked a little further through the tree-lined park leaving footprints in the snow, large and small behind them. Then, 'His name?'

'Sorry?' Her heart thumped.

Sean looked at her. 'I'm sorry, I have to know. What was his name? Did you ever think about giving him one?'

'Yes.'

'And did you give it to him? Did you tell him what his name was? Did he hear it?'

'Yes. I told him his name. I told him I loved him. I told him I was sorry.' *I cried it out to the skies and whispered it to the silence.* 'But then they took him away... and...I never got to hold him again.'

His lips a thin line, Sean dragged her to him. 'I'm so sorry. I'm sorry. I'm sorry.'

'It was a long time ago.' Her throat was thick with hurt, words were hard to find, even more difficult to speak. And her chest felt blown wide open.

Wrapped in his arms, she stood for a moment looking up at Sean, at his earnest face. The smooth line of strong jaw, the turmoil in his eyes. She hadn't wanted to put it there. Her gaze was drawn skywards to the fading light and the dance of snowflakes as they fluttered around them shrouding the cathedral in a magical white blanket.

The sound of bells ringing made her jump. She pulled away from him and started to walk again. As the light began to fade Isabel thought it was possibly the most beautiful place she'd ever visited. So serene through the gardens, the crisp crunch of snow the only real sound around them. Most of the tourists and hawkers had headed away, but a few stragglers remained. As they approached the stone bridge a man peeked out from behind a stall laden with postcards, mini Notre Dame cathedrals and paraphernalia.

'*Pour vous? Une serrure?* A lock? You buy?' His croaky voice made little sense.

'Keep walking. I don't know what he's talking about.' Isabel kept hold of Sean's arm as they stepped onto the bridge. The last dying rays of sun bathing the cathedral in an eerie light. 'Oh, my goodness. Look at that… What are they…? Are they locks?' Thousands and thousands of locks of all shapes and sizes covered the metal railings all along the bridge. She peered closer. 'They all have names on.'

'They're love locks, Izzy. Surely you've heard of them? People bring them here, write their names on the locks, attach them to the railings and toss the key into the Seine. Apparently if the key can't be found, the love can never be broken…or something like that.'

'"*A 4 M…*" "*Marry Me…*" "*Love You Always…*" "*Ever Mine…*" Oh, so sweet. But so many. There must be thousands.'

'And more. Look, there's another one just going on.' Sean pointed to the far end of the bridge where a bride and groom were having their wedding photographs taken, the sunset-captured cathedral in the background. The groom kissed something in his hand and then pressed it against his wife's lips and together they threw it into the gurgling water below.

'Wait here.' Sean left her side. She watched him jog back to the stallholder, who had almost finished packing up. From inside one of his bags he passed Sean something. Isabel's heart began thumping. Surely not. Surely Sean wasn't going to do something…something like… Looking over towards the bride and groom, she held her breath.

What the hell was he doing?

CHAPTER EIGHT

IF HE LET them go, Sean reasoned as he walked back to Isabel, if he pretended these keys held the past and hurled all the lies and the history and the hurt into the river, then that would be the end of it, right? He would let it all sink to the silted bottom, drowned in everyone's shared promises of everlasting love. Surely some of that would rub off onto him? Surely he'd be able to let her in? Surely he'd be able to stop thinking about it. Draw a line.

Maybe it was that easy. Maybe having her was as easy as that.

'Here.' He handed her a marker pen the guy had sold him for way more than it was worth. But how much was the price of casting off these emotions and facing her renewed? 'I want you to write our son's name on this lock.'

'What?' Her eyes widened, although there was some relief there too—he couldn't fathom why. 'Okay, I just thought…oh, never mind.'

'Write his name.'

Her hands were trembling as she tried to take the top off the pen. He took it from her, pulled it off with his teeth and handed it back. She wrote wobbly letters across the bronze lock.

Joshua.

'I hope you like it.' She was heaving great breaths while her whole body, his beautiful brave Isabel, shook.

'Yeah. Yes, I do. It's solid. Strong. It's a good name for a fine boy.' He'd had a son, and he'd been called Joshua. Sean's chest felt as if it were being squeezed in a vice. Above and to the left of the boy's name he wrote his own, to the right he wrote Isabel.

Damn it, if his own hand wasn't shaking too. Maybe it was the freezing weather.

'He was due at Christmas, right?' He'd done the maths. They'd only had sex a couple of times so by his reckoning their baby had probably been due around December.

'Yes.' She looked away, her eyes glittering. She gripped the top of the railings, for a moment he thought she might faint or tumble or scream, but she held her ground, staring into the distance along the river. Snow fell onto her shoulders, into her hair like tiny pearls. When she turned back her eyes were dry. 'He would have been a Christmas baby. He would have been seventeen this year. All games consoles and mobile phones. Maybe a girlfriend. Definitely smart and handsome.'

'And that's why you offered to work?'

She nodded. Her mouth about to crumple. 'Yep. I always work this time of year.'

'Oh, God, Isabel.' He pulled her close again, trying to protect her from something he couldn't stop. 'You spend every Christmas thinking about him? You must hate it.'

She let go of the railing and curled into his arms, her head shaking against his chest. 'No. Because it means I can think about him more. But...well, yes. I hate it.'

His chest constricted. She'd carried this for too long on her own. 'Okay. Let's do this.'

She nodded. Hauled in another breath; this one was stuttered as if her lungs were blocked. 'Okay. I'm ready.'

He lifted his fist to attach the lock to the tiny speck of space they'd found amongst the other locks bearing the love of thousands of people from around the world. All that love right here in this one place, all those promises, all that uplifting belief—he didn't know if he had it in him, but he'd damned well try.

But her hand closed over his, making him stop. 'Wait, Sean, look, there's a sign there saying the people of Paris don't want us to do this. It's damaging the bridge and the water, apparently. There's a picture of the railings collapsing under too much weight, of fish being poisoned by the toxins from the metal.'

Below them a pleasure boat chugged along, splaying dark water from either side, a commentary in French coming from speakers. When it had gone and the water smoothed out a little Sean peered as close as he could. There were no signs of any keys. No sign of damage. But he knew that you couldn't always see the damage. That nature had a habit of keeping that kind of thing locked deep, the harm seeping out slowly and steadily over the years, poisoning everything. Like his life. Like hers.

Not any more.

Rapidly blinking, she gave him a brave smile. 'I don't want to add to any more destruction. Can we do something else?'

He gazed down at the lock, at the names written there, and the sharp pain in his chest intensified. 'It's just a symbol, that's all.'

'Exactly. So… I suppose we should…just go.' She seemed deflated.

'Okay. I have an idea. Stay here.' He dashed back to

the gap-toothed man and bought another lock—a different one with a different set of keys. Then he walked back to where she was shivering. After writing the names in the same configuration he gave her the keys to his lock. 'Take these. Now, give me the keys to your lock.'

He wrapped her fist tight around his keys. 'You have the keys to my lock—I can never open it without you. Keep them safe. These are a symbol of what we had. *Who* we had. What we lost. All that love, Isabel. It was there, it was ours. We can't deny it or forget it, but we can honour it. And him. I want to honour him. Joshua.'

Still no tears, but her bottom lip quivered. How she held it all in was beyond him—not once had he seen her truly cry. As if it was some kind of weakness, he presumed, she wouldn't let herself break down. She took the keys and put them on a chain round her neck. 'Here. Take these keys, Sean. These are the keys to my lock. These are a symbol of what we shared. Of Joshua. Take them and keep them safe.'

'Always.' He fixed them to his key ring and put them in his inside top coat pocket.

'Next to your heart.' She pressed her palm against the pocket and he took the moment to shield her tight from the wind. From the snow that had continued to fall. From the past.

Now he had the keys to her lock, and, despite what he'd promised himself over the years, she had the keys to his heart again.

But then, the simple shocking truth was she'd always had them, hadn't she?

'Okay. No more of this. We have to get moving before we freeze our socks off.' He straightened up and gave her the first smile she'd seen from him in hours. It was gentle and honest and trusting. And with such intention Isabel watched Sean cast away the pain and the fear and the past. It was the right thing to do and yet somehow she couldn't quite let it all go. Almost all...but there was still a part of her, a tiny corner of her heart that clung to that long-ago night as if determined not to forget.

She took another huge breath and blew it out. Like cigarette smoke it plumed in the air, then was gone. The lump in her throat still lodged there though, but with every smile of Sean's it lessened just a little bit more.

'Okay.' He was right; it was time to move on. She took his hand and walked the length of the bridge, and onto the other side of the river, the lights from the old sandstone buildings reflected in the dark water. *Paris.* 'Yes. No more of this...we're in Paris for some fun and extracurriculars. Can I say, I particularly like the extracurriculars.'

His eyes glittered. 'Me too. Phil from Hastings does have a point. As did Jacob—this *entente cordiale* is good for the soul.' The hurt had gone; now all she could see as she looked at him was light and fun and teasing. His hand crept close to her bottom. 'I intend to fully indulge myself in *beaucoup d'entente cordiale.*'

'I am fully aware of your intentions, Dr Anderson. That poor lift. Those poor people waiting on the ground floor.' She grinned, remembering exactly why the lift had been halted. Dangerous. Exciting. Sex. 'So where to now, maestro?'

'The Latin Quarter,' Sean told her, filled with resolve. 'Full of quirky shops, decent cafés. There's a second-hand English bookshop along here you might like, too.

Or we could stop and get your portrait done. There will be lots of opportunity between here and the Louvre.'

Never. 'My God, you're going full-out tourist.'

'I thought you might like a memento of your visit.'

She didn't need one. She had every memory of this day engraved on her heart, and it was wide open for more. 'Not if it means staring at my ugly mug for ever more.'

At her frown he grinned. 'Okay, okay, no portrait. So it takes us about half an hour to walk to the Louvre. Of course, that depends on how many *chocolats chauds* you have between here and there. Or there's always cognac to chase away the chill. Chocolate and cognac, how's that for a combination?'

'Now you're talking.'

The afternoon was, indeed, filled with chocolate and cognac and a little red wine and a lot of kissing and many, many shops. By the time they took another taxi and did the rounds of the sparkling Christmas village at the Champs-Élysées Isabel's cheeks were pink, her legs tired and her arms filled with Christmas gifts, decorations and festive food. What a day, filled with extremes, some heart-wrenching lows and adrenalin-pumping highs. Some very, very highs.

'Okay, smile.' Sean snapped a selfie of them with nothing but dark sky and stars around them. It wasn't hard to smile; they were sitting at the top of a huge Ferris wheel—the central cog lit up like a shining Christmas star, or snowflake, Isabel hadn't quite decided—bright white in an inky-black night. Below them the streets of Paris stretched out in all directions, long straight roads of lights, a thin layer of snow on the rooftops as if someone had dusted the city with icing sugar. The tinny sound of a mechanical organ played the tune of 'O' Come All Ye Faithful' somewhere below them. And even though Isabel knew her nose was probably running she couldn't feel it because she was so very, very cold, and she didn't rightly care. She was high above the most beautiful city she'd ever visited, with a gorgeous sexy man at her side. For the first time in a long time she felt light and free and she had a sudden urge to scream out her joy, to release all the emotion knotted in her chest.

But she didn't, of course.

'That down there is the Tuileries Garden.' Sean pointed to the left, his voice raised because the breeze up here was quite strong…like being jabbed with tiny icicles down underneath her collar, on the tips of her ears, onto her cheeks. 'When I was here before we brought a picnic of baguette and cheese and some pretty rough red wine and ate down there. We had a packet of playing cards and spent hours playing blackjack and watching the world go by. Pretty cool. Mind you, it was July, so the temperature was a little different.'

She realised, then, that he hadn't talked much about those long intervening years. The focus of their conversations recently had been so much on their dark shared past and the now, but not on his life. The wheel jerked downwards and she was able to breathe a bit more evenly as the wind dipped. 'Where did you stay when you were here?'

'In a pretty scuddy backpackers' hostel in the fifth *arrondissement*. We couldn't afford much else. We did the cut-down tour of Paris, actually of Europe—mainly exploring cities on foot and on a very strict budget—so we never managed to go *in* to any of the tourist attractions, we just looked at them from the outside. Basic doesn't describe it. We spent a lot of time sleeping rough at train stations and during train journeys, to save money... which we spent, mostly, on beer.'

'I bet it was fun, though.' Intriguing. Carefree. A stab of envy ripped through her gut. 'Daddy always insisted on luxury travel so I've never done anything like that.' This trip had been safeguarded by a job—but now she felt as if she wanted to spread her wings a little, to live a little bit more, to move away from that very safe comfort zone she'd erected alongside the emotional walls. She wanted to breathe deeply, to fill her lungs with exotic air.

And then there was the question that had been forming on her lips for the last couple of minutes. 'We?'

He shrugged. 'Yeah. I travelled around with a friend.'

'Girl?'

His eyebrows rose. 'Yes.'

'Er...romantic friend?'

'Yes.'

It was silly to be jealous, and she wasn't really; after all she'd had her share of liaisons. None of them serious, she'd made sure of it...but she'd dabbled. And she couldn't help wanting to learn a little more about Sean's past. How much dabbling had he done? 'What happened to her?' *To your relationship. Your heart.*

'She went back to Brisbane. She's a GP now up on the Sunshine Coast.'

'Was it serious?'

He turned to look fully at her. 'Whoa, so many questions, Isabel. We broke up, a long time ago. So no, clearly it wasn't serious.'

'What happened?'

He looked away then, out over Paris, and she wanted so much to ask him again. *What happened to her? To you?* But then he turned back. 'Apparently I don't trust enough. Or commit...or something.'

'Because of me, what I did to you?' She waved that thought away. Too self-absorbed to think she'd be the reason his relationship had broken up. 'No, forget I said that, way too silly. I didn't mean it.'

'You really want to know?' His eyes blazed. 'Okay. Stacey—my ex—reckoned there was a part of me that was always looking backwards, comparing everyone to you. All that first love angst...yada-yada...'

'Oh. Wow. Really?'

His hand was on her arm now, which he squeezed, almost playfully. 'Of course, that's a whole lot of crock, so don't get any ideas of grandeur. Things just didn't work out. Now, after the day we've had, after what we've just done on the bridge, on a night like this—with the snow and the lights and the laughter everywhere—we are not going to talk about my old doomed relationships.' He shook his head and laughed, but Isabel got the feeling that there was a lot of truth in what he'd said and he was making light of it. That he had been affected by what had happened. Had she really ruined him for any other woman? 'Unless you want me to ask about your past lovers too? A pity fest?'

He had a point. Even though he was making a joke, what they'd shared all those years ago had been very real and raw and if she was honest she had been searching for that connectedness and never found it since. 'No, you really do not need to hear about my shabby love life.'

'Good.' The Ferris-wheel attendant opened the gate and let them out. Once on terra firma Sean shivered and stamped his feet. 'Okay, I'm hungry. You want to find something to eat?'

Isabel indicated the food in her brown paper sacks. 'We could have a picnic?'

He laughed. 'It's probably just about hit zero degrees Celsius. There's no way I'm having a picnic out here. The food will likely freeze, if we don't first.'

'I wasn't talking about outside, you idiot. I was talking about in my room. It's warm and dry and there's wine in the cupboard, Cognac in my bag.'

He took hold of the bags in one hand and wrapped his other round her waist. 'I like your thinking. Mine has a view of the Eiffel Tower. From the main room. Straight across.'

'Yours it is, then. But, Sean…' She rose on her tiptoes.

'Yes?'

'Don't think for a minute that I'm going to pretend that all those years haven't gone by. I want to know what you did. I want to know what you like. I want to know who you are now and what shaped you. I want to know everything.' Instead of creating a reality in her head that clearly wasn't true.

'Everything?'

'Everything.'

His grip on her waist tightened as he crushed her against him. She could feel his heat and his strength and she wanted to feel more of it. Preferably naked. His voice was rough with desire. 'I can tell you what I like if that helps? Actually…I can show you.'

If he meant what she thought he meant, they needed a taxi, and quick. 'That works for me.'

Within half an hour they were in Sean's room. The view was indeed breathtaking, but she'd come to realise that every view of Paris took her breath away— it was that kind of place: stunning buildings, amazing artworks, sophisticated people. Was any of it rubbing off on her? Was she becoming that nonchalant French-woman she'd tried to be? She sorely doubted it. But at least some of who she'd been had been stripped away a little. She was starting to feel new, different.

He'd found plates and knives in a drawer, opened a bottle of Bordeaux and sat in the middle of the bed with food on a blanket and two glasses in his hand. And with far too many clothes on.

Just the wall lights were lit and the way they high-lighted the dark curls of his hair and the ridges and shad-ows of his face made her want to lean in and kiss him. To run her fingers over his face, to explore the new terrain of his features. Breath left her lungs when he raised his head and his dark gaze locked with hers, his intentions very clear now. There was stark hunger in his eyes; de-sire, thick and tangible, filled the heavy air around them. The strength of her need shocked her. It took all of her resolve not to undress him right there. But this was a day she wanted to remember as much for the loving as the letting go—she wanted to take her time getting to know him properly.

'What are you waiting for, Isabel? You know, I still can't get used to calling you that. You'll be my Izzy for ever.'

Those words gave her a shiver of delight because, more than anything, she wanted to be his Izzy today.

As he lifted his glass to his lips she saw a bare patch of skin on his forearm, a linear scar about three inches long. 'Come sit down. I have wine.'

'You have a scar there. What's that about?'

'This?' He looked down at the place she was point-ing to. 'Geez, I can't even remember. Maybe a sports thing? Surfing, maybe? Yeah, probably surfing. I took a bad dunking down at Portsea, which ripped a layer of skin off. Years ago now.'

'You used to love surfing. Sometimes I thought there was no contest—you'd choose that board over me any day.'

'Nah…it was just a teenage obsession. I haven't done it for a while. Not since…' He ran his hand through his hair as he stared at the scar. 'Well, probably not since I did this.'

'Oh, well, I'll kiss it better anyway, seeing as I missed my chance when it happened.' When her lips made contact with his skin she tasted soap and imagined the salt and sunshine taste of the beach. She imagined him wet and bedraggled. Hot and languid from exercise. At the touch of her tongue on such a tender place he groaned. She smiled and pulled his thick sweater over his head, revealing a navy-blue body-hugging T-shirt. Her fingers trailed down to his hand, where she slid her fingers in between his. 'Any more injuries that need some care and attention from a very dedicated doctor?'

'Hmm… I like where you're going with his.' He levered himself up against the headboard. 'When I was nineteen I was playing Aussie rules footie and broke my wrist.'

'Poor you.' She picked up his left arm and kissed his wrist.

'It was the other one.'

'Oops.'

'Aha.' He slid his hand to the back of her head and pulled her in for a kiss; he tasted of wine and promise, and hot lust coiled through her gut. Her heart was beating hard and fast and the shaking had melded into confidence and daring. His eyes still didn't leave hers. 'When I was twenty-two I broke two left ribs in a motorbike crash.'

'Someone else's bike? No?' She guessed she must have looked pretty prim, with her mouth wide open at his admission, so she tried to look as if his having a death wish was the most acceptable thing in the world. 'You had a motorbike?'

'When I lived in Sydney, it was a lot cheaper to get around. I loved that motorbike.' His hands pressed under her top, around her waist—bare skin on skin making her shiver with more need—pulling her closer. 'Still do.'

'You have it here? No, surely not.' She crawled across him to straddle his lap; the warmth of his skin stoked her soul, spanning out from her core to her legs, arms, fingers. 'In Cambridge? How do I not know this?'

'Clearly I have a different one in Cambridge, but my old Triumph is waiting for me in Melbourne, at my parents' house.' He cupped her bottom and positioned her over his hardness. 'And why would you know? This is the first time we've really talked about anything in between the last end and the new beginning.'

Getting to know him all over again was very illuminating. Was there nothing about him that didn't excite her? 'Very dangerous. Very edgy…although most people have bicycles in Cambridge. I'd like to see you ride it. In fact, I'd very much like to see you in leathers.'

'I'd like to see you strip them off.' Pulling her top over her head, he palmed her bra, unclipped it, let it fall. 'About those ribs…'

'Oh, yes. Well, clearly this needs to go too.' Naked. She wanted him naked. Without wasting any more time she dragged the T-shirt over his head, exposing his broad, solid chest. She ran her fingers across to his back, skimming over muscles and sinews. Kissed her way from his spine forward to his solar plexus, her tongue taking a detour to his nipples where she sucked one in, making him groan all over again. 'Better?'

'Almost…' His voice raspy and deep. 'When I was twenty-four I had acute appendicitis…'

Giggling, she looked down at his perfect, unblemished abdomen, then back at him. 'You don't have a scar.'

He gave her a wry smile. 'No, it was just a stomach ache in the end, but I think you'd better kiss it better just in case. Just to avoid a flare-up.'

As she licked a trail from nipple to belly button her nipples grazed his jeans. The rough fabric against such sensitive skin made her pause. She was nose to…well, nose to bulge. 'Well, hello, hello… We seem to have a flare-up happening. You…you haven't had any injuries down here?'

'No. All in full working order, ma'am. As I'm sure you remember.'

'I most certainly do.' Thank the good Lord for that. She flicked the button and dragged his jeans off. Took a sharp intake of breath as she looked at him. So supremely sexy. Hard and hot.

'Anything else you want to know? Blood group?'

She knew enough, that he was rhesus negative, because she'd had a Rhesus immunoglobulin injection when she'd had Joshua. But he didn't need to know that. This wasn't the time or the place. 'I want to know…when are you going to kiss me again?'

Then his hands were under her arms, pulling her to face him, his mouth slanting over hers, whispering her name over and over, then fingers plunging into her hair as he kissed her throat, her neck. 'Isabel... *God*, Isabel, the way you make me feel...'

'I know.' Knew what he needed. Another kiss. Touch. The soft silk of skin against skin. The press of heat. Another kiss.

And another. It was in his eyes, in his words, in his voice, in a look. In the beat of his heart against hers. 'Isabel, no more questions... I *know* you now, here.'

'And I *know* you.' She had no care for thinking, for analysing the past, of worrying for the future. She knew him this moment and that was enough.

His teeth grazed her nipples and her head dropped back, her fists in his hair as he feasted. Then his hands moved over her body in a slow teasing study, as if in reverence, down her shoulders, over her breasts, down her belly, slipping to the inside of her thigh.

Oh, God. Yes. She kissed him again full and hard, clutching him closer, and closer still, erasing any space, any past.

'Wait.' He grasped for his jeans and took out a foil, turned onto his side a moment—too long...she couldn't wait. The ferocity of need stripped her lungs until she gasped for more air, more kisses, more him. He kissed her again and more, and more kisses, wet and greedy, mouths slipping, tongues dancing.

'Sean. I need you.'

'I know, baby. I need you too. So much. So much.' He laid her down and covered her with his body, his hardness so tantalisingly close, his fingers exploring her folds. His thumb skimmed her hard nub and she moaned, opening for him.

'Now, Sean. I need you inside me.'

He slid into her, stretching, filling her so completely

it was as if he were made for her. And she gasped again, fitting herself to his rhythm. Her orgasm rising, swelling with each thrust.

'Sean... I...' The rise of emotions thick and full in her chest, she couldn't put them into words.

'I know. I know, Izzy. I know.' This time his kisses were frenzied, hard, rough. And she loved it. Loved his taste and his touch and his scent. Loved the knot of muscles under her fist moving with every thrust. Loved this moment.

Her orgasm shook through her, unbearable and beautiful in equal measure. His thrusts became faster, deeper, as he too shook as his climax spiralled through him; he was calling her name and clutching her close as if he couldn't bear to ever let her go.

CHAPTER NINE

SEAN WOKE TO bright light filtering through the curtains. Down in the street below there was a siren, voices, the beep of a horn. Paris was awake and, apparently, it thought he should be too. Facing him, curled over onto her side, slept Isabel, blonde hair splayed over the pillow, sheets pulled tightly around her. She looked so peaceful, so rested, so damned perfect that his heart tightened as the questions that had stampeded through his head at midnight played over and over like a stuck record.

Did he want her?

Yes.

Were they rushing things?

Yes.

What did the future hold?

Damned if he knew.

She was everything he'd ever wanted in a woman—back at school and now—the ideal woman every male wanted to be with. Compassionate. Kind. Beautiful. Sexy. Fun. He'd never been able to believe his luck when she'd chosen him above all the other sixth formers. He could barely believe she was here right now.

Whatever it was that was developing between them was huge. Intense. But she'd broken him once and he'd spent so many years erasing her from his heart, so letting her fully in was causing some trouble. He wanted to. Man, he wanted to, but there was a part of him that just wouldn't let go. Even after yesterday. Such a symbolic and profound moment on the bridge—but that had been about Joshua, not about them. He knew she was scared too and, knowing Isabel, she was a definite flight risk. He couldn't even think about committing to someone who would always be looking over her shoulder and planning when to leave.

Like him, right now.

She reached a hand to his thigh, her voice groggy with sleep. 'Hey there, good morning. Don't even think of going anywhere. I have plans.'

'Me too.' He stroked the underside of her breast. She was so gut-wrenchingly beautiful. 'You wanted to go to see Marina and Teo, and I need to pack if I'm going to get that two o'clock train. Work waits for no man, so I'm told.'

'Do we have five minutes before we start to rush around? Yes, I'd like to see Marina and the boy, but can we just wait a few more moments? I'd like five. Just five.' She curled into his waiting arms and lay there, her breathing calm and steady, oblivious to the turmoil in his head. 'Thank you, Sean, for such a wonderful day yesterday.'

'My pleasure.' And it certainly had been. Just watching her smile had been worth every second. But he wanted more and more and more—and that wanting scared the hell out of him. 'It was a good day all in all.'

'I wish you didn't have to go back. I wish we could stay here like this, warm and cosy and...' she wiggled towards him, her fingers straying upwards along his thigh '…content.'

Content? With a juggernaut of questions steamrollering through his brain? 'How about you ring down for some room-service breakfast? We can have a quick shower, eat and then go?' And maybe with fresh air he'd get some more perspective.

'We can have a shower? Great idea.' Shoving the covers back, she bounded out of bed, then she stopped and looked back at him. 'Come on, what are you waiting for?'

'Just taking in the view…'

'Oh, and you like what you see?' She wiggled her backside at him. Naked. Pretty as a picture. Her long limbs stretching with ease, there were still the vestiges of her last Australian summer there in the fading freckles. Her breasts bobbed slightly as she moved and he remembered how they'd felt under his tongue, how she'd felt astride him.

Apparently perspective was difficult to come by when he was already hard for her again.

What sane man would walk away from this?

'Isabel, I have to leave today.'

The smile fell. 'I know.'

'So we have to talk—'

She came back to him, sat on the duvet and stroked a hand across his bicep. 'No, we don't.'

'Yes.' He anchored her to the bed, hands on her shoulders. 'Stop and listen—'

'No,' she interrupted him, her mouth on his lips now. 'I get it, you know. I totally know that when we leave this room, things will be different. When we go back to work things will be different. So don't go raining on my parade just yet, got it? Give me five damned minutes, that's all I'm asking…give me some of the fairy tale.'

'But—'

Now she'd climbed onto him, straddling his legs—her favourite position, it seemed—pressing herself over his erection. Her lips on his throat. Her glorious heat and wetness on him. Puckered pink nipples pressing against his chest. 'Please, Sean. Don't break the spell…not yet.'

Yes, that was how it felt—as if she'd bewitched him. She kissed him again and his resolve wavered. He cupped her bare cheeks and pulled her closer. The woman wanted five minutes.

Five lifetimes and he'd never have enough of her.

And, what the hell, he was all for a little magic every now and then…

And so she'd taken more than five minutes to savour Sean all over again. *So sue me.* But she'd had to do something to wipe that look from his face—the one that said *I'm sorry, but…*

She hadn't wanted to hear how much he regretted spending these past few days with her or that it had to end because they were going back to work. Or anything other than *let's do it all again.* Because she knew he'd wanted her as much as she'd wanted him—at least, his body had; his brain seemed to be working overtime trying to find problems. And she'd just had to kiss him one more time before the inevitable happened. But the kissing had led to so much more…and now she was in deeper than she'd ever intended.

As they walked up the paediatric ward corridor towards Teo's bed she saw Marina waving at her. She'd showered; her hair was in a neat plait down her back.

She was dressed in a hospital gown…and, wait? 'Sean,' Isabel almost screamed as she gripped his arm. 'She's had the baby. Oh, my God, she's had the baby.'

How the heck would Marina cope now?

Isabel dropped her bags, rushed forward and wrapped her new friend into a hug, tussled the grinning boy's hair and then stood back as mum unwrapped the bundle she held tightly in her arms.

'Izzbel…' Marina held the baby out to her, smiling. 'Lucia. Lucia.' And then she garbled something that Isabel didn't understand but she took the sleeping baby from Marina's outstretched hands and held it close. The distinct smell of newborns hit her and her heart melted at once at the tiny snub nose and the dark watchful eyes that seemed to know so much already. She thought about Isla and little Geo and felt a mixture of homesickness and pride. All these babies were true miracles. 'Boy?' She pointed at Sean because the white gown the baby wore gave no hint as to gender. 'Or girl?' She pressed a finger to her own chest, which was thick with joy at this little life, and fear for its future.

Marina pointed at Isabel. '*Fată…* Lucia.'

'Lucia? Her name is Lucia? It must be a girl. Oh, Sean, come and look.' He was sitting down and building bricks with Teo. Just watching him play so gently with the boy made her heart sing. He'd have made a wonderful father, she had no doubt.

She really had to stop berating herself about events of seventeen years ago and start to live for now. She'd promised herself that. She'd even kissed Sean's doubts away long enough to make love with him again, but she couldn't help having a few herself. And being with him brought all those memories to the forefront.

Could they survive the past?

'Sean, come look at this gorgeous girl.'

'Hey there, little one.' He stood and gave Marina a kiss on the cheeks and offered her a very proud smile, but, as with Isabel, there was a question there. What would Marina do now?

Just then, she noticed another woman hovering close by, in a smart straight black skirt and buttoned-up black jacket, dark hair pulled tightly back into a bun. 'Hi. I'm Isabel. I met Marina yesterday at the shelter—we brought her here.'

She didn't smile back. 'Yes, you are Izzbel. Good to meet you. I am Ana, translator.'

'Pleased to meet you. I'm so glad you're here to help.' Isabel nodded, cradling baby Lucia in one arm while she gingerly reached for her bag and brought out the nappies and babygros she'd purchased yesterday. 'Can you please tell Marina I'd like her to have these? And here's some toiletries for her too. Hospital ones are so basic, it's nice to have some luxury.'

Ana did as she was asked. 'Marina says, thank you very much.'

'How is Teo?'

Sean cut in, 'I've just checked through the notes—looks like his fever's settling. Still a bit high, but it's coming down and that's the main thing. He seems chirpier today.'

Isabel brought out the toy fire engine she'd bought for him, leaving the outfits she hadn't been able to resist in the bag. She'd just leave it all here for him rather than have him overwhelmed all at once. 'Here you go, buddy. Here's something for you to play with.'

He took it shyly from her hands and grasped it close

to his chest. Marina's eyes pricked with tears as she grabbed Isabel's sleeve and muttered something.

Ana translated in that mechanical voice. 'Again, she says thank you.'

Isabel knew she should probably not ask this question, it was none of her business, but she just couldn't help it. 'Can you tell me, what's the plan for her? Where are they going to be discharged to?'

Ana looked over at Marina, then took Isabel to one side. 'They want to check her for a few days. She has... high blood pressure from the birth—'

'I thought so—pre-eclampsia? They induced her too? That should resolve easily enough, but she has nowhere to live and two small children. It's freezing—'

Ana nodded. 'There is caseworker assigned now. She go to hotel and then to lodging in Éragny when available.'

The baby started to stir and Isabel felt the usual pull she felt when a baby cried, the ache in her breasts. Her milk had come in after a couple of days and she hadn't known what to do, how to deal with leaks...for the record, tissue stuffed down a bra just made everyone at school think you were trying to impress. She offered Lucia back to her mum. 'I think she might want you.'

Garbling again, Marina shook her head and pushed the baby back to Isabel.

'What's she saying?'

Ana shook her head and looked at the floor. 'She says you can have the girl.' Ana spoke to Marina in the lyrical language, her voice raised. '"Take her," she's saying. "You and your husband can give her better than I can."'

'Husband?' If she wasn't mistaken the look Sean threw her was one of abject horror at the suggestion.

Now a different beat began to play in her chest. He didn't
want her? Was that it? She wasn't wife material? Did she
want to be? She'd never thought about it before…images
flashed through her head of a wedding, and smiling Sean
and kids….all so inappropriate and yet, so wonderful.

But he didn't want it. And Marina wanted her to be
a mother, and Isabel didn't know if she could do that
either. Not that she'd ever accept a baby like this, but,
well… She walked to Marina and tried to place the baby
into her arms. 'No, Marina, take her, please.' It was all
becoming just a little too intense. The baby was snif-
fling now and no doubt preparing to wail for her lunch.
And yes, Isabel had material wealth and stability and
probably looked like a damned fine bet in Marina's eyes,
but she wasn't this baby's mother. And that was what
Lucia needed more than anything—her mother's love.
Isabel tried to reason with her, lowered her voice and
got her eye contact. 'Take your baby, Marina. You're a
good mum. Take her.'

Marina shook her head and turned her back as if the
deal had been settled.

'Marina, take your baby, please.' Sean's voice had
a ring of authority, but was laced with gentleness. He
took the infant from Isabel's shaking hands. 'Marina,
take your baby. Lucia. Needs. You.'

He handed the baby back to Marina and she took her
with tears streaking her face. She said something very
quietly and then turned away again, sat down and started
to breastfeed Lucia.

Ana explained, 'She said she had to try. She loves her
baby too much to keep her.'

Isabel fought tears of her own. She would not cry. She
would subsume this emotion and pretend it didn't exist.

But, oh, it was one thing to have your baby cruelly ripped away because you just couldn't nurture him, another altogether to be willing to hand your child over to strangers in the hope of a happier life. Isabel's heart just about broke into pieces. She sat down next to Marina and stroked her back. 'You'll be okay. You have so much strength and determination. Look at Teo, he's a happy boy chatting away to Sean, he's bonny and—oh, you poor, poor thing. You love her, and that's the most important thing. I'll help you. Somehow.'

Sean was by her side as she looked up; he gave her a soft smile. 'Does this happen a lot? People offering you their babies?'

'No, it's usually a one-way street. I hand the baby over at delivery—no one's ever offered it back to me.'

'Are you okay?' He ran a thumb down her cheek.

She curled into his touch as his fingers reached her neck. 'I think so.'

'Good.' He pressed a hand to her arm and urged her to stand. 'I think it's best if we leave now. Marina's probably feeling distraught and guilty and…well, I think we've done our best here.'

Isabel shook her head; she wasn't finished. 'I'd like to help her further. Maybe there's a charity I can contact? There must be.'

Ana nodded and gave her a business card. 'We have charities that can help with baby, with childcare and getting Marina job when she is ready. I have network of Romanian people who will help too. Contact me and I give you details.'

'Thank you. So much. I will.' Isabel decided that the formidable Ana would probably not want a hug, so she gave two to Marina instead. Then she kissed little

Lucia and knuckled Teo's cheeks gently. If there was one Delamere gene she was proud of it was the determination to help and to make things work out. She would do that for Marina. 'I'll come back soon, I promise. Tomorrow, hopefully.'

Once outside Isabel sucked in a deep breath. 'This was supposed to be just a conference and then some holiday time. I feel wrung out by it all. I think I'm going to need a holiday when I get back to Cambridge.'

Sean's arm was round her shoulder as they walked down the steps and towards the Metro station. 'You take everything to heart, and you shouldn't. She's not your responsibility. Are you like this with all your patients?'

Isabel laughed. 'As if! I'd never get through the day. I manage to keep a perfectly good professional distance but I do care. It's my job to care. But Marina's not my patient. She's…well, she needs a friend, everyone needs that.'

'You don't know anything about her.'

'I know that she loves her kids and that she'd do anything for them. I know that she's desperate and I've been there too.' And he was right, she shouldn't have got involved. But how could she not? Somehow the emotion of the week had got to her.

He'd got to her. Spending time with him had cracked open that barrier she'd so carefully built around her heart and now it seemed she was prey to every emotion out there. That had to stop. And right now.

They'd arrived at the Metro and her heart began its funny little thumping and her tummy began to whirl.

Sean looked at his watch then shrugged a shoulder. 'I'm going to have to go and get that train, but I want to make sure you're all right.'

And now he was going to leave and the moment she'd been dreading reared its ugly head. 'Of course, I'm fine. There are thousands of people like Marina all over the world and I can't help them all. I do understand.'

He pulled her collar around her ears and gave her a look she couldn't read. 'I didn't mean Marina. I meant us. This.'

Us. The thought of it made her hopeful...but then the doubt fairies started to circle again. 'Of course, I'm fine. After I've waved you off with my white handkerchief I'm going to do more shopping...'

He grinned. 'Oh, yes, of course. The deep and meaningful way of dealing with goodbyes.'

'The only way of dealing with anything, surely?' Part of her wanted to cling to his arm and refuse to let him go into the station, to drag him back to bed and replay last night, to never go back to Cambridge or Melbourne and stay here, in Paris, and just be *us*. Her throat was clogged with words she couldn't say to him out loud— the poor guy would run a mile.

But he wasn't going to let it go. 'That's not what I was asking, Isabel.'

Oh, she knew what he was asking, all right, she just didn't know how to answer. 'I mean, it's been really great, Sean, but...geez, husband? I had to chuckle to myself when she said that...'

He frowned. 'That stupid an idea, is it?'

She'd thought he'd have seen the joke too. Thought that the notion of them being married would have made him smile and raise his eyebrows in disbelief. 'What? No. I mean...well...'

His shoulders dropped a little. 'Things will change when we go back to work.'

She infused her voice with fake joy. 'No bed picnics and lie-ins for us…not when we're playing stork and delivering much-wanted babies. Busy on-call rosters. And, besides, in a couple of weeks I'll be heading back to Aussie. You'll be in Cambridge, then who knows where…?'

He nodded. 'You sound as if you're trying to convince yourself that it's not worth the effort.'

'No. That's not it at all.'

He tucked a lock of her hair behind her ear, then his hands skimmed her arms and locked her in place. 'I know you're scared. I understand—it's freaking me out too. So it's probably a good thing that we have this time to take stock. There's a lot to work through.'

'Yes. Of course, so much to think about.'

She thought he was going to walk away but he stepped closer, cupped her face in his hands and brought his mouth close to hers. 'I was angry about what happened, I admit that. I said some stupid things and I apologise. I was a jerk on the train and an idiot at the wine-tasting. It's taken some time for me to get used to the idea of what I missed out on—and it hasn't been easy. Isabel, I'm not a heart-on-my-sleeve kind of bloke, but…it could work, you know. If we wanted it to. We just have to believe. Can you do that?'

The kiss he gave her was lingering and warm. It told her without any doubt that he was willing to do anything to make this work, that he wanted her, that he wanted this.

Did she? *Yes.* Her heart was cheering. Yes.

And still the questions buzzed in her head along with the one true belief she'd kept all those years: *you'll get hurt.*

Plain and simple.

'Can you do that, Izzy? Can you believe?'

Izzy. Oh, yes, in his arms she was Izzy again, she couldn't deny it—he had her down pat. He was the only guy who ever had. But was it enough? She'd done wrong by him and they would never get away from that, from that one night that changed everything. It happened; she couldn't pretend it hadn't. 'I don't know, Sean. I'm sorry.'

He pulled away. 'You need to stop apologising for everything and start to believe in us again.'

She grasped the keys on the chain round her neck. 'I'm going to try. I promise. I'll try.'

'Good. Me too. When are you back in Cambridge?'

'Twenty-third, late…then I'm on call Christmas Eve, dinner at Bonnie's in the evening if I can get away…' She watched him try to keep up and it sounded like a load of excuses, but it was her life—just her life. This was how it was going to be if anything became of *us*— two busy professionals trying to fit each other in—none of the all-consuming togetherness they'd shared here. None of what they'd had all those years ago when life was theirs for the taking. 'I'm at work Christmas Day.'

He pecked a kiss onto her nose and tilted her face up to his. 'I'll see you on Christmas Day then, at work— maybe we can do something after our shifts? I don't want you to be on your own.'

'Thank you, that would be wonderful. I don't want to be alone, either. Dinner, maybe?'

'Yes, dinner. And the rest…everything.' At her smile he found one too. 'Believe, Izzy. Take a chance.' Then he let her go and turned away, his duffle bag high on his back, taking long, long strides into the busy tube station. And taking, along with him, her heart.

CHAPTER TEN

'OOH, LOVELY, MORE CHOCOLATES!' Isabel reached across the labour suite nurses' station desk and grabbed a chewy toffee from the box before they all disappeared. 'From another grateful client?'

'Hmm, yes.' Bonnie looked up from her seat in front of the computer screen, popped a chocolate into her mouth and sucked; she had a pair of red velvet reindeer ears on a band over her lovely russet-coloured hair. 'It's the best bit about working at Christmas—all the patients get nostalgic about gifts and babies and mangers and we get the benefit. Although there only ever seems to be strawberry creams left when I get to choose.'

'Aww, that's because, as labour suite sister, you make sacrifices for your staff. It's very noble of you.'

Bonnie laughed. 'It's because I'm too busy to stop and eat, more like.'

She did indeed have a busy life, what with a little daughter and now Jacob in her life, plus this unit to run. But, if anyone could make it work, Bonnie could. Isabel felt a wee pang of jealousy—it looked like Sister Bonnie had managed to get it all: family, a man who adored her and a job she loved. Some people really could put their past behind them and believe things could work out. 'Don't worry, sweetie, I'll bring a box of yummy French choccies tonight just for you, specifically with no strawberry creams.'

'Oh, good, are you still coming over for dinner? Freya's so excited to see you—but be warned... Father Christmas is on his way so she'll be hyped-up beyond belief.'

After her now ex-husband's tawdry affair with her best friend, Bonnie had made a fresh start in Cambridge, bringing her daughter away from everything familiar. She had worked hard to make her happy here and to provide everything the girl needed. Isabel had to admit to having fallen just a little bit in love with the little tyke... hyped or not. 'Okay...no worries at all, I'm looking forward to it. Christmas Eve is so special when you're five. How's Jacob bearing up with it all? Must be strange for him to be sharing his house with a ready-made family?'

Bonnie sighed. 'Don't tell him I said so, but he loves it. Underneath that brooding exterior is a sucker for candy canes and Santa sacks. Between you and me he's about as hyped-up as Freya.'

Isabel laughed, imagining their straight-as-a-die, oh-so-professional boss in a Santa outfit. Somehow the image just didn't fit. 'There's a side to him we don't get to see, obviously. I got Freya some gorgeous dresses in Paris...you'll just die when you see them!'

'Oh, that's so sweet, but you know you didn't have to buy her anything, really. Anyway, never mind my terrible twosome, tell me about Dr Dreamcakes. I'm all ears and green with envy. A vacation with him in Paris...' Bonnie put the back of her hand to her forehead and pretended to swoon. 'Naughty Jacob for setting you two up like that. I swear he had an ulterior motive, but he denies all agendas other than a work one. And I'm sorry he couldn't go to Paris with you—that may have been my fault. I wanted to make the build-up to Christmas a special one for Freya, and I put some pressure on Jacob not to go. Still, up close and very personal *à la* France, with a hunk like Sean, what's not to like? How was it?'

Bless her, all loved-up and finally with the full fairy tale, Bonnie hadn't got a clue about the state of Isabel's mind. Her history with Sean had been a well-kept secret from day one and, truth was, Isabel didn't know how it was.

The few extra days in Paris had been filled with thinking and shopping and worrying. And helping Marina, Teo and Lucia move into temporary accommodation. And then there had been a lot more thinking and wishing and panicking about how she really felt. Which was…confused. She'd spent the last few hours at work grateful that Sean had the day off today and that she wouldn't have to face him until tomorrow, because no doubt he'd want some kind of an answer. One more sleepless night to try to sort out her head. 'Oh, you know…it was…Paris.'

'Hey, you're back!' Hope Sanders, one of the other unit midwives, walked out of a side room and wrapped Isabel into a big hug. 'How're you doing? Have you seen the crazy amount of stuff we've got for the first Christmas baby?'

'I know, lucky winner! How on earth they'll get that lot home I don't know. They're going to need to call in Santa and his sleigh.' A huge mountain of gifts now swamped a shopping trolley; the generosity of the unit staff, clients and relatives had been amazing. 'We could halve it and give a prize for the first baby of the new year too.'

'What an excellent idea, Isabel. We could do that and share the love.'

For a moment Isabel thought that her trip might well have been forgotten. Prayed so. Alas no… Hope squeezed a drop of sanitiser onto her hands, rubbed them vigorously and grinned. 'So, come on, how was it? How was Dr Sex-On-Legs? How was Paris? Oh… Wait… Hang on, I've just got to go to the ladies'. Don't say a single word until I get back.'

'Don't worry, I won't…' *Won't say anything at all, if I can help it.* Isabel smiled at her friends. Gosh, she was going to miss this lot when she went home. There was nothing quite like a group of warm and welcoming women to bridge that homesickness gap. They'd all made her very welcome despite their own troubles, and, God knew, they'd all had their fair share over the last year. Bonnie had moved from Scotland and moved in with Jacob before she even knew him; Hope had met and fallen for Aaron, the totally gorgeous American infertility specialist; and rumour had it that midwife Jess Black was also loved up with sexy SCBU doc Dean Edwards, if their spectacular kiss at the Christmas party was anything to go by; but not without a few road bumps along the way for all of them. Somehow they'd survived, the better and happier for it. Apart from Isabel, of course. She was just muddled.

Bonnie smiled as she watched Hope walk down the corridor towards the bathrooms. 'Not that I'm counting, but that's the third time Hope's been to the loo this morning. I hope she's okay. None of my business, of course.'

'No, none whatsoever.' Isabel raised her eyebrows in question, which was girl code for *tell me what you're thinking.*

Bonnie's eyebrows rose in response. 'She seems very happy. Glowing, I'd say.'

'What? D'you think…? No, not Hope…and Aaron? And…pitter-patter?'

'I have no idea…but peeing a lot is one of the first telltale signs…'

Really, nothing was terribly secret on this unit. They all worked long hours and much of their social time was spent together too; they were like family. Everyone knew how gooey Hope went over the newborns, how much she desperately wanted one of her own…and the heat between her and Aaron had been off the scale every time those two had laid eyes on each other. She'd had IVF planned to become a single mum and no one had dared ask her how it had gone; they thought she'd tell them when she had news. Maybe Hope had finally got her dream too?

After a few minutes Isabel watched Hope sauntering back onto the ward, smiling to herself, her hand gently rubbing her abdomen. 'I think if she had anything to tell us she would. It's not for us to speculate.'

Bonnie shrugged and winked. 'All I was saying was that she's spent a lot of time on the loo this morning. And she seems quite happy about it. Nothing gossipy about that, it's all just facts.'

Hope reached them. 'Sorry about that. Now, Isabel, tell me about Paris. Was it wonderful?'

'We had a very interesting conference, thank you.'

'*Interesting?* What exactly does that mean?' Bonnie

checked her watch, stood and walked across to Isabel. 'Come on, you can dish the dirt on the way.'

'To lunch? Aww, no, sorry, ladies, much as I'd love to come with you I have so much paperwork to catch up on, emails and stuff, I don't have time today.'

Bonnie's arm looped through Isabel's. 'I thought you'd say that. As it happens we need some extra personnel downstairs…so you're coming with us. We won't keep you too long. I said we'd meet Jess down there.'

'Jess?' Isabel sensed mischief. 'Down where? The cafeteria? I said I can't do lunch. Are we doing lunch?'

'Not so much.' As they strolled towards the hospital main exit Jess walked towards them, arms full of Santa hats.

'Oh, great, you made it.' Jess gave them all a big grin. Another one in the unit to have had a difficult year, but for whom things were very definitely looking up. 'Thank you so much. I have some extra people coming down from SCBU too, a backing track and some collection boxes. We should make quite a bit, fingers crossed.'

Oh-oh. Isabel felt as if she'd been duped into something she might not enjoy. 'Make what? Doing what?'

'Carol singing.'

'Really? At lunchtime? Why?' *Me? Sing?* 'It's not my thing, really. I have work to do.'

'Oh, come on, sweetheart. You're a long way from home and we thought you might enjoy it.' Bonnie draped some glittery red tinsel over Isabel's shoulder while Jess stuck a red hat on her head. 'Because this is what we do at Christmas. Here's some tinsel—wrap it round your stethoscope. You are going to have a taste of our lovely British traditions. No beach and prawns on the barby…'

She put on a terrible Australian accent. 'It's all mince pies, roast chestnuts and lots and lots of singing.'

'We sing. I just don't like doing it all that much.' It was too much of a reminder, all that little baby Jesus stuff. Away in a manger. Lay down his sweet head.

'You'll love it, honestly, and it's for a good cause.' Jess grinned. 'I've even managed to coerce Dean to help out, and that's got to be a first.'

Isabel had had a few professional dealings with Dean Edwards over preemies in SCBU; he was a damned fine doctor and a pretty decent colleague. A bit of a heart-throb too, if she was honest. But no one ever seemed to match up to Sean, no matter how much she looked. And she'd look a heck of a party-pooper if she didn't join in now. Better to get it over with and then leave. 'Dean Edwards, singing? Well, if he's in then I guess I am. I have got to see this.'

'Oh, there he is.' Jess walked towards him as if she were floating on air. She gave him a shy smile and he gave her one in return, oblivious to anyone else in the room. Jess handed him a hat. More *facts* in the department: Jess and Dean were now dating... 'Thank you for coming down.'

Hope stopped mid-tinsel-wrapping. 'Oh...hang on. I just need...wait. I just need to pee. I'll be right back.'

Bonnie threw Isabel a look as if to say *I told you so*, then back at Hope. 'You just went.'

Looking a little sheepish, Hope stuck out her tongue, but the smile stuck. 'Who are you, my mother?'

'Sometimes it feels like I'm everyone's mother here— it comes with the job description.' Bonnie looked at her seriously. 'Hope, are you okay?'

'Yes... Yes, I'm fine. Oh...come here all of you. I

need to tell you something.' Hope steered the three of them, Isabel, Jess and Bonnie, across to a quiet corner, took their hands. 'Listen, ladies, this has so got to be a secret, but I can't think straight unless I tell you… I'm pregnant! Sorry, *we're* pregnant, me and Aaron…'

Isabel pretended to look blown away with surprise. 'Wow! That's so fabulous, honey. Well done you. The IVF worked?'

Hope looked as if she was going to burst with excitement. 'No…no, that's just it… I never thought it would happen like this… I went for the implantation and I didn't need it. I was already pregnant. I'm so excited.'

Jess gave her a cuddle and squealed a little. 'Wow, that's just so brilliant. What a Christmas present. You look amazing—feeling okay? No nausea?'

'Not yet. Apart from needing the loo a lot, I'm fine.'

'Okay, yummy mummy, you nip off to the ladies' while we set up. Now, gather round, or we're going to run out of time. I have to get back in twenty minutes.' Jess got them all together into a semicircle by the main doors, in front of a beautiful scented floor-to-ceiling pine Christmas tree, and flicked on the sound system. Handing out sheets of lyrics, she joined them and started to sing 'Away In A Manger'.

Just peachy. As she read through the words Isabel wondered about little Lucia and how she was doing in the new crib that she'd found for her in a Paris baby shop. For some reason the thought of that little scrap of life made her feel a bit heartsore. Or it could have been the excitement of Hope's pregnancy. Or, it could have been, as Sean had suggested, that perhaps she still had that small part inside her that wanted a baby of her own. That perhaps that dream hadn't died along with Joshua after all. Maybe she could open her heart to thinking about that, some time, in the future. She decided as she stood there surrounded by all this love that maybe she would.

As they moved into the second chorus people stopped rushing about and started to listen, and they were smiling and joining in. Beyond the doors the sky was thick and heavy as more snow threatened. Isabel knew that by three-thirty it would be dark outside and that every child in the country would be counting down the hours until that very special jolly man paid them a visit. And so it wouldn't be a swim, then champagne and a barbecue, it wouldn't be sunbathing and lounging around with her family. She'd be here, with this new family of hers, having a very different time, delivering babies and making some people's Christmas a very happy one indeed.

And, as the saying went, a change was as good as a rest.

She watched Hope wipe her eyes as the carol came to an end. The audience had grown quite large and people were generously donating into the buckets at their feet.

Then, at the back of the crowd, she saw a face that sent her heart into overdrive.

He wasn't supposed to be here.

His gaze caught hers and he watched her sing, a small smile on those sensual lips. The world seemed to shrink a little and she felt herself singing the words just to him, and she felt the heat in his gaze. From this distance he probably looked, to everyone else, just like any other guy. But she knew differently.

She knew he was capable of great things, the greatest things anyone could ever do; he was capable of forgiving, of trying to let go, of believing in something that not everyone had the chance to experience in their lives; he was capable of believing in love. With her. He was offering her a chance to have what Hope had, what Jess and Bonnie had, what Isla had, and what everyone deserved: a rich, fulfilling future.

And no, nothing had changed in those last few days, damn it, nothing had changed in those last seventeen years, she still felt gloriously attracted to him; she still craved his touch. Her heart still swelled at the sight of him. She wanted to lean into those shoulders and feel his arms around her; she wanted to lie next to him and talk about the day. She wanted to grow old by his side and somehow make up for the lost years without him. She just had to pluck up the courage to say yes. That was the problem.

After two more songs he gave her a slow wink and walked away.

'What the hell was that about?' Bonnie whispered out of the corner of her mouth as she too watched Sean's back disappear up the corridor. 'What just happened between you two?'

'Shut up and sing.' Isabel smiled through gritted teeth.

And she did. And nothing more was said as they went through another five carols and raised a couple of hundred pounds for the SCBU.

But later, when just the two of them were walking back to the labour suite, Bonnie stopped and looked straight at Isabel. 'I know it's none of my business—'

'No, it's not.' But she knew her friend had the very best intentions.

'So here are the facts as I see them.' Bonnie smiled gently as heat hit Isabel's cheeks. 'Every time you and Sean are in the same room there are sparks. Tensions soar so high we all feel a need to switch on the fans and get ice. Fact number two: you were heard arguing about your past, about a relationship you had. About lies you told, apparently. And he said he didn't want to see you again. But you went to Paris together. And it was *interesting*.' Another girl-code stare. 'Fact three: the way he looked at you out there just about set the hospital alight. I was torn between decking the halls with boughs of holly and phoning the fire brigade. The man clearly wants you and yet, here you are, looking glum and worried. You want to talk? Because I can listen, very well.'

It would help, Isabel knew, just to say the words out loud. 'Maybe later?'

'Later it'll be Freya and Father Christmas and Jacob and chaos. Trust me, we won't get a chance. I have time now. My office?'

'You hate your office.' Everyone knew that Bonnie never went in there unless she could help it.

'I know, which means no one will find us, so we won't be disturbed.'

Thirty minutes and two cups of strong black coffee later Isabel felt as if she'd bled all over Bonnie's desk. 'So now I have to decide what to do. Take a chance on him, or walk away. I have a plane ticket to Melbourne on New Year's Eve, so essentially I have a week to decide the rest of my life.'

'When are you seeing him again?'

'Tomorrow.'

'So, in reality, you have twenty-four hours.'

'Geez, girlfriend, you are not helping.'

Bonnie shook her head and with a formidable glint in her eye she leaned forward. Isabel could see why she was a very good match for Jacob—Bonnie would fight for what she wanted, tooth and nail. 'Do you think that if you had a hundred more years to decide it would help? If you love the man you have to take a chance. Do you love him?'

Well, wow, that was a question. She'd tried to put him behind her, she'd tried to erase those feelings, ignored them, subsumed them, but in the end the real question was: had she ever stopped loving him? 'But, Bonnie, how could you dare to let go after what you went through?'

Bonnie's shoulders rose then fell. 'Sometimes you've got to take a risk, and, believe me, I didn't do that lightly. I had Freya to think of. But, well, once I realised I loved him and he loved me I wasn't prepared to let that chance slip through my fingers.' She covered Isabel's hand with her own, and it was almost as if Isla were here talking sense to her. They'd get on well, she thought, her sister and this woman who was fast becoming like one. One day she'd get them to meet, somehow. What a party that would be. 'Come on, Isabel, I understand what you've been through, but that's all in the past. You have a lot of living to do. What have you got to lose?'

Isabel nodded, fighting the lump in her throat. Bonnie was right, of course—what did she have to lose by loving Sean Anderson? 'Everything. That's the problem.'

'And if he's worth that much to you, you'll take that risk.'

CHAPTER ELEVEN

'ANY ROOM AT the inn?' Johnny, one of the paramedics, breezed into the labour suite, stomping snow from his boots while pushing a young woman on a trolley. For five o'clock in the morning, Christmas Day, the man looked remarkably chipper. The girl, not so.

'Yeah, yeah, very funny. I've never heard that one before. Happy Christmas to you, too.' Sean shook his head and laughed, giving an extra-special smile to the girl on the gurney. She looked so young, pale and frightened. And on her own. Who the hell wanted to be here instead of unwrapping presents? Which was where she should have been right now, with her family looking after her—she barely looked old enough to be out on her own. 'Hello there. Who do we have here?'

The girl gave him a grimace and curled up around her distended belly. Tears streaked her face as she sucked on portable gas and air. Sean took her in—straggly hair, clothes that were scruffy, long thin bones, skin stretched tight over her cheekbones. Man, she was way too thin.

Johnny handed over a copy of his observation chart. 'This is Phoenix Harding. She's eighteen years old and, we think, about thirty-two weeks pregnant. She's had lower abdominal pain for the past week increasing over time. Lower back pain too. Using gas and air to good effect. Contractions started at around midnight, getting closer together and stronger, every two to three minutes.'

'Okay, thanks, Johnny. We'll take it from here. Hi there, Phoenix, my name's Sean and I'm one of the doctors here. Can you manage to tell me what's been happening?'

She shook her head. Terrified.

'Are you okay if I do some prodding and poking around? I need to have a listen to baby—that will help us work out what to do next.'

She nodded, but hid her face in her hands.

Sean began his assessment, had Hope attach the heart monitor across Phoenix's belly, and heard a strong quick heartbeat. 'That's sounding good. Baby seems to be quite happy.' But the girl doubled up in pain. He tried to get her to look at him. 'Phoenix, he's not as cooked as we'd like, so we'd prefer to keep him in a little longer. But it looks like he's keen to meet you.'

Phoenix shook her head. Still no words. She looked so young. So frightened. And, as he watched Hope leave the cubicle with an apologetic raise of her eyebrows, in need of a friend and a chaperone.

'Have you got anyone we can call to come and be with you? Friends? Family? Baby's dad?'

Again she shook her head. It was going to be difficult if he had to conduct the assessment by telepathy. 'Hey, missy, just a quick question: can you recall whether your waters broke? It'd have been like a gush of water…an unexpected trickle?'

There was a knock on the door. Isabel stepped into the cubicle and Sean's heart felt as if it were tumbling, mixed with a sharp sense of relief. He never could get used to seeing her without having some kind of reaction. 'Hope's just had to pop out—she thought you'd need a chaperone, everyone else is busy so she asked me to come in.'

After he brought her up to speed with Phoenix's case he added, 'But Phoenix isn't feeling like talking at the moment, so we're taking things slow.'

Isabel nodded, as if she understood exactly what he meant. Thirty-two weeks meant a risk to baby—it was too immature to be born yet. But if it was, they'd need extra care—usually a stint in the SCBU to monitor progress and for special feeding; babies that young often didn't quite get the hang of sucking at a nipple or a teat. Never mind the dangers of immature lungs trying to suck in hospital air.

Isabel smiled at the girl. 'Oh, that's okay, we can take all the time you like, Phoenix.' She paused and stroked the girl's back as she curled into another contraction. 'Although we can't do anything to help if we don't know what's happening. That baby is a bit young to be born yet—so we need to try to keep it in there a bit longer. Phoenix, do you mind if I examine you?' Time was running out if they wanted to stall the labour; obviously Isabel was fully aware of this.

The girl shook her head and turned onto her back. She looked grateful to have Isabel there at least and when Isabel had done her examination she breathed out a big breath. 'Eight centimetres—wow, you're doing well. And your waters must have broken some time? You don't remember? Can you try to think?'

'No.' Finally a voice.

'Never mind, honey. The main thing is, your cervix is dilating quickly, your baby's on the way. We'll have to give you an injection of steroids to make his lungs good and strong for when he's born. He's going to be a bit small as yet, so we have to give him all the help we can. Is that okay? And I'd like to work out why this is happening now... Have you had any problems or anything over the last few days? Taken any different medicines, drugs? Alcohol? Any accidents, bumps? Done anything really strenuous?'

'No.' As if grabbing onto a life raft Phoenix took hold of the hand Isabel offered to her. 'I've been going to the toilet more. I thought it was just the pregnancy— I read somewhere that you pee more often. But looking back it was twice as many times for half as much wee.'

'In which case we'll need to test your urine as soon as we can. Any fever? Lower back pain?' Isabel reached for a thermometer to continue her assessment.

'Pain, yes.' She pointed to her lumbar region. 'And when I pee.'

'It sounds as if you might have a kidney infection. We'll set up some intravenous antibiotics to help you and to prevent baby getting an infection too.' Isabel inhaled sharply as she helped Phoenix to sit, revealing her skeletal frame under her nightie. 'Have you eaten recently?'

The girl clung to Isabel's arm. 'No, not really. I'm so stupid. I'm so stupid.'

'No, you're not.'

'I should have been more careful. I should have looked after him instead of pretending it wasn't happening.' Then she began to cry thick tears. Isabel held Phoenix as her chest racked with deep sobs for a few minutes. When she'd finished the girl managed to force a few more words out. 'I'm sorry. I'm sorry. I didn't know what to do. I was scared so I didn't tell anyone and I haven't been doing the right things. Have I killed him? Hurt him? Will he be okay?'

'Hey…hush now. We'll sort you out. Don't worry.' Sean watched for Isabel's reaction. It must have been like a rerun of her own life. Which she steadfastly would not allow to interfere here, that much he knew.

She pressed her lips together, took a long deep breath. 'I understand. I do. I know you were scared and that you're scared now. But it will be fine. It will. The main thing is that baby has been growing—clearly. Maybe you'd like a little walk around? Sometimes it's easier if you move.'

Make yourself useful, Sean was telling himself. *Find someone to help her.* 'It's okay. Really, we're here to help. Are you sure you don't want me to phone anyone?'

The girl shook her head vehemently. 'There isn't anyone.'

'There must be someone, surely, sweetheart?'

She was gripping onto Isabel's hand now as pain ripped through her. 'No.'

Damn. Whether there was or wasn't anyone in her life to help her was clearly not up for discussion. 'What are you doing in Cambridge? On your own? Working? Student?'

Phoenix took a deep breath. 'It was supposed to be a fresh start for me and my ex—things hadn't been going well between us in Manchester—he got a job down here so we came. But as soon as he found out about the baby he ran a mile. Or a hundred miles. I have no idea where he is.' She cradled her belly as another contraction rippled through her. When she got through it she asked, her voice weak with fear, 'Have I done something bad to him? Why is he coming so early? I'm not due until March. I can't have him now. I can't.'

Sitting down in the chair next to her, Isabel stroked the girl's arm. 'Sometimes infections can bring on an early labour. All sorts of things can—not eating properly…'

'I was trying to lose weight to hide the bump when I went for job interviews.' Looking defeated, Phoenix slumped forward. 'It didn't work—I never got any job, I'm starving, he's coming now and I've made a mess of everything.'

'Look, sweetheart, sometimes babies come early. We'll do everything we can to make sure he's okay. But what about you? Have you got any friends to come and help you?'

Their patient shook her head. 'You don't make many friends when you don't go out.'

'What about your midwife? Who did you register with?'

'I didn't. I didn't think. I just wanted it all to go away.' She blinked up at them both with frightened eyes. 'Will you stay with me? And him.'

'Of course we will. Whatever you need, Phoenix.' After giving her the injections Sean stepped forward and took the girl's other hand as another, stronger contraction ripped through her. They were coming thick and fast. No woman should have to face this on her own. 'We'll stay with you, and Hope—the midwife—she'll be back soon and we'll all help you get through this. You'll see.'

Isabel looked across the bed and he felt the punch to his heart as she gave him a weak smile; gratitude shone from her eyes. It gave him some hope for their next conversation. Although there was that nagging sensation again, the one that said she would run as fast as she could, far away from him, all over again. And even though he knew that, the familiar warmth curled through his gut. What was it about her that held him captivated?

He dragged his eyes away from that mass of blonde hair that he loved to run his hands through and turned to listen to Phoenix. Her voice was starting to sound panicked. 'What if I can't do it? What if I'm not strong enough? I'm scared.'

'Don't worry, really. You'll manage. You're young...' He was going to say *and fit and healthy*...but she'd neglected herself a little too much. He had only to hope that the little one had got what it needed from her.

Her body began to tense and she screwed her face up. 'Owwww. I feel like it's pressing down, like I need to push it out. But I don't want to. He's too little. It's too soon. What if it's...what if he...?'

Isabel gave her a warm smile. 'You're fully dilated now, sweetheart. Your body will work whether you think it's the right time or not, honey. Whatever happens we'll deal with it. You can do this. You can do this.'

But there was a catch in her throat that made Sean lift his head and look at her. She blinked and turned away, shaking her head. Then she turned back, in full control again. 'It's okay, Phoenix. You have me and Sean. We can do this together. Okay? So I need you to breathe like this.'

Isabel began to pant and count.

When Phoenix screamed and bore down, squeezing against Isabel, Sean took over. 'Okay, so breathe with me, Phoenix. Breathe with me. That's a good girl. Lift your legs a little. Well done. I can see the head. Not long to go now.

The girl began to cry. 'Owwww. I don't want to push.'

'You have to push when I say so. Okay? Okay? Okay, Phoenix…you need to push now.' Cradling the head with one hand, he caught the body as it slithered out. He laid it on Phoenix's chest, but she turned away as he cut the cord. Closed her eyes tight shut as tears trickled anyway down her cheeks.

'A girl, you have a daughter, Phoenix.' But the little one wasn't happy to be out in the big wide world. He rubbed her chest with a towel. And again. *Come on. Come on. Breathe for me. Breathe, damn it.*

His gut twisted as he carried her to the Resuscitaire, worked on her until she took a short breath and squawked. A river of relief ran through him. He would not have been able to look at Isabel if this little one hadn't made it. God knew what she was feeling. Dealing with a young desperate teenager and a preemie baby. Although not as preemie as Joshua…

Isabel seemed to have overridden any emotion and was handling the situation with warmth and professionalism; she'd delivered the placenta and was clearing up with a sunny smile. But he could see the stretch in her shoulders, the clench of her jaw. It was costing her a lot to be here, he knew. She'd done that ever since he'd been back in her life again: borne every emotional insult with fastidious grace. She might have called it coping. He called it denial. She refused to be broken. No, she refused to allow anything to reach her emotionally.

'She's beautiful, Phoenix. Do you want to hold her just for a few moments?' He carried the little one over. 'Just hold her against your chest, skin to skin. They love that.'

'No. I don't know what to do. I don't know what to

do.' The girl was shaking. 'She's so small. Her skin's too big. She looks…she looks so tiny.'

'Look, she'll love being against your skin.'

She turned away. 'No. I don't… I can't. I'm too scared.'

'It's okay to be scared, sweetheart. But you have the strength to do this. She needs you. She needs her mum.' Isabel cast a worried flicker of her eyes to Sean. This teenager was experiencing the most traumatic experience possibly of her young life—having a premature baby with no emotional support. She needed someone she knew and loved to be with her. 'Hey, are you sure you don't have a friend, your mum, someone who you can at least talk to on the phone? You need someone here for you, Phoenix. You and…your daughter. Have you chosen a name yet?'

'No. I don't know… I thought it was going to be a boy… I thought she was going to die. I thought—'

'Look, she's doing okay. Your daughter is perfect.'

Clearly Phoenix was struggling and needed time to get to grips with all this. And baby needed to be looked after properly—she needed a full assessment, warmth and care. Sean bent to speak to her. 'Okay, so she's managing to breathe fine on her own, she's a trooper, but she's quite little and may not be able to feed properly as yet. I'd like to get her along to the Special Care Baby Unit as soon as we can—get her checked out and warm and looked after. How about I run her along there now and you come with Isabel or Hope when you're a bit more settled?'

Phoenix looked up at Isabel, saw the quick nod of her head. 'Okay. Yes. Okay. Thank you.'

'I'll stay here with Phoenix.' Isabel caught his gaze.

She looked as shaken as he felt. He didn't miss the irony—that Isabel had been almost in the same situation, with no one experienced to help her. She'd been through months of worry and anxiety. She hadn't told a soul about her pregnancy. And yet here she was dealing with this.

Her face was fixed in a mask, her emotions hidden so deep that it made his chest ache. Was this how she'd been? Had she shaken like this? Cried? Or had she internalised it all? Damn, he didn't want to think about any of that. Like her, he didn't want to meet those emotions head-on.

But they were there, glittering brightly within him. He wanted to comfort her. He wanted to stroke her worries away. Goddamn, he wanted her, body and soul, more than anything he'd wanted in his whole life.

So, yeah, he loved her. Which was hardly a surprise given that he'd probably been in love with her for most of his life.

Which was a dumb move on his part, because he knew that loving Isabel Delamere was the single most destructive thing he could do. Because she wouldn't allow herself to love him back.

But still, all he wanted to do was take her in his arms and hold her, soothe her pain away. To make her believe how much she meant to him. But he couldn't. He had a professional responsibility to Phoenix and the little scrap of new life in his hands. He also had a responsibility to himself. 'Excellent, I'll see you up there in a little while.' And that would give him a few precious minutes to get his act together too.

CHAPTER TWELVE

HOLD IT IN, Isabel reprimanded herself as she walked to the SCBU. Hopefully he'd have gone by the time she got there. Hopefully she wouldn't see the love in his eyes and feel the need to walk straight into his arms and cry like a baby over things that had happened too long ago. To be held in arms that she still longed to be wrapped inside. To let herself go and love him right back.

No such luck. He was lifting the tiny baby from the incubator; she looked so frail in his strong hands. 'Hi, Isabel. Where's Phoenix?'

'She's having some food and going to have a shower. She's exhausted, poor thing, and overwhelmed.'

'She doesn't want to come?'

Avoiding eye contact, she walked to the baby and gave her a wee stroke on her head. Someone, one of the nurses, she assumed, had popped a little knitted red Santa hat on her head. It just about broke her heart. 'I think she will. She needs some TLC herself. She's just getting her head around everything. I managed to get a bit of history from her. Basically she has no one. Her mum died a couple of years ago and her dad's been pretty absent for most of her life. There are no siblings. She needs a lot of support. I've warned her about the bells and whistles up here, and the feeding tube and the oxygen. But she's terrified, poor thing.' Then she remembered about the good news she had to tell him. 'But, after all that, she won the first baby of Christmas prize, so at least she's got a few things to tide her over.'

'You don't think she'll decide to put this little one out for adoption?'

'I don't know. She needs a little time to work it all out.'

Cradling the baby in the crook of his arm, he rocked side to side as he spoke. 'How are you?'

'Bearing up, thanks.' She would not break down. She would not let the pain in. And he had no right to look so damned beautiful standing there with a baby in his arms. Her heart thumped with desire, with emotion she did not want to recognise.

'You don't have to hide it from me, you know.' He leaned close enough that, if she'd wanted to, she could have touched him. She could smell his scent, the one that had clung to her body after he'd left her in Paris, and her heart thumped a little more.

She shivered. 'I'm not hiding anything. I'm at work, is all.'

'Isabel, it's been a very emotional morning. You're about at boiling point.'

Thankfully, Dean sauntered over. There was safety in numbers. 'Hey, Happy Christmas!'

'Thanks, you too.'

Dean tickled the baby girl under her chin. 'Is mum coming soon? This little one needs some cuddles.'

'No. She's having a rest.' Grateful for the chance to speak and not to feel Sean's insistent, concerned gaze on her, she filled Dean in on Phoenix's history. 'She's scared stiff and feeling guilty all round, so we need to be gentle with her. I think she'll come round. I'll pop down in an hour or so and see if she wants to come up then.'

'And in the meantime this one needs a cuddle. You want to hold her, Isabel?' He took the baby from Sean and gave her a quick check over. 'Kangaroo care. She really needs some love—especially on Christmas Day. Who doesn't?'

Whoa. Skin-to-skin contact? No. No way was she cradling this baby against her bare skin. That would be the worst thing she could ever do. That would bring back so many memories—she shook her head vehemently. 'No—oh, no, I couldn't.' The little thing was wiggling and her bottom lip had started to shake and Isabel's instinct was to reach out and comfort her, but she couldn't, wouldn't…but, oh, suddenly Dean was helping her to sit and lowering the baby into her arms, onto her chest, which—as bad luck would have it—was covered with a blouse that easily stretched open. She felt the tiny little shudder and curl into her breast, felt the warmth and smelt the just-born fresh scent. For a moment she held her there skin to skin, feeling the life force in this tiny thing, the beating heart where she'd felt none with her own child. And suddenly everything was swimming and blurred from tears she'd steadfastly refused to shed. Ever. It was all too much for her to deal with. The baby. Her memories. Sean. All on Christmas Day. 'I—I just can't.'

And then Sean was there taking the baby and in his eyes he was telling her it was okay, that everything would be okay. He was telling her all the things she'd said to Phoenix. That she was strong enough to deal with it, that she'd be okay.

But she wasn't. She wasn't okay at all. None of this was okay.

'I'm sorry, I think I might… I just… I need to go.' And she hurried out of SCBU, down the stairs and out into the falling snow, trying to force cold air into her lungs.

'Isabel! Izzy, wait. Stop.' It was Sean behind her, his footsteps muffled by the deadening snow. Where it had been beautiful and magical in Paris, now it just felt grey. Ice. The thick air suffocating. 'Isabel.'

She turned. 'I'm going for a walk.'

Warm hands skimmed her arms. 'You have no coat. You're shivering. You shouldn't be out here.'

'Please, Sean, just leave me alone.'

'I can't. I won't.' He caught her up again and pulled her round to face him. 'I know you enough that I feel the pain inside you, Isabel. Talk to me. Let it out.'

If she did she might crumble. She started to walk again, with no idea where she was headed. But the words just tumbled out; she couldn't stop them. 'I used to think it was something I'd done, you know. I thought it was my fault he didn't make it. That I could have saved him if I'd only done…this…or that. But I know he wasn't ever going to make it, Sean. Not like that little one in there. So tiny, so precious and perfect.'

'I understand.'

She came to a halt, whipped round to rail at him. 'Do you? Did you fight against your own body, trying to keep him inside you? To protect him? When you failed at that, did you hold him against your bare chest and sing to him? Did you whisper his name over and over? Did you pray for someone to hold you too? And did you have no one who was capable to take care of you? Oh, yes, Isla was brilliant and so was Evie…but in the end it was me. Just me, and this little lifeless thing that I loved with all my heart. And that broke it into tiny pieces that will never ever mend. And just when I had survived and was getting on with my life, just when I was okay, this is reminding me all over again.'

'You will mend and grow again, Isabel. Look at everything you've achieved with your life so far—what an amazing and compassionate doctor you've become. What a beautiful, sensational woman. Just think of what a tour de force we'll be together.' That was a promise from him for the future. He believed in them, that this could work. His arms were round her now and he'd found a bench in the white-coated garden and she was sitting on it and hadn't even noticed. He was warm and safe and for a moment she let him hold her, let him soothe her memories away with a kiss against her throat. He was here, he was making his claim, his stand, his promise and she felt so close to letting go, to believing him. To feeling that everything would turn out fine.

That realisation was enough to jolt her away from him.

She stood. Closed down every emotion, just as she always had, because it was safer that way. Because she had never felt as if her heart had been wrenched from her chest until today—and that surely must mean that she'd allowed herself to get lulled into feeling too much again.

She'd seen him hold a baby, seen the look of contentment on his face, the joy. And she knew she would be unable to commit herself to give him that or anything like it. Ever. Because it couldn't be fine, because she would always be thinking about the worst things that could happen, never giving herself totally to protect herself from breaking into pieces again, and he deserved more than that. So much more.

She'd been too close to the edge just now and she did not want to fall from it. She was too scared, too darned terrified because it would be too hard, so very, very hard to pull herself up from it again. Life had been fine before she'd met Sean again. Empty, but fine. Monochrome, but liveable. She could survive without colour and a full heart and making love, without Paris and without Sean. Without memories and pain and the risk that she could feel so lost again without him. Some time. Once had been enough for any lifetime.

She did not want to bleed for him again. 'I'm so sorry, Sean. I can't do this. *Us.* I'm sorry. There isn't a future and I don't want to let you think there could be.'

'What?' He stood to face her. 'After everything we've been through? You're saying you don't want to try?'

She took a deep breath of the cold, cold air, filled her insides with ice, let it infuse her veins, her blood, because that way she would be able to say these things. 'Yes, that's exactly what I'm saying. It's over, whatever it was, in Paris—whatever I let you believe, I'm sorry.'

But instead of giving the understanding, thoughtful gentle response she expected, he frowned. His voice was laced with anger. 'No, you're not sorry at all. You just want to protect yourself. You want to live a half-life. You want to hide. That's not living, Isabel.'

'Please don't make this harder than it is. It's what I want.'

'And what about what I want? Ever think about that?' When she looked away he huffed out an irritated breath. 'No. I didn't think so.'

'It's not you—' Then she shut up, because all that *it's*

not you, it's me gumpf was just a sweetener, and nothing about this was sweet. He had so much to offer, so much promise, so much capability to love—he deserved far more than what she could give him. It made her stomach hurt. It made everything inside her twist and contort and knot. He was right: she hadn't given much thought to how he would be after all this. It had all been about her.

How selfish. How typically Delamere girl. But there it was… She had to do what was right for her; there was no point letting him believe in something that she just couldn't do.

He glared at her. 'Really? You were going to trot out some well-worn phrase? Don't we deserve more than that?' And even though she'd made him cross he was still devastating to look at. His dark eyes still entranced her. There was still that magnetic pull to him that was so hard to resist. She'd been resisting it for too long already. Snow whirled around him like a vortex sticking to his scrubs. He didn't seem to notice. 'You really mean it, don't you? You don't want any of it.'

'No. I don't.'

'You're a coward, Isabel Delamere. You have closed off your life, shut down, checked out. You don't have to bury yourself along with Joshua, you know. You deserve to live.'

'I do live.'

'Hardly. I mean, sure, you get involved with your patients, because that's safe, you know where the line is and you never cross it. You allow yourself to feel their pain, like some sort of proxy for actually feeling things inside you, and then you try to fix them—because you couldn't do that for yourself. But with someone who really cares for you, with me, you totally shut down. You're afraid. I get that, but you have to let people in some time or you'll end up sad and lonely and, well...dead inside.' He pulled her towards him, anger and desire mingling in his eyes. 'I love you. I just think you should know that before I go.'

'Don't—' She put her hand out to his lips, trying to erase his words. 'Don't say that.'

He shrugged her hand away. 'I love you. And I know you love me. I saw it in Paris. I saw it in the way you looked at me. I saw it when we made love. For God's sake, Isabel, don't run away from it this time.'

'No—' She couldn't love him; she'd tried so hard not to. She'd fought and fought to stop him affecting her, to stop him reaching inside her soul and meeting her there, raw and pure. But here she was, out in the snow, having almost lost the plot with him and a preemie and a young girl on Christmas Day. In Paris she'd almost felt that things could be perfect; she'd let them be. She'd almost believed him.

She remembered that feeling at the top of the Ferris wheel—the freedom, the joy of being with him. The way her whole body craved him, and still did now, even more than ever.

And she was struggling to let him go, because she wanted him so much to stay. She did...she did love him.

She closed her eyes against the bitter reality. She loved him totally, utterly...needed him in her life. It was the single worst thing she could do. She hated that she needed him, that she wanted him so much. She hated that they'd become *us* and she couldn't allow herself to be part of that. She'd fallen further under his spell, with his total faith in things working out okay. She needed to go home, to be with Isla—the only person in the world who understood. She needed to put herself back together again.

When she opened her eyes he was closer, his gaze smoky with intent despite the layer of snowflakes in his hair, on his cheeks, on his shoulders. Despite the freezing gale both outside and in her gut. 'Tell me you don't love me and I'll walk away. Tell me, Isabel, that Paris meant nothing to you and I won't stay here another moment.'

'I… What does it matter? I don't want to love you. I can't love you. There it is. Now go, please.'

He stood for a moment, not moving, just looking at her as if willing her to change her mind.

She didn't.

Then he shrugged his shoulders and took one last step towards her. She'd never seen him like this—so coiled and taut, so angry and explosive. And, damn her hormones, she wanted him even more for it. This Sean loved her. This formidable man had been there for her years ago and she hadn't taken him then, this man who had come to find her, who had loved her once, loved her again. It was a second chance.

But he wasn't taking it any more than she could. 'You know what? I'm done chasing you, Isabel. All those years ago you thrashed my heart to pieces because you didn't trust that I would look after you, you couldn't trust me with your secret or your love. All those wasted years we could have been together, exploring the world. Living. Being. Together. That was all I ever wanted from the moment I first saw you in that classroom. And even now, when I've told you again that I love you, you throw it back in my face. Well, that's me done. If you're not willing to take a risk and let me in then I'm gone.' His fingers ran across her throat to the chain that held the keys to his lock. He looked at them, then shook his head. 'I'm finished trying to fight for you, Isabel. I'm finished loving you.'

No. Don't go. She wanted to call to him, to cling to him. To make him stay. He had been her constant. He loved her, still. After everything, he still wanted her. All she had to do was take a step. But she was scared, terrified, so deep-down frozen that she stood there and looked at him. And said nothing.

Don't go. In her head, a tiny voice. *Don't go.* That got louder until it was all she could hear, all she could feel. She clasped the keys on her chain into her fist and tried to swallow through the thick wedge of sadness. *I love you with every beat of my heart.*

But then he swivelled in the snow, stomping long wide footprints back to the hospital entrance, to the happy smiling relatives, to the big sparkling Christmas tree and the jingle-jangle music of Christmas songs. Leaving, in his wake, her frozen body and broken heart.

And only then, when she knew she'd truly lost him, when there was no scrap of hope left, did she crumble to the bench and let the tears fall.

CHAPTER THIRTEEN

Happy bloody Christmas?

Yeah, right. Happy bloody life. The growing pressure in Sean's chest almost stopped his breath. He had to get away from her.

It was like Groundhog Day. It was as if he'd gone right back to being seventeen again, only worse because, hell—he'd been forewarned and forearmed, he'd known exactly what she was like and yet he'd loved her anyway.

Fists clenched tight against his sides, Sean walked back into the warmth of the hospital, kept on going past the cafeteria, past the labour suite, past the wards and the cleaners' department, past the delivery bay and out to the street at the other side. Then he ran. Along deserted roads covered in a thickening layer of snow. Past closed shops, further past magnificent colleges and the cathedral and onwards to the river.

Along the footpath he ran past laughing families out throwing snowballs, screeching kids on their new bikes struggling with too-big wheels and too-high seats. He ran past hedges of brambles asleep until spring. Past punts, empty of passengers until summer sun hit the city. Past riverside pubs that murmured with laughter and cheer that he did not feel in any cell in his body, past trees and parks and fields. He ran and then he ran some more.

And eventually, when he no longer had the energy to put one foot in front of the other, he came to a stop.

Goddamnit, he had no clue where he was. 'Isabel.' He shouted her name to the sky, to the empty field, as if she might hear him and look for him. Louder, like a lunatic, like a desperate man. 'Isabel!'

But he wasn't desperate; he'd just made a fatal error in falling in love with someone who didn't know how to do the same. He'd tried, he'd laid his heart on the line and she'd stomped on it again. He'd been so close— they'd been so close—to having it all. And she just didn't want it.

Then he realised he had no breath left and he was doubled over trying to fill his lungs, but all he got were icy vocal cords and a searing hacking cough. He was supposed to be on call. He was supposed to be at the hospital doing his job. Not running to get Isabel out of his system—because she was there, indelibly printed on his heart and it was all pointless. He loved her, for God's sake—how bloody stupid. He loved her, needed her, wanted her more than ever and she couldn't see what a wonderful gift the two of them could be together. And even though he'd known this going in, he'd fooled himself into believing it wouldn't happen. Well, no more. He straightened up, looked at the clear blue sky, emptied of its white load, a thin weak sun. But sun nevertheless. He would go onwards, travel some more. See the world. He would put her behind him, forget Paris and Cambridge and the hope and the love. He would recover from the hurt.

Somehow.

He stamped his feet and began to walk back to work.

'How's she doing?' Five hours and a couple of less straightforward Christmas deliveries later and Isabel had managed to find some time to visit SCBU again. Better that than to wallow in her own troubles. He was gone from her life—she had a week to endure working on side with him, loving him. Then she'd be home in Melbourne and she could put today behind her.

She would get through this, start her life again. In the meantime she just had to make sure she didn't come face to face with him. The crying had eventually stopped—although she had never known that a person could sob so hard for so long. And after she'd splashed her face with water and drunk two cups of fortifying coffee she'd filled her voice with Christmas cheer and come back to her world. She couldn't leave the hospital, but she could certainly fill her day with people so she wasn't free to face him again alone. She could do this. She could. 'Baby Harding? Is she okay?'

'Absolutely fine.' Dean jerked his thumb towards the incubator and gave a wry smile. 'Mum seems to be taking her time, but she's getting there.'

Dressed in some over-large clothes that Isabel guessed were from the goodwill cupboard, Phoenix was sitting on a chair staring at the cot while her baby gurgled in her incubator kicking her waif-like legs in the air. Poor mite. Both of them. They needed each other and neither of them knew how to go about it. Hoping she could perhaps set them on a path, Isabel crossed the unit and bent down next to Phoenix. 'Hey, there. You made it.'

Phoenix shrugged. 'I couldn't leave her here, not on her own.'

'You did good. Now you can watch over her.' And hopefully feel a mother's need to hold her, some time soon. 'How are you feeling?'

'A bit better.'

Isabel nodded and gave her what she hoped was a reassuring smile. 'That's good, isn't it?'

'Yes. I think so. Hope said she'd speak to a social worker and get me some help.' Phoenix looked at her hands. 'I need it. I'm not sure I can do this on my own. It's a big responsibility—a life. Someone else's.'

'You'll be okay. There are people who can support you. I'll make sure of it.'

But Isabel felt guilt settle on her shoulders. Phoenix had no one. No family, no partner, no one to care for her. She'd thought that she'd been in a similar situation, once, but there had been people there for her if she'd asked. Isla, of course. Her parents, if she'd taken a chance. Sean.

Not any more. The sharp stab in her stomach was startling.

Baby Harding started to stir; her body went rigid as she prepared to bawl. 'I think she needs some company.' Isabel gestured towards Dean, asking if she could pick her up. He nodded and winked.

'Phoenix, is it okay if I pick her up?'

'Sure.'

Isabel bent into the crib and scooped up the little one. This time she would keep her feelings out of it. This time there would be no skin to skin—at least not hers. 'Come here, sweetie. You want a cuddle?' She cradled the baby in her arm, trying to soothe her. Singing a soft lullaby as Phoenix watched from behind her fringe.

'You see this tube?' Isabel pointed to the nasogastric tube, managing to keep it together. But, oh, how she wished she didn't keep having that image of Sean in her head—the one where he'd looked at her so angrily and walked away. Where he'd finally, totally, given up on her. 'This is to help with her feeds. She hasn't mastered the art of sucking yet, so she needs a bit of help. If you get a chance, hold her close to your breast so she can smell your milk, try popping the tip of your little finger into her mouth and see if she tries to suck. Oh, and that tube in the crib is just for oxygen, if she needs it. But, as you can hear, her lungs are in pretty good condition.'

As bub wailed Isabel continued to chat, inching closer and closer to Phoenix… 'She's got your hair colouring. Look at all that dark fluff. She's gorgeous.'

Tears filled Phoenix's eyes. 'Why won't she stop crying?'

'I think she needs her mum. Maybe?' Dragging a chair next to Phoenix, she sat, still cradling the baby, grateful to have a distraction from Sean—and a little bit of interest from Phoenix if the flicker in her eyes was anything to go by. 'Have you chosen a name for her yet?'

'I was thinking of Sarah. After my mum.'

'It's a pretty name. For a pretty girl.'

Isabel could see Phoenix's fingers twitching. Then the young mum sat on her hands. Maybe she did want to hold her baby, but didn't know how to ask. Didn't dare. Some people were like that; some people had to be guided and were slow to build their confidence, whereas others dived right in. *Like me,* Isabel thought; no confidence whatsoever when it came to relationships. And then she tried again to rid her mind of all thoughts of Sean.

But it wasn't working. She couldn't not think of him. Her heart swelled at the memory of his face, of his promises. Then it broke all over again.

Noticing all the staff were busy, Isabel tried her strategy to help Phoenix. 'I don't suppose... No. It's okay. I'll ask someone else...'

'What?' Phoenix sat up straight.

'I need to go to the loo. I don't suppose you'd want to take Sarah for a moment. Just for a moment, mind you. I wouldn't ask...only everyone seems busy with feeds and those poor babies needing extra care...'

Biting her lip, Phoenix gave a little smile. 'I...well, I suppose I could. Try.'

'Oh, thank you. You'd be doing me a huge favour.' Very slowly she handed the baby over. 'I thought I'd be useless at holding them when I first started doing this job, but babies are very easy... Look, just support her head here, and keep that hand under her little tush. Good. That's great. You're a natural, Phoenix.'

The baby began to turn her head towards Phoenix's breast and nuzzled in.

'Oh, she knows you're her mum, all right.' Isabel glanced up at Phoenix's face, trying not to place too much emphasis on this because she didn't want to frighten her, or put pressure on her. Gentle was the way to go. But Phoenix's eyes were glittering with tears again. 'She's so small.'

'But you watch, she'll soon put on weight. Now, just sit tight and I'll be back in a mo.'

As Isabel stood she caught a glimpse of Sean's reflection in the entrance-door glass.

Oh. She sucked in a breath. Wow. It was a physical pain in her heart.

She did not want to see him. Did not. 'I…er… I think I'll stay a minute.'

She could do this. She sat back down.

Phoenix watched her. 'Dr Delamere, are you hiding from Dr Anderson?'

'No. I'm just…well, I'm just trying to…'

'I know it when I see it. I've been doing it for the last seven months. Trouble is, it catches up with you in the end.' The girl grinned and lifted Sarah as evidence. 'There are some things you just can't deny any more.'

'Don't be so clever.' Isabel didn't know if he'd seen her, but he hadn't come into the room.

And Phoenix just wouldn't let it drop. 'So, he's a nice guy. Helpful. Good with his hands…'

She would not discuss her personal life with a patient—that would be absolutely stepping over the line. 'Yes, well, I think you need to focus on Sarah.'

'She's asleep.' Phoenix craned her neck to watch the door.

'Ah, yes…anyway…'

Phoenix turned back and grinned again. 'It's okay, he's going now.'

Relief flooding through her, Isabel breathed out and started to relax. 'Good. Thank you.'

'But if I were you I wouldn't run too far away from him. Sexy guy like that.'

'And none of your business.'

Phoenix raised an eyebrow. 'Just saying…if I had a guy look at me the way he looks at you I'd be walking towards him not hiding in a wing-backed chair. You're lucky to have someone like him looking out for you. You're lucky to have someone, full stop.'

So it turned out that young Phoenix was wise beyond her years—and so very alone. And in stark contrast Isabel could have had everything. He'd been there offering her a future regardless of their past but she'd pushed him away. Again.

How lucky was she to have someone like him in her life, someone to share everything—good times and bad—to walk with her through whatever life threw their way? How very selfish to wallow in the past and not take a chance on loving someone, and having them love you right back. Just because she was scared. Scared of feeling something…but wasn't she feeling things right now? Despair, mainly. Loss. Broken. As if she'd ripped her own heart out of her chest, because it had all been her doing after all.

Isabel turned and watched him disappear down the corridor. Was he avoiding her too? Did he really not want to see her again?

And it hit her with force that she couldn't bear the thought of not having him in her life. Of not loving him for ever. Because she had, it dawned on her now; she'd loved him her whole life. And it was painful and beautiful and every colourful emotion in between. The joy of it all was that he loved her too.

Isabel glanced at Phoenix, who was now pressing her lips against the baby's chest and murmuring the words to a Christmas song that was playing through the speakers. This girl had been so frightened to love her daughter and now it seemed she had decided to. Just like that. She was going to do it alone and it was going to be hard, but she was taking her first steps along that road. She was brave and strong and everything Isabel could be too—if she let it all in. If she let Sean in. Miracles could happen if you let them. Isabel brushed the rogue tears from her cheeks. Maybe it was her turn for one.

But she couldn't find him. She'd tried the labour suite, the cafeteria, the postnatal ward. She'd popped into Theatre and he wasn't there. Which was probably a good thing because she had no idea what she was going to say to him when she caught up with him.

She wandered along the second-floor corridor with her heart beating too fast, panic setting in, looking in every room—stopping short of calling his name. And then, there, he was calmly ambling along towards her, deep in thought, hands in pockets.

She stopped by the chapel and waited for him to see her, watching his reaction as he slowly came to a halt in front of her. She tried to read his face—but it was a mask. It seemed she wasn't the only one who could hide their feelings. 'Isabel. Hello.'

'Sean.' She didn't know how to begin. What to say.

But he spoke first. 'Phoenix seems to be doing okay.'

So he was keeping it professional. 'Yes. Yes, she's getting there. As am I.'

His forehead crinkled as he frowned. 'Sorry, I don't understand.'

'I wanted to tell you that I do love you. That being with you in Paris was the happiest I've ever been in my life.'

He gave a sharp nod. 'Good to know. Now, I need to go—'

'Wait. Please. Don't go, Sean.'

'Is there any point to this?'

'Yes. Yes, Sean...' Pressing her palms against his chest, she made him stand still—because this was her only chance to say how she felt. Out loud to him. This was the only chance and she was going to grab it—and him and their love, whatever it took. 'I was so scared, so very scared to love you—but it happened anyway. In fact, I don't think I ever stopped loving you all these years. But I didn't know how to let you in. I've spent so long pushing people away, not letting myself feel anything, in case I got hurt... I'm sorry. It's taken some time for me to realise, but I know now that I don't want to live my life without you.'

He shook his head and confirmed all hope was gone. He took her hands in his and she thought he was going to drop them, but he spoke, his voice weary. 'I'm tired, Isabel.'

'It's Izzy.' She squeezed her eyes closed to press back the tears, but this time she just couldn't hold them back. Because she was his Izzy. 'To you.'

'I'm tired, Izzy.'

She opened her eyes, because he'd used her pet name. A flicker of hope bloomed bright in her chest. 'Of me?'

'Of having to fight for you, of having to believe for two people. I'm tired of trying to be that person, the one you trust, the one you choose. And then you not choosing me anyway. I'm over that. I need a life for me. I can't do this any more.'

Her hands stilled against his heart. It was there, solid and strong. He'd been so strong for them both. 'I trust you.'

'Do you, really? Because I haven't seen any sign of that.' He looked as if he didn't believe her, didn't want to. 'Since when?'

'Since for ever.'

'But I need to see it, you needed to show me instead

of bottling everything up inside. I love you, but I won't go through that again. I don't want to.'

So she'd pushed him to the edge and he'd stepped right over. 'I see. So there's no chance…?'

There's a small chance, she thought, because he was still holding her hands.

She gripped his tightly and peered up into his dark eyes that shone with light. 'I know I've been a Delamere disaster to live with, but you've got to understand, I love you with all my heart—and I always will. You, me and Joshua—we were a family, even if just for such a short time, and somewhere along the line I stuffed that up. Big time. I lost you and I don't ever want to lose you again, because that would be too much to bear. You remember those dreams we used to have when we were younger? Those happy, silly dreams that we had a lifetime ahead of us, all the things we could do together? Conquer the world and have fun in the process? I know I lost that— it's taken me all these years to find that again—and you've reawakened it. I know we can do great things, we can be great together. Look at how we helped Teo and Marina…'

'That's charity, Izzy. You can do that on your own.'

'Like hell I can. You give me the confidence to do that. You believe I can do that. You make every day worthwhile—waking up with you is the best gift I've ever had.' She wrapped her fist around the keys on the chain at her throat. 'I want to spend the rest of my life with you. I want to wake up with you every day. So, please, Sean—I love you. I want you in my life. I choose you. Please…don't make me beg.'

His eyes widened. 'Why the hell not?'

She swallowed. 'Really? You want me to beg? Is that

how it's going to be?' God knew, she'd really, really stuffed up. 'Okay—if that's what it's going to take—'

'Not on your life. I'm joking.' Sean let his hands slip out of hers and made a decision. It was one he'd been toying with in Paris. One he'd made years ago and one he hoped he'd never have to make again. He could hardly believe what she was saying—but he had to. He had to take the chance. She loved him and wanted him.

And he knew it was early days, that she had a long way to go—but he believed she wanted to walk that journey with him. He reached into his pocket and pulled out the box he'd been carrying with him ever since he'd arrived in Cambridge.

'In that case, Isabel Delamere...' Then he took one of her hands and knelt onto one knee. The look on her face was one of love and joy—and he knew he'd seen that before, in Paris, and he would never tire of seeing it. She loved him. He knew it, he felt it.

'Oh, my God, Sean?'

At that moment the chapel doors opened and out streamed a congregation of smiling people who came to a standstill at what they were witnessing. Great. Now he had an audience.

'Izzy, I know this is soon for you—but I want you to know that I will be here for you, I will walk this road with you. I want nothing more than to be part of your family. I will give you all the time in the world for you to choose whether you want more children to add to it, or if you want our family to be just the two of us. But whatever you decide, I will be by your side. I love you, Izzy. Will you marry me?'

He offered her the ring and his solemn promise.

Her soft green eyes were brimming with tears. 'Is that…is that the ring you gave me when I was sixteen?'

'The very same.'

'You kept it?'

A collective *awww* had him turning his head towards the grins and smiles—everyone seemed to be silently cheering him on.

He was starting to get stage fright. 'I guess I always hoped…one day we'd get to use it.' He took her hand again. 'The wait is killing me… And everyone else?'

A murmur of *yes* rippled around the space.

She laughed, her mouth crumpling. 'Oh, Sean, I couldn't imagine a life more wonderful than being with you.' Then she was pulling him up and in his arms and the congregation gave a cheer and a round of applause. As she pressed her lips to his all the other people melted away and he was alone again with her. Just her. The thought that had come back to him time and again over too many wasted years. Just her. His Izzy.

Something akin to the joy he'd seen on her face roared through him. 'I guess that's a yes?'

'Yes. Yes. Yes! When?' Her arms were round his neck.

'Whoa…someone's keen.'

'I want to start now… I want to be with you from now until for ever.'

'Let's start with today, then. Merry Christmas, Izzy.'

'Oh, yes. A very happy Christmas to you, Sean.' Then she gave him a long lingering kiss that left him in no doubt that this would be the happiest Christmas ever.

EPILOGUE

'I CAN'T BELIEVE it's happening…' Isabel looked out of her old bedroom window at her parents' house down to the manicured garden below. If they weren't quick the flowers would droop in the lovely summer heat. She turned to Isla, who looked so exquisitely beautiful in her long pale lilac silk dress, her hair woven with white flowers, eyes glistening with tears, it made Isabel's heart ache. In fact, her heart hadn't stopped aching—in a good way—for the last three hundred and sixty-four days. 'It's like a fairy tale down there.'

'It's your fairy tale—and we need to get on with it. I love you. I'm so proud of you.' Her sister squeezed her hand; her voice was tender and calm and so not the way Isabel was feeling inside. Calm had left her somewhere around the rehearsal dinner last night when nerves and excitement had taken over. Then sleep had evaded her, not because she was scared—those days were long gone—but because she was just counting down the hours until she could see him again and become Mrs Anderson.

'Okay, let's do this.' Isabel swallowed, inhaled deeply and then walked to the door. Would it be too unbridely to just run down there and jump into his arms? She guessed it probably would.

As she took her father's arm and began to walk up the makeshift petal-strewn aisle behind cute-as-a-button flower girl Cora Elliot, Isabel kept her focus on Sean up ahead waiting for her.

He smiled at her.

He had no idea.

She smiled back, hugging to herself the new secret she'd kept from him for the last two days. And she kept that smile as she nodded to the guests who sighed as she walked by. To Darcie, who had become a firm friend and job-share partner over the last year. The part-time role giving her lots of opportunity to volunteer at the homeless clinic and to raise money for those charities that supported pregnant teenage girls.

And she smiled at Lucas, the dashing man by Darcie's side, who was grinning proudly at his little niece, Cora. Then on to Alessi, who was trying—and failing—to wrestle a wriggling Geo into some sort of quiet. Her gorgeous nephew had taken his first steps recently and was causing every kind of mayhem in their household.

The only piece missing from their day was the staff from Cambridge Royal Maternity Unit, who had been such a huge part of their lives, but they'd had a long email from Bonnie this morning wishing them all the luck in the world; news that Hope's baby had been born, a lovely boy for her and Aaron, and that Jess and Dean were just back from honeymoon with very big smiles. Bonnie and Jacob had some good news of their own—a wedding and adoption plans approved.

Gosh, she missed them all. One day…one day, somehow they'd all be together again, but if not in person they talked regularly over the Internet and their friendships were solid and lasting.

But it was so lovely to be here, sharing this day with these special people she loved, at home in Melbourne—and since opening her heart out to Sean she had truly never felt so loved in her life.

And then she was there, facing him, in front of the celebrant and surrounded by so much love.

As she said her *I wills* and *I dos* she kept her secret tight inside her.

As her husband kissed her she didn't say a word.

But as the speeches were made and she had to raise a glass she just couldn't hold it in any more. 'Hey, husband of mine, this has been the best day of my life.'

'Mine too. Now chink my glass and drink...they're waiting.' He gave her a kiss and a very sexy wink that had her looking forward to her wedding night at the plush vineyard hideaway they'd booked for a honeymoon.

'I...er... I don't think I should do that.' She leaned in closer, careful not to mess up his dark charcoal suit that made him look very definitely the most handsome man in the world. 'Not for the next nine months or so anyway.'

He looked at her, dark eyes shining. 'What? Really?'

'Yes,' she whispered. 'I'm pregnant. And I have a clean bill of health, all going exactly to plan. Perfect? Yes?'

'Yes, you are, my darling.' Then he kissed her again as if he would never have enough.

When he put her down she clinked his glass and the crowd cheered all over again. But still they didn't share their news...because, well, because some things just needed to be enjoyed in private for a while.

The marquee provided decent shade from the searing

summer sunshine, but there was a barbecue and music and later a plan for a trip to the beach. Sean surveyed the mayhem as their friends and family began the informal part of the proceedings. 'A little bit different from last Christmas?'

'And next year will be different again, with a little one.' She patted her tummy, which was as flat as it ever was, but she *knew*…she just knew that everything was going to be fine.

Sean ran his thumb down her cheek and she honestly didn't think it could be possible to be any more happy. But she was, a little more every day, by his side, and now as his wife.

'A baby would be totally perfect, but, Izzy, I don't care where we are or what we do or who we're with, just as long as you and I spend the rest of our lives together.'

'Oh, yes, I promise with all my heart.' She picked up her glass and, one last time, clinked it against his. 'Together. For ever.'

* * * * *

HIS LITTLE CHRISTMAS MIRACLE

EMILY FORBES

PROLOGUE

'AND SO IT BEGINS,' Kristie said as she stuck her head into her cousin's bedroom.

'So what begins?' Jess asked as she tied off her plaits and pulled a red knitted hat over her white-blonde hair. She picked up her sunglasses and ski gloves and followed her cousin out of their family's five-star apartment.

'Operation Find Jess a Boyfriend,' Kristie replied.

'What! Why?'

'Because you're almost eighteen and you have no idea what you've been missing. It's time to find you a gorgeous boy. One you won't be able to resist, someone who can kiss their way into that ivory tower of yours and sweep you off your feet. We've talked about this.'

They had but Kristie was always talking about boys in one way or another and Jess mostly ignored her. Kristie was boy crazy—she fell in love every couple of weeks—but Jess was different. Most boys Jess met seemed immature and silly. She didn't see what all the fuss was about. Seventeen- and eighteen-year-old boys were just that. Boys. And Jess wanted Prince Charming. And Prince Charming would arrive in his own time. She didn't think Kristie was going to be able to conjure him up.

'I think you're forgetting something,' Jess said as they dropped their skis onto the snow and clicked their boots into the bindings, ready to tackle their first day on the slopes of the Moose River Alpine Resort.

'What's that?'

'I'd never be allowed to find my own boyfriend. Everyone I've ever dated has been a friend of the family.'

'*You're* not going to find him, I'm going to find him for you,' Kristie explained. 'And let's be honest, you'll never get laid if you only date guys your dad picks out. For one they'd be too terrified of what he'd do to them if he found out and, two, I'm sure your dad deliberately picks guys who are potentially gay.'

'That's not true,' Jess retorted even as she wondered whether maybe it was.

But surely not? Some of those boys had kissed her and while the experiences certainly hadn't been anything to rave about she'd always thought that was her fault. The boys had been cute enough, polite and polished in a typical trust-fund, private-school, country-club way, but not one of them had ever set her heart racing or made her feel breathless or excited or any of the things she'd expected to feel or wanted to feel, and she'd decided she was prepared to wait for the right one.

'Maybe I don't want a boyfriend,' she added.

'Maybe not, but you definitely need to get laid.'

'Kristie!' Jess was horrified.

'You don't know what you're missing. That's going to be my eighteenth birthday present to you. I'm going to find you a gorgeous boy and you're going to get laid.'

Kristie laughed but Jess suspected she wasn't joking. Kristie didn't see anything wrong with advertising the fact that she wanted to hook up with a boy but Jess could think of nothing more embarrassing. Despite the fact that they spent so much time together their personalities were poles apart. Less than three months separated them in age but Kristie was far savvier than Jess, not to mention more forthright and confident.

'This is your chance,' Kristie continued. 'We have one week before your parents arrive. One week with just my parents, who are nowhere near as strict. That's seven days to check out all the hot guys who'll just be hanging around the resort. You'll never get a better opportunity to hook up with someone.'

'Maybe I don't want to hook up with anyone. Promise me you won't set me up,' Jess begged. Kristie's seven-day deadline coincided with Jess's eighteenth birthday. Her parents were coming up to the resort to celebrate it with her and once they arrived Jess knew she wouldn't have a chance to be alone with a boy. Surely not even Kristie could make this happen in such a short time even if Jess *was* a willing participant. And while she wasn't averse to the *idea* of the experience, she wanted it her way. She wanted the romance. She wanted to fall in love. She wanted to be seduced and made love to. *Getting laid* did not have the same ring. Getting laid was not the experience she was after.

But then she relaxed. She might get a chance to kiss a boy but even though Kristie's parents were far more lenient than her own she still doubted that she would get an opportunity to lose her virginity.

'We won't be allowed out at night,' she said when Kristie didn't answer.

Kristie laughed again. 'Do you think you're only allowed to have sex after midnight?' she called back over her shoulder as she skied over to join the lift line for the village quad chair. 'No one is keeping tabs on us during the day. We could sneak off whenever we wanted.'

Sex during the day! Jess hadn't considered that possibility. But it still wasn't going to happen. As much as Kristie wanted her project to get off the ground, Jess couldn't imagine getting naked in the middle of the day. In her fantasy she imagined soft lighting, perfumed candles, the right music and a comfortable bed. Preferably her own bed. With clean sheets and a man who adored her. A quick fumble in the middle of the day with some random guy from the resort, no matter how cute, just wasn't the same thing.

'Today is the beginning of the rest of your life. It's time you had some fun,' Kristie told her as she joined the line. 'This place will be crawling with good-looking boys. We'll be able to take our pick.'

Getting a boy's attention was never a problem. Jess knew she was pretty enough. She was petite, only one hundred and sixty centimetres tall, and cheerleader pretty with a heart-shaped face, a chin she thought was maybe a bit too pointy, platinum-blonde hair, green eyes and porcelain skin. Finding a boy who ticked all her boxes was the tricky part. And if one did measure up then getting a chance to be alone was another challenge entirely.

Kristie's joke about Jess's ivory tower wasn't completely inaccurate. Jess did have dreams of being swept off her feet, falling madly in love and being rescued from her privileged but restricted life. It seemed to be her best chance of escaping the rules and boundaries her parents imposed on her. She couldn't imagine gaining her freedom any other way. She wasn't rebellious enough to go against their wishes without very good reason.

But she couldn't imagine falling in love at the age of seventeen and she wasn't about to leap into bed with the first cute guy who presented her with the opportunity. That didn't fit with her romantic notions at all. But although Jess could protest vigorously, it didn't mean Kristie would give up. And she proved it with her next comment.

'What about him?' she asked as they waited for the quad chair.

Jess looked at the other skiers around them. It was just after nine in the morning. The girls had risen early, keen to enjoy their first morning on the slopes, but everyone else in the line was ten years younger or twenty years older than them. They were surrounded by families with young children. All the other teenagers were still in bed, and Jess couldn't work out who Kristie was talking about.

Her cousin nudged her in the side. 'There.' She used her ski pole to point to the front of the line and Jess realised she meant the towies.

Two young men, who she guessed to be a year or two older than she was, worked the lift together. They both wore the uniform of the mountain resort, bright blue ski jackets with a band of fluorescent yellow around the upper arm and matching blue pants with another yellow band around the bottom of the legs. A row of white, snow-covered mountain peaks was stitched across the left chest of the jacket with 'Moose River Alpine Resort' emblazoned beneath. Their heads were uncovered and Jess could see one tall, fair-headed boy and another slightly shorter one with dark hair.

They had music pumping out of the stereo system at the base of the lift. It blasted the mountain, drowning out all other noise, including the engine of the chairlift. Jess watched as the boys danced to the beat as they lifted the little kids onto the chair and chatted and flirted with the mothers.

The fair one drew her attention. He moved easily, in time with the music, relaxed, unselfconscious and comfortable in his skin. Jess couldn't ever imagine dancing in front of strangers in broad daylight. She wasn't comfortable in a crowd. But there was something erotic about watching someone dance from a distance. She wouldn't normally stare but she was emboldened by her anonymity. He didn't know her and from behind the security of her dark sunglasses she could watch unobserved. Like a voyeur.

Kristie shuffled forward in the line and Jess followed but she couldn't tear her eyes away from the dancing towie. Watching the way his hips moved, she felt a stirring in her belly that she recognised as attraction, lust, desire. Watching him move, she could imagine how it would feel to dance with him, how it would feel to be held against him as his hips moved in time with hers. She found her hips swaying to the beat of the music, swaying in response to this stranger.

The song changed, snapping her out of her reverie, and she watched as he mimicked some rap moves that had the kids in front of her in stitches. The dark-haired one was chatting to a mother while the fair one lifted the woman's child onto the seat before giving him a high five. He lifted his head as he laughed at something the child had said and suddenly he was looking straight at Jess.

Jess's pulse throbbed and her stomach ached with a primal, lustful reaction as his eyes connected with hers. They were the most brilliant blue. A current tore through her body, sending a shock deep inside her all the way to her bones. She was aware of Kristie moving into position for the lift but she was riveted to the spot, her skis frozen to the snow. She was transfixed by eyes the colour of forget-me-nots.

'Careful. Keep moving unless you want to get collected by the chair.' It took Jess a second or two to realise he was talking to her. He had an Australian accent and in her bewildered and confused state it took her a moment to decipher it and make sense of his words. While she was translating his speech in her head he reached out and put one hand on her backside and pushed her forward until she was standing on the mat, ready to be swept up by the chairlift. Jess could swear she could feel the heat of his hand through the padding of her ski suit. She was still standing in place, staring at him, as the chair swung behind her and scooped her up, knocking into the back of her knees and forcing her to sit down with a thump.

'Have a good one.' He winked at her as she plopped into the seat and Jess felt herself blush but she kept eye contact. She couldn't seem to look away. *Let me off*, she wanted to shout but when she opened her mouth nothing came out. Her eyesight worked but she appeared to have lost control of all her other senses. Including movement. She was enchanted, spellbound by a boy with eyes of blue.

'They were cute,' Kristie said as the lift carried them up the mountain and Jess forced herself to turn her head and look away. Maybe that would break the spell.

'I guess,' she said. She felt like she had a mouthful of marbles as she tried to feign indifference. Kristie would have a field day if she knew what Jess had really been thinking.

'What do you think?' Kristie asked. 'Worth a second look?'

The girls had the quad chair to themselves but that didn't mean Jess wanted to have this discussion. She knew if she agreed it would only serve to encourage Kristie's foolish plan.

'You're not serious!' she cried. 'I don't think they're my type.' She suspected she'd have nothing in common with them. She knew she wouldn't be cool enough.

'Why not?'

'You know the reputation those guys have.' The towies—usually an assortment of college students taking a gap year, locals and backpackers—had a reputation as ski-hard-and-party-harder people.

But Kristie was not about to be deterred. 'So…' she shrugged '…that all adds to the excitement and the challenge.'

'I'm not going to hook up with a total stranger,' Jess said. Obviously the lessons of her upbringing were more deeply ingrained in her than she'd realised. Her movements were carefully orchestrated, her whereabouts were always mapped out, and she'd never really had the opportunity to mingle with strangers. Prince Charming was going to have his work cut out for him.

'I know your parents want to know where you are every minute of the day but they're not here,' Kristie replied, 'and despite what they tell you, not every spontaneous situation is dangerous and not every stranger is a psychopath. I'm not saying you have to marry the guy, just have some fun.'

'He looked too old for me,' Jess protested.

'You're always complaining about how immature boys our age are. Maybe someone a bit older would suit you better. Shall we head back down? Take another look?'

The quad chair took them to the basin where all the other lifts operated from. No one skied straight back down to the bottom of this lift unless they'd forgotten something and needed to return to the village. Jess didn't want to be that overtly interested. She needed time to think. 'No. I want to ski,' she said as they were deposited in the basin.

The slopes were quiet at this hour of the day and it wasn't long before Kristie decided she was overheating from all the exercise and needed to discard some layers. Jess suspected it was all an act designed to invent a reason to return to their apartment and hence to the quad chair, but she was prepared to give in. She knew she didn't have much choice. She could have elected to stay up on the mountain but they had a rule that no one skied alone and she had to admit she was just a tiny bit curious to have another look at the boy with the forget-me-not-blue eyes. After all, there was no harm in looking.

But by the time they had changed their outfits and returned to the quad chair there were two different towies on duty. Disappointment surged through Jess. It was silly to feel that way about a random stranger but there had been something hypnotic about him. Something captivating.

They rode the lift back to the basin where they waited in line for another quad chair to take them to the top of the ski run. As they neared the front the two original towies appeared, each with a snowboard strapped to one foot as they slipped into the singles row and skated to the front of the line.

'G'day. Mind if we join you?'

Jess and Kristie had no time to reply before the boys had slotted in beside them and Jess found herself sandwiched between her cousin and the boy with the tousled, blond hair and amazing blue eyes. He shifted slightly on the seat, turning a little to face her, and the movement pushed his thigh firmly against hers.

'Have you had a good morning?' he asked her. 'You were up at sparrow's.'

'Pardon?' Jess frowned. His voice was deep and his accent was super-sexy but the combination of his stunning eyes and his Aussie drawl made it difficult to decipher his words. Or maybe it was just the fact that she was sitting thigh to thigh with a cute boy who was messing with her head. Either way, she couldn't think straight and she could make no sense of what he was saying.

'Sparrow's fart,' he said with a grin before he elaborated. 'It means you were up really early.'

His blue eyes sparkled as he smiled at her but this time it was the twin dimples in his cheeks that set Jess's heart racing. His smile was infectious and she couldn't help but return it as she said, 'You remember us?' She was surprised and flattered. The boys would have seen hundreds of people already today.

'Of course. Don't tell me you don't remember me?' He put both hands over his heart and looked so dramatically wounded that Jess laughed. She'd have to watch out—he was cute and charming with more than a hint of mischief about him.

And, of course, she remembered him. She doubted she'd ever forget him, but she knew his type and she wasn't about to stroke his ego by telling him that his eyes were the perfect colour—unforgettable, just like him. She knew all the towies were cut from the same cloth, young men who would spend the winter working in the resort and then spend their time off skiing and drinking and chasing girls. They would flirt with dozens of girls in one day, trying their luck, until eventually their persistence would pay off and they'd have a date for the night and, no matter how cute he was, she didn't want to be just another girl in the long line that would fall at his feet.

'Well, just so you don't forget us again, I'm Lucas and that's Sam,' he said, nodding towards his mate, who was sitting on the other side of Kristie.

'I didn't say I'd forgotten you,' Jess admitted. 'I remember your accent.' But she wasn't prepared to admit she remembered his dancing or had been unable to forget his cornflower-blue eyes. 'You're Australian?'

'Yes, and, before you ask, I don't have a pet kangaroo.'

'I wasn't going to ask that.'

'Really?'

'I might not have been to Australia but I know a bit about it. I'm not completely ignorant.'

'Sorry, I didn't mean to imply that,' Lucas backtracked.

'It's okay.' She'd stopped getting offended every time people treated her like a cheerleader but while she was one she was also a science major. 'I know most of you don't have pet kangaroos and I know you eat that horrible black spread on your toast and live alongside loads of poisonous snakes, spiders and man-eating sharks. Actually...' she smiled '...I'm not surprised you left.'

Lucas laughed. 'I'm not here permanently. I'm only here for the winter. It's summer back home. I'll stay until the end of February when uni starts again.'

'So where is the best place to party in the village?' Kristie interrupted. 'What's popular this season?'

Kristie knew the village as well as anyone—she didn't need advice—but Jess knew it was just her cousin's way of flirting. To Kristie that came as naturally as breathing.

'How old are you?' Sam replied.

'Nineteen,' she fibbed. She was only three months older than Jess and had only recently turned eighteen but nineteen was the legal drinking age.

'The T-Bar is always good,' Sam told them, mentioning one of the après-ski bars that had been around for ever but was always popular.

'But tonight we're having a few mates around,' Lucas added. 'We're sharing digs with a couple of Kiwis and Friday nights are party nights. You're welcome to join us.'

'Thanks, that sounds like fun,' Kristie replied, making it sound as though they'd be there when Jess knew they wouldn't. Which was a pity. It did sound like it might be fun but there was no way they'd be allowed out with strangers, with boys who hadn't been vetted and approved. Although Kristie's parents weren't as strict as hers, Jess's aunt and uncle knew the rules Jess had to live by and she didn't think they'd bend them that far.

'We're in the Moose River staff apartments. You know the ones? On Slalom Street. Apartment fifteen.'

'We know where they are.'

They were almost at the top of the ski run now and Jess felt a surge of disappointment that the ride was coming to an end. The boys were going snowboarding and Jess assumed they'd be heading to the half-pipe or the more rugged terrain on the other side of the resort.

They wouldn't be skiing the same part of the mountain as she and Kristie.

She pretended to look out at the ski runs when she was actually looking at Lucas from behind the safety of her sunglasses. She wanted to commit his face to memory. He was cute and friendly but she doubted she'd ever see him again. He wasn't her Prince Charming.

CHAPTER ONE

JESS ZIPPED UP her ski jacket as she stood in the twilight. She was back.

Back in the place where her life had changed for ever.

Back in Moose River.

She remembered standing not far from this exact spot while Kristie had told her that day marked the beginning of the rest of her life, but she hadn't expected her cousin's words to be quite so prophetic. That had been the day she'd met Lucas and her life had very definitely changed. All because of a boy.

Jess shoved her hands into her pockets and stood still as she took in her surroundings. The mountain village was still very familiar but it was like an echo of a memory from a lifetime ago. A very different lifetime from the one she was living now. She took a deep breath as she tried to quell her nerves.

When she had seen the advertisement for the position of clinic nurse at the Moose River Medical Centre it had seemed like a sign and she'd wondered why she hadn't thought of it sooner. It had seemed like the perfect opportunity to start living the life she wanted but that didn't stop the butterflies in her stomach.

It'll be fine, she told herself as she tried to get the butterflies to settle, *once we adjust*.

In the dark of the evening the mountain resort looked exactly like it always had. Like a fairy-tale village. The streets had been cleared of the early season snow and it lay piled in small drifts by the footpaths. Light dotted the hillside, glowing yellow as it spilled from the windows of the hotels and lodges. She could smell wood smoke and pine needles. The fragrance of winter. Of Christmas. Of Lucas.

She'd have to get over that. She couldn't afford to remember him every few minutes now that she was back here. That wasn't what this move was about.

In a childhood marked by tragedy and, at times, fear and loneliness, Moose River had been one of the two places where she'd been truly happy, the only place in the end, and the only place where she'd been free. She had returned now, hoping to rediscover that feeling again. And while she couldn't deny that Moose River was also full of bittersweet memories, she hoped it could still weave its magic for her.

She could hear the bus wheezing and shuddering behind her, complaining as the warmth from its air-conditioning escaped into the cold mountain air. It was chilly but at least it wasn't raining. She was so sick of rain. While Vancouver winters were generally milder than in other Canadian cities there was a trade-off and that was rain. While she was glad she didn't have to shovel snow out of her driveway every morning, she was tired of the wet.

Jess could hear laughter and music. The sound floated across to the car park from the buildings around her, filling the still night air. She could hear the drone of the snow-making machines on the mountain and she could see the lights of the graders as they went about their night-time business, grooming the trails. She glanced around her, looking to see what had changed and what had stayed the same in the seven years since she had last been here. The iconic five-star Moose River Hotel still had pride of place on the hill overlooking the village but there were several new buildings as well, including a stunning new hotel that stood at the opposite end of Main Street from the bus depot.

The new hotel was perched on the eastern edge of the plaza where Main Street came to an end at the ice-skating rink. There had been a building there before, smaller and older. Jess couldn't recall exactly what it had been but this modern replacement looked perfect. The hotel was too far away for her to be able to read the sign, although she could see the tiny figures of skaters gliding around the rink, twirling under the lights as snow began to fall.

She lifted her face to the sky. Snowflakes fell on her cheeks and eyelashes, melting as soon as they touched the warmth of her skin. She stuck out her tongue, just like she'd done as a child, and caught the flakes, feeling them immediately turn to water.

But she wasn't a child any more. She was twenty-four years old, almost twenty-five. Old enough to have learned that life was not a fairy tale. She didn't want a fairy-tale ending; she didn't believe in those any more but surely it wasn't too late to find happiness? She refused to believe that wasn't possible.

Seven years ago she'd had the world at her feet. She'd been young and full of expectation, anticipation and excitement. Anything had seemed possible in that winter.

In the winter that she'd met Lucas. In the winter that she'd fallen in love.

Sometimes it seemed like yesterday. At other times a lifetime ago. On occasions it even seemed like it was someone else's story but she knew it was hers. She was reminded of that every day. But as hard as it had been she wasn't sure that she would do anything differently if she had her time again.

She could still remember the first moment she had laid eyes on him. It was less than two hundred metres from where she now stood. She'd been seventeen years old, young and pretty, shy but with the self-assurance that a privileged lifestyle gave to teenagers. In her mind her future had already been mapped out—surely it would be one of happiness, wealth, prosperity and pleasure. That was what she and her friends, all of whom came from wealthy families, had been used to and they'd had no reason to think things would change. She'd been so naive.

At seventeen she'd had no clue about real life. She'd been happy with her dreams. Her biggest problem had been having parents who'd loved her and wanted to protect her from the world, and her biggest dream had been to experience the world she hadn't been allowed to taste.

To her, Lucas had represented freedom. He'd been her chance to experience the world but the freedom she'd tasted had been short-lived. And the real world was a lot tougher than she'd anticipated. Reality had slapped her in the face big time and once she'd been out in that world she'd found there had been no turning back.

Reality was a bitch and it had certainly killed her

naivety. She'd grown up awfully quickly and her clueless teenage years were a long way behind her now.

She was still standing in the car park, mentally reminiscing about that winter, when an SUV pulled up in front of her at a right angle to the bus. The driver put down his window. 'Jess? Jess Johnson?' he said.

Jess shook her head, clearing the cobwebs from her mind. 'Sorry,' the driver said, misinterpreting the shake of her head. 'I'm looking for a Jess Johnson.'

'That's me.'

The driver climbed out of the car. 'I'm Cameron Baker,' he introduced himself as he shook Jess's hand. Cameron and his wife, Ellen, owned the Moose River Medical Centre. He was Jess's new boss. 'Let's get your gear loaded up. Is this everything?'

Jess looked down at her feet. The bus driver had unloaded her belongings. Three suitcases and half a dozen boxes were piled beside her. All the necessities for two lives.

'That's it,' she replied. 'I'll just get Lily.'

She climbed back into the bus to rouse her sleeping daughter.

She scooped Lily up and carried her from the bus. She was keen to introduce her to Moose River but that would have to wait until tomorrow.

This was Lily's first visit to the mountain resort. Jess had avoided bringing Lily here before now. She'd made countless excuses, telling herself Lily was too young to appreciate it, but she knew that was a lie. Jess had been skiing since she was four and Lily was now six and there were plenty of other activities here to keep young children entertained for days. Lack of money had been another excuse and even though Jess hadn't been able to afford to bring her that was still only part of the truth. The reality was that Jess hadn't wanted to return. She hadn't wanted to face the past. She'd thought the memories might be too painful. But it was time to give Lily a sense of where she had come from. It was time to come back.

Cameron loaded their bags and Jess climbed into the back of the vehicle, cradling a sleepy Lily in her arms as he drove them the short distance to their accommodation. The job came with a furnished apartment, which had been one of a number of things that had attracted Jess to the position, but she hadn't thought to enquire about any specifics, she'd just been relieved to know it had been organised for her and she was stunned when Cameron pulled to a stop in front of the Moose River staff apartments.

She picked Lily up again—fortunately Lily was small for her age and Jess could still manage to carry her— and followed Cameron inside the building, counting off the apartment numbers as they walked down the corridor. Thirteen, fourteen, fifteen. Cameron's steps started to slow and Jess held her breath. It couldn't be. Not the same apartment.

'This is you. Number sixteen.'

She let out her breath as Cameron parked the luggage trolley, loaded with boxes and bags, and unlocked the door. There'd been a brief moment when she'd thought she might be staying in apartment fifteen but she might just be able to handle being one apartment away from her past.

She carried Lily inside and put her on the bed.

'I'm sorry, they were supposed to split the bed and

make up two singles,' Cameron apologised when he saw the bedding configuration.

'It doesn't matter,' Jess replied. 'I'll fix it tomorrow.' She couldn't be bothered now. She had enough to think about without fussing about the bed. She and Lily could manage for the night.

'Ellen has left some basic supplies for you in the fridge. She promised me it would be enough to get you through breakfast in the morning,' Cameron said, as he brought in the rest of Jess's luggage.

'That's great, thank you.'

'I'll let you get settled, then, and we'll see you at the clinic at eleven tomorrow to introduce you to everyone and give you an orientation.'

Jess nodded but she was having trouble focusing. She was restless. There were so many memories. Too many. More than she'd expected. Thank goodness Lily was dozing as that gave her a chance to shuffle through the thoughts that were crowding her brain. She paced around the apartment once Cameron had gone but it was tiny and in no more than a few steps she'd covered the kitchen and the dining area and the lounge. All that was left was the bedroom and a combined bathroom-laundry. There wasn't much to see and even less to do as she didn't want to disturb Lily by beginning to unpack.

She crossed the living room, opened the balcony doors and stepped outside. Night had fallen but a full moon hung low in the sky and moonlight reflected off the snow and lit up the village as if it was broad daylight. To her left was the balcony of unit fifteen, the two-bedroom apartment that Lucas had stayed in seven years ago. The apartment where she and Kristie had gone on the night of the party was only metres away.

She could see the exact spot where she'd been standing when Lucas had first kissed her.

He had been her first love. He had been her Prince Charming. She'd fallen hard and fast but when he'd kissed her that first time and she'd given him her heart she hadn't known there would be no turning back.

Now, at twenty-four, she didn't believe in Prince Charming any more.

CHAPTER TWO

'MUMMY?'

The sound of Lily's voice startled her. Jess was still on the balcony, standing with her fingers pressed against her lips as she recalled the first kiss she and Lucas had shared. She shivered as she realised she was freezing. She had no idea how long she'd been standing out there in the cold.

She didn't have time for reminiscing. She had responsibilities.

Lily had wandered out of the bedroom and Jess could see her standing in the living room, looking around at the unfamiliar surroundings. She was sucking on her thumb and had her favourite toy, a soft, grey koala, tucked under one arm. With white-blonde hair and a heart-shaped face she was the spitting image of Jess, just as Jess was the image of her own mother.

'I'm hungry,' Lily said, as Jess came in from the balcony and closed the doors and curtains behind her.

'You are?' She was surprised. Lily wasn't often hungry. She was a fussy eater and didn't have a good appetite and Jess often struggled to find food that appealed to her daughter, although fortunately she would eat her vegetables.

'Let's see what we've got.' Jess opened the fridge, hoping Cameron had been right when he'd said that his wife had left some basics for them. She could see bread, milk, eggs, cheese and jam.

'How about toasted cheese sandwiches for dinner?' she said. 'Or eggs and soldier toast?'

'Eggs and soldier toast.'

Jess put the eggs on to boil and then found Lily's pyjamas. By the time she was changed the eggs were done. Lily managed to finish the eggs and one soldier. Jess slathered the remaining soldier toasts with jam and polished them off herself.

Lily was fast asleep within minutes of climbing back into bed, but even though Jess was exhausted she found she couldn't get comfortable. Lily, who was a restless sleeper at the best of times, was tossing and turning in the bed beside her and disturbing her even further. She would have to split the bed apart tomorrow; she couldn't stand another night like this.

She got up and put the kettle on, hoping for the hundredth time that she'd made the right decision in moving to Moose River.

It seemed surreal to think that returning to the place where things had started to go wrong had been the best solution, but she'd felt she hadn't had much choice. She'd needed a job with regular hours and this one had the added bonus of accommodation, which meant she could be home with Lily before and after school and she wouldn't need to leave Lily with a childminder or take extra shifts to cover the rent or babysitting expenses. She also hoped that living in Moose River would give Lily the opportunity to have the childhood she herself had missed out on. A childhood free from worry, a childhood of fun and experiences.

She carried her decaf coffee over to the balcony doors. She drew back the curtains and rested her head on the glass as she gazed out at the moonlit night and let the memories flood back. Of course they were all about Lucas. She couldn't seem to keep thoughts of him out of her head. She hadn't expected Moose River to stir her memory quite so much.

What would he be looking at right now? Where would he be?

Probably living at Bondi Beach, running a chain of organic cafés with his gorgeous bikini-model wife, she thought. They would have three blue-eyed children and together his family would look like an advertisement for the wonders of fresh air and exercise and healthy living.

But maybe life hadn't been so kind to him. Why should it have been? Why should he be glowing with health and happiness?

Perhaps he was working in a hotel restaurant in the Swiss Alps and had grown fat from over-indulging in cheese and chocolate. He could be overweight with a receding hairline. Would that make her feel better?

What was it she wanted to feel better about? she wondered. It didn't matter where Lucas was or what he was doing. That was history. She'd woken up to herself in the intervening years. Woken up to real life. And he wasn't part of that life. He was fantasy, not reality. Not her reality anyway.

Jess shook herself. She needed to get a grip. Her situation was entirely of her own choosing and she wouldn't change it for anything, not if it meant losing Lily.

She sighed as she finished her coffee. Her father had

been right. Lucas hadn't been her Prince Charming and he wasn't ever coming to rescue her. Wherever he had ended up, she imagined it was far from here.

Their first fortnight in Moose River went smoothly. Lily settled in well at her new school. She was thriving and Jess was thrilled. She loved the after-school ski lessons and Jess was looking forward to getting out on the slopes with her this weekend and seeing how much she'd improved in just ten days. It was amazing how quickly children picked up the basics.

She wondered about Lily's fearless attitude. If Lily wanted something she went after it, so different from Jess's reticence. Was that nature or nurture?

Jess had vowed to give Lily freedom—freedom to make her own friends and experience a childhood where she was free to test the boundaries without constant supervision or rules. A childhood without the constant underlying sense that things could, would and did go wrong and where everything had to be micromanaged.

Moose River was, so far, proving to be the perfect place for Lily to have a relaxed childhood and Jess was beginning to feel like she'd made a good decision. Lily had made friends quickly and her new best friend was Annabel, whose parents owned the patisserie next to their apartment building. By the second week the girls had a routine where Lily would go home with Annabel after ski school and have a hot chocolate at the bakery while they waited for Jess to finish work. Jess had been nervous about this at first but she'd reminded herself that this was a benefit of moving to a small community. She'd wanted that sense of belonging. That sense that people would look out for each other. She wanted somewhere where she and Lily would fit in.

Initially she'd felt like they were taking advantage of Annabel's mother but Fleur was adamant that it was no bother. Annabel had two older siblings and Fleur insisted that having Lily around was making life easier for everyone as Annabel was too busy to annoy the others. Jess hated asking for favours, she preferred to feel she could manage by herself even if she knew that wasn't always the case, but she was grateful for Fleur's assistance.

Her new job as a clinic nurse was going just as smoothly as Lily's transition. Her role was easy. She helped with splints, dressings, immunisations and did general health checks—cholesterol, blood pressure and the like. It was routine nursing, nothing challenging, but that suited her. It was low stress and by the end of the two weeks she was feeling confident that coming here had been the right decision for her and Lily.

Not having to work weekends or take extra shifts to cover rent or child-care costs was paying dividends. She could be home with Lily in time for dinner and spend full, uninterrupted days with her over the weekends. It was heaven. Jess adored her daughter and she'd dreamt of being able to spend quality time with her. Just the two of them. It was something she hadn't experienced much in her own childhood and she was determined that Lily would have that quality time with her. After all, they only had each other.

She checked her watch as she tidied her clinic room and got ready to go home. Kristie was coming up for the weekend—in fact, she should already be here. She was changing the sheet on the examination bed when Donna, the practice manager, burst into the room.

'Jess, do you think you could possibly work a little later today? We've had a call from the new hotel, one of their guests is almost thirty-six weeks pregnant and she's having contractions. It might just be Braxton-Hicks but they'd like someone to take a look and all the doctors are busy. Do you think you could go?'

'Let me make some arrangements for Lily and then I'll get over there,' Jess said when Donna finally paused for breath. Jess was happy to go, provided she could sort Lily out. She rang Kristie as she swapped her shoes for boots and explained the situation as she grabbed her coat and the medical bag that Donna had given to her.

Thank God Kristie was in town, she thought as she rang Fleur to tell her of the change in plans. Of course, Fleur then offered to help too but Jess didn't want to push the friendship at this early stage. She explained that Kristie would collect Lily and take her home. She could concentrate on the emergency now. It was always a balancing act, juggling parenting responsibilities with her work, but it seemed she might have the support network here that she'd lacked anywhere else.

Jess hurried the few blocks to Main Street. The five-star, boutique Moose River Crystal Lodge, where her patient was a guest, was the new hotel on the Plaza, the one she'd noticed on the night they'd arrived. She and Lily had walked past it several times since. It was hard to miss. It wasn't huge or ostentatious but it was in a fabulous position, and she'd heard it was beautifully appointed inside.

In the late-afternoon light, the setting sun cast a glow onto the facade of the lodge, making its marble facade shine a pale silver. On the southern side of the main entrance was an elevated outdoor seating area, which would be the perfect spot for an afternoon drink on a sunny day; you could watch the activities in the plaza from the perfect vantage point.

A wide footpath connected the lodge to the plaza and in front of the hotel stood a very placid horse who was hitched to a smart red wooden sleigh. Lily had begged to go for a ride when they had walked past earlier in the week but Jess had fibbed and told her it was for hotel guests only because she doubted she could afford the treat. She had meant to find out how much it cost, thinking maybe it could be a Christmas surprise for Lily, but she had forgotten all about it until now.

She walked past the horse and sleigh and tried to ignore the feeling of guilt that was so familiar to her as a single, working mother, struggling to make ends meet, but walking into the lobby just reinforced how much her life had changed from one of privilege to one much harder but she reminded herself it was of her own choosing.

The lobby was beautifully decorated in dark wood. Soft, caramel-hued leather couches were grouped around rich Persian rugs and enormous crystal chandeliers hung from the timber ceiling. It looked expensive and luxurious but welcoming. Although it was still four weeks until Christmas, festive red, green and silver decorations adorned the room and a wood fire warmed the restaurant where wide glass doors could open out onto the outside terrace. Jess tried not to gawk as she crossed the parquet floor. She'd seen plenty of fancy hotels but this one had a warmth and a charm about it that was rare. Maybe because it was small, but it felt more like an exclusive private ski lodge than a hotel.

She shrugged out of her coat as she approached the reception desk.

'I'm Jess Johnson, from the Moose River Medical Centre. Someone called about a woman in labour?'

The young girl behind the desk nodded. 'Yes, Mrs Bertillon. She's in room three zero five on the third floor. I'll just call the hotel manager to take you up.'

'It's okay, I'll find it.' Jess could see the elevators tucked into a short hallway alongside the desk. The hotel was small so she'd have no trouble finding the room. She didn't want to waste time waiting.

She stabbed at the button for the elevator. The doors slid open and she stepped inside.

Jess found room 305 and knocked on the door. It swung open under her hand. There was a bathroom to her left with a wardrobe on the right, forming a short passage. Jess could see a small sofa positioned in front of a large picture window but that was it.

She called out a greeting. 'Mrs Bertillon?'

'Come in.' The faceless voice sounded strong and Jess relaxed. That didn't sound like a woman in labour.

A woman appeared at the end of the passage. She was a hotel employee judging by her uniform. 'She's through here.' The same voice. This wasn't Mrs. Bertillon. 'I'm Margaret. I was keeping an eye on Aimee until you got here,' she explained, and Jess could see the relief on her face. She'd obviously been waiting nervously for reinforcements. 'I'll wait outside now but you can call for me if there's anything you need,' she said, hurriedly abdicating responsibility.

Jess introduced herself to Aimee and got her medical

history as she washed her hands and then wrapped the blood-pressure cuff around her patient's left arm. This was her first pregnancy, Aimee told her, and she'd had no complications. Her blood pressure had been fine, no gestational diabetes, no heart problems. 'I've had some back pain today and now these contractions but otherwise I've been fine.'

'Sharp pain?' asked Jess.

'No. Dull,' Aimee explained, 'more like backache, I suppose. Ow...'

'Is that a contraction now?'

Aimee nodded and Jess looked at her watch, timing the contraction. She could see the contraction ripple across the woman's abdomen as the muscles tightened. This wasn't Braxton-Hicks.

'Your waters haven't broken?' she asked, and Aimee shook her head in reply.

Once the contraction had passed she checked the baby's size and position, pleased to note the baby wasn't breech. But she wasn't so pleased when she discovered that Aimee's cervix was already seven centimetres dilated. Aimee was in labour and there was nothing she could do to stop it.

'Where is your husband?' Jess asked. She'd noticed a wedding ring on Aimee's finger but wondered where Mr Bertillon was.

'He's out skiing,' Aimee replied. 'Why?'

Jess smiled. 'I thought he might like to be here to meet your baby.'

'It's coming now?'

'Mmm-hmm.' Jess nodded. 'You're about to become parents.'

'Oh, my God.'

'Does your husband have a mobile phone with him? Would you like me to call him for you?' Jess asked.

'No. I can do it. I think.' Aimee put a hand on her distended belly as another contraction subsided. 'If I hurry. Jean-Paul will be surprised. This was supposed to be our last holiday before the baby arrived and it wasn't supposed to end like this.' She gave a wry smile. 'Maybe we've been having too much sex. Is it true that can bring on labour?'

Jess couldn't remember the last time she'd had too much sex. She could barely remember the last time she'd had *any* sex. She nodded. 'But not usually at this stage. I think your baby has just decided to join the party.' She concentrated on Aimee. Thinking about sex always made her think about Lucas, especially since she was in Moose River, but now wasn't the time for daydreaming. Aimee needed all her attention.

Aimee's cell phone was beside the bed. Jess passed it to her and then picked up the hotel phone and asked for an ambulance to be sent. Aimee needed to go to the nearest hospital that had premature birthing facilities, which meant leaving Moose River.

Another contraction gripped Aimee and Jess waited as she panted and puffed her way through it. Jess checked her watch. The contractions were two minutes apart. How long would the ambulance take? She had no idea.

Once that contraction had passed and Jess saw Aimee press the buttons on her phone to call her husband she went to gather towels from the bathroom. She stuck her head out into the corridor and asked Margaret to fetch more towels from Housekeeping.

'How did it go? Did you reach Jean-Paul?' Jess asked when she returned to Aimee's side.

'No. It goes straight to his message service.' Aimee gasped and grabbed her belly as another contraction ripped through her. 'He's gone skiing with a snowcat group so I can only assume he's out in the wilderness and out of range.'

Margaret came into the room with an armful of towels and Jess asked if there was any way of getting a message to Jean-Paul.

'Yes, of course,' Margaret replied. 'Will you be all right on your own with Aimee while I organise that?'

Jess nodded. Margaret wasn't going to be of any further use. It was the ambos Jess wanted to see. Jess tucked several of the towels underneath Aimee. She knew it was probably a futile exercise but if Aimee's waters broke she was hoping to limit the damage to the hotel bedding. Another contraction gripped Aimee and this one was accompanied by a gush of fluid. Fortunately it wasn't a big flood and Jess suspected that meant the baby's head was well down into Aimee's pelvis.

Jess used the time between contractions to check Aimee's cervix. Eight centimetres dilated. This was really happening. If the ambos didn't hurry she would have to deliver the baby. What would she need?

She'd need to keep the baby warm. She put a couple of the clean towels back on the heated towel rail in the bathroom.

Aimee's cries were getting louder and she had a sheen of perspiration across her forehead. 'I want to push,' she called out.

'Hang on,' Jess cautioned, and she checked progress again.

Oh no. The baby's head was crowning already.

Jess felt for the cord. It felt loose and she just hoped it wasn't around the baby's neck.

'Okay, Aimee. This is it. You can push with the next contraction.'

Jess saw the contraction ripple across Aimee's skin. 'Okay, bend your knees and push!'

The baby's head appeared and Jess was able to turn the baby to deliver one shoulder with the next contraction and the baby slid into her hands. 'It's a girl,' she told Aimee. Jess rubbed the baby's back, checking to make sure her little chest rose and fell with a breath and listening for her first cry before she placed her on Aimee's chest and fetched a warm towel. She took one-minute Apgar readings and clamped the cord just as the ambos arrived. Relief flooded through her. She'd done the easy bit, now they could finish off.

'Congratulations, Aimee.'

'Thank you.' Aimee's smile was gentle but she barely lifted her eyes from her baby. She was oblivious to the work the ambos were doing. Nothing could distract her from the miracle of new life.

Jess could remember that feeling, that vague, blissful state of euphoria. She tidied her things, packing them into her bag as she thought about Lily's birth. Like Aimee, she'd done it without the baby's father there.

She hadn't wanted to do it alone but she hadn't had a lot of choice. She hadn't expected their relationship to end so suddenly. She hadn't expected a lot of things.

By the time she'd discovered she was pregnant the ski fields had closed for the season and Lily's father had been long gone, and despite her best efforts she hadn't been able to find him. So she'd done it alone and she'd done her best.

She snapped her medical bag closed with shaky hands. Now that the drama was over her body shook with the adrenalin that coursed through her system. She stripped the bed as the ambos transferred Aimee and her baby onto a stretcher and wheeled them out the door.

She could hear voices in the hallway and assumed that Jean-Paul had been located. That was quick. She could hear an Australian accent too. That was odd. Jean-Paul didn't sound like an Australian name. She listened more carefully.

A male voice, an Australian accent. It sounded a lot like Lucas.

Her stomach flipped and her heart began to race. She was being ridiculous. It had been seven years since she'd heard his voice, as if she'd remember exactly how he sounded. She only imagined it was him because he'd been in her thoughts.

It wouldn't be him. It couldn't be him.

But she couldn't resist taking a look.

She picked up the medical bag and stepped out into the hallway. The ambos had halted the stretcher and a man stood with his back to her, talking to Aimee.

'We've got a message to your husband,' he was saying. 'We'll get him back as quickly as possible and I'll make sure he gets brought to the hospital.'

The man was tall with broad shoulders and tousled blond hair. Jess could see narrow hips and long, lean legs. His voice was deep with a sexy Aussie drawl. Her heart beat quickened, pumping the blood around her body, leaving her feeling light-headed and faint.

It was him. It was most definitely him.

She steadied herself with one hand against the wall as she prayed that her knees wouldn't buckle.

It was Lucas.

She didn't need to see his face. She knew it and her body knew it. Every one of her cells was straining towards him. Seven years may have passed but her body hadn't forgotten him and neither had she. She recognised the length of his legs, the shape of his backside, the sound of his voice.

The ambos were pushing the stretcher towards the elevator by the time she found her voice.

'Lucas?'

CHAPTER THREE

Jess felt as if the ground was tipping beneath her feet. She felt as if at any moment she might slide to the floor. She could see the scene playing out in front of her, almost as though she was a spectator watching from the sidelines. She could see herself wobbling in the foreground and she could see Lucas standing close enough to touch. If she could just reach out a hand she could feel him. See if he really was real. But she couldn't move. Life seemed to be going on around her as she watched, too overcome to react.

He turned towards her at the sound of his name.

'JJ?'

She hadn't been called JJ in years. It had been his nickname for her and no one else had ever used it.

She couldn't believe he was standing in front of her. Lucas, undeniably Lucas. He still had the same brilliant, forget-me-not-blue eyes and the same infectious, dimpled smile and he was smiling now as he stepped forward and wrapped her in a hug. She fitted perfectly into his embrace and it felt like it was only yesterday that she'd last been in his arms. Memories flooded back to her and her stomach did a peculiar little flip as her body responded in a way it hadn't for years. She tensed, taken by surprise by both his spontaneous gesture and her reaction.

He must have felt her stiffen because he let her go and stepped away.

Her eyes took in the sight of him. He looked fabulous. The years had been kind to him. Better than they'd been to her, she feared. His hair was cut shorter but was still sandy blond and thick, and his oval face was tanned, making his blue eyes even more striking. He had the shadow of a beard on his jaw, more brown than blond. That was new. He wouldn't have had that seven years ago, but he hadn't got fat. Or bald.

Her heart raced as she looked him over. He was wearing dark trousers and a pale blue business shirt. It was unbuttoned at the collar, no tie, and he had his sleeves rolled up to expose his forearms. He looked just as good, maybe even better, than she remembered.

Her initial surprise was immediately followed by pleasure but that was then, just as quickly, cancelled out by panic. What was he doing here? He wasn't supposed to be here. He was supposed to be in Europe or Australia. Eating cheese in Switzerland or surfing at Bondi Beach. He wasn't supposed to be in Canada and especially not in Moose River. *She* was the one who belonged here. *She* was the Canadian.

'What are you doing here?' she asked him.

'I'm the hotel manager.'

'In Moose River?'

'It would seem so.' He grinned at her and her stomach did another flip as heat seared through her, scorching her insides. He didn't seem nearly as unsettled as she was about their unexpected encounter. But, then, he'd always adapted quickly to new situations. He seemed to thrive on change, whereas she would rather avoid it.

The ambos and Aimee and her baby had disappeared and a second elevator pinged as it reached their floor.

'Are you finished up here?' he asked.

Jess nodded. It seemed she'd lost the power of speech. It seemed as though Lucas had the same effect on her now as he'd had seven years ago.

'I'll ride down with you,' he said.

He waited for her to enter the elevator. She tucked herself into the corner by the door, feeling confused. Conflicted. She wasn't sure what to think. She wasn't sure how she felt. One part of her wanted to throw herself into his arms and never let him go. Another wanted to run and hide. Another wanted desperately to know what he was thinking.

Lucas stepped in and reached across in front of her to press the button to take them down to the lobby. She hadn't remembered to push the button, so distracted by him she wasn't thinking clearly.

He was standing close. She'd expected him to lean against the opposite wall but he didn't move away as the elevator descended. If she reached out a hand she could touch him without even straightening her elbow.

He was watching her with his forget-me-not-blue eyes and she couldn't take her eyes off him. His familiar scent washed over her—he smelt like winter in the mountains, cool and crisp with the clean, fresh tang of pine needles.

The air was humming, drowning out the silence that fell between them. She clenched her fists at her sides to stop herself from reaching out. She could feel herself being pulled towards him. Even after all this time her body longed for his touch. She craved him.

They stood, for what seemed like ages, just looking at each other.

'It's good to see you, JJ.' His voice was a whisper, barely breaking the silence that surrounded them.

He stretched out one hand and Jess held her breath. His fingers caught the ends of her hair and his thumb brushed across her cheek. The contact set her nerves on fire, every inch of her responding to his touch. It felt like every one of her cells had a memory and every memory was Lucas.

'You've cut your hair,' he said.

'Many times,' she replied.

Lucas laughed and the sound was loud enough to burst the bubble of awareness and desire and longing that had enveloped her.

She didn't know how she'd managed to make a joke. Nothing about this was funny. She was so ill prepared to run into him.

Last time he'd seen her she'd had long hair that had fallen past her shoulders. She'd cut it short when Lily had been born and now it was softly feathered and the ends brushed her shoulders. She'd changed many things about herself since he'd last seen her, not just her hair. It was almost a surprise that he'd recognised her. She felt seventy years older. Not seven. Like a completely different person.

She *was* a different person.

She was a mother. A mother with a secret.

The lift doors slid open but Jess didn't move. Lucas was in her way but even so she didn't think she was capable of movement. She needed the wall to support her.

Her legs were shaking. Her hands were shaking. She knew her reaction was a result of the adrenalin that was coursing through her system. Adrenalin that was produced from a combination of attraction and fear. Why had he come back? And what would his presence mean to her? And to Lily?

'Mr White.' A hotel staff member approached them. Lucas had his back to the doors but he turned at the sound of his name and stepped out of the elevator. 'Mr Bertillon is nearly back at the lodge. He's only a minute or two away. What would you like me to do?'

'I'll meet him here. Can you organise a car to be waiting out the front? We need to get him down the mountain to the hospital asap.'

Jess pushed off the wall and forced her legs to move. One step at a time, she could do this. Lucas turned back to face her as she stepped into the lobby. 'Have you got time for a coffee? Can you wait while I sort this out?'

Jess shook her head. 'I have to get back to the medical centre,' she lied. She had no idea how to deal with the situation. With Lucas. She had to get away. She needed time to process what had just happened. To process the fact that Lucas was here.

'Of course. Another time, then.' He put a hand on her arm and it felt as though her skin might burst into flames at his touch. Her pulse throbbed. Her throat was dry. 'We'll catch up later,' he said.

Jess dropped the medical bag off at the clinic before trudging through the snow back to her apartment. Seeing Lucas had left her shaky and confused and she used the few minutes she had to herself to try to sort out her feelings.

He said they'd catch up later. What would he want?

She definitely wasn't the naive teenager from seven years ago. She wasn't the person he would remember.

What would she do? She needed to work out what to tell him. How to tell him.

She shook her head. This was all too much.

She'd have to try to avoid him. Just for a while, just until she worked out what having all three of them in the same place would mean for her and Lily. Just until she solved this dilemma.

Seven years ago she'd fallen in love. Or she'd thought she had. Seven years on she had convinced herself that maybe it had just been a bad case of teenage hormones. Lust. A holiday romance. But seeing him today had reinforced that she'd never got over him. How could she when she was reminded of him every day?

She knew she wouldn't be able to avoid him for ever. Moose River wasn't big enough for that. They were bound to bump into each other. But even if avoidance was a possibility she suspected she wouldn't be able to resist him completely. Curiosity would get the better of her. She'd been thinking about him for seven years. She would have to fill in the gaps. But as to exactly what she would tell him, that decision could wait.

She opened her apartment door and was almost knocked over by an excited Lily.

'Mum, where have you been? Kristie is here. We've been waiting for you for ages.'

'Yes, darling, I know. I'm sorry I'm late,' she said as she kissed her daughter.

Normally, seeing Lily's little face light up when she arrived home after a long day at work was enough to lift her spirits. Normally, it was enough to remind her of why she worked so hard and why she'd made the choices she had, but today all she could think of was all the secrets she had kept and wonder how much longer she had until the secrets came out.

She felt ill. The living room was warm but she was shivering. Trembling, Kristie got up and hugged her and Jess could feel herself shaking against her cousin's shoulder.

Kristie stepped back and looked at Jess while she spoke to Lily. 'Lily, why don't you go and try on that new skisuit I got for you? I think your mum would like to see it.' She waited for Lily to leave the room and then said to Jess. 'What's going on? Did it go badly with the patient?'

'No, that was all fine,' Jess replied. She'd been going to stop there but she knew Kristie would get the news out of her eventually. She'd always known when something was bothering her and she'd always been able to wheedle it out of her. She decided she may as well come clean now. 'It's Lucas.'

'What do you mean, "It's Lucas"? What's he got to do with anything?'

Jess collapsed onto the couch. 'He's not in Switzerland or on Bondi Beach. He's here.'

'Here? In Moose River?'

'Yes.'

'What's he doing here?' Kristie sat down opposite Jess.

'He's managing the Crystal Lodge.'

'The new hotel? How did you find that out?' she asked, when Jess nodded.

'I saw him there.'

'You've seen him?'

She nodded again.

'Oh, my God! What did he say? How did he look? What did *you* say?'

'Not much. Good. Nothing.' She couldn't remember what she'd said. All she could remember was how he'd looked and how she'd felt. How those eyes had made her catch her breath, how her knees had turned to jelly when he'd smiled, how her heart had raced when he'd said her name, and how he'd wrapped her in his arms and she'd never wanted to leave. How, after all these years, she still fitted perfectly in his embrace.

'Look, Mum, it's pink.' Jess jumped as her reverie was interrupted by Lily modelling her new skisuit. 'Isn't it pretty?'

'It's very nice, darling,' she replied, without really looking at her mini-fashionista. She was finding it hard to focus on anything other than Lucas. 'Now, why don't you get ready for a bath while I do something about dinner.'

Lily stamped her foot. 'I want to stay in my suit and I don't want dinner.'

'You need to eat something and you don't want to get your new suit dirty, do you?'

Lily folded her arms across her chest and scowled at her mother. 'I don't want dinner.'

'I bought Lily a burger and fries after school. She won't be going to bed hungry,' Kristie said.

'She ate it?'

'She ate the fries and about half the burger.'

Jess was pleased. Maybe the fresh mountain air was stimulating her appetite. Maybe a compromise could be reached.

'Okay, you don't need to eat but you do need to have a bath and put your pyjamas on. Then you can hop into bed, put the headphones on and watch a movie on the laptop.'

That was a bribe and a compromise but it worked. Lily thought she was getting a treat and she stopped complaining. It worked for Jess too as it meant she and Kristie could talk without fear of being overheard. She knew Kristie would continue to pump her for information and she didn't want to discuss Lucas in front of Lily.

By the time Jess had bathed Lily and got her settled with her movie Kristie had ordered a pizza and poured them both a glass of wine. The moment Jess emerged from the bedroom she could tell she was in for a grilling.

'What are you going to do?' Kristie asked, as Jess drew the curtains on the balcony doors and shut out the night.

'Nothing.'

'You can't do nothing! He deserves to know.'

'Why? My father was right. Obviously the week we spent together didn't mean as much to him as it did to me. If Lucas wanted to be a part of my life he's had plenty of time to look for me before now.'

'You know you don't believe that,' Kristie said. 'You didn't believe your father seven years ago and you don't believe that now. If we could have found Lucas all those years ago he'd be part of your life already.'

'But we couldn't find him and my life is fine as it is,' she argued.

'But what about Lily? Doesn't she deserve to know?'

Jess greeted Kristie's question with stony silence.

'You can't put off the inevitable,' Kristie added. 'It's not fair to Lucas and it's not fair to Lily.'

'But I have no idea what type of man he is now,' Jess countered. He might not be the person she remembered. *Did* she even remember him? Maybe everything she remembered had been a product of her imagination but she knew one thing for certain—she wasn't the person he would remember.

She'd dreamt of Lucas coming back into her life but now that he was here she was nervous. His return brought complications she hadn't considered and consequences she wasn't ready for. She wasn't ready to deal with having him back in her life. She rolled her eyes at herself. Who said he would even want to be part of her life? Or Lily's? This wasn't a fairy tale. This was reality.

She sighed. One thing at a time. That was how she would deal with this. She would gather the facts and then work out her approach, and until then she would stay as far away from him as possible.

'I need some answers before I tell him anything,' she said.

'You can't avoid him for ever.'

'I just need some time to process this,' she said. No matter how much she'd wished for one more chance, now that the moment was here she wasn't ready. 'Whatever we had was over a long time ago. It was a teenage romance—it's water under the bridge now.'

'It might be,' Kristie argued, 'except for the fact that the bridge is sleeping in the other room. There's always going to be something connecting you to him.'

And Jess knew that was the crux of the matter.

Lily.

'You can't keep her a secret any more, Jess.'

CHAPTER FOUR

IT TOOK A lot to frustrate Lucas. He was normally a calm person, level-headed and patient, all good attributes when working in hospitality, but right now he was frustrated. Seeing Jess again had hit him for six. It was a cricketing term but one that perfectly matched how he was feeling. He could cope with the day-to-day issues that arose with the hotel, he'd even coped with the delays and revisions while it had been redeveloped, but he couldn't cope with Jess's disappearance. Not again.

By the time he'd waited for Aimee Bertillon's husband and seen the ambulance off, all the while itching to return to Jess but doing his best to hide his impatience, she had vanished. She had said she couldn't wait and it seemed she'd meant it.

He knew he wouldn't be able to settle, he wouldn't be able to concentrate on work, not while thoughts of Jess were running rampant through his head. He told his PA that he was going out. No excuses, no reasons. He needed to think and he always thought better if he was outside in the fresh air. If she wasn't going to wait for him, he'd go and find her. He changed his shoes and grabbed his coat and walked to the medical centre.

'Can I help you?' The lady behind the desk had a name badge that read 'Donna'.

'I hope so. I'm looking for one of your doctors, Jess Johnson.'

'She's not a doctor,' Donna told him.

Now he was confused as well as frustrated. 'I've just seen her. I'm Lucas White from the Crystal Lodge. I called for a doctor and she came.'

'Jess is a nurse. All our doctors were busy so she agreed to go and make an assessment. Was there a problem? She's gone for the day but is there something I can help you with?'

A nurse.

Lucas shook his head. 'No. Nothing. Thank you.' The only thing he wanted was to know where she was and he didn't imagine that Donna would give him that information. He'd have to come back.

Jess was a nurse. He wondered what had happened. She'd been planning on becoming a doctor—why hadn't she followed her dream?

Night had fallen when he stepped back outside and the temperature had dropped. He pulled his scarf and gloves out of his coat pocket—he'd learnt years ago to keep them handy—and wandered the streets, still hoping to find her.

If he'd known on the day she'd been yanked from his life that he wasn't ever going to see her again he would have tried harder to keep hold of her. When she'd disappeared he'd been left with nothing. Nothing but a sense that he needed to prove himself.

He had left Moose River to return home, vowing he would make it back one day. Vowing to make something of himself. For her. It had been an impulsive, young man's promise, one that seven years later he might have thought would be long forgotten, but even though there had been plenty of other women over the years he'd never got Jess out of his system. She'd been an irresistible combination of beauty, brains, innocence and passion. She had worn her heart on her sleeve and she'd shared herself with him without reservation.

At times it was almost impossible to believe they'd only had seven days together. That one week had influenced him profoundly. It had made him the man he was today, determined to succeed. Determined to find Jess again and prove himself worthy.

It had taken longer than he would have dreamed. If someone had told him at the age of twenty that it would take him almost seven years, he would have thought that was a whole lifetime. But he had done it and he was back.

When the opportunity had presented itself in Moose River he'd jumped at it. At the time it had seemed as though all the planets had aligned. The timing had been right, he'd been ready to spread his wings, and the opportunity to be back in Moose River had been too good a chance to pass up. He'd wanted to prove himself and what better place to do it than in the very place where his dreams had all begun.

He'd returned as a successful, self-made man but things hadn't gone quite as he'd expected. The hotel hadn't been the problem. It had been Jess. He'd been back in Moose River for nine months and hadn't caught sight of her until today. He hadn't imagined that he'd find her, only to have her disappear again. Maybe she didn't feel the same desire to catch up. Maybe she hadn't kept hold of the memories, as he had. Maybe she barely remembered him.

Although he'd seen in her face that she hadn't forgotten him. He'd held her in his arms and it had felt like yesterday and he knew she'd felt it too.

But things had not gone according to his plan. The reunion he'd always pictured had gone quite differently.

But he wasn't a quitter, he never had been, and he wasn't about to start now. He'd found her and he wasn't going to let her disappear again.

He walked past the building where Jess's family had had their apartment all those years ago. He'd called in there before but this time he knew she was in town. She had to be staying somewhere. He pushed open the lobby door and pressed the buzzer for the penthouse.

No answer. That would have been far too easy.

He continued walking and eventually stopped and leant on a lamppost. He looked across the street and recognised the building. He was in front of the Moose River staff apartments. He counted the windows and stopped at unit fifteen. It was in darkness but he could see lights in the gap between the curtains in apartment sixteen. His gaze drifted back to the dark windows of fifteen as his memory wandered.

Jess had given him her heart but he hadn't really appreciated it at the time. He'd been young and hungry for adventure. He hadn't realised what he'd had with her. Not until she'd been long gone. And by then it had been too late.

No one else had ever measured up to her. Or not to his idealisation of her anyway. Perhaps he was looking back on the past with rose-tinted glasses but there had been something special about her and he'd never

met anyone else like her. And he'd travelled to almost
every corner of the globe. He'd been constantly on the
go since he'd left Moose River. He'd immersed himself in the hospitality trade before he'd even finished
studying, learning the lessons that enabled him to take
the next step, getting the knowledge and experience to
embark on a solo project. Getting ready to prove himself to Jess and her father.

But he wasn't to know his efforts were to be in vain.

Apartment fifteen remained dark. He wasn't going to
solve the puzzle that was life or even the problem that
was Jess and her whereabouts while standing out here
in the cold. There were plenty of issues waiting for his
attention back at the lodge. He could make better use
of his time. He pushed off the lamppost and trudged
back through the snow. He'd continue to search for her
tomorrow.

Lucas had been up since five. He'd been unable to sleep
and he'd done half a day's work already. It was Thanksgiving weekend in the United States and the official
start of the ski season in Moose River, Canada. Crowds
were building and the Crystal Lodge was fully booked.
This was what he'd wanted. What he'd been working
towards. No vacancies. He wanted Crystal Lodge to
become one of the premier hotels in the resort. But
now he feared that wasn't enough. Jess was back and
he wanted her too.

He loved his job, he loved his life and he'd thought
that he was happy with his success, but seeing Jess yesterday had shown him that all his success was nothing
if he had no one to share it with. Seeing her yesterday
reinforced that he'd spent seven years making some-

thing of himself, of his life, and he'd done it for her. But had she moved on? What would be the point of making himself worthy of Jess if she didn't want to have anything to do with him?

He stood by the window of his office and watched the snow fall. It had started early this morning and the forecast was for heavy falls over the weekend. It was perfect for the start of the season.

Next week all the Christmas decorations would be up around the village. They were already multiplying at a rapid rate and Lucas knew his tradesmen were at work this morning, building a frame for the thirty-foot tree that would be on display in front of the hotel on the plaza. He planned to switch on the lights on the tree next weekend to coincide with the opening of the Christmas market that was to be held in the plaza. There were plenty of things needing his attention, he had plenty to keep him occupied, but all he could think about was Jess.

He needed a break from the indoors. He muttered something to his PA about inspecting the progress on the framework for the tree and then wandered through the village, retracing his steps to all the places he and Jess had spent time seven years ago. Not that he expected to find her in the same places but he was happy to let his feet lead the way as it left his mind free to reminisce.

He headed up the hill, past the popular après-ski venue, the T-bar, and skirted the iconic Moose River Hotel, which set the standard for accommodation and was the hotel that Lucas measured the performance of Crystal Lodge against. The village was blanketed in snow. It was as pretty as a picture but everyone was bundled up against the weather and he knew he could walk right past Jess and never know it. He may as well return to the lodge and do something more productive.

He was halfway down the hill, passing the tube park, when he spotted her. She was leaning on the railing at the bottom of the slope and he could see her profile as she watched people sliding down the hill in the inflatable rubber tubes. She was wearing a red knitted cap and he had a flashback to the day he'd first met her. How the hell did he remember that? The sound of laughter floated up to him as people raced down the lanes and Lucas felt like laughing along with them. He'd found her.

'JJ!'

Jess turned around at the sound of her nickname. Her heart was racing even before she saw him. Just hearing his voice was enough to make her feel like she was seventeen once more and falling in love all over again. He was smiling at her and she couldn't help but smile back, even as she cursed her heart for betraying her brain.

'I was hoping to bump into you.'

That was ironic. She'd been hoping to avoid him.

'You were? What for?'

'Old times' sake. I wanted to invite you for coffee. Or dinner?'

'I don't think so,' Jess replied. She was nowhere near ready to spend one-on-one time with Lucas. She knew she owed it to him to catch up but she wasn't ready yet. She needed time to prepare. She needed time to plan a defence. And she definitely needed more than twenty-four hours.

'Jess!'

Kristie was flying down the slope towards them in a double tube. The snow had been falling too heavily to make for pleasant skiing with a beginner so she and Kristie had opted to bring Lily to the tube park instead. But she hadn't anticipated that they'd bump into Lucas. Not here.

She used the interruption to her advantage, choosing to wave madly at her cousin and hoping to divert Lucas's attention.

'Is that Kristie?'

'Yes.' Kristie had Lily tucked between her knees and she was screaming at the top of her lungs as they raced alongside the person in the adjacent lane. Kristie always took things to the extreme and Lily was yelling right along with her, looking like she was having the time of her life.

Jess could remember coming to the tube park with Lucas. She could remember sitting in the tube between his thighs with his arms wrapped around her and yelling with delight, just like Lily was now. Life had been so much simpler then but she hadn't appreciated it at the time.

'Who's that with her?' Lucas asked, as he spotted Lily.

Jess had successfully diverted Lucas's attention away from herself, only to focus it on Lily. The one thing she didn't want.

She was tempted to tell him that Lily was Kristie's but she knew she'd be caught out far too easily in that lie. 'That's my daughter,' she said.

'You have a daughter?'

Kristie and Lily hopped out of the tube and Kristie started dragging it back to the conveyor belt that would take them back to the start of the lanes at the top of the hill. Lily waved to Jess but followed Kristie. Luckily, she wasn't ready for the fun to end yet so didn't come over to her mother. Jess was relieved. She didn't want to have to introduce Lily to Lucas. Not yet. She definitely wasn't prepared for that.

'She's the image of you,' Lucas said, as Lily stepped onto the conveyor belt. 'How old is she?'

'Five.' Jess's heart was beating at a million miles an hour as she avoided one lie only to tell another.

Lily was, in fact, six, but luckily she was small for her age. While Jess didn't want to give Lucas a chance to put two and two together, she wasn't completely certain why she'd lied. She didn't expect him to remember that it had been seven years ago that they had spent one week together. It was obvious he hadn't forgotten her but to think he would remember exactly how many years had passed might be stretching things. Just because that time had become so significant to Jess, it didn't mean it would be as important to him. Why should it be? It had been just one week for him. For her it had been the rest of her life.

'Is that the reason you don't want to catch up? You're married?'

Jess shook her head. 'No.'

'Divorced?'

'No, but I still can't go to dinner with you. Life is more complicated now.' She had to think of Lily. But she knew she was also thinking of herself. She wasn't ready for this.

'I guess it is.' He nodded his head slowly as he absorbed her words. 'But, if you do find yourself free at any time, or if your complications become less complicated, you know where to contact me.'

He didn't push her. He didn't suggest she bring Lily

along to dinner and Jess knew he wanted to see only her. Alone.

Was it possible that her father had been right? If she'd been able to find Lucas all those years ago would he have wanted to know about Lily or would he have chosen to have nothing to do with her? She didn't think that was the sort of person he was. But what would she know? It wasn't like they'd had time to really get to know each other.

She wondered if he'd ever thought about being a father. Maybe he already was one. The question was on the tip of her tongue but she bit it back. Did she want to know more about him? Did she want to know what his life was like now? What if he had children of his own? Other children? Would that be too painful?

Surely it was better, safer, easier if she kept her distance.

He smiled. His forget-me-not-blue eyes were shining and his dimples flashed briefly, tempting her to say, *Wait, yes, of course I'd love to have dinner with you.* But she nodded and let him go.

She watched him walk down the hill and thought about how different her life could have been.

Jess stood at the balcony doors as the last rays of the sun dipped behind the mountain. She had thought that spending the morning at the tube park would have exhausted Lily but she seemed full of beans and Jess didn't have the energy to cope with her at the moment. Thank goodness for Kristie. She had taken Lily off to the shops, leaving Jess alone to think.

She looked to her left, down to the village. In the foreground she could see the balcony of apartment fifteen,

Lucas's old apartment. She tried to look past it as she didn't want to think about him but she knew she couldn't help it. Her mind had been filled with memories of him all day and right there, on that balcony, was where they had shared their first kiss.

When Lucas and Sam had invited them to their party Jess had never imagined actually going. But Kristie had managed to come up with a semi-believable story about a school friend's birthday and before she'd known it Jess had been at Lucas's door.

He and Sam had been sharing the apartment with two other boys and it had already been crowded when they'd arrived. People had spilled out of the living room into the corridor between the flats, overflowing into the bedrooms and out onto the balcony. But somehow Lucas had met her and Kristie at his front door.

He'd smiled at her and his blue eyes had lit up. His grin had been infectious and full of cheek and Jess had known right then that he would love creating mischief and mayhem. 'You look great,' he told her.

She and Kristie had spent ages getting ready, all the while ensuring that it had looked effortless. Kristie had straightened Jess's hair so that it hung in a shiny, platinum cascade down her back. She had coated her eyelashes with mascara to highlight her green eyes and swiped pink gloss over her lips.

She'd been nervous about coming to the party, worried about being in a room full of strangers, but one smile from Lucas and all her nervousness had disappeared. He hadn't felt like a stranger. She'd felt safe with him. She'd trusted him. All those years of listening to her parents telling her to be wary of strangers, of forbidding her to go out alone, and what had she done at the first opportunity—she'd disappeared to a party with a stranger just because he'd been cute and he'd flirted with her. He'd been so gorgeous and she'd been pretty sure she was already in trouble but she'd been unable to resist.

Even Kristie couldn't have predicted this turnaround in such a short time. Jess, who'd never gone against her parents' wishes, had been rebelling big time because a cute boy had smiled at her and made her laugh. She hadn't known him but she hadn't cared. She would get to know him. She'd felt like she'd been where she was supposed to be. Here. With him.

He took the drinks they carried, opened one for each of them and handed them back before stashing the rest into a tub that had been filled with snow. Kristie had used a fake ID to buy the pre-mixed cans of vodka and soda and they'd shared one as they'd walked to the party. Jess had needed it for courage; she hadn't really planned on having another one but she supposed she could nurse one drink for the evening. It's not like anyone would pay attention to what she was doing.

'I'm glad you could make it,' he said to her, as Kristie spotted Sam and made a beeline for him.

'We almost didn't.'

'How come?'

'We're not normally allowed to go to random parties.'

'Who would stop you?'

'Our parents.'

'So you're not nineteen, then?'

Jess frowned. What did her age have to do with anything? 'What?'

'If you were nineteen you'd be making your own decisions.'

They'd fibbed to her aunt and uncle about where they were going but she'd forgotten that Kristie had also lied to the boys about their age.

'I'll be eighteen next week.' She hoped that wouldn't matter. She wasn't sure what she wanted to happen but she wanted a chance to find out. She didn't want Lucas to decide she was too young but he didn't mention her age again.

'So you've sneaked out and no one knows where you are. Are you sure that's wise?'

'You seemed trustworthy.' Jess smiled. 'And as long as we're home before midnight, everything should be fine,' she added, aware that she was babbling. Normally if she was nervous she'd be tongue-tied but she had forgotten to be nervous. Was it the half a drink she'd had or was there something about Lucas that made her feel comfortable?

'What trouble can you get into after midnight that you can't get into before?' he asked.

'You sound like Kristie.'

'You have to admit I have a point.' Lucas was standing very close to her. When had he closed the distance? She was leaning with her back against a wall and he was standing at a right angle to her, his left shoulder pressed against the same wall, inches away from her. His voice was quiet and he had a mischievous look in his blue eyes.

'I don't know the answer,' she said. 'I just know we need to be home before our curfew. I don't want anyone looking for us and finding out we're not where we said we'd be. I don't tend to get into trouble.'

'Not ever?' He grinned at her and suddenly Jess could imagine all sorts of trouble she could get into.

Trouble, mischief and mayhem. All sorts of things she'd never exposed herself to before.

She shook her head. 'I've never had the opportunity.'

Her parents knew where she was every minute of the day and Jess knew how stressed they would be if she ever sneaked off and went against their wishes. She had never wanted to test the boundaries before, aware of how upset they would be. But neither they nor her aunt and uncle had any idea where she was tonight. If she was careful she could have some fun and they would be none the wiser.

'Maybe you just haven't recognised opportunity when she's come knocking,' Lucas said. 'Or maybe you need to create it.'

His last sentence was barely a whisper. His head was bent close to hers and she held her breath as he dipped his head a little lower. He was going to kiss her! She closed her eyes and leant towards him.

'Hey, Lucas,' someone interrupted. 'Your shout.'

'You've gotta be kidding me.' He lifted his head and turned to face the room. Over his shoulder Jess could see a couple of his mates holding empty beer bottles up in the air and laughing, and she knew they'd deliberately interrupted the moment. Jess could have screamed with frustration. She'd never forgive them if she'd missed an opportunity that she couldn't get back. What if the moment was gone for ever?

'Come on.' He took her by the hand and her skin burned where his fingers wrapped around hers. He pushed through the crowd until they came to a pair of doors that opened onto a balcony. He led her outside to where there were more tubs filled with snow and beers.

He let her go as he grabbed a couple of beers in each hand and asked, 'Will you wait here?'

She wasn't sure what she was waiting for but she nodded anyway. She seemed destined to follow his lead. Something about him made her finally understand what got Kristie all hot and bothered when it came to boys. Her hormones were going into overdrive and she was certain she could still feel the imprint of his fingers on hers. She couldn't think about anything except what it would be like to be kissed by Lucas. He was cute and confident, his accent was completely sexy and the way he looked at her with those brilliant blue eyes made her want to leap in, even though she didn't have the faintest idea about how to do that. But she suspected he knew what to do and she would happily let him teach her.

He took the beers inside and when he came back to her he was holding two coats and another drink for her that she didn't really want. He handed her the can, not realising she hadn't finished her first drink.

'You're not having anything?' she asked.

'I don't feel like drinking tonight.'

He was looking at her so intensely that even with her limited experience Jess knew exactly what he did feel like doing and the idea took her breath away.

'I don't want this either,' she said.

Lucas reached out and closed his hand around hers. It was warm, really warm in contrast to the cold drink. He took the can from her and stuck it into a tub with the beers.

Lucas was making Jess feel light-headed and giddy and she didn't want alcohol to interfere with her senses. She wanted to remember this moment, how it made her feel. She finally felt as if the world made sense.

She had always believed in love at first sight. She didn't know why, but she liked the idea that people could recognise their soul mate the very first time they saw them and she imagined that this was how it would feel. Like you couldn't breathe but you didn't need to. She felt as if she could exist just by looking into Lucas's eyes. She felt as though she didn't need anything more than that. Ever.

'I thought we could stay out here,' he said. 'There'll be fewer interruptions and, you never know, we might find the only thing that interrupts us is opportunity.' He was standing only inches from her. She could see his breath coming from between his lips as little puffs of condensation that accompanied his words and it was only then she noticed the cold. He opened one of the coats and held it for her as she slipped her arms into the sleeves. It smelt like him, fresh and clean with a hint of pine needles, but it swamped her tiny frame.

'How long are you staying at the resort?' he asked, as he rolled the sleeves up for her. He had closed the balcony doors and while they could still see the party through the glass the music was muted and they had the balcony to themselves.

'A little over two weeks. Until the New Year.'

'Do you come here often?'

'We spend most Christmas vacations here.' That was true of the past nine years. Prior to that, when her brother had been alive, they'd spent every second Christmas in California with her mother's family. But that had all changed after Stephen had died. But she didn't think Lucas needed to hear that story. Tonight wasn't about her family. It wasn't about her past. Tonight was about her. Tonight was her chance to experience all the things that Stephen's early death had robbed her of.

'Christmas in the snow,' he said. 'I'm looking forward to seeing what all the fuss is about. This will be my first white Christmas.'

'Really?'

He nodded.

'I'll have to make sure you get the full festive season experience, then,' Jess said with a smile. She'd worry about how to actually achieve that later.

'Don't worry, I intend to.'

He was watching her closely and she started to wonder if she had food caught between her teeth. Why else would he be staring at her like that? 'What is it?' she asked.

'I want to know what you're thinking,' he told her.

'About what?'

'About me.'

She hesitated before answering. She could hardly tell him she thought he was gorgeous or that he might well be her soul mate. He might appreciate her honesty but then again he might think she was completely crazy. She played it safe. 'I don't know anything about you.'

'What would you like to know?'

'I have no idea.' She wasn't very good at social conversations. She'd never really had to talk to a stranger before. She usually only got to talk to people with whom she already had some sort of connection—family, school friends or family friends. There was never anything new to learn about any of them. Every one of them was the same. Rich, well educated and well spoken, they all lived in Vancouver's exclusive suburbs, had private school educations, holiday homes, overseas vacations and were gifted new cars on their sixteenth birthdays. She was surrounded by trust-fund children. Lucas was a clean slate and she didn't know where to begin.

'Well, why don't I start?' he said.

'All right.'

'Do you have a boyfriend?'

She shook her head. 'No. Why?'

'I want to kiss you and I want to know if that's okay.'

Jess's green eyes opened wide. He was offering her a chance to experience freedom. To do something spontaneous, something that hadn't been sanctioned by her parents.

She'd broken so many rules tonight, what was one more? And, besides, there wasn't actually a rule forbidding her to kiss boys. It was more that she was rarely given the opportunity. And that was what it was all about, wasn't it? Opportunity.

Her freedom in Moose River was on borrowed time and if she didn't grab the opportunity with both hands now she knew she'd miss it altogether. She didn't have time to stop and think. She didn't have time to weigh up the options and the pros and cons. Her time was finite. It was now or never.

She didn't do anything she would regret. Not that night at least. Lucas was cute and he was interested in her and there was no one in the background, keeping tabs on her. For the first time ever she could do as she pleased. And she wanted to kiss Lucas.

'Have you made up your mind yet?' he asked.

He bent his head. His lips were millimetres from hers.

She'd wanted a chance to make a decision for herself. But some decisions, once made, couldn't be reversed. Right then, though, she wasn't to know that this kiss would mark the moment when she stood at the cross-roads of her life. She wasn't to know that this would be the moment when she decided on a path that would change her life for ever.

She nodded, ever so slightly, and closed her eyes in a silent invitation.

His lips were soft. The pressure of his mouth on hers was gentle at first until his tongue darted between her lips, forcing her mouth open. She let him taste her as she explored him too. She felt as though he'd taken over her body. She felt as if they had become one already, joined at the lips. Her nipples hardened and a line of fire travelled from her chest to her groin, igniting her internally until she thought she might go up in flames. Her body was on fire as she pushed against him, begging him to go deeper, to taste more of her.

She could feel herself falling in love with each second.

He could kiss her as much as he liked for the rest of for ever if he kissed like that.

CHAPTER FIVE

'JESS? JESS!'

Jess turned around from the window as the sound of Kristie's voice dragged her back to the present. She needed to focus. Judging by Kristie's tone, it seemed she might have been calling her for a while. 'What?'

'Lily was talking to you.'

'What are we doing tonight, Mummy?' Lily asked, but Jess couldn't think. Her mind was still filled with thoughts of Lucas and it took her a moment to come back to the present. She was distracted but that wasn't Lily's fault and it wasn't a good enough reason to ignore her daughter.

Kristie rescued her. 'How would you like to do something special with me, Lily?' she offered.

'Like what?'

'It'll be a surprise. I know you love surprises. Go and pack a bag with your pyjamas and a toothbrush while I think of something.'

Kristie waited for Lily to leave the room. 'You should ring Lucas and see if he's free for dinner.'

'What? Why?' How was it possible that Kristie could read her mind?

'I know you haven't stopped thinking about him

since this morning, probably since yesterday. I know you said you were going to avoid him but you can't pretend you don't want to see him. You've been miles away all afternoon. So the way I figure it is you might as well go and see him while I'm here to look after Lily. I'll take her on a sleigh ride, she's desperate to do that—she won't even care what you're doing.'

'She told you she wants to go on a sleigh ride?' That was enough to stop Jess from thinking about Lucas. 'Would you mind doing something else? I really want to do that with her. I'm saving up to take her as a Christmas surprise.' Her heart ached. She knew Lily wanted to take a sleigh ride from Crystal Lodge more than anything and even now that she knew Lucas's involvement with the lodge she wasn't going to let it derail her plans. Logistics weren't the issue but money was. She didn't have the cash to spare so, until she got her first pay cheque, the sleigh ride would have to wait.

Jess could see Kristie biting her tongue and knew she wanted to offer to pay for it but she'd learnt the hard way that Jess was determined to make it on her own.

Kristie looked at her but didn't argue the point. 'Sure. Can I take her to our apartment?' she asked. 'I won't tell her it belongs to our family—we can drink hot chocolate and toast marshmallows in front of the fire and watch the replay of the Thanksgiving parade. She can have a sleepover and then you can have the night free to do as you please.'

Jess wasn't convinced this was a good idea. 'You know what happened last time we hatched a plan like that,' she said. 'I ended up pregnant.'

Kristie just shrugged and smiled. 'Lily would like a sibling. She'd probably like a father too. I think this is fate intervening. Leading you to decisions that I know you don't want to make. Perhaps you should let fate dictate to you. I think you owe it to Lucas to meet up. Don't you?'

'No,' Jess replied.

She'd refused to wear a dress. As if that meant she had some control over the situation. She didn't want to feel like she was going on a date. They were just two old acquaintances catching up. She tucked her jeans into her boots and tugged a black turtleneck sweater over her head. Jess did put on make-up—she was too vain not to—but kept it simple. Foundation, mascara, some blush and lip gloss. She still wanted to look pretty but not desperate. Adding a red scarf for some colour, she headed out the door.

She'd insisted on meeting him at the hotel. This wasn't a date so he didn't need to collect her, she was quite capable of walking a few streets. She stepped from the plaza into the lodge. Tonight she had more time to take in her surroundings and she stopped briefly, gathering her thoughts as she admired the room. There were two beautifully decorated Christmas trees in the lobby, one at each end, and the lobby itself was festooned with lights, pine branches, red bows and mistletoe.

The lodge was celebrating Christmas in style and decorations were multiplying in the village too. The Christmas spirit was alive and flourishing in Moose River and Jess smiled to herself. As a child she had loved Christmas. She had looked forward to it all year, partly because the festive season also included her birthday, but it had been her favourite time of year for so many reasons. Until her brother had died.

After Stephen's death Christmas had lost its sparkle. She knew he was always in her parents' thoughts, particularly her mother's, especially at certain times of the year, including Christmas, and that had taken the shine off the festivities. Even though he wasn't spoken of for fear of further upsetting her mother there was always the underlying sense that someone was missing and Christmas had never been the same. Until Lily was born. And now Jess was desperate to have the perfect Christmas. She wanted to create that for Lily and she had hoped that being in Moose River would give her that chance. This was her opportunity to put the sparkle back.

She felt someone watching her and she knew it was Lucas. Jess turned her head. He had been waiting for her by the bar and now he was walking towards her, coming to meet her in the lobby.

Seeing him coming for her made her feel as if she was coming home but she resisted the feeling. She belonged here in Moose River so she should already feel at home, she shouldn't need Lucas to make her feel that way.

He was wearing a navy suit with a crisp white shirt and a tie the colour of forget-me-nots. She'd never seen him in a suit before. His hair had been brushed, it wasn't as tousled as she was used to, and she fought the urge to run her fingers through it and mess it up a bit. He looked handsome but she preferred him more casually styled. But perhaps the old Lucas wouldn't have fitted into this fancy hotel. She wondered how much he'd changed. Probably not as much as she had. The thought made her smile again.

He smiled in response. A dimple appeared in his

cheek, a sparkle in his eye. Now he looked like the Lucas she'd fallen in love with.

He reached out and took both her hands in his then leaned down and kissed her cheek, enveloping her in his clean, fresh scent. The caress of his lips sent tingles through her as her body responded to his touch. She could feel every beat of her heart and every whisper of air that brushed past her face as his lips left their imprint on her skin. Despite what she thought, her body didn't seem to remember that this wasn't a date or that seven years had passed. Her body reacted as if it had been yesterday that Lucas had been in her bed.

She'd been on a few dates over the past few years but she'd eventually given up because no one else had ever had the same effect on her as Lucas had. The attraction she'd felt for Lucas had been immediate, powerful and irresistible, and she'd never felt the same connection with anyone else. Not one other man had ever made her feel like she might melt with desire. Not one of them had made her feel like she was the centre of the universe, a universe that might explode at any moment. What was the point in dating? she'd asked herself. Why waste time and energy on someone who wasn't Lucas? If she couldn't have Lucas she'd rather have nothing.

And it seemed he hadn't lost the ability to make her feel truly alive. Just a touch, a glance, a kiss could set her off. She'd need to be careful. She'd need to keep her wits about her and remember what was at stake.

'JJ,' he said, and his voice washed over her, soft and deep and intimate. How could she feel so much when so little was said? 'Thank you for coming.'

As if she'd had a choice.

Despite her show of determination to Kristie earlier

in the day, she'd known her resolve wasn't strong enough to withstand the temptation of knowing that Lucas was only a few streets away. She'd known she'd pick up the phone and call him.

'I hope you don't mind if we stay in the hotel to eat?' he asked.

'I'm not dressed to eat here,' she said, as she took her hands out of his hold and shrugged out of her coat. Jeans and an old sweater were not five-star dining attire, even if the jeans hugged her curves and the black top made her blonde hair shine like white gold.

He ran his eyes over her and Jess could feel her temperature rise by a degree for every second she spent under his gaze. She could see the appreciation in his eyes and the attention felt good.

'You look lovely,' he said as he took her coat. It had been a long time since she'd wanted to capture a man's interest and despite telling herself this wasn't a date it was nice to know that Lucas liked what he could see. 'And you're safe with me. I can put in a good word for you if need be.' He was laughing at her and she relaxed. His words reminded her of their first night together all those years ago. She'd felt safe then and she felt safe now.

'Are you sure? I don't want to drag down the standards.'

'Believe me, you're not lowering our standards.' He ran his gaze over her again and Jess's breath caught in her throat as she saw his forget-me-not-blue eyes darken. 'We're fully booked for the weekend and I'd like to be close to hand in case there are any issues.'

She was worried that eating in the hotel would give him the upper hand. He would be in familiar surroundings and she felt underdressed and out of place. But, then again, she consoled herself, this wasn't a competition, it was a friendly dinner.

'Are you expecting problems?' she asked, as she walked beside him into the restaurant. He had his hand resting lightly in the small of her back, guiding her forward. His touch was so light she should hardly have felt it but she could swear she could feel each individual fingertip and her skin was on fire under the thin wool of her sweater.

'There are always teething problems with a new project—the only unknown is the scale of the disaster,' he said, as he checked in her coat and greeted the maître d'.

She followed him to a table positioned beside the large picture windows looking out over the outdoor terrace and onto the plaza. Lucas pulled out her chair for her and reached for a bottle of champagne that was chilling in a bucket next to her. He popped the cork and poured them each a glass.

'To old friends,' she said, as they touched glasses.

'And new memories,' he added. 'It's good to see you, JJ.'

She took a nervous sip of her champagne as the waiter approached their table.

'We're not ready to order yet,' Lucas told him.

'It's fine, Lucas,' Jess told him. 'You must know what's good—why don't you choose for us both?' She sounded breathless. She was nervous, on edge from conflicting emotions—guilt, lust, fear and desire—and she doubted she'd be able to eat anything anyway. The sooner he ordered the sooner she'd be able to escape before she said or did something she might regret. She'd been desperate to see him but now she was worried that she'd made a mistake.

She looked out the window as Lucas gave the waiter their order. Christmas lights were strung up around the terrace and stretched across to the plaza. They surrounded the ice-skating rink and looped through the bare branches of the trees. The ice and snow sparkled under the glow of the lights as skaters glided around the rink. It was the perfect image of a winter wonderland.

'It's a beautiful view,' she said, as the waiter departed, leaving them alone again. She got her breathing under control and returned her gaze to Lucas. 'It's a beautiful hotel.'

'You like it?'

'It's perfect. Just looking at it makes me happy. Someone has done a very good job.' The entire lodge—the furnishings in the rooms, the decorations in the lobby and the views from the restaurant—all conspired to make her feel as though the hotel was giving her a warm hug. Or maybe that was Lucas.

'Thank you,' he said.

'You?'

Lucas nodded. 'This is my vision.'

'Really? I thought you were the hotel manager.'

'That's my official title but this is my hotel.'

'Yours? You own it?'

'Yes. This is my baby.'

'You dream big, don't you?' she said.

'What do you mean?'

'You told me you wanted to work in the hospitality industry when you finished university. You never said you actually wanted to own a hotel.'

'You remember that?'

I remember everything about you, she thought, but she said nothing. She just nodded as the waiter placed their first course on their table.

'I have you to thank for that,' he told her.

'Me?'

'I started planning this the day you vanished from my life.'

'I didn't vanish,' she objected. 'My father dragged me away. I didn't have a choice.'

'In my mind you vanished. I never saw you again. I looked for you, every day, until the end of the season, until the day I left, but you had disappeared.'

'You looked for me?' She'd never dared to imagine that he would have thought about her.

'Of course. Did you think I would just let you go? Especially after what happened that day. I went back to your apartment the next day but there was no answer. Eventually I found the caretaker and he told me you'd all left. I was sure you would get in touch with me and I kept looking, thinking maybe you'd be back before the season ended. When that didn't happen I started writing to you, long letters that I was going to post to your family's apartment, but I never finished them.'

'Why not?' How much simpler might things have been if he'd done that. Then she might have been able to find him when she'd needed to.

'I was never good with words. I decided that words were empty promises and that I was better off showing you what I wanted you to know. It's taken longer than I thought. But now we have a chance to fill in all the gaps. To catch up on what happened that day and in the past seven years.'

Jess could remember every second of that day. Every

moment was imprinted on her brain, each glorious moment, along with every humiliating one. It had certainly been a birthday to remember.

She had wanted to sleep with him from the moment he'd kissed her. After that first night at his party she would have gladly given him anything he'd asked for but for as long as she could remember she'd fantasised about her first sexual experience and it had involved a big bed, clean sheets, flowers, music and candles. Not a single bed in a shared flat. Getting naked in Lucas's flat in a bedroom he'd shared with Sam had not been an option and so she'd had to wait and hope for a different opportunity. And then, on the morning of her birthday, her aunt and uncle had announced they were going cat skiing, leaving the girls on their own, leaving Jess free to spend the afternoon with Lucas.

They had spent any spare moments they'd had together since meeting seven days earlier. With Kristie's help Jess had sneaked off at every chance she'd had. She'd never done anything like that before but being with Lucas was more important than being the perfect daughter. Lucas had unleashed another side to her personality and she hadn't been able to resist him.

On her eighteenth birthday her aunt and uncle's plans had given her the ideal opportunity to create the perfect setting in which to let Lucas seduce her. It had to be that way. Lucas would have to seduce her as she didn't know where to start. She would create the opportunity for seduction and Lucas would have to do the rest.

And, just as Kristie had predicted several days earlier, Jess found herself planning sneaky afternoon sex. Only it had been more than that. She had gifted her virginity to Lucas. She had offered herself to him. She had offered him her body and her heart and he had taken them both. She had given herself to Lucas and in return he had given her Lily. It had been the perfect birthday. Up to a point.

'That day didn't end quite how I'd expected,' she said.

'No. Me neither. But I have to know what happened to you. Where did you go?'

'We left Moose River that night.'

'All of you?'

Jess nodded.

'Because of me?' Lucas asked.

'Because of both of us,' Jess said. 'But mostly because of my father. I still don't know how I'd forgotten they were arriving that night. I can't believe I lost track of time so badly.' She'd been swept away by Lucas and once she'd had a taste of him she hadn't been able to get enough. He had brought her to life. Her body had blossomed under the touch of his fingers and the caress of his lips. He had introduced her to a whole new world. A world of pleasure, fulfilment and ecstasy. He had consumed her body, her mind and her heart, and she had forgotten about everything else, including the imminent arrival of her parents.

Everyone had got more than they'd bargained for that day.

Jess could still remember the moment she'd heard them arrive. The moment her ecstasy had turned to dread. The moment her fantasy had become a nightmare.

Lucas's head had been buried between her thighs and he had just given her another orgasm, her second of the day, when she'd heard the front door of the apartment slam. And then she'd heard Kristie's loud, panicked voice welcoming them. Jess had known Kristie had been trying to warn her. Thank God she'd been there and had been able to stall them just long enough for Lucas to scramble to the bathroom. Jess could still recall how his round white buttocks, pale in contrast to his Aussie tan, had flexed as he'd darted to the bathroom. She'd just had time to throw his clothes in after him and then pull on her sweatpants and a T-shirt before her father had come into her room to wish her a happy birthday.

Their hurried dressing hadn't been enough to fool him. He'd taken one look at their semi-dressed state and the rumpled bed and had gone completely berserk. Being caught out by her parents hadn't been anywhere near how she'd imagined that afternoon would end.

Her father had been furious with her, upset and disappointed, and disparaging of Lucas. He'd thrown him out without ceremony after a few well-chosen remarks before making Jess pack her bags. Her aunt and uncle had arrived home from their day of cat skiing in the middle of the circus and both girls had then been bundled into the car and returned to Vancouver, where Jess had been subjected to endless lectures about abuse of trust and lack of respect for her aunt and uncle as well as for her parents' rules.

'I was so worried about you.' Lucas's words broke into her reverie. 'I thought your father was going to have a fit.'

'He was always over-protective but his reaction was extreme, even by his standards. I was so embarrassed by the way he spoke to you. I still haven't forgiven him for that.'

Lucas smiled as the waiter delivered their appetisers. 'I feel I should thank him.'

'*Thank* him?'

Lucas nodded. 'His diatribe started me on this mission. He accused me of being a good-for-nothing bum and I wanted to prove him wrong.'

Jess looked around her at the opulent hotel. 'You did all this to get back at my father?'

'I wanted to prove to him that I was worthy of his daughter. He was my inspiration but I did this for you.'

'For me?'

He picked up her hand and Jess felt his pulse shoot through her. His thumb traced lazy circles in her palm and her body lit up in response to his touch. It gave life to her cells and awakened her dormant senses. She felt seventeen again, full of newly awakened hormones.

'Your father suggested I would never measure up to his expectations. But it was your expectations I was worried about. I wanted to be someone who was important to you. I wanted to be someone who could fight for you. Who could protect you. I didn't stand up for you that night and I want you to know that won't happen again.'

'I'm not the same person I was then, Lucas.'

She remembered that awful day as if it were yesterday. The shame. The heartbreak. She had felt as though things could never be worse. Until she'd found out that, really, they could. In fact, they could be a *lot* worse.

Everything had changed after that, including her. The only thing that hadn't changed, apparently, over the past seven years was how Lucas affected her. As his eyes locked onto hers she knew she would jump right back into bed with him tonight if he asked. She could feel every cell in her body yearning for him. She felt as though if she didn't keep tight control of her emotions her body would dissolve. The heat between them was enough to melt her core and she could feel herself burning.

She could get lost in him so easily and she couldn't let that happen. She needed to resist him, needed to keep her distance, but when he looked at her like he was doing now, like she was the only person in the world, she didn't think she had the willpower to stay away. Sitting there, looking in to his blue eyes, she could pretend that her life was still simple and easy and privileged.

But that wasn't the truth.

She fought the urge to give in to him. To do so would mean telling him all her secrets. She knew that it was inevitable but she was terrified of what he would think when he found out. Would he forgive her? Would he reject her? Would he reject them both?

What a complicated situation. Coming back was supposed to be the answer. It was supposed to help her get her life on track, to give her and Lily the freedom she craved, but all she'd got were complications and confusion. All she'd got were more questions and fewer answers.

She suspected it would be impossible to get out of this with her heart intact and she wasn't sure if she could stand to lose him a second time. But that wasn't going to be her choice to make.

She picked up her glass as it gave her a chance to remove her hand from his, which was the only thing to do if she wanted to think straight. There were things she needed to tell him.

Jess sipped her champagne, steadying the glass on her lip to disguise the shake in her hand. All the times she'd wished he'd been with her and now here he was.

It was time for the truth. She couldn't keep her secret any longer. She took a deep breath and put her glass down on the table. Starting the tale would be difficult but she feared it wouldn't be the worst part.

'Lucas, there's something I need to tell you.'

CHAPTER SIX

'I'M SORRY TO INTERRUPT, Mr White, but there's an emergency.'

Before Jess could begin to explain, before she could begin to divulge the secrets she'd been keeping, she was interrupted by a tall, thin, young woman dressed impeccably in a tailored black skirt suit, who appeared beside their table. The gold name tag on her lapel read 'Sofia' and her dark hair, cut in a shiny blunt bob, brushed her shoulders as she leant over to speak to Lucas.

'What is it?'

'A child is missing.'

Lucas was out of his seat before Sofia had finished her sentence. 'Are they hotel guests?' he asked.

'No.' Sofia named one of the smaller lodges and Jess recognised the name. It was an old lodge on the edge of the village. 'The search and rescue team has been mobilised but because of the heavy snowfalls they are having trouble finding tracks and have requested all hands on deck.'

'Of course.' Lucas turned to Jess. 'I'm sorry, I'll have to go. I'm part of the volunteer S&R team. We assist the professionals when we're needed.'

'Is there anything I can do?' Jess asked.

'What did you have in mind?'

'I don't know. I could help to look or at least make cups of tea. Someone always does that job.' There had to be something she could do.

'Sofia, can you see if you can rustle up some warmer clothes for Jess and some snow boots while I get changed?'

Jess took that to mean he had given permission for her to accompany him and she followed Sofia and got changed as quickly as possible. She didn't want to hold Lucas up.

Outside the snow was still falling. The Christmas lights around the plaza were doing their best to shine through the weather as Jess wondered what sort of Christmas the family of the little boy would get. She hoped he'd be found.

She could see pinpricks of light throughout the village and up and down the mountain. The lights bobbed in the darkness as the searchers panned their flashlights across the snow. There had to be hundreds of them.

The snow muffled all sound but Jess could hear the occasional voice calling out a name. Otherwise, the village was eerily quiet and Jess guessed that the S&R team didn't want any unnecessary noise that might mask something important. Like the cry of a young child.

Lucas strode out, heading for the lodge where the little boy had gone missing and where the S&R was now being co-ordinated. Jess hurried along beside him. When she slipped on the snow he reached for her hand to steady her. He kept hold of her as they approached the lodge from the rear but he wasn't talking. Jess assumed he was focusing on what lay ahead and she kept quiet too. She didn't want to disturb him or any of the other people who were out searching.

They reached the lodge and Lucas held the door open for her and followed her inside. He made his way directly to a table that had been set up in a lounge area to the right of the entrance and introduced himself to the man who was sitting there. He had a two-way radio in one hand and a large map spread out in front of him.

'The boy's name is Michael. He is seven years old and he was reported missing twenty minutes ago.' The search co-ordinator gave them the little information he had.

'Where was he last seen?'

'He and his brothers were playing in the snow behind the lodge. His brothers came inside thinking he was behind them but he wasn't.'

'Where is the search area?' Lucas peppered the man with questions.

'The lodge is at the epicentre of the search and we've spread out from here. There are people searching at one-hundred-metre intervals from here.' The co-ordinator pointed to concentric circles that had been marked on the map with red pen. 'This is the area we're covering so far.'

'Can someone show me exactly where he was last seen?'

'If you go around the back of the lodge you'll see the snowman the boys were making. That was the last confirmed sighting.'

'I'd like to start from there,' Lucas said, 'unless there's anywhere more specific you want me to begin?'

'There was no sign of him there.'

'I'd like to check again.' Something about Lucas's tone suggested he wasn't really asking for permission. He was a man with a plan.

The co-ordinator nodded. 'Okay. Take these with you,' he said, as he handed him a whistle and a torch.

Lucas turned to Jess. 'JJ, come with me.'

Jess followed him back outside with no real idea about what he expected of her or how much help she could be. She'd have to trust him to direct her.

She hurried to keep up with him as he stomped through the snow around to the back of the lodge. Jess's borrowed boots sank into the snowdrifts that had formed against the walls of the lodge and she was out of breath by the time she rounded the back corner. A lonely, misshapen snow-man stared at her as she gulped in the cold air.

Lucas was standing beside the snowman, looking left and right. The snow around the snowman had been flat-tened and trampled by dozens of feet, the searchers' feet, Jess assumed, although most traces were already being covered by the fresh snow that continued to fall. Jess knew the footsteps of Michael and his brothers would have been obliterated long ago, making the search even more difficult.

Lucas lifted his head and Jess could see him look-ing up at the roof of the lodge.

'What are you looking for?' she asked.

He took three steps towards the lodge and stopped beside a large mound of fresh snow, which looked as though it had been pushed into a heavy drift by a snow-plough. 'This pile of snow has fallen from the roof.' He pointed up to the roof. 'See how that section of roof is clear of snow?' Above their heads a large section of the lodge roof was bare. The weight of the fresh snowfall had caused the snow beneath to slide off the roof and land in a heap on the ground, a heap that was five or six feet high. 'I've seen this once before. We need to check this drift. Michael could be buried under here.'

Lucas knelt in the snow and started digging with his gloved hands while Jess stared at the huge mound. She felt her chest tighten with anxiety and she struggled to breathe. She felt as though she was the one trapped and suffocating.

How long had Michael been missing? It must be close to half an hour by now. *How long can someone survive without air?* Not long.

She knew that. She'd lived that. Her own brother had suffocated.

Jess was frozen to the spot, paralysed by the memories. She couldn't go through this again.

'JJ, give me a hand.' Lucas was looking at her over his shoulder. His busyness was in stark contrast to her immobility but she didn't think she could move.

'JJ, get down here.'

Lucas raised his voice and his words bounced off the walls of the lodge and echoed across the snow, jolting Jess out of her motionless state.

She knelt down beside him and started digging. If she didn't want to go through this again she only had one option and that was to do everything in her power to save this child. Digging like a mad woman now, she could feel the sweat running between her breasts and her arms ached with the effort of shifting the snow, but she wasn't going to let this be another tragedy. She hadn't been able to save her brother but she'd been eight years old then. She wasn't going to let another little boy die.

'Michael, are you there, buddy? Hang on, we're

going to get you out.' Lucas was talking constantly as he frantically tore at the snow.

Jess's vision was blurring as the blood pumped through her muscles. Her breaths were coming in short bursts and her heart was pounding but she wasn't about to stop. She dug her hands into the pile of snow again and her fingers hit something hard. Something firmer than the recently fallen snow.

'Lucas! There's something here.'

Lucas helped her to scrape the snow away and Jess could see something dark in the snow pile. Clothing? A jacket?

'It's a boot,' he said. 'Keep clearing the snow,' he told her as he pulled the whistle from his pocket and blew into it hard. The shrill sound pierced the still night air and Jess knew it would be heard for miles. Lucas gave three, short, sharp blasts on the whistle before yelling, 'Some help over here.'

Jess's movements intensified. She had to hurry. She had to clear this snow.

'What is it?'

'Have you found him?'

They were bombarded with questions as other searchers arrived on the scene.

'He's here,' Lucas replied. 'We need to clear this snow.'

Jess had cleared the snow to expose Michael's foot and ankle and now that they could work out in which direction he was lying Lucas could direct others to start clearing the snow to expose Michael's head. There was a sense of urgency, though the snow muffled the sound so there was nothing loud about the panic but it was there, under the surface. Every minute was vital, every second precious.

In under a minute the snow had been cleared to reveal a child's body. A young boy, curled into a foetal position with one arm thrown up to cover his face. He wasn't moving.

'Call the ambos,' Lucas said to the crowd that had gathered around them. He whipped off one of his gloves and placed his fingers on the boy's neck to feel for a pulse. 'Pulse is slow but present.'

Jess bent her head and put her cheek against Michael's nose. 'He's not breathing.'

'We need to roll him,' Lucas said. 'Clear some snow from behind him.'

'I can't let this happen again, Lucas. We have to save him.'

'We're doing everything we can, JJ.'

'We have to hurry.'

The snow had been cleared now and Jess held the boy's head gently between her palms as Lucas rolled him. Stuffing her gloves into her pocket, she started mouth-to-mouth resuscitation as they waited for the ambulance. She had to do something. She had to try to save his life.

Clearing Michael's airway, she tipped his head back slightly and breathed into his mouth, watching for the rise and fall of his chest. She was aware of his parents arriving on the scene as she continued to breathe air into their son's lungs. She heard them but she couldn't stop to look up. Everything else had to be blocked out. She could feel tears on her cheeks but she couldn't stop to wipe them away, she had to keep going.

'JJ, the ambos are here.' Lucas rested his hand on her shoulder and finally she could stop and hand over to someone who was better qualified than her.

She was shaking as Lucas helped her to her feet. She knew the tip of her nose was red and cold and she could feel the tightness of the skin on her cheeks where the tears had dried and left salt stains. Her toes were numb and her fingers were freezing.

Lucas put his arm around her. 'Come on, let's get you warmed up.'

She knew Lucas wanted to get her out of the cold and she knew she should probably listen to him but she couldn't do it. 'I can't leave yet,' she told him, as she pulled her gloves back onto her hands. She had to stay. She had to know how this ended.

Lucas didn't argue. He kept his arm around her as they stood together while the ambulance officers inserted an artificial airway and attached an ambu bag and Jess was grateful for his additional warmth. She could hear that the ambos were worried about head and thoracic injuries but they weren't giving much away. They ran a drip of warm saline and loaded Michael onto a stretcher as they continued to bag him. At least they hadn't given up.

Jess and Lucas waited until the ambulance drove away, heading for the hospital, and then, somehow, Lucas wangled a lift for them back to Crystal Lodge.

Jess was exhausted and Lucas practically carried her inside when they reached the lodge. 'Do you want me to run you home?' he asked.

'Not yet.' She could barely keep her eyes open but she wanted to stay in Lucas's embrace for just a little longer.

'Come to my suite, then, and I'll organise something warm to drink.'

Jess didn't have the energy to argue, even if she'd wanted to. He led her into an office behind the reception desk and unlocked a door in the back wall. The door opened into the living room of his suite. The room was cosy and, even better, it was warm.

Lucas steered her towards the leather couch that was positioned in front of a fireplace. A wood fire burned in the grate. It was probably only for decoration—Jess assumed there would be central heating—but there was something comforting about a proper wood fire.

He undid her boots and pulled them from her feet. He rubbed the soles of her feet, encouraging the blood back into her extremities, and Jess almost groaned aloud with pleasure.

There was a knock on the door as Lucas propped her feet on the ottoman and one of the housekeeping staff wheeled in a small trolley. 'Dessert, Mr White.'

Lucas lifted the lid to reveal a chocolate pudding, apple pie and a mug of eggnog.

He took the eggnog and added some brandy and rum to it from bottles that stood on a small sideboard. 'That'll warm you up,' he said, as he passed it to Jess before pouring himself a shot of rum. He dropped a soft blanket over Jess's lap and sat down beside her. She lay next to him with her feet stretched out to the fire and his arm wrapped around her shoulders. Lying in front of the fire in Lucas's embrace with a warm drink and warm apple pie, she thought this might be heaven.

'Do you think Michael will be all right?' she asked.

'He has a good chance. His pulse was slow but the cold temperature means his systems had shut down and that may save him.'

'But we have no idea how long he wasn't breathing.'

'Maybe he'd only just stopped breathing. If there was an air pocket in front of his face he could have survived for thirty minutes or maybe a little longer in those conditions, provided the snow wasn't heavy enough to crush him. We'll just have to hope that we found him in time.'

'How did you know where to look for him?'

'I saw a similar scenario once before in Australia when a child was in the wrong place at the wrong time and was buried by a pile of snow that slid off a roof. No one picked up on it at the time so people were searching in the wrong places. It's stuck with me. I'll never forget the possibility that that can happen.'

'What happened that time?'

Lucas shook his head. 'We weren't so fortunate back then. By the time we found him it was too late. We were lucky tonight.' He took a sip of his rum. 'You said you couldn't let this happen again. You know what it's like, don't you? To lose someone. You've been in that situation before too, haven't you?'

Jess nodded.

'Do you want to talk about it?'

'It was my brother.'

'Your brother?' She could hear the frown in his voice and his arm around her shoulders squeezed her against him a little more firmly.

She let her head drop onto his shoulder. 'He died when he was six.'

'In an accident?'

'Yes, one that had a lot of similarities to tonight.'

'Was it here?'

'No. We spent most of our winter holidays here but Mum used to take my brother and me to spend our summer holidays in California with her family. Dad would join us for a week or two but it was usually just Mum and her sisters and our cousins and we'd spend the summer at my grandparents' beach house. We loved it. We were pretty much allowed to do as we pleased for six weeks. That summer we were digging a big hole with tunnels under the sand. We'd done this before but not with tunnels and one of the tunnels collapsed, trapping Stephen and one of my cousins in it. We managed to get my cousin out but not Stephen. The weight of the sand crushed him and he suffocated. His body was recovered but it was too late.'

'JJ, that's awful. I'm so sorry.' Lucas dropped a kiss on her forehead, just above her temple. It felt like a reflex response but it lifted her spirits. 'How old were you when it happened?'

'Eight.' Jess sipped her eggnog. She could feel the warmth flow through her and the kick of the added brandy gave her the courage to continue. 'My mother has never gotten over it. I think she feels a lot of guilt for not watching us more closely but we'd done similar things plenty of times before without any disasters. I think the combination of stress and guilt and trauma was all too much. We've never been back to California. Stephen's death cast a shadow over our family, a shadow I've grown up under, and it's shaped my life. I didn't want another family to go through what we've been through.'

'What did it do to you?'

'After he died my mother changed. She couldn't be around people. She couldn't bear the thought that they would ask about Stephen or ask how she was coping. She wasn't coping. With anything. She shut herself off from everyone, including me. Dad said she couldn't cope with the idea that something might happen to me too so her way of coping was to ignore the outside world and me.

'Dad, however, was determined that nothing was going to happen to me. One tragedy was enough. So I was protected, very closely and very deliberately. I wasn't allowed any freedom. Mum and Dad had to know where I was and what I was doing every minute of the day, which is why Dad flipped out when he caught us together. His whole mission in life had become to protect me from harm and there I was, in bed with a stranger. His reaction was completely out of proportion with what we'd been doing but it was a case of his mind jumping to the worst possible conclusions of not knowing what else I'd been up to without his knowledge. My whole life has been influenced by Stephen's death. In a way it's still influencing me.'

'How?'

'It had a lot to do with why I came back here with Lily.'

'Lily? That's your daughter?'

Jess nodded. She hadn't realised she hadn't told him her name. She wondered if he liked it.

'Before Stephen died I was allowed to walk to school with my friends and go on sleepovers and school camps. After he died that all changed. I didn't want Lily to grow up like that. But because I'd spent most of my childhood being taught to be fearful I found it hard to relax. When she was a baby I was very uptight, I was worried about what she ate and panicked every time she got a cold.

'I was nervous about leaving her with childminders while I studied and worked and when she started school I realised that I was bringing her up the same way my parents had brought me up. I was wrapping her in cotton wool and I didn't want that. I wanted her to have the childhood that I'd missed out on. I wanted her to be able to walk to school and to her friends' houses without me worrying that something would happen to her. I wanted her to grow up somewhere safe.'

'And what about Lily's father? What does he think about you moving here?'

'Lily doesn't know her father.'

'Really? What happened to him?"

Was now the right time to tell him? No, she decided, she needed to have a fresh mind.

'Sorry,' he apologised, when she didn't answer straight away. 'It's probably none of my business.'

If only he knew how much of his business it actually was.

She had to tell him something. 'Nothing happened to him. I was young. We both were.' She tipped her head up and looked at Lucas, met his forget-me-not-blue eyes and willed him to understand what she was saying. 'I loved him very much but our timing was wrong. It was no one's fault but Lily and I have been on our own for as long as she can remember.'

She knew she had to tell him about Lily but where did she start? *How* should she start?

She stifled a yawn. It was too late to have this conversation tonight; they were both exhausted. A little voice in her head was telling her that she was making excuses but she didn't have the emotional energy to have the discussion now.

She pushed herself into a sitting position. 'It's getting late,' she said, making yet another excuse. 'I'd better get home.'

'Are you sure? I hate to think of you going out in the cold just when you've thawed out.' She could hear the smile in his voice and knew she couldn't afford to look at him. If she saw him smiling at her she'd find it hard to refuse. Although he might not be intending to cause trouble he'd done it once before and she suspected it could easily happen again.

Mischief and mayhem. That's how she'd first thought of him and it still seemed to fit. Mischief, mayhem and trouble.

She was tempted to stay right where she was, on the couch in front of the fire wrapped in Lucas's arms. It felt safe. Lily was having a sleepover with Kristie so she could do it but she knew that it would just complicate the situation. Seven years ago she'd fallen for the charms of a good-looking boy and she knew she could easily fall again. She couldn't let herself get involved.

She reached for her boots, busying herself with putting them back on. 'I have to go. I have Lily, remember?'

'I'll walk you home, then.' Lucas stood and took her hand to pull her to her feet. He helped her into her coat and then took her hand again as they walked through the village. She kept her hand in his. There was no harm in that, right?

'This is where you're living?' He sounded surprised to find she was in the old accommodation block. 'We're back where it all began.'

He pushed open the door and Jess knocked the snow from her boots before stepping into the foyer. She hesitated inside, not wanting Lucas to walk her to her door, afraid of too much temptation.

'Thanks for getting me home safely and thank you for an interesting evening.' She sounded so formal but that was good. She was keeping her distance.

'My pleasure. We should do it again.' Lucas's voice was far from formal. It was full of promise and suggestion and Jess could feel her body respond. If he could do that to her with his voice she hated to think what he could do with a touch.

'Without the drama,' she said, as she fought for control. She was still conflicted and confused. She could feel the attraction but she knew she couldn't pursue it. Not yet. She couldn't let her hormones dictate to her.

'Definitely.' Lucas's voice was a whisper. He bent his head and his lips were beside her ear. Then beside her mouth.

Her hormones took over again as confusion gave way to desire. She wasn't strong enough to resist him. She never had been.

She turned her head and then his lips were covering hers. He wrapped his arms around her waist and pulled her close. Her hands went behind his head and kept him there. She parted her lips and tasted him. He tasted of rum and chocolate. He tasted like a grown-up version of the Lucas she'd fallen in love with.

His kiss was still so familiar and it made her heart ache with longing. She had seven years of hopes and dreams stored inside her and Lucas's lips were the key that released them. They flooded through her and her body sang as it remembered him. Remembered how he tasted and felt.

His body was still firm and hard. His hair was thick. He smelt like winter and tasted like summer. He felt like home.

She clung to him, even though she knew she shouldn't be kissing him. She knew she was only complicating matters further but she had no resistance when it came to Lucas. Absolutely none. She knew she'd have to find some.

She pulled back.

'We should definitely do *that* again,' he said as he grinned at her, and she was tempted to take him up on his suggestion there and then.

No. Find some resistance. Find some resolve, she told herself, and find it right now. 'I'm not sure that's wise.'

'Don't blame me.' He pointed up and she saw a sprig of mistletoe hanging from the ceiling. 'Someone has gone to all that effort, I thought it would be a shame to let it go to waste.'

A shame indeed. She smiled but she'd have to let it go for now. She wanted the fantasy but she was worried that the reality might be very different.

CHAPTER SEVEN

'LUCAS, WE HAVE a situation.'

Lucas looked up from his computer screen. His PA was standing in his doorway, smiling. She didn't look too perturbed by the 'situation'.

'What is it?'

'I think you'd better come and see,' Sofia replied.

Lucas followed her out of his office. He glanced around as he crossed the lobby. Everything looked to be in order. Sofia continued across the floor and exited the lodge out onto the plaza. It was late in the afternoon, the ski runs had closed and streams of people were coming and going through the village. Sofia gestured with an open palm towards the bay where the lodge sleigh was parked. Three young girls, one with her platinum blonde hair tied in two short pigtails, stood beside it.

Lily. Even if he hadn't seen her at the tube park last weekend he would have recognised her. She was just a down-sized version of her mother.

Lucas frowned. What possible reason could Lily have for being here? It had been almost a week since he'd seen Jess and he'd never met her daughter.

Since the kiss, he'd been snowed under with work, the hotel was at full capacity and he'd had some staffing and maintenance issues that had taken up a lot of his time, and although he had invited Jess and Lily to dinner during the week Jess had graciously refused. He wasn't sure if she was avoiding him or not but he'd been too busy to push the invitation. Nevertheless, his curiosity was now piqued.

'What do they want?' he asked Sofia.

'A sleigh ride.'

'I've got this,' he told her.

He'd been kicking himself since last weekend when he'd discovered that Jess had a child. He couldn't believe he'd been such an idiot. He should have come back to Moose River sooner. He'd thought he'd had time, he'd thought he could afford to wait until he'd achieved his goals. They were both young and he hadn't considered for one moment that Jess would have moved on. Not to this extent.

But a child wasn't a deal-breaker. Not in any way. If Jess had been married, that would be a different ball game but he could work with her being a mother. If she'd let him. And he was intrigued to find out more about Lily. This might be the perfect opportunity.

He approached the girls. One looked to be Lily's age, maybe a year older, and the other he guessed to be twelve or thirteen.

'Lily?' he asked. 'I'm Lucas. This is my hotel. Is there something I can do for you?'

Lily looked up at him and he was struck again by the resemblance to Jess. She was frowning and she got the same little crease between her eyebrows that her mother got when she was unsure of something. 'How did you know my name?' she asked.

Lucas smiled to himself. He'd been imagining that

Jess had mentioned him to Lily. He'd been flattered and encouraged to think she might have but obviously that wasn't the case.

'I know your mum. You look just like her. What can I do for you?'

'Is this your sleigh?' Lily asked, as she pointed at the brightly painted red sleigh that had 'Crystal Lodge' stencilled across the back of it in ornate gold lettering.

Lucas nodded. 'It is.'

'We wanted a sleigh ride. We have money but this man…' Lily looked up at François, the sleigh driver with an accusatory expression '…says he can't take us.'

'François isn't allowed to take you unless you have an adult with you,' Lucas explained.

Lily folded her arms across her chest and frowned. Lucas expected her to stamp her tiny feet next and he almost laughed before realising that would probably not be appreciated. Not if she was anything like her mother. Lily looked up at him with big green eyes that were nearly too big for her face. She was a *lot* like her mother. 'You could come with us,' she said.

'Me?'

Lily nodded. 'You said you know my mum. You could take us. We have money.'

'Where did you get the money from?'

'Annabel's mum,' Lily said.

Lucas turned to the other two girls. 'Is one of you Annabel?' he asked.

The older girl pointed to the younger one. 'She is,' she said. 'I'm Claire, her sister.'

'Is the money supposed to be for a sleigh ride?' Lucas asked.

Claire shook her head. 'No. We were going ice skating but Lily and Annabel ran off here.'

'Where is your mum?'

'She's at work,' Claire told him. 'She owns the bakery.'

'The patisserie?' he asked.

Lily giggled and her laughter set her pigtails swinging. 'You don't say it right,' she told him.

'Don't I? That's probably because I'm Australian. I don't speak French.'

'That's why you sound funny,' she said, as if everything made perfect sense now. 'I know all about Australia.'

'How much can you know? You're only five.'

'I am not. I'm six.'

Lucas was curious. He was sure Jess had told him Lily was five. 'How do you know about Australia?'

'My mum told me.'

Now he was even more curious. He'd been wondering about Jess's circumstances, he'd spent too much time in the past week thinking about her if he was honest, but there was a lot to consider. Why wasn't she living in her family's apartment? Why had she taken basic accommodation? And what had happened to Lily's father? Why wasn't he in the picture? And why would she talk to Lily about Australia? He couldn't ask Lily directly but he had another solution.

'I need to call your mum,' he told Claire. 'Would you girls like to meet Banjo while I do that?' he asked.

'Who's Banjo?'

'He's the horse.'

Lily and Annabel jumped up and down and clapped their hands.

'You've met François,' Lucas introduced the sleigh driver, 'and this is Banjo.' He was a handsome draught horse. He was dark brown but had distinctive white lower legs with heavy feathering and white markings on his face. Lucas rubbed his neck and the big horse nuzzled into his shoulder. 'Would you like to feed him? He loves apples.'

'Yes, please.' The girls all answered as one.

'Hold your hand flat like this,' Lucas took Lily's hand and flattened her fingers out. François passed him an apple that had been cut in half and he placed it in the centre of her palm. 'Banjo will take it off your hand but keep your hand flat.' He guided Lily's hand to the horse and held her fingers out of the way. 'He won't be able to see the apple so he'll sniff for it.'

Lily giggled as the horse's warm breath tickled her hand. He took the apple and Lucas let Lily rub his neck as he crunched it. Banjo shook his head and Lily pulled her hand away.

'François will give you each an apple to feed Banjo while I ring the patisserie,' Lucas said, as he took his cell phone from his pocket. He got the number and spoke to Fleur. He explained the situation and also explained he was an old friend of Jess's and offered to drop the girls off to her.

As he finished the call Sofia reappeared, carrying a small cardboard cake box, a flask and some takeaway coffee cups. 'What are those for?' Lucas asked.

'I thought the girls might like some hot chocolate and something to eat on their sleigh ride.'

Lucas raised an eyebrow. 'How did you know?'

Sofia smiled and shrugged. 'You're a soft touch.'

'All right,' he asked the girls, 'who would like a lift home in the sleigh?'

'Really?'

'Yep.'

His offer was met with a chorus of squeals and as Banjo had finished all the apples that were on offer to him Lucas helped the girls into the sleigh before climbing up to sit on the driver's seat beside François.

The sleigh had been decorated with pine wreaths, bells and ribbons, and François had also decorated Banjo's harness with bells and tinsel. The shake of his head as he started to pull the sleigh set the bells ringing. Lucas asked François to take them for a turn around the plaza before heading to the patisserie. He'd acquiesced on the ride as he wanted a chance to chat to Lily, wanted to find out what she knew about Australia, but sitting up next to François while Lily sat in the back wasn't going to get him the answers he wanted.

He delivered Annabel and Claire to their mother and told Fleur that he would take Lily to collect Jess.

'Banjo can take you to your mum's work, Lily. Would you like to sit up front next to François?' Lucas asked, and when Lily nodded he lifted her onto the driver's seat. This seat was higher than the passenger seat to allow François to see over Banjo, and the position afforded Lily an uninterrupted view of the Village. The sun had set and the streets and the plaza were glowing under the Christmas lights. Lucas grabbed a fur blanket from the back of the sleigh and tucked it over Lily's lap.

On the seat next to them was the cardboard box Sofia had given him. Lucas peeked inside. Sofia had packed some pieces of cake and Lucas's favourite chocolate biscuits. The girls had finished their hot drinks but hadn't had time to eat anything. He showed the contents of the box to Lily as Banjo set off again, pulling the sleigh through the snow. 'Would you like a piece of cake?'

'No, thank you, I don't really like cake.'

'How about chocolate biscuits, then? I know you like chocolate.'

'How do you know that?'

'Who doesn't like chocolate? And these are the best chocolate biscuits ever. I get them sent over to me from Australia,' he told her.

'Really?' she asked, as she picked one up and bit into it.

'Do you like it?'

Lily nodded.

'So that's something you know about Australia—we make good chocolate biscuits. Tell me what else you know.'

'I know about the animals.'

'Do you have a favourite?'

Lily nodded again. 'Mum says I remind her of a platypus but I like the koala best,' she said with a mouthful of chocolate biscuit, 'because it's so cute. I know what the flag looks like too but I like our flag better. Did you know you've got the same queen as us?'

'I did know that.' Lucas smiled. She really was adorable.

'I can sing "Kookaburra sits in the old gum tree".'

'Did your mum teach you?'

'No, I learnt it in school. Mum taught me "Waltzing Matilda".'

Lucas remembered teaching that song to Jess and explaining what all the words meant. Why had Jess told Lily so much about Australia? 'Did you know that in

Australia it's summertime now? It's so hot at Christ-mastime we all go to the beach for a swim.'

'That's silly. Who would want to go to the beach on Christmas?'

'Yeah, you're right.' Lucas had come to love a white Christmas but that might be because it reminded him of Jess. It was far more romantic to think of cuddling by a warm fire with snow falling outside than sweating under a blazing sun, battling flies and sand. He loved summer but he didn't have to have it at Christmastime.

Lucas checked his watch. It was almost five. 'We'd better get you to the medical centre,' he told Lily. 'Your mum will be finishing work soon and I promised Fleur I would have you there on time.'

'Oh.' Lily pouted. 'Is that the end of my sleigh ride?'

'I have an idea. Does your mum like surprises?'

Lily nodded. 'She likes good surprises. She says I was a good surprise.'

'Excellent. Why don't we go and pick her up from work in the sleigh? Do you think she'd like that?'

Lily nodded, her green eyes wide.

'That's healed up nicely, Oscar,' Jess said as she removed the stitches in the chin of a teenage boy. He had come off second best in a tussle between the snow-boarding half-pipe and his board and Jess had assisted Cameron when he'd fixed him up a week earlier. She snipped the last stitch and pulled it from the skin. 'See if you can stay out of trouble now, won't you?' Oscar was a regular visitor to the clinic and Jess suspected his skills on his snowboard didn't quite match up to his enthusiasm.

'I'll try,' he said, as he hopped up from the examination bed. 'But maybe I should make a time for next week just in case I need it.'

'I don't want to see you again for at least two weeks.' She laughed. 'Off you go.'

Oscar was her last patient for the evening and she checked her watch as she typed his notes into the computer. She was finishing on time and was looking forward to collecting Lily from Fleur's and getting home. Sliding her arms into her coat, she switched off the computer and pulled the door closed as she prepared to leave for the day. Heading into the reception area to say goodnight to Donna, she was surprised to find Lily there.

'Hi, Lil, what are you doing here?' She frowned as she bent down to give her daughter a kiss.

'We have a surprise for you.'

'We?'

Lily took her hand and led her outside. Lucas was standing on the porch.

He looked gorgeous. He was wearing a grey cashmere coat that contrasted nicely with his forget-me-not-blue eyes. His coat looked smart and expensive. Her own coat was several years old and Jess was well aware of the contrast in their wardrobes.

'Lucas,' she greeted him.

'Hello, JJ.' He smiled at her and her heart beat a tattoo in her chest.

She hadn't seen him for a week and the sight of him took her breath away all over again. How was it possible that she could forget the effect his smile had on her? It was like seeing the sun coming out when she hadn't noticed it was missing. She'd never thought her day needed brightening until Lucas had popped into it.

But that didn't explain what he was doing there. In front of her work. With her daughter. Lily didn't know Lucas. He didn't know Lily. She had deliberately kept them apart. She didn't want him getting to know Lily. Not until she'd decided what to do. So what on earth were they doing together? What was going on?

'Why are you here?' she asked. 'Why are you *both* here?'

'Lily went walkabout.'

'What's walkabout?' Lily wanted to know.

Lucas looked at Lily as he explained. 'It's something we say in Australia. It means you went wandering.'

'What? Where?' Jess was worried. She had wanted Lily to be able to roam around the village safely, she'd felt confident that it would be possible, but she realised now that she'd assumed Lily would be wandering with her permission. Not taking off on a whim whenever the mood struck her. 'Did you find her?'

'No.' Lucas was shaking his head. 'She came to the lodge.'

'Why? What for?' Why would Lily go to Lucas? Jess turned to her daughter. 'Lily, what's going on?' She could hear the note of panic in her voice but there was nothing she could do to stop it.

'Jess, it's all right.'

Lucas's voice was calm, his words measured. He was always very calm, very matter-of-fact and practical. A whole lot of personality traits that Jess was sure she could use but it wasn't his place to placate her.

'Don't tell me it's all right!' she hissed at him.

'Lily, Banjo looks hungry.' Lucas turned to Lily, ignoring Jess's outburst. 'Why don't you go and ask François if he has another apple that you can give him?'

Jess watched as Lily went down the steps at the front of the clinic to where the Crystal Lodge sleigh was waiting in the snow. She hadn't even noticed it she'd been so distracted by Lucas and Lily arriving on her doorstep. She assumed Banjo was the horse, a very large but fortunately placid-looking horse.

Once Lily was out of earshot Lucas turned back to Jess. 'Lily was quite safe. I thought this was what you wanted—for her to be able to feel safe in the village?'

'Within reason,' Jess snapped. 'I didn't expect her to roam the streets alone or take off without notice.' Who knew what might happen? All Jess's insecurities, deeply embedded into her psyche by her parents, came to the fore.

'Is this about Stephen?' Lucas asked. He was watching her carefully with his gorgeous eyes. Was he waiting to see if she was going to explode with anger or dissolve into tears?

Jess had to admit that in a way it did all relate back to her brother. She nodded. 'I wanted Lily to have the freedom I never had but I expected to know where she was. She's too young to be getting about on her own. She'd supposed to have someone with her.'

'She wasn't alone. Annabel and Claire were with her. Claire was supposed to be taking them ice skating.'

'So what happened? How did Lily end up with you?'

Lucas shrugged. 'She wanted a sleigh ride so I gather she convinced Annabel to take off with her and they came to the lodge to see if they could use their ice-skating money for a ride instead.' he said, as if that was a perfectly natural request to make of a complete stranger.

'And you said yes, I see.' Jess was annoyed. Not only had Lily gone and found Lucas, she'd also managed to wangle a sleigh ride out of him. She'd been planning that as a holiday surprise and Lucas had taken that gift away from her. She knew it wasn't his fault—he hadn't done it deliberately—but it still irked her.

'I did clear it with Fleur first,' he told her. 'You should be proud of Lily. She wanted something badly enough to go after it. That shows initiative, determination and commitment, and I thought she deserved to be rewarded.'

He would think that, Jess thought, even though she knew her bitchy attitude was unfair.

'And I didn't think you'd mind, especially if you got to share it with her.'

'What do you mean?'

'We've come to give you a lift home in the sleigh. We thought we'd take the long way around. What do you say? Am I forgiven?' He held his hands out, palms open, beseeching her, and she couldn't stay mad. She knew she shouldn't be cross with him anyway, he had only been trying to do something nice for Lily and for her.

And he was right. Did it matter that she hadn't organised it? She should be happy. Lily was safe and she was getting her treat. And it wasn't costing her anything. Well, not money at least. It was costing her some pride and now she would owe Lucas a favour.

He smiled at her. His dimples flashed and his blue eyes twinkled. She would owe him a favour, but when he smiled at her she figured she could live with that.

She sighed. 'I'm sorry I snapped at you. And, yes, you're forgiven.'

'Good. Shall we?' He bent his elbow and Jess tucked her hand into the crook of his arm as he led her down the steps to the sleigh. She put one foot onto the running board and felt Lucas's hands on her hips as he helped her up. She sank into the soft leather seat as Lucas lifted Lily up beside her. He climbed in on the other side of Lily and tucked rugs around them all.

François clicked his tongue at Banjo and the big horse moved off slowly, bells jingling.

'Mummy, I can't see,' Lily complained.

She was tucked between Jess and Lucas and was too small to see past them or over the front of the sleigh.

'Hold up, please, François, while we do some reshuffling,' Lucas said.

Lily and Jess swapped seats so Lily could see out of the side of the sleigh but this meant that Jess was now sitting beside Lucas. Their knees were touching under the blanket and Jess was very aware of the heat of his body radiating across to her. He took up a lot of space and she could have shifted closer to Lily to give them both some room but she didn't want to. It felt good to sit this close to him.

'How has your week been?' he asked, as Banjo set off again.

'It was busy. Apparently the resort is almost at full capacity, I suppose you know that, but we also really notice the influx of the tourists as we get an increase in patient load.'

'Do you still think you've made the right choice taking this job?'

'Definitely. It's so much better than my old job in so many ways. No shift work, no weekends. Three minutes from home. It's heaven.'

'What are your plans for the weekend?'

'I'm not sure. Nothing much. We'll probably do a bit of skiing. Lily has been having lessons after school so I like to see how she's progressing. She's been pestering me for a sleigh ride since we arrived in Moose River but I won't need to do that now.' She smiled at him, all traces of her earlier irritation having vanished. The sleigh ride was relaxing and romantic, even with Lily in tow. It was a lovely end to the working week and sitting beside Lucas was the icing on the cake. 'Thank you.'

'My pleasure.'

She could see his forget-me-not-blue eyes shining in the light of the streetlamps. He looked very pleased with himself. As he had every right to be.

He was humming carols—something about it being lovely weather for a sleigh ride together—as François took them on a circuit around the village. Lucas's hand found hers under the blanket. He squeezed it gently and didn't let go.

Jess rested her head on his shoulder. She didn't stop to think about what she was doing. It just felt natural. It felt good. Banjo headed up the hill where François stopped to let them take in the view of the village, which was spread out before them. The lights sparkled and danced and the sounds of happiness drifted up to them on the breeze. Jess sighed. Sitting in the sleigh, listening to Lucas humming, and seeing Lily's smile, she imagined this could be what her life would be like if they were a real family. Cocooned in their own little bubble of contentment.

She suspected that anyone looking at them now would assume that's what they were. A blond family, bundled up in their furs, being pulled through the snow on a sleigh. They could be the perfect image on a festive season card.

Only it wasn't the truth.

Lucas wasn't her reality. He wasn't her Prince Charming.

She still didn't know if he even wanted a family.

Telling him everything might ruin it all.

Banjo had begun picking his way back down the hill and within minutes François had guided him to a stop in front of her apartment block. It was late now. It was time for dinner.

Lucas helped them down from the sleigh and walked them to the door.

'I know you have other priorities and I don't want you to feel as though I'm intruding on your life, but I would really like to spend some time with you. With you and Lily,' he said, as he held the door open. 'Tomorrow evening is the first Christmas market for the season and we're switching on the lights on the Christmas tree out the front of the lodge. I'd like the two of you to be my guests for the tree lighting. What do you think?'

Jess thought she should refuse politely but she couldn't. She wanted to see him too and Lily would love it.

If Lily and Lucas wanted something badly enough, they would both go after it. That was definitely a trait of nature, not nurture, but why shouldn't she do the same? She and Lily could spend time with Lucas, it would give her another chance to see how he interacted with Lily, another chance to watch him. Was it her fault if having Lily there meant she had to hold onto her secret for one more day?

'We'd love to,' she said. 'Thank you.'

CHAPTER EIGHT

THE THIRTY-FOOT FIR tree stood sentinel over the plaza. Lily craned her head to see to the very top where the star was perched, and even Jess looked up in awe. She'd noticed the framework being erected—that had been difficult to miss too—but the tree itself, with its spreading limbs, was simply enormous. Its dark green foliage had been decorated with myriad silver balls and shining stars and bells that rang when the breeze stirred the branches. A light, shaped like a candle, was attached to the end of each branch. It must have taken hours to decorate but the effort was well worth it. It was beautiful.

Lucas came to them as they stood under the tree. He had his grey cashmere overcoat on again with a black scarf wrapped around his throat. Jess had made more of an attempt to dress up tonight. She'd chosen her smartest woollen coat in a winter white and had taken time with her make-up.

'Ladies, your timing is perfect.' Lucas greeted them with a smile and Jess was pleased she'd made the extra effort.

Lucas had reserved a table for them on the outdoor dining terrace in front of the lodge. They had an uninterrupted view across to the tree as well as down to the plaza, where the colourful tented market stalls had been set up. Carol singers were performing at the edge of the terrace and Lucas ordered eggnog for everyone as they sat down.

As the eggnog was served Lily handed Lucas a box wrapped in Christmas ribbon.

'What's this for?'

'For you,' Lily told him. 'To say thank you for the sleigh ride.'

Lucas undid the ribbon and lifted the lid to reveal cookies in various Christmas shapes—stars, angels, reindeer, bells and sleighs. Each cookie had been decorated with icing and had a small hole in the top through which red ribbon had been threaded.

'Mum and I made gingerbread for the school Christmas cookie swap and I thought you might like some.'

'Thank you, Lily, they look delicious,' he said, as he lifted out a star.

'You can't eat them yet!' Lily admonished him. 'You're supposed to hang them on the tree. That's why they've got ribbons in them.'

'I see that now. Have you hung some on your tree?'

'We don't have a tree.'

'You don't?'

'I haven't got around to it,' Jess told him. She wasn't actually planning on having a tree, mainly because she didn't have any decorations for it. She hadn't brought decorations with them to Moose River—that hadn't seemed a necessity when she'd been choosing which belongings needed to fit into their luggage—but now that she was immersed in the festive spirit of the village she regretted her decision. It wasn't likely to change, though. She could get a tree but she still didn't have the money to splash out on new decorations. Of course, she wasn't about to tell Lucas that. Fortunately Lily piped up and redirected the conversation.

'Do you have a Christmas tree inside?' she asked.

'I do,' Lucas replied.

'I think you should hang them inside, then, so they don't get snowed on.'

'I think that's a very good idea.'

The carol singers were singing 'O Christmas Tree' and as they neared the end of the song Lucas stood up.

'That's my cue,' he said. 'Would you like to come with me, Lily? We need to start the countdown for the lights.'

He took Lily's hand and a lump formed in Jess's throat as she watched the two of them make their way to the tree. He was being so sweet with her. She didn't know what she was worried about. He would love Lily.

Actually, she did know what she was worried about. She was worried he'd think less of her for keeping the secret. She didn't want that but there was no way around it. She knew she had to tell him the truth. She just hadn't decided when.

Lucas took a cordless microphone from his pocket and switched it on. He looked confident and relaxed and very sexy.

'Welcome everyone to the inaugural lighting of the Crystal Lodge Christmas tree. I'd like to invite you all to help count us down from ten to one before we flick the switch. Lily, would you like to start us off?'

Lily looked up at Lucas and beamed. Jess thought her smile was so wide it was going to split her face in two. She was looking at Lucas as if he was the best thing that had ever happened to her, and Jess knew Lily would only benefit from having Lucas as a father. There would be no downside for Lily. Jess had to do the right thing.

Lucas handed Lily the microphone. 'Ready? From ten.'

'Ten!' Lily's voice rang out across the plaza and then the crowd joined in.

'Nine, eight, seven, six, five, four, three, two, one!'

As they reached 'one', the lights were switched on, accompanied by a massive cheer. The tips of the candle lights were illuminated and now glowed brightly against the night sky. The tree had a light dusting of snow and looked magical.

As the carol singers launched into another set of carols Lucas and Lily returned to their table.

'Did you see that, Mum?'

Jess had tears in her eyes as she got out of her chair and hugged her very excited daughter. 'I did, darling, you were fabulous.' Over the top of Lily's head she mouthed 'Thank you' to Lucas.

'Can we go to the market now?' Lily asked, and Jess knew she wasn't going to be able to sit still.

'Would you like to come with us or are you busy?' she invited Lucas.

'No, my duties are all done for the evening. I'd love to walk with you.'

They strolled through the market, stopping at any stall that caught their attention. There was a good variety selling food and gifts, everything from scarves, knitted hats and delicate glassware to souvenirs, Christmas decorations, hot food and candies.

Lucas stopped at a stall selling decorations. 'Lily, I think I need a few more decorations for my inside trees, to go with your cookies. Would you like to choose some for me?'

Lily agonised over her choices but eventually had filled a bag with a varied assortment of ornaments. Jess wasn't sure how they would match in with the smartly decorated trees in the lodge's lobby but seeing the pleasure on Lily's face she knew that wasn't the point. Lucas was doing all sorts of wonderful things for Lily that Jess couldn't afford to do but she couldn't begrudge him. Not when she could see how much pleasure Lily was getting from it.

Jess stopped at the next stall, which was selling barley candy. This was a Canadian Christmas tradition and one she could afford. It was also one she'd shared with Lucas years ago. She chose three sticks of the sugary sweets, one shaped like Santa, one a Christmas tree and the third a reindeer, and let Lily and Lucas choose one each.

They sucked on the candy as they wandered through the market. Lily skipped in front of them, in a hurry to see what lay in the stalls ahead. She stopped at one that displayed some intricate doll's houses, complete with delicate furniture and real glass windows, and spent ages admiring the display as Lucas and Jess talked.

'What are your plans for Christmas?' Lucas asked. 'Are your parents coming up to the resort?'

Jess shook her head. 'I don't think so.'

'Really? I thought that was a family tradition for you?'

Jess had no idea what her parents' plans were. They could be spending Christmas here but even if they were their celebration wouldn't include her and she wasn't going to explain why that tradition had come to an end.

She stopped to buy a bag of hot cinnamon doughnut holes, hoping that would distract him from any further questions.

'What about you?' she asked, as Lily traded her barley sugar for the bag of doughnuts.

'I'll be hosting the Christmas lunch at the lodge. A buffet extravaganza.'

'A bit different from your traditional Christmas,' she said.

'I've grown to prefer a white Christmas.' Lucas smiled. 'It feels more like a celebration to me.'

They had reached the ice-skating rink at the end of the first row of market stalls and they sat on a bench to eat doughnut holes and watch the ice skaters. Lily leant on the railing, leaving Jess and Lucas free to talk. Jess sat at one end of the bench, which was a long bench with plenty of room, but Lucas chose to sit right next to her.

'What has Lily asked Santa for?'

'It's the same thing every year, a baby sister.'

'I take it from your tone you have no plans to give her what she wants.' He was smiling.

Jess shook her head. 'I'm not doing that again. Not on my own.'

Lily came back to Jess and handed her the empty doughnut bag. 'Can we go ice skating?' she asked.

'I guess so.' Jess knew it was only a few dollars to hire the skates.

'I might have to sit this one out. I'm a terrible ice skater. I'm Australian, remember, there's not much ice where I come from.'

Disappointment flowed through Jess. She hadn't stopped to think that this might be something Lucas wouldn't enjoy. But, taking a leaf out of his book, she decided persistence might pay off. 'Lily and I will help you,' she suggested. 'We can hold your hands.'

Lucas flashed his dimples at her as he grinned and said, 'There's an offer too good to refuse. Let's do it.'

He scooped Lily up and she squealed with delight as he carried her over to the hire kiosk to choose skates. It seemed his charm worked equally as well on Lily as it did on her.

Jess tied Lily's skates and then she and Lily each took one of Lucas's hands and stepped onto the ice. Lucas struggled to get the idea of gliding on the slippery surface but his innate sense of balance meant she and Lily had no trouble keeping him upright as they skated around the rink.

They'd managed to negotiate their way twice around the rink before Lily saw one of her friends from school and skated off, leaving Jess alone with Lucas.

'Did you want to keep skating?' she asked him.

'Definitely,' he replied. 'I'm not going to pass up an opportunity to have you all to myself.' He pulled his gloves off his hands and put them into his pocket. He held out his hand and Jess slipped her gloves off too and gave them to him before putting her hand in his outstretched palm. His skin was warm but Jess knew she wouldn't care how cold it got, she wasn't going to put her gloves back on.

They did a couple more laps of the rink hand in hand and then Lucas let her go.

'Are you going to try by yourself?' she asked.

'No,' he said, as he put his arm around her waist and pulled her in closer. 'I still need to lean on you.'

Jess knew that was a bad idea—he wasn't steady enough on his skates yet—but before she could protest he'd pushed off and within a few feet their skates had tangled. Lucas stumbled and grabbed the railing that ran around the edge of the rink and just managed to keep his feet, but his momentum as he tried to regain his balance spun Jess around so that she was now facing him. They leant together on the railing as Lucas straightened up.

He was laughing. 'Sorry about that,' he said. 'Actually, I'm not sorry, it's put you right where I want you.'

She was almost nose to nose with Lucas and she could feel her cheeks burning but it wasn't from the cold. It was from being so close to him. Jess lifted her chin and looked into his forget-me-not-blue eyes. She could feel his breath on her cheek. Warm and sweet, it smelt of cinnamon doughnuts. She was close enough to kiss him.

Lucas dipped his head. She knew what he was going to do. But she couldn't let him kiss her. Not here. Not yet. But she couldn't move away. She was transfixed by his eyes. She held her breath as she watched his eyes darken from blue to purple as he closed the distance.

Jess felt something tugging on her coat.

'Mummy, I feel sick.'

Jess looked down. Lily was beside her. 'Lily? What's the matter?'

'I feel sick,' she repeated.

Was she dizzy from skating? Jess wondered. She did look a bit pale. Jess let go of Lucas to put her hand on Lily's forehead. She felt warm but Jess found it hard to tell if that was just because of all the layers she was bundled up in.

'Too much sugar, probably,' Jess said. 'We'd better get you home.'

'I can't walk,' Lily grumbled.

'I'll give you a piggyback,' Lucas offered, and Jess looked at him gratefully.

Lily didn't need to be asked twice. She whipped her skates off, pulled her boots back on and wasted no time hopping onto Lucas's back, where she held on tight and buried her face in his neck as he carried her home.

'You're making a habit of getting us home safely,' Jess said, as Lucas put Lily onto the couch.

'I'm happy to be of service,' he said with a smile. 'Are you going to be all right?'

'We'll be fine. Thank you.' It wasn't quite the ending she'd pictured to the night but there wasn't anything she could do about that.

Jess was browning onions to add to the meatballs she was planning to make when there was a knock on the apartment door. 'Can you answer that, please, Lily?'

'Who is it?' she called out to Lily as she heard the door open.

'It's a Christmas tree!'

Jess wiped her hands on a tea towel and stepped out of the kitchen. A pine tree filled the doorway. 'What on earth…?'

Lucas's face appeared around the side of the tree. He was grinning at Lily. 'G'day.'

'Lucas!' Lily jumped up and down and clapped her hands as she shouted. All trace of yesterday's illness had well and truly disappeared. 'Who's the tree for?'

'You. I thought it might cheer you up if you were sick but you look like you're feeling much better.'

'I am better but, please, can I still have it? I *love* Christmas trees, they're so pretty.'

'It's not pretty yet but it will be once we decorate it.'

'That's very sweet of you,' Jess interrupted before the excitement took over completely, 'but I haven't got time to be fiddling around with a tree.'

'What's the problem?' Lucas asked, as he leant the tree against the door frame and stepped into the apartment.

He looked as disappointed as Jess knew Lily would be but as much as she would have loved to have a Christmas tree she hadn't the budget for one. She'd thought about decorating the room with a small pine bough and maybe spending an afternoon making kissing balls with Lily as a compromise, but that was as far as she'd got. 'It's always so difficult to get it secure and then in a couple of weeks I'll just have to work out how to get rid of a dead tree.'

'That's why I'm here. I will make sure it won't topple over and I promise I will dispose of it when you're ready. All you need to do is tell me where you'd like it.'

'Lucas, have a look.' Jess waved an arm around at the cramped living space. 'There's nowhere for it to go.'

'Why don't I put it in front of the balcony doors? How much time do you spend out there in this weather anyway?'

He smiled at her and Jess remembered how it had been when she'd been seventeen. She would have given him the world when he'd smiled at her. She had. And she thought she still might.

But she wasn't ready to give in just yet. 'I like to look at the village lights,' she protested.

'How about, for the next three weeks, you look at the lights on the tree instead?'

He made a fair point but she didn't have any decorations and that included lights. 'I don't—'

'Have lights,' Lucas interrupted. 'No dramas. I do. I have everything you need. Just say yes.'

Did he have everything she needed? Should she say yes? It was a tempting offer.

'Please, Mum?'

Why was she refusing? She'd dreamt of giving Lily a perfect Christmas and Lucas was here, offering to help make that happen. She'd offer him one last chance to excuse himself. 'I'm sure you've got better things to do too,' she said to Lucas.

'Nope. It's Sunday. I'm taking the day off. This'll be relaxing.'

Jess laughed. 'You think? Why don't you go out snowboarding? Wouldn't that be more fun?'

'It'll be snowing for the next four months, there's plenty of time for that. Christmas is in three weeks, which makes this a priority.'

She couldn't resist a combined assault. 'All right, if you're sure.' She gave in. 'But you and Lily will have to manage without me. I've got a mountain of mincemeat waiting to be turned into dinner.'

'No worries. We'll be right, won't we, Lily?'

Lily nodded her head eagerly.

Jess would actually have loved to help but she'd already said she didn't have time. But Lucas didn't argue—he didn't seem to mind at all, leaving Jess feeling mildly disappointed. Had he only come to see Lily?

Lucas tossed his coat onto the sofa and then Lily helped him to carry all the paraphernalia into the apartment. He'd brought everything they would need, including all the decorations Lily had bought at the market the day before plus candy canes and some of the gingerbread. The tree was only small, maybe a touch over five feet tall, and Jess had to admit it was perfect for the compact apartment.

Jess watched out of the corner of her eye, unable to resist an opportunity to watch Lucas. She forgot all about the onions on the stove as she watched his arms flex and his T-shirt strain across his shoulders as he hefted the tree inside and fitted it into the stand.

The smell of burning onions eventually returned her focus to the kitchen and she pitched the singed batch and chopped a second lot as Lucas and Lily trimmed the tree. He had even brought Christmas music—Jess could hear it playing on his phone while they worked.

'What are you listening to?' she asked.

He named a well-known Australian children's group. 'This is their Christmas album.'

'Why do you have their music?'

'I downloaded it for Lily. I thought she'd enjoy it,' he explained. 'Surely you recognise the songs, even if you're not familiar with the artists?'

'I will by the end of the afternoon,' Jess quipped. 'You seem to have it stuck on repeat.'

Lucas laughed and the sound filled the space. It was a lovely sound, better than the music, and Jess wished she could hear that whenever she liked.

'We like it, don't we, Lily?'

'Yes, it's fun.'

Jess felt even more left out as she listened to them laugh and sing along to Lucas's music. But she'd had six years of having Lily to herself. It was time Lily got to know Lucas.

But was she ready to share? What implications would

it have? He said he'd come back for her but what if he changed his mind? What if he only wanted Lily? What if he wanted to take her away? What was best for Lily? Should she turn her world upside down? Could Lucas give her things that she couldn't?

She knew he could.

He already had.

The tree was finished and Lily had switched the lights on. It looked very pretty and lifted Jess's spirits. 'Would you like to stay for dinner?' she invited Lucas. 'We're having spaghetti with meatballs.'

'I don't want to be rude but I don't eat pasta.'

'Oh.' Her heart dropped. It seemed he didn't want to spend time with her.

'Would it be all right if I just had the meatballs?'

'I don't want spaghetti either,' Lily said, but Jess wasn't all that surprised. Lucas was Lily's new idol so, of course, she'd want to imitate him. She hadn't stopped talking about him all day and it had almost been a relief when he'd arrived at their door. At least then Jess hadn't had to listen to Lily's running commentary any more, but having Lucas there in the flesh had added other frustrations. She could see him and smell his winter-fresh pine scent but she couldn't touch him.

Lucas and Lily sat opposite Jess with their bowls of meatballs sprinkled with cheese. Jess could see some similarities. Lily may look just like her but her green eyes were more changeable. Tonight, sitting next to Lucas, Jess could see that flash of forget-me-not blue in them. It was odd that she'd never noticed that before.

Looking at them sitting opposite her, Jess had an-other glimpse of what it would be like to be a family, and she wondered what Lucas would say if she told him the truth tonight.

But she couldn't tell him in front of Lily. Despite how he'd treated Lily over the past couple of days, she couldn't assume that his reaction would be positive. Being nice to an old friend's daughter was one thing, finding out he was a father might be another thing entirely. Jess couldn't risk upsetting Lily if Lucas's reaction wasn't what she hoped. This wasn't a conversation she could launch into on the spur of the moment. They needed time alone, without interruption. She needed a plan.

Perhaps she should ask Fleur if Lily could have a sleepover with Annabel. She didn't like to ask for favours but given the circumstances it was probably her best option. Either that or get Kristie to come up to the resort to babysit. Kristie had been right. Lucas deserved to know the truth.

Christmas was fast approaching and Lily's calendar was chock-full of activities, far more so than Jess's was. In the past week alone she'd had the Christmas cookie swap, a Christmas lunch, yesterday had been Annabel's birthday party and tonight she was supposed to be going back to Annabel's for a sleepover, but right now it didn't look as though that was going to happen.

Lily had started vomiting after the party and fifteen hours later she hadn't stopped and Jess was beginning to worry. She called the clinic for advice as she spooned ice chips into Lily's mouth. She tried to think what she would advise a stressed parent in this situation if she was the nurse who took the call, but sleep deprivation and worry made it difficult to think clearly.

Donna answered the clinic phone and put her straight through to Cameron.

Jess explained the situation and Lily's symptoms. 'She's been vomiting since four o'clock yesterday, she's complaining of abdominal pain—that's not unusual but she's extremely lethargic.'

'Do you think it could be her appendix?'

Jess had thought about that but Lily's symptoms didn't fit and she'd just assumed it was a usual childhood stomach ache, which Lily seemed to get plenty of, but what if it was more serious than that?

'I've checked but what if I've missed something?'

'I'll come over as soon as I can.'

Jess sat with Lily and fretted while she waited for Cameron. This was one of the things she hated about being a single parent. There was no one to share the worry with.

'Has she had a temperature overnight?' Cameron asked when he arrived.

'No.'

'No, not now or, no, not at any stage?' Cameron clarified.

'Not at any point.'

'Any urine output in the last four to six hours?'

'No.'

'When was her last bowel movement?'

'Yesterday?' Jess wasn't one hundred per cent sure.

Cameron examined Lily and checked for signs of appendicitis. 'I agree with you. I don't think it's her appendix. How quickly did she get sick after the party?'

'Pretty quick. A couple of hours.'

'Too soon for it to be food poisoning. And no one else has had any gastro?'

Jess shook her head. She'd spoken to Fleur and between the two of them they'd rung and checked with the other parents.

Cameron motioned for Jess to follow him out of the bedroom. 'I think it would be best to take her down to the hospital. They should run some tests. She could have a bowel obstruction but she'll need an X-ray to check that out.'

'A bowel obstruction!' That was not good news.

'It's one possibility and I think it should be investigated. The hospital will be able to run blood tests and get the results faster than I can up here on the mountain. I can treat her for dehydration but that's treating the symptoms, not the cause. Would you like Ellen to drive you? She's not working today.'

'Thanks, but I'll call a friend.' Jess didn't want to impose on Cameron or his wife any more than necessary. She had made plans to have dinner with Lucas tonight and it looked like she was going to have to call him to cancel but she hoped he would offer to drive them down the mountain. 'If he can't take us, I'll call Ellen.'

'All right, I'll let the hospital know to expect you.'

Just as she'd hoped, Lucas offered to drive them. She'd rather he was with her than Ellen. They were both busy and probably neither had the time to spend being her taxi service but Lucas had more invested in Lily—he just didn't know it yet.

Lily didn't vomit at all on the hour-long trip to the hospital, which Jess was grateful for. Lucas dropped them at the entrance to the emergency department and went to park the car. The hospital was small. At the bottom of the mountain it was still more than an hour out of Vancouver, but it did have modern facilities. Jess carried Lily inside and walked straight up to the desk.

'This is Lily Johnson. Dr Cameron Baker was calling ahead for us.'

The nurse on duty took them straight into a partitioned cubicle. There wasn't a lot of privacy but Jess knew most patients in an emergency department had bigger priorities than to be fussing about privacy. Jess ran through all Lily's symptoms with the nurse while she took Lily's obs and then listened as the nurse repeated them to the doctor, who had introduced himself as Peter Davis.

'This is Lily. Age six, weight sixteen kilograms. She has been vomiting since yesterday afternoon but nothing for the past two hours. Complaining of stomach pains. Afebrile. BP normal. No diarrhoea.'

'Current temperature?'

'Thirty-seven point two.'

'No allergies?' He looked at Jess.

'No,' she replied.

'What has she eaten?'

'Nothing since yesterday afternoon.'

'What did she eat yesterday?'

'I don't really know. She went to a party but none of the other children are sick, I checked.' Jess knew the doctor was thinking about food poisoning as one option.

'Has there been any gastro at the school?'

'No. Nothing.'

'No major illnesses? No surgeries?'

Jess shook her head again.

'Any episodes of rumbling appendix?' Peter continued to question her.

'No, and her GP didn't seem to think it was her ap-

pendix. He thought she could have a bowel obstruction.'
Jess was getting distressed. She didn't want to tell the
doctor what to look for—she knew there was a routine,
she knew he would want to eliminate more common
possibilities first, and there was no need to run unnecessary tests if Lily's problem was something simple, but
she wanted to make sure he didn't miss anything or ignore something more significant. A bowel obstruction
could be nasty and Jess really hoped it wasn't the case
but nothing else seemed to fit.

'No diarrhoea, you said?' he asked as he conducted
the rebound test, checking for appendicitis.

'No.'

'Can you cough for me, Lily?'

Lily coughed obediently and didn't show any signs
of discomfort.

'Is there any past history of recurrent diarrhoea or
blood in her stools?'

'No.'

'I'll run a drip to counteract her dehydration and
organise an abdominal X-ray. See if that can shed any
light on the situation.'

Jess held Lily's hand as the nurse inserted a canula
and connected a drip. Lily was very flat but that might
have been related to lack of sleep. Jess wasn't feeling
so bright herself.

The nurse fixed a drip stand to a wheelchair and
helped Lily into the seat, explaining she would take her
over to the radiology department. Jess walked beside the
wheelchair and tried to keep a positive frame of mind,
but it was difficult when she could see Lily so pale and
quiet, with needles and tubes sticking out of her.

Jess waited as the X-ray was taken. Then she waited for the result.

'The X-ray was inconclusive,' Dr Davis told her. 'We'll do a CT scan next but I'm not sure we're looking in the right place.'

'What do you mean?' Jess was confused.

'Her pain has eased considerably and she's stopped vomiting. I don't think it's all as a result of the medication. I think she may have purged her system of whatever was upsetting her. Has she *ever* had any allergy testing done?'

Jess shook her head.

'Is there any family history of allergies or gastro-intestinal problems?'

'She's a fussy eater with the usual childhood stomach aches but no allergies that I know of.'

'Any auto-immune deficiencies?'

'Not on my side, but I'm not sure about her father's side.' It was obvious that the tests weren't giving the doctor the answers he was expecting but Jess didn't have any other answers for him. She would have to talk to Lucas. She had to know what was wrong with Lily and Lucas could hold the key. 'I'll see what I can find out,' she said.

Knowing Lily wouldn't be able to see her while she was in the CT scanner, Jess returned to the waiting room to see if Lucas had appeared. She needed to find him. She needed answers. The time had come. She had secrets that needed to be told.

He was in the waiting room when she returned. He stood up when she walked in and came towards her with his arms open. She stepped into his embrace.

'How're you doing?' he asked. 'How's Lily? Do they know what's wrong?'

'They're still not sure. The doctor was thinking appendicitis or a small bowel obstruction but the X-ray was inconclusive. They're doing a CT scan now but the doctor seems to be leaning towards an allergy of some sort. He was asking about her family history but, of course, I only know half of the answers.'

'Well, there's not much you can do about that,' Lucas said, 'unless you can track down Lily's father.'

Jess took a deep breath. The time had come. 'I have,' she told him.

'What? Have you spoken to him?'

'Yes and no. Will you come outside with me? I need some fresh air.' She knew she had some explaining to do but she wasn't about to go into the details in the middle of the emergency department. Jess stepped out through the automatic sliding door. There was a bench just outside. She sat and waited until Lucas was sitting beside her.

It was time.

'I know where Lily's father is,' she said. She took another deep breath. 'It's you. You're her father.'

CHAPTER NINE

'WHAT?' LUCAS SHOT straight back up off the bench as if it was electrified. 'What the hell are you saying?'

'Lily is your daughter.'

'What? No. She can't be.'

Jess nodded. 'You're her father.'

'She's mine?' He shook his head in disbelief. 'I have a daughter?'

Lucas paced backwards and forwards in front of the bench while Jess waited nervously. What was going through his head?

He stopped and looked at her, a puzzled expression in his forget-me-not-blue eyes. 'You're sure about this?'

'Of course I'm sure.'

'But why haven't you told me?' Lucas stood in front of her, rooted to the spot. He ran his hands through his hair and stared at her with a fixed, unseeing expression. 'How could you keep this from me? *Why* would you keep this from me?'

'I'm sorry.'

'What for?' He was looking at her now, his blue eyes boring into her as if he was searching for any more secrets she had yet to divulge. 'For telling me? For not telling me? For keeping her a secret? Which one of those things are you apologising for?'

Jess felt ill. She swallowed nervously and she could taste bile in her throat. 'I'm sorry for telling you the way I did. I didn't mean to blurt it out like that.'

'How could you have kept this a secret?'

'I didn't mean to. I tried to find you.'

'When?'

'When I found out I was pregnant. Kristie and I hired a private investigator but after a month the PI told us we were wasting our time. Do you know how many Lucas Whites there are in Australia? And not one of them was you.'

'When was this?'

'It was April. The ski season was over, the resort had closed for the summer and you would have been home in Australia.'

Lucas's legs folded and he sat back down on the bench. His face was pale. He looked ill. 'I...'

'What is it? Are you okay?' Jess asked.

He looked up at her and she could see dismay in his blue eyes. 'April?'

Jess nodded.

'I wasn't in Australia then,' he said.

'What? I thought you were going back to university?'

Lucas was shaking his head. 'That was my plan. But my plans changed. I went home but I couldn't settle into uni. The father of one of my mates offered me a job in his new hotel and I jumped at the chance. It was a fantastic opportunity, I was going to get to do everything from housekeeping to bartending to running the activities desk and administration, so I took a year off uni. That April, I was in Indonesia.'

'I was looking in the wrong place.' Jess sat on the bench beside him. She was close to tears. All that time spent searching for Lucas, only to find now that she'd been looking in the wrong haystack.

'I'm sorry, JJ. I should have written like I'd planned to, but I thought I had time. I hadn't expected consequences.'

'Neither of us did, I guess,' she sighed. 'But I had to deal with the consequences and I've done the best I could.'

'But what about more recently? Did you look for me again?'

'Of course. I was eighteen, pregnant and alone—do you think I wanted to do this by myself? I searched again when Lily was born but I was still concentrating on Australia and the harder I looked without success the more I believed you didn't want to be found. My father told me you wouldn't want a baby, that you wouldn't want to become a father with a girl you barely knew, and I didn't want to believe him but in the end I didn't have a choice. I couldn't find you.'

'Lily is my daughter.' Lucas stood up and Jess could see him physically and mentally settling himself. He straightened his back and squared his shoulders and focused his forget-me-not-blue eyes on her. 'I need to speak to the doctor.'

'What for?'

'You said he was asking about allergies and family history. We need to tell him to test Lily for celiac disease.'

'What? Why?'

'I'm a celiac and if I really *am* her father then there's a good possibility she has it too.'

'Lucas…' Jess was about to say 'Trust me' but she decided that was a poor choice of phrase. 'Believe me, you're her father.'

'You said Lily had a lot of parties last week. If she has celiac disease and she's overloaded on gluten, that could explain the vomiting. We need to let the doctor know. He needs to run tests.'

'What sort of tests?' Jess felt she should know the answers but it was strange how everything she'd ever learnt seemed to have vanished from her head. Right now she was a patient's mother, not a nurse, and her head was filled with thoughts of Lily and Lucas. There was no room in it for facts about a disease she'd never had to deal with. A disease that quite possibly her daughter had inherited from her father.

Jess needed to focus. Lily was the priority here; she'd have to sort through all the other issues later, when her head had cleared and the dust had settled.

'I think it's just a blood test initially,' Lucas was saying. 'It's been fifteen years since I was diagnosed. We'll have to speak to the doctor.'

He headed back into the hospital with Jess at his heels. Dr Davis was standing beside the triage desk.

'Do you have the CT results?' Jess asked.

He nodded. 'There was no sign of a blockage on the CT scan either.'

'We'd like you to test Lily for celiac disease,' Lucas said.

'Why?' he asked Jess. It was his turn to be puzzled now.

'Apparently her father has celiac disease,' Jess replied.

Dr Davis frowned. 'And you didn't think to tell me?'

'I didn't know.'

'Lily is my daughter,' Lucas interrupted, 'and I have celiac disease.'

'She's never been tested?' Dr Davis asked.

'We were estranged,' Jess said.

At the same time Lucas said, 'I didn't know I had a daughter.'

Neither of the answers made things any clearer for the doctor.

'Look, that's all irrelevant,' Lucas continued. 'The bottom line is I have celiac disease, Lily is my daughter and her symptoms sound consistent with celiac disease. Even if she was asymptomatic, there's a high possibility she has it too. We'd like her tested.'

Dr Davis was nodding now. They'd managed to get his attention but if Jess thought she was going to be the one in control she was mistaken. Lucas was used to being in charge; she'd forgotten how much he relished it and he didn't mince his words with the doctor. He'd become like a wild animal protecting his offspring and nothing was going to stop him from getting what he wanted for Lily. Not this doctor and certainly not her.

If Lucas thought there was a strong chance that Lily had celiac disease they needed to find out for sure, but listening to him now and looking at his body language she knew that if she thought he would bow out of their lives, out of Lily's life, without a whimper, she was mistaken. She knew he would want to be involved, she knew he would fight for Lily, but where would that leave her?

'A blood test isn't conclusive. There are other digestive diseases with similar presentations,' the doctor explained.

'I know that but it's a start,' Lucas replied.

'What do you test for?' Jess asked.

'The best test is the tTG-IgA test. It's the most sensitive and is positive in about ninety-eight per cent of patients with celiac disease.'

'Positive for what?'

'Tissue transglutaminase antibodies. They'll be present if the celiac patient has a diet that contains gluten. But if they've already been avoiding gluten you may get a false negative. Does Lily eat food that contains gluten?'

Jess nodded.

'The result might still depend on whether or not she eats *enough* gluten.'

'It's our best chance,' Lucas insisted. 'Can you run the test?

'I can order it but I'm also going to admit her overnight. I want to keep her here while we run the tests. If it turns out to be appendicitis or a bowel blockage, she's better off here. I'll go and make the arrangements.'

'Now what?' Jess asked Lucas, as they watched the departing figure of the doctor.

'We wait. The important thing is finding out what's wrong with Lily. Celiac disease isn't life-threatening but if left untreated or undiagnosed it can cause irreversible damage to her small intestine. You know that—you're a nurse. If that's all it is it can be controlled by diet. Just cut out gluten. It's much easier to manage now than it was years ago. The important thing is to get it diagnosed.' He ran his hands through his hair, making it more tousled than it normally was. He sighed and shook his head. 'I'm going to wait outside. Come and get me if there's any news.'

That didn't sound like he wanted company.

He headed for the exit and Jess waited inside. Alone. And wondered if she'd done the right thing. But she'd done what she'd had to for Lily's sake.

Lily was brought back from the radiology department and Jess sat with her as the nursing staff got her settled into a ward bed. Her blood was taken and a sedative was added to her drip and Jess stayed with her until she fell asleep.

Lily hadn't vomited since they'd arrived at the hospital and Jess would have been happy to take her home. She would have gladly put all this behind them but the doctor's reasons for admitting Lily were valid ones. She would stay at the hospital for as long as it took to diagnose Lily's problem. But what about Lucas? Had he waited? Was he still in the hospital or had he got out while he still could? She couldn't have blamed him, her announcement must have come as quite a shock. She should have broken the news differently.

She owed him an apology.

She found him sitting on a bench outside the emergency department with his head in his hands. He lifted his head as she sat beside him but he didn't look at her. He ran his hands through his hair as he stretched his legs out, before tipping his head back and resting it against the wall. He was casually dressed in jeans and lace-up workman's boots with a T-shirt under his coat. His hair was tousled but his infectious grin was missing. What had she done?

He sighed and finally looked at her. His forget-me-not-blue eyes were dark purple. He looked exhausted. 'You should have told me.'

'I know.'

'I understand you couldn't find me but for the past two weeks I've been right here. You've had plenty of opportunity to say something and you still chose not to. Why? Why would you continue to keep this a secret? Did you not think I deserved to know I had a child?'

'I was waiting for the right time. I didn't know what you'd think. I needed to find out what kind of person you had become. I didn't know if you wanted to be a father. If you didn't want Lily then she would be better off never knowing about you. Better that than for her to know that her father didn't want her.'

'Of course I would want her. How could you think otherwise?'

'You don't miss what you've never had. She might not matter to you.'

'How can you say that? Of course she matters, and think of all the things I've missed. I missed her being born, I missed her starting school, losing her first tooth, taking her first step, saying her first word. My God, JJ, I don't even know when her birthday is.' He listed all the milestones that Jess had witnessed. She hadn't taken them for granted but she had revelled in them.

'Her birthday is September thirteenth.'

He ignored her olive branch. 'And what about Lily?' he continued, as if she hadn't spoken. 'You thought I wouldn't miss her but what about her? Do you think she doesn't miss having a father?'

Jess had felt the absence on Lily's behalf and Lily herself commented when she saw her friends' families. But did she really know what she was missing? Jess suspected she did—Lily knew what other people's fathers were like. She just didn't know her own.

He had made a good point.

'Yes, she misses it,' she admitted. 'She would love to have a father. She would love you.' Jess could feel tears of regret welling in her eyes but she tried to fight them back. She didn't want to turn on the waterworks, she didn't want Lucas to think she was looking for sympathy—she didn't deserve sympathy. But she did hope to make him understand. She was scared that if he didn't understand he was going to hate her, and how would she live with that?

'And when she asked about her father? What were you planning on telling her?'

'I hadn't worked that out yet. I didn't think we'd ever see you again.' Jess's voice was quiet. There were so many things she'd refused to think about. So many things she'd just tried to ignore. It looked like those days were over now.

'Did you think you were the only one who could love her?'

Jess shook her head. 'No.' *But I was worried you wouldn't love me.*

'I thought I knew you, JJ. I came back here to prove myself to you but I wasn't prepared for this.'

'What are you going to do?'

'I don't know but I want to see Lily.'

'What are you going to say?' Jess was worried. Was she about to lose everything?

'Nothing yet,' he said as he stood up. 'I'm not an idiot. This is a shock for me, it's going to be a shock for her too. I just want to see my daughter. Is that too much to ask?'

Jess shook her head and walked with him to the ward. She hesitated outside the door to Lily's room.

'Aren't you coming in?' Lucas asked.

'I wasn't sure whether you wanted me to.'

'Lily might think it's odd if she wakes up to find me by her bed. You're the one she'll be looking for.'

Lily was still asleep. Lucas stood by her bed. He didn't speak, just stood and watched her. Jess knew that feeling. She used to spend hours just watching Lily sleep when she'd been a baby. She looked like a little angel.

She stirred and murmured. She opened her eyes and recognised Jess but didn't wake fully. 'I need Ozzie,' she said.

Jess pulled the little grey koala with white-tipped ears and a shiny black nose out of her handbag and tucked it under Lily's arm. Lily never liked sleeping without Ozzie. She hugged the soft toy into her chest and closed her eyes again.

'Is that…?' Lucas spoke.

Jess nodded. It was the koala he'd given her for her eighteenth birthday seven years ago.

'You've kept it?'

'It was all I had of you.' Jess could hear the catch in her throat. The little koala had been the cutest thing she'd ever seen, aside from Lucas, and it had become her most treasured possession throughout her pregnancy, and now it was Lily's.

'Does Lily know where you got it?'

'No.' Jess shook her head and turned as she heard the door open.

Dr Davis stepped into the room and he held a piece of paper in his hand. 'I have the blood-test results,' he told them. 'Lily has tested positive for TTG antibodies and the test also showed elevated antigliadin antibodies.

'What does that mean?'

'It means Lily *could* have celiac disease.'

'Could?'

'The blood test isn't definitive,' he reminded her.

'So what do we do now?'

'You can take her home once this drip has run through, provided she has something to eat and keeps it down.'

'She doesn't need to stay overnight?'

'No. With her history and the blood test and scan results I think a bowel obstruction is unlikely so provided she eats, doesn't vomit and can urinate, you can take her home. But she will need an endoscopy and biopsy of her small intestine in order to confirm the diagnosis.'

'A biopsy? What for?'

'To look for inflammation of the intestinal lining and changes to the villi. That's a more definitive indication of celiac disease. Lily will need to see a specialist for the endoscopy. It will be done under a GA. I'll organise a referral. Has she seen a gastroenterologist in the past?'

Jess shook her head. 'No.'

'Who would you recommend?' Lucas asked. 'Who is the best paediatric gastroenterologist in Vancouver?'

'Stuart Johnson.'

Jess had known that would be the answer. 'Is there anyone else?' she asked.

'Of course,' Dr Davis replied, 'but you asked who the best is and in my opinion Dr Johnson is. But I can give you some other names if you prefer.'

Lucas jumped in before Jess could protest any further. 'He will be fine. We'll take that referral.'

'Okay. Do you have any other questions? I'm not an expert but at this stage I wouldn't panic. It looks like celiac disease may be the problem and if that's the case it's one of the easier gastrointestinal problems to control. Just make sure you keep Lily eating some gluten. If you stop before she sees the specialist they may not be able to make an accurate diagnosis. If she has a diet that is already low in gluten we could see a false negative. The recommendation is that she should continue to eat two slices of bread, or the equivalent amount of gluten, per day.'

Lucas waited until the doctor had left the room before he turned to Jess. She knew what he was about to say.

'What is the matter with Stuart Johnson?' he asked. 'Do you know him? Is he a relative? What's wrong with him?'

'He's my father.'

'Your father! Your father is a gastroenterologist?'

'Yes.'

'And he's the top dog?'

'What's going on, JJ? If your father is the best in his field, why did you ask for a different referral? Why don't you want to take Lily to him?'

Jess had managed to delay the discussion until Lily had been discharged and they were in Lucas's car on the way home. Lily seemed to have fully recovered from whatever it was that had upset her. There was no trace of the vomiting, she'd had a good sleep and appeared to have no lingering ill-effects. Jess, on the other hand, was exhausted, physically and emotionally, but she knew Lucas wasn't going to let matters lie.

Lily was cuddling Ozzie while she listened to Lucas's Christmas music through the headphones on his cell phone when he raised the subject again, and Jess figured she might as well get the conversation over with while Lily was out of earshot and otherwise occupied. Maybe it would be easier if Lucas was concentrating on driving and couldn't interrogate her or pin her down with eye contact. 'What do you remember about my father?' she asked.

'That's a loaded question. The only time I came across him was on your birthday when he called me all sorts of colourful names and threw me out. You probably don't want to know my impressions of him as a person.'

'And you're asking why I don't want him to be Lily's specialist?'

'If he's the best in the business then I assume his behaviour that night isn't a reflection on his skills as a doctor. I'm prepared to separate the two. If he's the best I want him to see Lily.'

'My father and I aren't in contact any more.'

'What?' Lucas slowed the car as he took his eyes off the road and looked at her. 'At all?'

Jess shook her head.

'Since when?'

'Since Lily was born. I haven't seen him for six years. He's never met Lily.'

Lucas flicked his gaze back to her a second time. 'If we are going to have any chance of working things out between us, for Lily's sake, we need to operate on a policy of full disclosure. No more secrets. I think it's time you told me everything.' His hands were tight on the steering-wheel and Jess could hear in his voice the effort he was making to stay calm.

She took a deep breath and said, 'Remember I told you how Stephen's death shaped us into the family we became? How I was protected, supervised, guarded almost, from that day on? I went to school, I spent time with Kristie and we came up here as a family. I went to parties but only if Dad had thoroughly researched the event. I understood his reasons—he was determined to do everything he could to keep me safe—and it didn't really bother me until I met you.

'That was when I finally understood Kristie's point of view when it came to boys. For the first time I was prepared to disregard my parents' wishes. For the first time I was prepared to take risks, to ignore their rules, to lie to them or to my aunt and uncle. I couldn't resist you and I couldn't forgive my father for dragging me away from you, for separating us. You were my first love. I couldn't resist you and I gave you everything. My heart and my soul.'

'You gave me everything except for our child,' Lucas said, as he glanced in the rear-vision mirror.

Jess clenched her hands in her lap as she willed herself not to cry. Lucas's words were like a sledgehammer against her already brittle heart and she could feel how close it was to shattering. She had done her best but it didn't seem as though he was prepared to believe that. Maybe, given time, he would trust her again. She'd never deliberately kept Lily from him and maybe one day he would realise that.

She checked back over her shoulder to where Lily lay with her eyes closed. She was either sleeping or listening to music but either way she wasn't paying them any attention. Jess needed Lucas to understand what had happened. She needed to try to explain.

'That's not fair. I told you I tried to find you. If my father had had his way you wouldn't have Lily now either. She is the reason I haven't seen him for six years.'

'Lily is?'

Jess nodded. 'My relationship with Dad had been strained ever since we left Moose River. He was still furious that I'd lied to my aunt and uncle and that I hadn't followed the rules, and finding out I was pregnant was the icing on the cake. I thought that maybe it would be good news, maybe it would help to ease the pain of Stephen's loss, but Dad was convinced it was going to ruin my life. He didn't want me to keep the baby and, as I've explained, he convinced me that you wouldn't want to be a father. He used the argument that you'd never tried to contact me. He was quite persuasive and I even started to question whether you'd given me your real name.'

'Of course I had.'

'I know that now but you have to understand that I was only eighteen and not a very mature eighteen. I was naive and uncertain and scared, and Dad's argument was quite convincing.'

'What did he want you to do? Did he want you to terminate the pregnancy?'

'No! He would never have asked me to do that. We may have had our differences of opinion on lots of things but that wasn't one of them. After losing a child of his own, he wouldn't have wanted me to terminate a pregnancy. He wanted me to give the baby up for adoption.'

'But why?

'He was worried that I was too young. That having a baby at the age of eighteen would ruin my life, my plans for the future. He tried to convince me that there were other options, that I didn't have to be a single mother. Obviously, I refused to give her up. I hadn't planned on getting pregnant but I had a baby growing inside me and it was my job to protect her. Plus she was yours— I couldn't give her up.

'So I decided to keep the baby and prove to my father that I could manage on my own, that I didn't need his help. I was going to prove I could handle the conse-

quences. It was stupid really. I had no idea about anything but I resented my father for taking me away from
you and I wasn't going to let him take my baby as well.
So I sacrificed the bond I had with my father for the
love I felt for Lily. I told my father I was keeping the
baby and if he thought I was making a mistake then I
would do it on my own and he need have nothing to do
with me or his grandchild.'

'Was it a mistake?'

'I certainly hadn't planned on getting pregnant but
being with you wasn't a mistake. And Lily isn't a mistake.' Jess glanced back again at her sleeping daughter. Their daughter. Lily was perfect and Jess had never
regretted her decision. 'I was a naive teenager with no
clue but a massive stubborn streak. It hasn't been easy
but I don't regret it.'

'I'm sorry, JJ. It's been tough on you and I'm sorry
to have to ask you this, but don't you think it's time you
swallowed your pride and moderated your stubborn
streak? Don't you think you should try to sort things
out with your father? For Lily's sake?'

Jess shook her head. 'No. Too much has happened.
I'm not sure I can go back.' Her entire life had changed
and all the decisions she'd made, for the right or wrong
reasons, had brought her to where she was now. She
didn't think her decisions could be reversed that easily.
She didn't know if she could do it. 'Couldn't we just ask
for a couple of other names? It would be a lot easier.'

'But your father is the best. You're telling me you don't
want your daughter, our daughter, to have the best medical attention we can give her? Because I sure as hell do.'

'Let me make some calls,' Jess begged, as Lucas
indicated and turned the car onto Moose River Road.

'Let me see what other specialists I can come up with. Please? Just give me twenty-four hours.'

'I'll do you a deal. I'd like to spend some time with Lily so assuming she's feeling okay tomorrow I will pick her up in the morning and she and I can do something together while you sort out a specialist. We both have some decisions to make.'

Jess was worried. Was this going to be the beginning of deals and bargaining? Was Lily's time now up for negotiation? But she couldn't refuse his request. Not if she wanted to win the argument over the specialist.

Lucas parked his SUV in front of the Moose River Apartments. He carried a drowsy Lily inside for Jess but he didn't stay. He didn't stop under the mistletoe and he didn't speak to Jess again. It was as if he didn't even notice she was there.

Whatever Jess had dreamt of having was surely gone. She wasn't going to get the fairy-tale ending. They weren't going to be the perfect family on a Christmas card. She'd be lucky if she was left with anything at all.

But was that just what she deserved?

CHAPTER TEN

'How did you get on?'

Lucas spoke to Jess as she walked into the stables behind the lodge but there was no 'Good morning'. No 'How are you?' There were obviously more important things on his mind.

Lily had spent the morning with Lucas while Jess was supposed to be organising a specialist appointment. Lily had chosen to groom Banjo and she barely looked up when Jess arrived. It was obvious that Lily had enjoyed the morning far more than Jess had. She seemed quite content with Lucas's company and Jess knew Lily was smitten with him. Why wouldn't she be? He had that same effect on her. Did neither of them need her? Would they be just as happy with each other? Without her?

Everything was changing and Jess was worried.

Jess shook her head in response to Lucas's question as she tried to stem the rising fear in her belly.

'Lily, why don't you finish up with Banjo and then François can bring you to the restaurant for a hot chocolate when you're all done? Your mum and I have some things we need to talk about.'

'Okay,' Lily said. She barely looked up, content just to be with Banjo.

'Have you made a specialist appointment?' Lucas asked as they left the stable to return to the lodge.

Jess had spoken to Cameron but she'd got nowhere with alternative options. She shook her head. 'I couldn't get anything until well into the New Year,' she admitted. 'The doctors Cameron could call in favours from are both on holidays and Lily's condition isn't considered serious so no one else would squeeze her in.'

'I'm sure your father would see her earlier,' Lucas argued. 'I understand your history with your father—you were eighteen and on your own—but I'm here now and if you think I'm not going to be an active part of Lily's life you're mistaken. One way or another I will make sure she gets a diagnosis and the treatment she needs. If she is a celiac then staying on a gluten diet could be doing her more damage. If she is a celiac she'll feel a whole lot better once gluten is eliminated from her diet and we can't do that until she's had the biopsy. We already have a referral to your father,' he continued. 'If you prefer I'll take Lily. You don't need to come. You owe me this much.'

Jess shook her head. She'd already come to the same conclusion. She didn't want Lily to suffer any more than necessary. She knew what she had to do. 'I know she needs the appointment. I'll make the call but I'll take her. Lily is my daughter. She'll need me there.'

'She is also my daughter and that is something else I wanted to speak to you about. When are we going to tell her the truth?'

'Can it wait until the holidays? There's a lot for her

to digest and I think it will be better if she has time to think about it.' Jess honestly felt it would be better to wait a little longer but she also didn't want to deal with the repercussions.

'I'll wait,' Lucas agreed. 'But only until the end of the school term. She finishes on Friday, right?'

Jess nodded.

'I'll take you both to dinner on Friday night, then,' he said, as he held the door for her to step into the lobby. 'We can speak to her together. I'd like to be able to tell my parents about her before Christmas. I was planning on going back to Australia at the end of the ski season and I would like to take Lily too.'

Jess stopped dead in her tracks. He wanted to take Lily!

Black spots danced in front of her eyes and she thought she might either faint or throw up but if she couldn't stand the idea of giving her baby up at birth there was no way she was going to give her up now after six years of being her mother. She might not be able to deny him but she wasn't going to give up without a fight. She stood up as tall as possible and willed her vision to clear. She clenched her fists and tightened her thigh muscles as she tried to stop her knees from shaking. 'No.'

Lucas was frowning. 'What do you mean, "No"?'

'I left Moose River seven years ago, heartbroken and pregnant. Lily was all I had left.' Her voice was quiet but firm. 'I'm sorry I couldn't find you. I'm sorry I didn't try again. I'm sorry that you never posted me those letters and I'm sorry that you've missed six years of her life. I was foolish and I'm sorry but I'm not going to let you take her away from me. I've lost my brother and my mother and my father. Lily is all I have left. I won't let you take her from me.'

'I don't think you were foolish.'

'You don't?' After everything she'd admitted to he wasn't going to crucify her?

'No.' He shook his head. 'I've never said that.' He put his hand on her elbow and guided her to one of the soft leather couches in the lobby. He sat beside her and put his hand on her knee and only then did Jess stop shaking.

'You've made it this far on your own and from what I can see you've done a great job with Lily. She's a great kid and she's lucky enough to have a mother who loves her. I admit I wish I'd known about her before now but I know I have to take some of the blame for that. And I don't intend to take Lily away from you. I'd like to take her to Australia—she's got a whole family over there who would love to meet her—but I'm only talking about going for a holiday. My life is here now. My business is here and my daughter is here. I'm not going to abandon her and I would never take her from you. I assumed you would come with us.'

'Really?' Relief flooded through Jess and she thought she might burst into tears. Her emotions had been running high for days and being close to tears was almost becoming a permanent state for her. 'Even after everything I've done?'

'What's done is done, JJ,' he replied. 'We can't undo the past. We need to move on and Lily has to be our priority. She's the important one. We need to do what's best for her. We need to make sure she feels loved and secure and we need to sort out her health. So will you make an appointment to take Lily to see your father?'

'Yes.' She had no choice. She owed it to Lily and to Lucas. She would have to mend the relationship with her father. After seven years of making all her own decisions it seemed as though her time was up. Fate, or maybe Lucas, was taking over.

Jess was sweating as she picked up the phone and dialled her father's office number. She had never forgotten it, even after all these years. She just hoped he still had the same secretary. How would she explain her request if her father's admin staff had changed?

She'd delayed phoning her father's office until this morning. She'd spent last night trying to work out how to word her request. It seemed strange to be calling to ask for a favour from her father when she hadn't spoken to him in over six years. But it looked like it was time for Jess to be the bigger person and put her stubborn streak to one side, as Lucas had suggested.

She sighed with relief when Gabrielle answered. Jess launched into the speech she'd rehearsed before she could chicken out and she had just hung up the phone when there was a knock on her door. It opened and Cameron stepped in to her clinic room.

'Jess, has Lily gone on the school excursion to go dog sledding?'

What a strange question. Jess frowned and nodded.

'I don't want you to panic, everyone is okay at this stage, but there's been an accident.'

You couldn't tell someone not to panic right before delivering that sort of news. Jess shot out of her seat. 'What is it? What's happened?'

'There's been an accident on one of the chairlifts.'

Jess's hand flew to her mouth as her heart plummeted in her chest. *'Lily.'*

'The children are all okay at this stage but the lift has stopped working and there are people trapped in the cars. I thought you might want to go up the mountain. I'm sure the authorities will contact everyone but I wanted you to know.'

Jess changed her shoes and grabbed her coat. She didn't need to be asked twice.

She raced out of the building and collided with Lucas.

'What are you doing here?' She looked up at him as his arms went around her to steady her. One look at his face told her that he'd heard about the accident too. Of course, he was part of the search and rescue unit.

'What have you heard?' she asked.

'Not a lot at this stage except that no one seems to be injured yet and that a group of six- and seven-year-olds are involved. I thought that might mean Lily. But no one will notify me because I'm not her next of kin. I didn't know if you would call me so I came to you.'

'Have you been called in to the rescue?'

He shook his head and let her go. 'No, this is a mission for the trained team. I came to find out if Lily was in the gondola and to take you up the mountain.' He gestured to his left where a snowmobile was parked at the bottom of the steps. 'It'll be faster than taking the chair lift to the basin and then walking.'

She didn't waste time arguing. She pulled a knitted cap from her pocket and tugged it onto her head as Lucas handed her a pair of snow goggles. She followed him down the steps and climbed onto the snowmobile behind him. She tucked herself against his back and wrapped her arms around his waist. He was solid and muscular. He felt safe. Maybe he really was her knight in shining armour after all.

There was no denying he was a good man. Maybe they would be okay. She and Lucas would work things out. She'd make sure of it. For Lily's sake.

After several minutes Jess felt the snowmobile slow and knew they'd reached the basin. She peered around Lucas's shoulder and saw a group of people, parents of children in Lily's class, gathered around the base of one of the gondola pylons.

Lucas switched off the engine. The lift was motionless and the silence was eerie. Jess had expected noise and activity but everyone seemed to be standing around. Immobile. Uncertain.

They dismounted and Jess removed her goggles. She needed a clearer picture.

They were close to the edge of a gully. The gondola cable stretched across the ravine and Jess's eye was drawn to where it dipped lower. She could see what looked like two cars close together. Weren't they normally further apart than that? Or was she just looking at it from a funny angle?

'What's going on? Why isn't anything happening?' she asked Lucas.

'I'm not sure. I'll go and find out.'

He was back within minutes, bringing Fleur and her husband, Nathan, with him. Fleur's eyes were puffy and her nose was red but she wasn't crying at the moment. Jess hugged her tightly. 'Where are the girls?' she asked.

Fleur pointed down into the ravine to where it looked as though two cars had collided. 'They're in one of those cars.'

'Oh, no!'

'The girls are okay, JJ,' Lucas told her. 'There's a teacher in the gondola with them and she is in contact via her cell phone. No one is badly injured. The second car hasn't come loose but access is difficult.'

Jess released Fleur and turned to Lucas. 'When will they get them out?'

'It's going to take time. It's complicated. No one is getting out of any of the cars until the rescue team are certain that it is safe to do so. They're worried that emptying or moving the cars that haven't been involved in the derailment may cause the unstable cars to fall.'

'They could fall?' Jess clutched Lucas's arm.

'At the moment they think the cars are stable.'

'At the moment! I don't understand how this could happen. How is something like this even possible?'

'Apparently the emergency brake was accidentally activated, which caused one car to derail. The grip holding that car to the cable must have been faulty and when the cable jolted the car bounced and the grip released, but when it slid back into the other car they locked together and so far that has prevented it from falling. But because of where the cars are, getting to them will be tricky. They're talking about rigging up a second cable from tower to tower so that the mountain rescue team can access the gondolas from above. They'll have to secure the cars and then use harnesses and stretchers to lower everyone to safety. It's going to take time,' he repeated.

Jess wrapped her arms around herself. Despite the chill in the air she could feel herself breaking into a sweat. Fear gripped her heart and squeezed it tight. She couldn't bear to think of all the things that could go wrong. She couldn't bear to think of Lily up there, scared and in danger.

Lucas pulled her against his chest. She didn't want to imagine going through this on her own. Whatever happened, she knew she could rely on him. He would be there for Lily and she knew he'd be there for her too. He had promised her that much. She needed to give him something in return.

'If Lily is okay I promise I will give you whatever you want,' she said as she looked up at him. 'We'll tell her the truth tonight.'

Lucas hated feeling useless. He hated not being needed. He'd organised the lodge to send up hot refreshments but that had been the sum total of his assistance, and he wished there was more he could do. Standing around waiting while other people were being constructive didn't sit well with him. His child was trapped in one of the cars and he could do nothing.

He knew this rescue required the expertise of trained personnel and he didn't want to put anyone at risk by having people who were not fully qualified sticking their oar in, and that included him, but it didn't stop him from feeling inadequate.

Fleur and Nathan had gone to get something to eat, leaving him alone with Jess. She hadn't wanted to join the larger group of parents who waited anxiously to hug their children. She said she didn't want to talk to anyone. She sat on the snowmobile and chewed her lip while he paced around in the snow.

The whole process was slow going. Lucas and Jess had been on site for two hours and the gondolas had only just been secured. It was bitterly cold and unpleasant but no one was going anywhere. Hot drinks, soup and blankets were being passed around to the parents and some shelters had been brought up the mountain in an attempt to provide some protection from the biting wind. The wind was blowing straight up the gully, rocking the cars. The wind was strengthening and in Lucas's opinion the rescue team had managed to secure the cars just in time. Any longer and the wind would have made the project even more difficult, treacherous even, but at least the sky was clear. No snow was forecast and that was something to be grateful for. That was one less thing for the mountain rescue team to have to contend with.

'Do you want to sit down for a while?' Jess asked him.

He shook his head. 'I can't sit still. I'm finding it hard enough knowing that other people are being useful while I'm hanging around, twiddling my thumbs.'

Jess had promised him that if they got through this they would tell Lily the truth and he had to believe that everything would be okay. But it was proving difficult. He'd only just discovered the truth and he wasn't prepared to have Lily taken away from him now. 'I wish there was more I could do.'

'You're helping me.' Jess smiled up at him and reached out one hand.

'How?' he asked as he took her hand in his.

'It's nice to know I'm not alone. I'm glad you're here.'

He let her pull him down to sit beside her on the snowmobile. He wrapped his arm around her shoulders and tried to be content with the moment while avoiding thinking about all the things that could go wrong. He could sit still if Jess needed him to. She could anchor him. Sitting with her tucked against his side would settle him.

'Talk to me about Lily,' he said. Talking might keep his mind occupied. It might keep him too busy to worry and there was so much he didn't know about his daughter. He was still coming to terms with the idea that he was a father. He felt the weight of responsibility, to both Lily and Jess, but he was looking forward to the changes this development would bring. He didn't expect it to be easy.

There was a lot he and Jess needed to sort out but he was determined they would manage. He wished he hadn't missed six years of his daughter's life but that was as much his fault as Jess's and all he could do now was make certain he got to share the rest with them both. He refused to think that he wasn't going to get that chance and, in the meantime, he needed to learn as much about Lily as he could. He needed to get to know his daughter.

'She was born at half past six in the morning, six twenty-eight, to be exact, and she weighed seven pounds, five ounces.' Jess's voice lifted as she spoke about their daughter. This conversation wasn't just helping him. It was keeping her mind occupied too. 'She was in a hurry and she didn't come quietly. She hasn't been afraid to let me know what she's thinking ever since. She can be quite stubborn.'

Lucas smiled. 'Sounds like someone else I know.'

Jess nudged him in the side and said, 'She's got plenty of you in her as well.'

'Really?' He was surprised at how pleased he was to hear that. 'Good traits, I hope?'

'Mostly,' Jess teased. 'She's becoming quite a confident skier. I suspect she got her sense of balance from you, and her fearlessness—those things definitely didn't come from me. She has a very strong sense of self and have you noticed she has your ears?'

'I'm glad she got a little bit of me. There's no doubting she's your daughter, but it's nice to know I had something to do with it.'

'Don't worry, there's plenty of you in her. Her eyes aren't always green, they change colour depending on what she wears and if she wears blue they can look like yours. She started walking when she was thirteen months old and lost her first tooth at the beginning of this year. She loves roast chicken and carrots and Disney princesses and her koala and your horse, Banjo. Her favourite colour is pink and she loves to sing.'

Jess paused as around them noise started building. Low murmurs became a buzz of anticipation and people were on the move. The rescue crews in their bright yellow jackets were going past, carrying harnesses, and the ski patrol and ambos carried stretchers and first-aid kits. Lucas knew what that meant.

He stood and reached for her hand. 'They're starting to evacuate the cars.'

They hurried closer and stood waiting. The derailed car was the first to be evacuated but eventually it was Lily's turn.

Jess burst into tears when she spied Lily being lowered from the gondola in a harness. She ran through the snow and scooped her into her arms.

'My precious girl, are you all right?'

'I'm fine, Mum.' She was beaming. 'That was the best excursion *ever*.'

'She sounds okay to me.' Lucas grinned but relief washed over him too.

Jess laughed and wiped the tears from her cheeks. 'You've only been on one other excursion, Lil.' She brushed Lily's hair from her forehead and dropped a kiss there. Her fingers ran gently over the spot she'd just kissed. 'You've got a nasty bump on your head here—are you sure you're okay?'

'I was leaning on the window when the other gondola car crashed into us and I bumped my head. You should have heard the big bang it made.'

'Your head or the car?' Lucas asked.

Lily giggled. 'The car. It sounded like thunder and we all fell on the floor.'

Snow cats had been sent up the mountain to ferry the children back to the medical centre, where they would be checked for any injuries, frostnip or concussion. Jess climbed into the vehicle with Lily, she wasn't prepared to let her out of her sight, and Lucas took the snowmobile back down the mountain and met them at the clinic.

'Is she *still* talking?' he said, as he watched Lily gossiping with a group of friends as they drank hot chocolate and waited to be given the all-clear after their ordeal.

'The whole adventure has given her plenty to say. This is the most excitement she's ever had. She definitely takes after her father.' Jess spoke quietly but her words were accompanied by a smile. 'I always avoided drama.'

'Nature versus nurture?' he asked.

'It looks that way.'

Lucas took Jess's arm and gently pulled her to one side of the bustling waiting room. The noise level was high and he was fairly sure they could talk without being overheard but he made sure he kept Lily within sight. For Jess's sake and his own. 'Will you bring her over to the lodge when you're finished here? I'd like to talk to her tonight.'

Jess frowned and a little crease appeared between her eyebrows, making her look exactly like her daughter. Their daughter. 'I don't know. Don't you think she's had enough for one day?'

'I was as worried as you were up on the mountain, JJ. I want to be part of Lily's life and I want that to start today. I don't want any more missed moments. She's resilient. Look at how she coped with the events of today. She'll cope with this. Besides, it's good news.'

Jess paused and Lucas held his breath. He didn't want to wait. He wanted to be acknowledged as Lily's father.

Finally she nodded. 'All right. I'll take her home for a warm bath and then we'll come over.'

'Lily, your mum and I have something to tell you.'

Lily paused momentarily with one hand on Banjo's neck. It had been Jess's suggestion that they go to the stable and he had agreed without reservation. Grooming Banjo was a soothing, familiar activity for Lily and it meant they didn't have to sit awkwardly in the hotel to have this conversation. 'Is it a surprise?' she asked. 'I love surprises.'

'It was a surprise for me,' Lucas told her. 'But it's something I'm very excited about. Something I've wished for for a long time.'

'Lil, you know how I've always said you were made up of bits and pieces?' Jess asked her.

Lily nodded and tilted her head as she replied, 'Like a platypus.'

'That's right. Well, the outside bits of you are just like me,' Jess said, 'but some of the inside bits of you are different. Parts of your insides are funny and other parts are curious and other parts are brave, much braver than me, and you get those parts from your dad.'

Lily frowned and Lucas was reminded of how Jess had looked earlier in the day. 'I don't have a dad.'

'Everyone has a dad somewhere, sweetheart. I just lost your dad for a while and it took me a long time to find him again.'

'Is he nice?'

'He's very nice.'

Jess smiled at Lucas as she spoke to their daughter, and Lucas finally had what he'd wished for. He remembered the expression on Jess's face the night she'd told him about her relationship with Lily's father. How she'd looked when she'd told him that she'd loved Lily's dad. He'd seen the love in her eyes that night and he'd wished she'd been talking about him. He hadn't known then that he was Lily's father but she had that same expression in her eyes tonight. She'd said she loved him then. Did she love him still?

'Will he like me?' Lily wanted to know.

'He will *love* you. Very much. But I think he might want to tell you that himself.'

'When can I see him?'

'He's right here, Lily.'

'Where?'

'It's me, Lily,' Lucas told her 'I'm your dad.'

'Really?'

'Really.' He nodded. 'And I think I'm the luckiest dad in the world.'

'This is the best day ever,' Lily said, as she threw her arms around his neck and burrowed in against his chest.

He'd been worried about her reaction to their news. Holding his child in his arms was the most incredible feeling and he would have been devastated if Lily hadn't wanted him. He didn't think he would be able to give her up after this. What would he have done if she hadn't been as thrilled about the news as Jess had assured him she would be? What if she hadn't been as excited as he'd hoped she would be?

He wondered how Jess was feeling. He looked over the top of Lily's head. Jess was smiling but he could see a glimmer of tears in her eyes. How did she feel about having to share Lily?

Lily had fallen asleep on his couch after polishing off her dinner. Lucas looked at his sleeping daughter. Her blonde head was resting on Jess's lap and she had Ozzie, the koala, tucked under her arm. She was beautiful. She was perfect.

'What is it?' Jess asked him.

'I think it's incredible that we made her.' He'd never felt that anything was missing in his life but now that Jess was back in it, and Lily too, he wondered how he could not have known that there should be more. 'And that she accepted me so easily.'

'She thinks you're fabulous.'

'She does?'

'Why wouldn't she? You own a horse and sleigh.' Jess was smiling at him and his heart swelled with love for her and their daughter. His family.

He needed to make that his reality.

Thinking of family made him think of hers. 'Have you spoken to your father yet?'

Jess shook her head. 'Not exactly. But I did speak to his secretary this morning. Luckily she's been working for him for ever and she has booked Lily in for the biopsy on the Wednesday before Christmas. I meant to tell you but with all the drama today I forgot,' she said as she stifled a yawn.

'But you didn't speak to your father.'

'No. I couldn't do it. Talking to him on the phone didn't seem right but I don't know what to do. I don't want to have our first conversation in six years just before Lily goes into the operating theatre—that won't be any good for any of us—but I'm running out of time.'

'Sleep on it,' he said, as she stifled another yawn. 'A solution will present itself.' He had an idea that might just work. 'And why don't you take my bed for the night?' he offered. 'There's no point in waking Lily to take her home.'

Jess shook her head. 'Thanks, but if you bring me a blanket I'll be perfectly happy to sleep in front of the fire. I need to stay close to her, I don't want her to wake up in unfamiliar surroundings without me. Not after the day she's had.'

'I'll move her to my bed, then, and I'll take the couch.'

He picked Lily up. She was feather-light in his arms and snuggled in against his chest, still fast asleep. Jess followed him into his bedroom and pulled the comforter back. He tucked Lily under it before dropping a kiss on her forehead.

They stood together and watched Lily sleep. 'I still can't quite believe I have a daughter. It's incredible.

Thank you, JJ. For giving me this gift. For being strong enough to make what must have been a tough decision. Do you mind sharing Lily with me?'

Jess shook her head. 'Of course not. I never wanted to do this on my own and having you in Lily's life will be a good thing for her—provided we can figure out how it's all going to work.'

'We will,' he agreed, 'but not tonight. There have been enough decisions made today.' He turned Jess to face him. 'But I do have one more question for you. I want to be a part of your life too.'

'You will be. We'll always be connected through our daughter.'

'I want more than that. I want a chance to have a relationship with you that goes beyond us as parents. I want more. I want you.'

'You want me? After everything I've done?'

'Look around you, JJ. Everything I've done has been with you in mind. I know I said I wanted to prove a point to your father but I wouldn't have bothered with that if it wasn't for you. You were the reason I've done this. You were the reason I came back. I admit I've got more than I bargained for but I'm thrilled about that. The past is the past. I meant it when I said there's no point dwelling on it. It can't be changed. We all had a hand to play in the mess we made—me, you and your father—but what's done is done. It doesn't change how I feel about you or Lily. All we can do is look to the future. We have the rest of our lives to make up for lost time.'

'Really?'

'That was my plan.' He was smiling, grinning like a lovestruck fool. He loved her and he wanted to be 'the one' for her. He wanted them to be a family. 'Do you have other plans that I should know about?'

Jess shook her head. 'No.'

'Good.' He took Jess's face in his hands, cupping her cheeks gently between his palms, and tipped her head up. Her green eyes were wide, her lips plump and pink. He wanted her to be his. He wanted to claim her for his own.

He bent his head and covered her lips with his, pouring his love into her and sealing it with a kiss. She tasted like vanilla ice cream, innocent and sweet, and he made a promise to himself that he would take care of her, of her and Lily, if she would let him. He would convince her, he would persuade her, he would charm her and love her until she agreed to give herself to him. And then he would be content.

CHAPTER ELEVEN

JESS'S HEART POUNDED in her chest and her arm felt as if it weighed a tonne as she reached for the door handle of the lodge suite. Her hand was shaking and her palms were clammy. 'I don't think I can do this,' she said to Lucas.

He'd told her he would take care of things but she hadn't expected him to do it so quickly and she also hadn't expected her father to agree to Lucas's suggestion, but it seemed as though she had been wrong on both counts because her father was here, in Moose River, and he was waiting for her.

'It'll be okay, JJ, and I'll be just outside if you need me. Remember, this time I've got your back.' Lucas's voice gave her the courage to turn the handle. 'You can do this.'

She pushed the door open. 'Daddy?'

He was halfway across the room, coming to meet her. He was tall and still trim, although his dark hair was greyer than she remembered. He was sixty now. She'd missed his sixtieth birthday and he'd missed her twenty-first. For what? Why?

Because she was stubborn.

But his arms were open, forgiving, inviting. She

burst into tears and stepped into his embrace. 'I'm sorry, Dad,' she said, as his arms tightened around her. He'd only ever wanted to protect her and she'd repaid him by cutting him out of her life.

She closed her eyes and sobbed and let him hug her as he'd done when she'd been a child. She could feel the tension in her shoulders ease. She could feel the forgiveness in his embrace and all the anxiety that had been building up, all her nervousness over this meeting slipped away as he held her.

'I'm sorry too, Jessie.' He stepped back to look at her, pulling a clean handkerchief out of his pocket and handing it to her.

She smiled through her tears. 'You still carry a handkerchief.' It was one of the many things she remembered about him. Her father wore cufflinks and always had a clean hankie in his pocket.

'Always,' he replied. 'Some things never change. It's good to see you, sweetheart.'

'You too, Dad.' Jess looked around the room. She could smell coffee. There was a pot and two mugs on the sideboard. Only two cups. 'Is Mum here?' she asked.

'No. I wasn't sure how receptive you were going to be. She wouldn't be able to handle any confrontation.'

Jess was disappointed and she felt her shoulders drop. 'I wasn't planning on being confrontational,' she told him. She hadn't been planning anything. This had all been Lucas's idea. But it was silly to feel disappointed about her mother's absence when she hadn't even been sure if she herself wanted to come to the meeting. Why should her mother feel any differently?

Her father must have heard the disappointment in her voice. 'I'm sorry, Jessie. But we'll work it out. This is the first step. I promise I'll do everything I can to make sure we will be a family again.' He reached into his pocket and pulled out his wallet. 'I have something I want to show you.' He flipped his wallet open and handed it to her.

He'd always had a photo of her and Stephen as children in the plastic sleeve but that was gone now. Jess stared at the replacement. Her own eyes stared back at her. The photo was one of her and Lily. It was a photo Kristie had taken on Lily's sixth birthday.

She sat on the sofa and slipped the photo out of the sleeve. Behind it was the old photo of her and Stephen. She held the picture of Lily in her hands and looked up at her father. 'Where did you get this?'

'Kristie gave it to Aunt Carol. She gave it to me.'

'Why?'

'I asked for it.' Her father dragged an armchair across the floor, positioning it at an angle to the sofa, so that he was nearby without crowding Jess. 'I know I wasn't very supportive when you told me you were pregnant and were planning on keeping the baby. I didn't understand how you could make that decision at the age of eighteen but when you cut me out of your life I felt like I'd lost both of my children, first Stephen and then you. Kristie was my link to you, to you and to Lily. I tried to keep in touch with you but when you returned all my letters I had to rely on your aunt and uncle to give me news over the years. I couldn't stand the thought of you being lost to me for ever.'

Her father had sent her a letter, along with a birthday card and a sizeable cheque for Lily, every year. Kristie had always delivered it for them but Jess hadn't realised things had been going back in the other direction. Jess had kept the cards—she had boxed them up and put them away for Lily—but she had returned the letters and the cheques, still determined to prove she could manage on her own. Determined to prove she didn't need anything from her father.

But all this time he'd been hearing about Lily. She didn't know why she was surprised. If she'd ever given it any thought she would have figured out that Aunt Carol would have passed on any information her parents asked for. All this time he'd been following Lily's progress. Despite Jess's actions he had never stopped being her father or Lily's grandfather. He had never given up hope.

'I'm sorry I was stubborn. I'm sorry I've kept you out of our lives,' she apologised. 'I returned your letters but I've kept your cards for Lily. I was going to give them to her one day.' She wanted him to know that. It was important.

'Thank you, Jessie.' Her father reached for her hand and Jess gave it to him. 'I've missed you. Do you think we might have a chance to start fresh?'

'I wasn't sure if I could forgive you for separating me from Lucas. I loved him then, I love him still.' Jess felt her father tense and she hurried to continue, to put his mind at ease. 'But he says we need to leave the past behind if we want to move forward and I think he's right. I would like a chance to start again.' She stood up. 'Would you like to meet Lily?'

'Now?'

Jess nodded.

'She's here?'

'She's in the lodge. Lucas is waiting outside. He'll fetch her.'

'I'd love to, Jessie, and if it's all right I'd like to meet Lucas too. After all, I have him to thank for bringing you back into my life.'

Jess nodded. 'Okay. Give me a minute.' She was smiling as she left the suite. Lucas was waiting for her, just as he'd promised.

'You look happy.'

She walked over to him and threw her arms around him, hugging him tightly.

He picked her up and held her close. 'What was that for?' he asked, as he set her back down on her feet.

'It's a thank-you. I think it's going to be okay. Dad wants to meet Lily.'

'That's good. I've already asked Sofia to bring her up and I've ordered some champagne and afternoon tea for you too.'

'You knew it would go well?'

'I could tell when I spoke to him on the phone that he was keen to reconcile. I was pretty sure this would all turn out okay and I'm glad it has so far.'

'He wants to meet you too.'

'Now?'

Jess nodded and Lucas followed her back into the room.

'Dad, this is Lucas White. Lucas, my father, Stuart Johnson.'

Jess's heart was in her throat. *Please, be nice, Dad.*

Stuart was looking at Lucas closely but he stayed silent. He extended his hand and Jess exhaled as they shook hands. They seemed far more relaxed than she was. Perhaps this would turn out all right after all.

'Good to meet you properly at last, sir. I apologise for not taking responsibility before now—'

Stuart cut him off and Jess held her breath again. 'That's all right. I think I owe you an apology. I was hasty in my judgement of you and it cost me my daughter and my granddaughter. Thank you for bringing them back to me.'

'I want you to know that I intend to make it up to Lily,' Lucas said. 'And to Jess. I have the means and the desire to make it up to both of them and I'm not one to shy away from my responsibilities.'

Lucas stood next to her and she took his hand and squeezed it. He circled her waist with his arm and pulled her close, and Jess could almost feel her life turning around. With Lucas beside her, perhaps things would be okay. With him beside her, anything seemed possible. She'd felt lost, adrift and alone with no one except Lily and Kristie. She never would have admitted it, she was too stubborn, but now perhaps she could. With Lucas back in her life and her father and maybe even her mother, she and Lily wouldn't be alone any more.

Maybe she had a chance of finding happiness after all.

Jess was wearing scrubs and was sitting in the operating theatre at the foot of the bed while her father prepared for Lily's biopsy. The anaesthetist gave Lily a very light general anaesthetic and when she gave Stuart the all-clear he slid a flexible tube, complete with a tiny camera, down Lily's oesophagus, through her stomach and into the small intestine. Jess could watch the images on the monitor above their heads. Stuart examined the intestinal lining and took half a dozen samples at various points.

'What are you looking for?' Jess asked. She'd researched the procedure and the disease and she knew she was asking just to hear her father's voice. It was hard to believe he was back in her life.

'Atrophy of the villi and inflammation of the mucosal tissue,' he explained. 'There's a pathologist waiting for the samples as we speak so the results should be back almost immediately.'

The whole process took less than fifteen minutes and the light anaesthetic Lily had been given was reversed quickly. Then it was just a matter of more waiting.

Lucas and Jess were sitting with a drowsy Lily in the day surgery recovery area when Stuart ducked in between surgeries.

He kept his mask on as he spoke to them.

'The results are back. The villi are shrunk and flattened, indicating partial atrophy, and there is an increased presence of lymphocytes and some other changes consistent with inflammation. The Marsh classification is given as Marsh III.'

'What does that mean?'

'It means Lily has celiac disease.'

'Should I have done something about this earlier?' Guilt swamped Jess again.

Her father shook his head. 'From what I've read in her history from the emergency department, any symptoms she did have were so mild they could have been attributed to any number of things. Because it is commonly an inherited condition, finding out Lucas's history was the red flag. I know it's called a disease but you should think of it more as a condition. It's easily controlled as long as you are prepared to be vigilant with Lily's diet. I'm sure Lucas will agree with me, it's not difficult to manage. Once Lily has a gluten-free diet the villi and her intestine will recover.'

'How long does that take?'

'Usually around three to six months, but provided she sticks to a gluten-free diet there won't be any long-term effects. If she doesn't adhere to a strict gluten-free diet there can be other complications but there'll be time to discuss those later. I'll tee up an appointment with a dietician and a counsellor. It'll be okay, Jessie, we'll get through this.' He squeezed her hand. 'I have to get back into Theatre. Will you be all right?'

Jess reached for Lucas's hand and smiled at her father. 'We'll be fine.'

Lily was up bright and early on Christmas morning. She'd had no ill effects following the biopsy and had taken the news about her celiac disease in her stride, just like everything else. In all honesty, Jess suspected Lily was pleased to know that she and Lucas had something tangible in common.

That had been one problem solved. Jess had been busy ticking boxes over the past few days and things were going well. With Lucas's help she was mending her relationship with her parents, both her mother and her father. Lucas had invited them to the lodge for Christmas lunch and they were coming, along with Kristie and her parents. It would be the first family Christmas in many years and Jess and Lily were both excited. Lucas was helping to repair all the damage Jess had done but fortunately everyone seemed prepared to forgive her.

The only other thing still to be finessed was her relationship with Lucas and how they would parent Lily. But Jess knew they would get there. One thing at a time.

Lily was bouncing up and down on Lucas's bed, where she and Jess had spent another night while Lucas had slept on the couch. Jess felt bad about kicking him out of his own bed yet again but he had insisted. He wanted to be there when Lily woke up, he said. He'd missed all of her Christmases to date and he didn't want to miss another one. It was a good argument and Jess had happily agreed.

'Is it time for presents yet?' Lily was asking.

'We'll go and see if your dad is awake.' It was going to take some time to get used to saying that but Jess liked how it sounded.

'Merry Christmas to my girls,' he said, as he kissed them both and handed Jess a coffee.

'Did Santa come?' Lily asked.

'There seems to be a very big present by the fireplace that wasn't there last night,' Lucas was grinning. 'Shall we take a look?'

An enormous gift sat in front of the fireplace and Lily wasted no time in tearing the paper off it to reveal a magnificent doll's house. It was one she had admired at the Christmas market and had working lights and delicate furniture. A curved staircase led from the first to the second floor and a hollow chimney ended in a small fireplace in the lounge that was complete with tiny logs that lit up with fake flames at the flick of a switch. It was elaborate and beautiful.

'I think Santa might have stolen your thunder,' Jess said with a smile as Lily flicked the lights on and off before picking up a tiny music box that was inside the doll's house. She turned the handle on its side and squealed with delight as it played 'Waltzing Matilda'. 'You might not be her favourite today,' Jess added.

'Santa had six years to make up for but I've still got a few tricks up my sleeve.'

He handed Lily a small box. Nestled in tissue paper was a carved wooden sleigh. It had been painted red, just like the Crystal Lodge sleigh. Lily lifted it carefully from the box. Attached to it was a perfect replica of Banjo. 'I love it, Daddy, it looks just like Banjo.'

'Okay, Dad's turn, Lil,' Jess told her, once they'd all finished admiring the tiny horse.

Lily handed Lucas a flat, heavy parcel and then went to play with her doll's house as he unwrapped his gift, revealing a photo album.

He turned the pages of the album. It was filled with photographs of Lily, beginning on the day she'd been born and continuing to her sixth birthday. As Jess described each picture, telling Lucas something about each occasion, Lily's curiosity got the better of her. Fascinated as always by photographs of herself when she'd been younger, she abandoned the doll's house temporarily and climbed onto Lucas's lap. She snuggled against his chest and added to the commentary as he turned the pages. 'That's me when I lost my first tooth,' she said, 'and that's me when I was in the nativity play last year. I was a shepherd. And that's me on the day I started school in Moose River.'

'It's brilliant, JJ,' Lucas said, as he reached the end of the album and closed the book. He leant behind Lily and kissed Jess lightly on the lips. 'Thank you.'

'I have something else for you too,' she said, as she handed him a large, thin envelope. Inside was one sheet of paper.

Lucas slid it out. 'It's Lily's birth certificate.'

Jess nodded. 'I've had it amended,' she said. She

pointed to the word 'Father'. In the box underneath it said 'Lucas White'.

'This is the most perfect gift.'

'It's going to be a perfect Christmas,' Jess replied.

'I hope so. But there's one more thing to do before we reach perfection.'

'What's that?'

'Your present.' Lucas turned to Lily, who had returned to play, and Jess had to smile when she saw that Lily was busy showing mini-Banjo through the house. 'Lil, it's time for Mum's surprise.'

Lily put Banjo down and dived under the Christmas tree to retrieve a gift bag.

Lucas picked up Jess's hand and looked into her eyes. 'JJ, I loved you seven years ago and I love you still. You are beautiful and smart and I never forgot you. I love you and I love Lily. I want us to be a family.' Without letting go of her hand, he got down on one knee beside the couch. Lily was bouncing up and down on the cushion beside Jess, clutching the gift bag. 'Jess Johnson, will you do me the honour of becoming my wife? Will you marry me?'

Jess's eyes filled with tears.

'No! Don't cry, Mum.'

'It's all right, Lil, these are happy tears,' Jess said as she choked back a sob. 'You are my first and only love,' she said to Lucas. 'I have loved you and only you since the moment you first kissed me and, yes, I will marry you.'

Lily threw her arms around them both. 'Hooray,' she shouted.

'Okay, Lily, you can hand over the bag now,' Lucas said, when Lily finally released them.

Inside the bag was a tiny jewellery box. Jess pulled it out and lifted the lid. A princess-cut diamond ring glistened in dark blue velvet. Lucas pulled it from the cushion.

'Just as you have rescued me I promise to always protect you for as long as you need me. I promise to love you and Lily and to keep you safe. Always,' he said, as he slid the ring onto her finger before kissing her.

'I think she likes it,' Lily said, as Jess held her hand out so they could all admire it.

'You knew about this?' Jess asked her.

'Lily helped me choose the ring,' Lucas replied. 'She's nearly as good at keeping secrets as you are.'

'No more secrets. I promise.'

Lily was tugging Jess's arm. 'Now do you think I can have a baby sister?'

Jess smiled and looked into Lucas's forget-me-not-blue eyes. 'We'll see what we can do.'

EPILOGUE

JESS LAY ON a beach towel and let the autumn sun warm her pale skin as she watched Lucas and Lily playing in the famous Bondi surf. Lucas had swapped his snow-board for a surfboard and he was giving Lily her first surfing lesson. She was proving to be a natural, showing Jess once again that nature was just as strong as nurture.

Lucas came out of the water, leaving Lily to practise her surf moves with his youngest brother. He jogged up the beach to Jess and she didn't bother to pretend she wasn't checking him out. They'd been in Australia for a month and Lucas was tanned and fit and gorgeous. And all hers. He stood over her, blocking the sun and giving her a very nice view of his sculpted chest and strong thighs. His board shorts dripped water on the sand as he towelled his hair dry, leaving it even more tousled than normal.

She smiled up at him. 'Lily's having a great time. She's picked it up really fast. She must take after her dad.'

'Your husband,' he said, as he flopped down onto the sand beside her and kissed her.

They had married in Moose River in February and had just celebrated their three-month anniversary with a second ceremony with Lucas's family. It had been a whirlwind few months and Jess was exhausted but elated. She wouldn't change a thing.

'Happy?' he asked.

'Extremely,' she replied, as she rolled onto her side to look at Lucas. Some days she still couldn't believe her good fortune. Lucas was back in her life, he'd given her back her family and he'd given her himself too. She was happy and she had everything she needed. She reached out and picked up her husband's hand. 'But, in the interest of full disclosure, because I promised no more secrets, there is something I need to tell you.'

'Is it that you love me?'

'I do. But that's not a secret.'

'I know, I just like to hear you say "I do".' Lucas laughed and kissed her fingers. 'Sorry, go on.'

'You know how Lily always asks for a baby sister for Christmas? I've been thinking…'

'You think we should make a baby?' Lucas's forget-me-not-blue eyes lit up.

Jess shook her head. 'That wasn't what I was going to say.' She smiled as Lucas's face fell. She knew he was going to love her news. 'It's too late for that. We've already done it.'

'What?'

'I'm pregnant.'

'You are?'

Jess nodded. 'The baby is due the week before Christmas. So it looks as though Lily will get her Christmas wish this year. She's going to have a sibling,' she said, as she brought Lucas's hand to her belly.

'That is fantastic news, JJ. The best.'

'All those things you missed out on with Lily, I

promise you'll be there for every one of them this time around. Do you think that sounds okay?'

'I do.'

Jess closed her eyes and smiled as his lips covered hers.

This was the perfect start to the first day of the rest of their lives.

* * * * *

FROM CHRISTMAS
TO FOREVER?

MARION LENNOX

To the many people who've already made us
welcome in our new home.

To Jacky, to Gail, to Colleen, to Alison, and to
all on Fisherman's Flat, to all who welcome us as
we walk our dog, paddle our kayaks, or simply
yak over the front fence.

You're stuck with us for life, and we love it.

CHAPTER ONE

CHRISTMAS IN THE middle of nowhere. Wombat Valley. *Hooray!*

Dr Pollyanna Hargreaves—Polly to everyone but her mother—beefed up the radio as she turned off the main road. Bing Crosby's 'White Christmas' wasn't exactly appropriate for Christmas deep in the Australian bush, but it didn't stop her singing along. She might be a long way from snow, but she was happy.

The country around her was wild and mountainous. The twisting road meant this last section of the journey could take a while, but the further she went, the further she got from the whole over-the-top celebration that was her parents' idea of Christmas.

'You can't be serious!' She could still hear her mother's appalled words when she'd broken the news that she wouldn't be spending Christmas with them. 'We've planned one of the most wonderful Christmases ever. We've hired the most prestigious restaurant on Sydney Harbour. All our closest friends are coming, and the head chef himself has promised to oversee a diabetic menu. Pollyanna, everyone expects you.'

Expectation was the whole problem, Polly thought, as she turned through the next curve with care. This road was little more than a logging route, and recent rain had gouged gutters along the unsealed verge. The whole of New South Wales had been inundated with weeks of subtropical downpours, and it looked as if Wombat Valley had borne the brunt of them. She was down to a snail's pace.

But she wasn't worried. She wasn't in Sydney. Or in Monaco, where she'd been last Christmas. Or in Aspen, where she'd been the Christmas before that.

Cute little Pollyanna had finally cut and run.

'And I'm not going back,' she told the road ahead. Enough. She felt as if she'd been her parents' plaything since birth, saddled with a preposterous name, with nannies to take care of every whim and loaded with the expectation that she be the perfect daughter.

For Polly was the only child of Olivia and Charles Hargreaves. Heiress to the Hargreaves millions. She was courted and fussed over, wrapped in cotton wool and expected to be...

'Perfect.' She abandoned Bing and said the word aloud, thinking of the tears, the recriminations, the gentle but incessant blackmail.

'Polly, you'll break your mother's heart.' That was what her father had said when Polly had decided, aged seven, that she liked chocolate ice cream, eating a family tub behind her nanny's back and putting her blood sugars through the roof. And ever since... 'You know we worry. Don't you care?'

And then, when she'd decided she wanted to be a doctor...

'Pollyanna, how can you stress your body with a demanding career like medicine? Plus you have your inheritance to consider. If you need to work—which you don't—then at least take a position in the family company. You could be our PR assistant; that's safe. Medicine! Polly, you'll break our hearts.'

And now this. Breaking up with the boy they wanted her to marry, followed by Not Coming Home For Christmas. Not being there to be fussed over, prettied, shown off to their friends. This was heartbreak upon heartbreak upon heartbreak.

'But I'm over it,' she said out loud. 'I'm over families—over, over, over. I'm an independent career woman so it's time I started acting like one. This is a good start. I'm five hours' drive from Sydney, in the middle of nowhere. I'm contracted to act as locum for two weeks. I can't get further away than this.'

And it was exciting. She'd trained and worked in city hospitals. She didn't have a clue about bush medicine, but the doctor she was relieving—Dr Hugo Denver—had told her things would be straightforward.

'We're usually busy,' he'd said in their phone interview. 'The valley could use two doctors or more, but over Christmas half the population seems to depart for Sydney or the coast. We run a ten-bed hospital but anything major gets helicoptered out. Mostly we deal with minor stuff where it's not worth the expense of sending for the Air Ambulance, or long-termers, or locals who choose to die in the Valley rather than in acute city hospitals.'

'You provide palliative care?' she'd asked, astonished.

'Via home visits, mostly,' he'd told her. 'Most of our oldies only go to the city under duress, and it's an honour to look after them at home. I also deal with trauma, but the logging industry closes down for three weeks over Christmas and the place is quiet. I doubt if you'll have much excitement.'

'But I wouldn't mind a bit of excitement,' she said aloud as she manoeuvred her little sports car around the next bend. 'Just enough to keep me occupied.'

And then, as if in answer to her prayers, she rounded the next bend—and got more excitement than she'd bargained for.

Dr Hugo Denver was well over excitement. Hugo was cramped inside a truck balanced almost vertically over the side of a cliff. He was trying to stop Horace Fry from bleeding out. He was also trying not to think that Ruby was totally dependent on him, and his life seemed to be balanced on one very unstable, very young tree.

The call had come in twenty minutes ago. Margaret Fry,

wife of the said Horace, had managed to crawl out of the crashed truck and ring him.

'Doc, you gotta come fast.' She'd sobbed into the phone. 'Horace's bleeding like a stuck pig and there's no one here but me.'

'He's still in the truck?'

'Steering wheel jabbed him. Blood's making him feel faint.'

'Bleeding from where?'

'Shoulder, I think.'

'Can you put pressure on it?'

'Doc, I can't.' It was a wail. 'You know blood makes me throw up and I'm not getting back in that truck. Doc, come, fast!'

What choice did he have? What choice did he ever have? If there was trauma in Wombat Valley, Hugo was it.

'Ring the police,' he snapped. 'I'm on my way.'

Lois, his housekeeper, had been preparing lunch. She'd been humming Christmas carols, almost vibrating with excitement. As was Ruby. As soon as the locum arrived they were off, Lois to her son's place in Melbourne, Hugo and Ruby to their long-awaited two-week holiday.

Christmas at the beach… This was what his sister had promised Ruby last year, but last year's Christmas had become a blur of shock and sorrow. A car crash the week before. A single car accident. Suicide?

Hugo's life had changed immeasurably in that moment, as had Ruby's.

Twelve months on, they were doing their best. He was doing his best. He'd moved back to Wombat Valley so Ruby could stay in her home, and he fully intended to give her the longed-for beach Christmas.

But commitment meant committing not only to Ruby but to the community he lived in. The locals cared for Ruby. He cared for the locals. That was the deal.

Lois had been putting cold meat and salad on the table.

She'd looked at him as he disconnected, and sighed and put his lunch in the fridge.

'Ring Donald,' he'd told her. Donald was a retired farmer who also owned a tow truck. It was a very small tow truck but the logging company with all its equipment was officially on holidays since yesterday. Donald's truck would be all the valley had. 'Tell him Horace Fry's truck's crashed at Blinder's Bend. Ring Joe at the hospital and tell him to expect casualties. Tell him I'll ring him as soon as I know details, and ask him to check that the police know. I need to go.'

'Aren't you expecting the new doctor?' Lois had practically glowered. She wanted to get away, too.

'If she arrives before I get back, you can give her my lunch,' he'd said dryly. 'I'll eat at the hospital.'

'Should I send her out to Blinder's? She could start straight away.'

'I can hardly throw her in at the deep end,' he'd told her. 'Hopefully, this will be the last casualty, though, and she'll have a nice quiet Christmas.' He'd dropped a kiss on his small niece's head. 'See you later, Ruby. Back soon.'

But now…

A quiet Christmas was just what he wanted, he thought grimly as he pushed hard on the gaping wound on Horace's shoulder. The steering wheel seemed to have snapped right off, and the steering column had jabbed into Horace's chest.

And he'd bled. Hugo had stared in dismay into the truck's cab, he'd looked at the angle the truck was leaning over the cliff, he'd looked at the amount of blood in the cabin and he'd made a call.

The truck was balanced on the edge of the cliff. The ground was sodden from recent rain but it had still looked stable enough to hold. He'd hoped…

He shouldn't have hoped. He should have waited for Donald with his tow truck, and for the police.

It didn't matter what he should have done. Margaret had been having hysterics, useless for help. Hopefully, Donald and his tow truck were on their way but he'd take a while. The police had to come from Willaura on the coast, and he hadn't been able to wait.

And then, as he'd bent into the cab, Horace had grasped his wrist with his good arm and tried to heave himself over to the passenger seat. He was a big man and he'd jerked with fear, shifting his weight to the middle of the cabin…

Hugo had felt the truck lurch and lurch again. He'd heard Margaret scream as the whole verge gave way and they were falling…

And then, blessedly, the truck seemed to catch on something. From this angle, all he could see holding them up was one twiggy sapling. His life depended on that sapling. There was still a drop under them that was long enough to give him nightmares.

But he didn't have time for nightmares. He'd been thrown around but somehow he was still applying pressure to Horace's arm. Somehow he'd pushed Horace back into the driver's seat, even if it was at a crazy angle.

'You move again and we'll both fall to the bottom of the cliff,' he told Horace and Horace subsided.

To say his life was flashing before his eyes would be an understatement.

Ruby. Seven years old.

He was all she had.

But he couldn't think of Ruby now. He needed to get back up to the road. Horace had lost too much blood. He needed fluids. He needed electrolytes. He needed the equipment to set up a drip…

Hugo moved a smidgen and the truck swayed again. He glanced out of the back window and saw they were ten feet down the cliff.

Trapped.

'Margaret?' he yelled. 'Margaret!'

There was no reply except sobbing.

His phone… Where the hell was his phone?

And then he remembered. He'd done a cursory check on Margaret. She'd been sobbing and shaking when he'd arrived. She was suffering from shock, he'd decided. It had been an instant diagnosis but it was all he'd had time for, so he'd put his jacket across her shoulders and run to the truck.

His phone was still in his jacket pocket.

'Margaret!' he yelled again, and the truck rocked again, and from up on the cliff Margaret's sobs grew louder.

Was she blocking her husband's need with her cries? Maybe she was. People had different ways of protecting themselves, and coming near a truck ten feet down a cliff, when the truck was threatening to fall another thirty, was possibly a bad idea.

Probably.

Definitely?

'That hurt!' Horace was groaning in pain.

'Sorry, mate, I need to push hard.'

'Not my shoulder, Doc—my eardrum.'

Great. All this and he'd be sued for perforating Horace's eardrum?

'Can you yell for Margaret? We need her help.'

'She won't answer,' Horace muttered. 'If she's having hysterics the only thing that'll stop her is ice water.'

Right.

'Then we need to sit really still until help arrives,' he told him, trying not to notice Horace's pallor, deciding not to check his blood pressure because there wasn't a thing he could do about it. 'The truck's unstable. We need to sit still until Donald arrives with his tow truck.'

'Then we'll be waiting a while,' Horace said without humour. 'Donald and his missus have gone to their daughter's for Christmas. Dunno who's got a tow truck round here. It'll have to be a tractor.'

'Can you get Margaret to ring someone?'

'Like I said, Doc, she's useless.'

* * *

There was an SUV parked right where she wanted to drive.

It was serviceable, dirty white, a four-wheel drive wagon with a neat red sign across the side. The sign said: 'Wombat Valley Medical Service'.

It blocked the road completely.

She put her foot on the brake and her car came to a well-behaved standstill.

The road curved behind the SUV, and as her car stopped she saw the collapse of the verge. And as she saw more, she gasped in horror.

There was a truck below the collapse. Over the cliff!

A few hundred yards back she'd passed a sign declaring this area to be Wombat Valley Gap. The Gap looked to be a magnificent wilderness area, stretching beneath the road as far as the eye could see.

The road was hewn into the side of the mountain. The edge was a steep drop. Very steep. Straight down.

The truck looked as if it had rounded the curve too fast. The skid marks suggested it had hit the cliff and spun across to the edge. The roadside looked as if it had given way.

The truck had slipped right over and was now balanced precariously about ten feet down the cliff, pointing downward. There were a couple of saplings holding it. Just.

A woman was crouched on the verge, weeping, and Polly herself almost wept in relief at the sight of her. She'd escaped from the truck then?

But then she thought… SUV blocking the road. Wombat Valley Medical Service… Two vehicles.

Where was the paramedic?

Was someone else in the truck? Was this dramas, plural? *Help!*

She was a city doctor, she thought frantically. She'd never been near the bush in her life. She'd never had to cope with a road accident. Yes, she'd cared for accident victims, but that had been in the organised efficiency of a city hospital Emergency Room.

All of a sudden she wanted to be back in Sydney. Preferably off-duty.

'You wanted to be a doctor,' she told herself, still taking time to assess the whole scene. Her lecturers in Emergency Medicine had drilled that into her, and somehow her training was coming back now. *'Don't jump in before you've checked the whole situation. Check fast but always check. You don't want to become work for another doctor. Work out priorities and keep yourself safe.'*

Keeping herself safe had never been a problem in the ER.

'You wanted to see medicine at its most basic,' she reminded herself as she figured out what must have happened. 'Here's your chance. Get out of the car and help.'

My, that truck looked unstable.

Keep yourself safe.

The woman was wailing.

Who was in the truck?

Deep breath.

She climbed out of her car, thinking a flouncy dress covered in red and white polka dots wasn't what she should be wearing right now. She was also wearing crimson sandals with kitten heels.

She hardly had time to change. She was a doctor and she was needed. Disregarding her entirely inappropriate wardrobe, she headed across to the crying woman. She was big-boned, buxom, wearing a crinoline frock and an electric-blue perm. She had a man's jacket over her shoulders. Her face was swollen from weeping and she had a scratch above one eye.

'Can you tell me what's happened?' Polly knelt beside her, and the woman stared at her and wailed louder. A lot louder.

But hysterics was something Pollyanna Hargreaves could deal with. Hysterics was Polly's mother's weapon of last resort and Polly had stopped responding to it from the age of six.

She knelt so her face was six inches from the woman's. She was forcing her to look at her and, as soon as she did, she got serious.

'Stop the noise or I'll slap you,' she said, loud and firm and cold as ice. Doctor threatening patient with physical violence... *Good one*, Polly thought. *That's the way to endear you to the locals*. But it couldn't matter. Were there people in that upside down truck?

'Who's in the truck?' she demanded. 'Take two deep breaths and talk.'

'I...my husband. And Doc...'

'Doc?'

'Doc Denver.'

'The doctor's in the truck?'

'He was trying to help Horace.' Somehow she was managing to speak. 'Horace was bleeding. But then the ground gave way and the truck slid and it's still wobbling and it's going to fall all the way down.'

The woman subsided as Polly once again took a moment to assess. The truck was definitely...wobbling. The saplings seemed to be the only thing holding it up. If even one of them gave way...

'Have you called for help?' she asked. The woman was clutching her phone.

'I called Doc...'

'The doctor who's here now?'

'Doc Denver, yes.'

'Good for you. How about the police? A tow truck?'

The woman shook her head, put her hands to her face and started loud, rapid breathing. Holly took a fast pulse check and diagnosed panic. There were other things she should exclude before a definitive diagnosis but, for now, triage said she needed to focus on the truck.

'I need you to concentrate on breathing,' she told the

woman. 'Count. One, two, three, four—in. One, two, three, four—out. Slow your breathing down. Will you do that?'

'I…yes…'

'Good woman.' But Polly had moved on. Truck. Cliff. Fall.

She edged forward, trying to see down the cliff, wary of the crumbling edge.

What was wrong with Christmas in Sydney? All at once she would have given her very best shoes to be there.

CHAPTER TWO

TRIAGE. ACTION. SOMEHOW POLLY made herself a plan.

First things first. She phoned the universal emergency number and the response came blessedly fast.

'Emergency services. Fire, ambulance, police—which service do you require?'

'How about all three?' She gave details but as she talked she stared down at the truck.

There was a coil of rope in the back of the truck. A big one. A girl could do lots with that rope, she thought. If she could clamber down...

A police sergeant came onto the phone, bluff but apologetic.

'We need to come from Willaura—we'll probably be half an hour. I'll get an ambulance there as soon as I can, but sorry, Doc, you're on your own for at least twenty minutes.'

He disconnected.

Twenty minutes. Half an hour.

The ground was soggy. If the saplings gave way...

She could still see the rope, ten feet down in the back of the truck tray. It wasn't a sheer drop but the angle was impossibly steep.

There were saplings beside the truck she could hold onto, if they were strong enough.

'Who's up there?'

The voice from the truck made her start. It was a voice she recognised from the calls she'd made organising this job. Dr Hugo Denver. Her employer.

'It's Dr Hargreaves, your new locum, and you promised

me no excitement,' she called back. She couldn't see him. 'Hello to you, too. I don't suppose there's any way you can jump from the cab and let it roll?'

'I have the driver in here. Multiple lacerations and a crush injury to the chest. I'm applying pressure to stop the bleeding.'

'You didn't think to pull him out first?'

There was a moment's pause, then a reply that sounded as if it came through gritted teeth. 'No.'

'That was hardly wise.'

'Are you in a position to judge?'

'I guess not.' She was assessing the saplings, seeing if she could figure out safe holds on the way down. 'But it does— in retrospect—seem to have been worth considering.'

She heard a choke that might even have been laughter. It helped, she thought. People thought medics had a black sense of humour but, in the worst kind of situations, humour was often the only way to alleviate tension.

'I'll ask for your advice when I need it,' he retorted and she tested a sapling for strength and thought maybe not.

'Advice is free,' she offered helpfully.

'Am I or am I not paying you?'

She almost managed a grin at that, except she couldn't get her sandals to grip in the mud and she was kind of distracted. 'I believe you are,' she said at last, and gave up on the shoes and tossed her kitten heels up onto the verge. Bare feet was bad but kitten heels were worse. She started inching down the slope, moving from sapling to sapling. If she could just reach that rope...

'I'd like a bit of respect,' Hugo Denver called and she held like a limpet to a particularly shaky sapling and tried to think about respect.

'It seems you're not in any position to ask for anything right now,' she managed. She was nearing the back of the truck but she was being super-cautious. If she slipped she could hardly grab the truck for support. It looked like one push and it'd fall...

Do not think of falling.

'I need my bag,' Hugo said. 'It's on the verge where the truck...'

'Yeah, I saw it.' It was above her. Quite a bit above her now.

'Can you lower it somehow?'

'In a minute. I'm getting a rope.'

'A rope?'

'There's one in the back of the truck. It looks really long and sturdy. Just what the doctor ordered.'

'You're climbing down?'

'I'm trying to.'

'Hell, Polly...'

'Don't worry. I have really grippy toenails and if I can reach it I might be able to make the truck more secure.'

There was a moment's silence. Then... 'Grippy toenails?'

'They're painted crimson.'

He didn't seem to hear the crimson bit. 'Polly, don't. It's too dangerous. There's a cord in my truck...'

'How long a cord?' Maybe she should have checked his truck.

'Twelve feet or so. You could use it to lower my bag. Horace needs a drip and fast.'

There was no way she could use a twelve-foot cord to secure the truck—and what use was a drip if the truck fell?

'Sorry,' Polly managed. 'In every single situation I've ever trained in, triage is sorting priorities, so that's what I've done. If I lower your bag and add a smidgen of weight to the truck, you may well be setting up a drip as you plummet to the valley floor. So it's rope first, secure the truck next and then I'll work on getting your bag. You get to be boss again when you get out of the truck.'

'You've got a mouth,' he said, sounding cautious—and also stunned.

'I'm bad at respect,' she admitted. If she could just get a firmer hold... 'That's the younger generation for you. You want to override me, Grandpa?'

'How old do you think I am?'

'You must be old if you think a ride to the bottom of the valley's an option.' And then she shut up because she had to let go of a sapling with one hand and hope the other held, and lean out and stretch and hope that her fingers could snag the rope...

And they did and she could have wept in relief but she didn't because she was concentrating on sliding the rope from the tray, an inch at a time, thinking that any sudden movements could mean...

Don't think what it could mean.

'You have red hair!'

He could see her. She'd been so intent she hadn't even looked at the window in the back of the truck. She braved a glance downward, and she saw him.

Okay, she conceded, this was no grandpa. The face looking out at her was lean and tanned and...worried. His face looked sort of chiselled, his eyes were deep set and his brow looked furrowed in concern...

All that she saw in the nanosecond she allowed herself before she went back to concentrating on freeing the rope. But weirdly it sort of...changed things.

Two seconds ago she'd been concentrating on saving two guys in a truck. Now one of them had a face. One of them looked worried. One of them looked...

Strong?

Immensely masculine?

How crazy was that? Her sight of him had been fleeting, a momentary impression, but there'd been something about the way he'd looked back at her...

Get on with the job, she told herself sharply. It was all very well getting the rope out of the truck. What was she going to do with it now she had it?

She had to concentrate on the rope. Not some male face. Not on the unknown Dr Denver.

The tray of the truck had a rail around it, with an upright at each corner. If she could loop the rope…

'Polly, wait for the cavalry,' Hugo demanded, and once again she had that impression of strength. And that he feared for her.

'The cavalry's arriving in half an hour,' she called back. 'Does Horace have half an hour?'

Silence.

'He's nicked a vein,' he said at last, and Polly thought: *That's that, then.* Horace needed help or he'd die.

She wedged herself against another sapling, hoping it could take her weight. Then she unwound her rope coil.

'What are you doing?' It was a sharp demand.

'Imagine I'm in Theatre,' she told him. 'Neurosurgeon fighting the odds. You're unscrubbed and useless. Would you ask for a commentary?'

'Is that another way of saying you don't have a plan?'

'Shut up and concentrate on Horace.' It was unnerving, to say the least, that he could see her, but then Horace groaned and Hugo's face disappeared from the back window and she could get on with…what…? Concentrating not on Hugo.

On one rope.

Somehow she got the middle of the rope looped and knotted around each side of the tray. Yay! Now she had to get back to the road. She clutched the cliff as if she were glued to it, scrambling up until her feet were on solid ground. Finally she was up. All she had to do now was figure out something to tie it to.

She had the shakes.

'Are you safe?' Hugo called and she realised he couldn't see her any more. The truck was too far over the lip. 'Dr Hargreaves?' There was no disguising his fear.

'I'm safe,' she called back and her voice wobbled and she

tried again. This time her voice was pleasingly smug. 'Feet on terra firma. Moving to stage two of the action plan.'

'I thought you didn't have a plan.'

'It's more exciting without one, but I'm trying. Indeed, I'm very trying.'

Plans took brains. Plans required the mush in her brain to turn useful. To stop thinking about Hugo plunging downward…

It wasn't Hugo. It was two guys in a truck. *Take the personal out of it*, she told herself.

Plan!

She needed a solid tree, or at least a good-sized stump. She had neither.

Attach the rope to her car? Not in a million years. Her little yellow sports car would sail over the cliff after the truck.

Margaret looked kind of buxom. How would she go as an anchor?

She gave a wry grin, wishing she could share the thought with Bossy In The Truck. Maybe not.

Bossy's truck?

The thought was no sooner in her mind than she was running up the road to Hugo's car. Blessedly, his keys were in the ignition. *Yes!* A minute later, his vehicle was parked as close as she could manage to the point where the truck had gone over.

It was an SUV. She'd once gone skiing in an upmarket version of one of these—her boyfriend's. Well, her ex-boyfriend, she conceded. They'd been snowed in and the tow truck had had to winch them out.

Polly had been interested in the process, or more interested than in listening to Marcus whinging, so she'd watched. There'd been an anchor point…

She ducked underneath. Yes! She had the ends of the rope fastened in a moment.

Maybe she could pull the truck up.

Maybe not. This wasn't a huge SUV.

'Polly…' From below Hugo's voice sounded desperate. 'What are you doing?'

'Being a Girl Guide,' she yelled back. 'Prepare to be stabilised.'

'How…?'

'Pure skill,' she yelled back. 'How's Horace?'

'Slipping.'

'Two minutes,' she yelled back, twisting the rope and racking her brain for a knot that could be used.

Reef Knot? Round Turn and Two Half Hitches? What about a Buntline Hitch? Yes! She almost beamed. Brown Owl would be proud.

She knotted and then cautiously shifted the SUV, reversing sideways against the cliff, taking up the last slack in the rope. Finally she cut the engine. She closed her eyes for a nanosecond and she allowed herself to breathe.

'Why don't you do something?' It was Margaret—of course it was Margaret—still crouched on the verge and screaming. 'My Horace's dying and all you do is…'

'Margaret, if you don't shut up I'll personally climb the cliff and slap you for Polly,' Hugo called up, and Polly thought: *Uh oh.* He must have heard her previous threat. Some introduction to his new employee. Medicine by force.

But at least he was backing her and the idea was strangely comforting—there were two doctors working instead of one.

'Let's get you somewhere more comfortable,' she told the woman. She had a jacket draped over her shoulders. 'Is this Doc Denver's jacket?'

'I…yes. His phone's in the pocket. It keeps ringing.'

You didn't think to answer it? she thought, but she didn't say it. What was the point now? But if Emergency Services were trying to verify their location…

'I want you to sit in Doc Denver's truck,' she told Margaret. 'If the phone rings, can you answer it and tell people where we are?'

'I don't…'

'We're depending on you, Margaret. All you have to do is sit in the car and answer the phone. Nothing else. Can you do that?'

'If you save Horace.'

'Deal.' She propelled her into the passenger seat of the SUV and there was a bonus. More ballast. With Margaret's extra, not insubstantial, weight, this vehicle was going nowhere.

'I think you're stable,' she yelled down the cliff, while she headed back to the verge for Hugo's bag. She flicked it open. Saline, adrenaline, painkilling drugs, all the paraphernalia she'd expect a country GP would carry. He must have put it down while he'd leaned into the truck, and then the road had given way.

How to get it to him?

'What do you mean, stable?' he called.

'I have nice strong ties attaching the truck tray to your SUV,' she called. 'The SUV's parked at right angles to you, with Margaret sitting in the passenger seat. It's going nowhere.'

'How did you tie…?'

'Girl Guiding 101,' she called back. 'You want to give me a raise on the strength of it?'

'Half my kingdom.'

'Half a country practice in Wombat Valley? Ha!'

'Yeah, you're right, it's a trap,' he called back. 'You know you'll never get away, but you walked in of your own accord, and I'm more than willing to share. I'll even include Priscilla Carlisle's bunions. They're a medical practice on their own.'

Astonishingly, she giggled.

This felt okay. She could hear undercurrents to his attempt at humour that she had no hope of understanding, but she was working hard, and in the truck Hugo would be working hard, too. The medical imperatives were still there, but the flavour of black humour was a comfort all on its own.

Medical imperatives. The bag was the next thing. Horace had suffered major blood loss. Everything Hugo needed was in that bag.

How to get the bag down?

Lower it? It'd catch on the undergrowth. Take it down herself? *Maybe.* The cab, though, was much lower than the tray. There were no solid saplings past the back of the tray.

She had Hugo's nylon cord. It was useless for abseiling—the nylon would slice her hands—but she didn't have to pull herself up. She could stay down there until the cavalry arrived.

Abseiling… A harness? *Nope.* The nylon would cut.

A seat? She'd learned to make a rope seat in Abseil Rescue.

Hmm.

'Tie the cord to the bag and toss it as close as you can,' Hugo called, and humour had given way to desperation. 'I can try and retrieve it.'

'What, lean out of the cabin? Have you seen the drop?'

'I'm trying not to see the drop but there's no choice.'

His voice cracked. It'd be killing him, she thought, watching Horace inch towards death with no way to help.

'Did you mention you have a kid? You're taking your kid to the beach for Christmas? Isn't that what this locum position is all about?'

'Yes, but…'

'Then you're going nowhere. Sit. Stay.'

There was a moment's silence, followed by a very strained response.

'Woof?'

She grinned. *Nice one.*

But she was no longer concentrating on the conversation. Her hands were fashioning a seat, three lines of cord, hooked together at the sides, with a triangle of cord at both sides to make it steady.

She could make a knot and she could let it out as she went…

Wow, she was dredging through the grey matter now. But it was possible, she conceded. She could tie the bag underneath her, find toeholds in the cliff, hopefully swing from sapling to sapling to steady her...

'Polly, if you're thinking of climbing...you can't.' Hugo's voice was deep and gravelly. There was strength there, she thought, but she also heard fear.

He was scared for her.

He didn't even know her.

He was concerned for a colleague, she thought, but, strangely, it felt more than that. It felt...warm. Strong.

Good.

Which was ridiculous. She knew nothing about this man, other than he wanted to take his kid to the beach for Christmas.

'Never say *can't* to a Hargreaves,' she managed to call back. 'You'll have my father to answer to.'

'I don't want to answer to your father if you're dead.'

'I'll write a note excusing you. Now shut up. I need to concentrate.'

'Polly...'

'Hold tight. I'm on my way.'

CHAPTER THREE

IT NEARLY KILLED HIM.

He could do nothing except apply pressure to Horace's shoulder and wait for rescue.

From a woman in a polka dot dress.

The sight of her from the truck's rear-view window had astounded him. Actually, the sight of anyone from the truck's rear-view mirror would have astounded him—this was an impossible place to reach—but that a woman…

No, that was sexist… That anyone, wearing a bare-shouldered dress with a halter neck tie, with flouncy auburn curls to her shoulders, with freckles…

Yeah, he'd even noticed the freckles.

And yes, he thought, he was being sexist or fashionist or whatever else he could think of being accused of right now, but he excused himself because what he wanted was a team of State Emergency Personnel with safety jackets and big boots organising a smooth transition to safety.

He was stuck with polka dots and freckles.

He should have asked for a photo when he'd organised the locum. He should never have…

Employed polka dots? Who was he kidding? If an applicant had a medical degree and was breathing he would have employed them. No one wanted to work in Wombat Valley.

No one but him and he was stuck here. Lured here for love of his little niece. Stuck here for ever.

Beside him, Horace was drifting in and out of consciousness. His blood pressure was dropping, his breathing was becoming laboured and there was nothing he could do.

He'd never felt so helpless.

Maybe he had. The night they'd rung and told him Grace had driven her car off the Gap.

Changing his life in an instant.

Why was he thinking about that now? Because there was nothing else to think about? Nothing to do?

The enforced idleness was killing him. He couldn't see up to the road unless he leaned out of the window. What was she doing?

What sort of a dumb name was Polly anyway? he thought tangentially. Whoever called a kid Pollyanna?

She'd sent a copy of her qualifications to him, with references. They'd been glowing, even if they'd been city based.

The name had put him off. Was that nameist?

Regardless, he'd had reservations about employing a city doctor in this place that required definite country skills, but Ruby deserved Christmas.

He deserved Christmas. Bondi Beach. Sydney. He'd had a life back there.

And now...his whole Christmas depended on a doctor in polka dots. More, his life depended on her. If her knots didn't hold...

'Hey!'

And she was just there, right by the driver's seat window. At least, her feet were there—bare!—and then her waist, and then there was a slither and a curse and her head appeared at the open window. She was carefully not touching the truck, using her feet on the cliff to push herself back.

'Hey,' she said again, breathlessly. 'How're you guys doing? Would you like a bag?'

And, amazingly, she hauled up his canvas holdall from under her.

Horace was slumped forward, semi-conscious, not reacting to her presence. Polly gave Horace a long, assessing look and then turned her attention to him. He got the same glance. Until her assessment told her otherwise, it seemed he was the patient.

'Okay?' she asked.

'Bruises. Nothing more. I'm okay to work.'

He got a brisk nod, accepting his word, moving on. 'If you're planning on coping with childbirth or constipation, forget it,' she told him, lifting the bag through the open window towards him. 'I took stuff out to lighten the load. But this should have what you need.'

To say he was gobsmacked would be an understatement. She was acting like a doctor in a ward—calm, concise, using humour to deflect tension. She was hanging by some sort of harness—no, some sort of seat—at the end of a nylon cord. She was red-headed and freckled and polka-dotted, and she was cute...

She was a doctor, offering assistance.

He grabbed the bag so she could use her hands to steady herself and, as soon as he had it, her smile went to high beam. But her smile still encompassed a watchful eye on Horace. She was an emergency physician, he thought. ER work was a skill—communicating and reassuring terrified patients while assessing injuries at the same time. That was what she was doing. She knew the pressure he was under but her manner said this was just another day in the office.

'Those bruises,' she said. 'Any on the head? No concussion?'

So he was still a patient. 'No.'

'Promise?'

'Promise.'

'Then it's probably better if you work from inside the truck. If I work on Horace from outside I might put more pressure...'

'You've done enough.'

'I haven't but I don't want to bump the truck more than necessary. Yell if you need help but if you're fine to put in the drip then I'll tie myself to a sapling and watch. Margaret is up top, manning the phones, so it's my turn for a spot of R and R. It's time to strut your stuff, Dr Denver. Go.'

She pushed herself back from the truck and cocked a quizzical eyebrow—and he couldn't speak.

Time to strut his stuff? She was right, of course. He needed to stop staring at polka dots.

He needed to try and save Horace.

Polly was now just as stuck as the guys in the truck.

There was no way she could pull herself up the cliff again. She couldn't get purchase on the nylon without cutting herself. The cord had cut her hands while she'd lowered herself, but to get the bag to Hugo, to try and save Horace's life, she'd decided a bit of hand damage was worthwhile.

Getting up, though… Not so much. The cavalry was on its way. She'd done everything she could.

Now all she had to do was secure herself and watch Hugo work.

He couldn't do it.

He had all the equipment he needed. All he had to do was find a vein and insert a drip.

But Horace was a big man, his arms were fleshy and flaccid, and his blood pressure had dropped to dangerous levels. Even in normal circumstances it'd be tricky to find a vein.

Horace was bleeding from the arm nearest him. He had that pressure bound. The bleeding had slowed to a trickle, but he needed to use Horace's other arm for the drip.

It should be easy. All he needed to do was tug Horace's arm forward, locate the vein at the elbow and insert the drip.

But he was at the wrong angle and his hands shook. Something about crashing down a cliff, thinking he was going to hit the bottom? The vein he was trying for slid away under the needle.

'Want me to try?' Polly had tugged back from the truck,

cautious that she might inadvertently put weight on it, but she'd been watching.

'You can hardly operate while hanging on a rope,' he told her and she gave him a look of indignation.

'In case you hadn't noticed, I've rigged this up with a neat seat. So I'm not exactly hanging. If you're having trouble... I don't want to bump the truck but for Horace...maybe it's worth the risk.'

And she was right. Priority had to be that vein, but if he couldn't find it, how could she?

'I've done my first part of anaesthetic training,' she said, diffidently now. 'Finding veins is what I'm good at.'

'You're an anaesthetist?'

'Nearly. You didn't know that, did you, Dr Denver?' To his further astonishment, she sounded smug. 'Emergency physician with anaesthetist skills. You have two medics for the price of one. So...can I help?'

And he looked again at Horace's arm and he thought of the consequences of not trusting. She was an anaesthetist. They were both in impossible positions but she had the training.

'Yes, please.'

Her hands hurt. Lowering herself using only the thin cord had been rough.

Her backside also hurt. Three thin nylon cords weren't anyone's idea of good seat padding. She was using her feet to swing herself as close to the truck as she dared, trying to balance next to the window.

There was nothing to tie herself to.

And then Hugo reached over and caught the halter-tie of her dress, so her shoulder was caught at the rear of the window.

'No weight,' he told her. 'I'll just hold you steady.'

'What a good thing I didn't wear a strapless number,' she said approvingly, trying to ignore the feel of his hand against her bare skin. Truly, this was the most extraordinary position…

It was the most extraordinary feeling. His hold made her feel…safe?

Was she out of her mind? *Safe?* But he held fast and it settled her.

Hugo had swabbed but she swabbed again, holding Horace's arm steady as she worked. She had his arm out of the window, resting on the window ledge. The light here was good.

She pressed lightly and pressed again…

The cannula was suddenly in her hand. Hugo was holding her with one hand, acting as theatre assistant with the other.

Once again that word played into her mind. *Safe*… But she had eyes only for the faint contour that said she might have a viable vein…

She took the cannula and took a moment to steady herself. Hugo's hold on her tightened.

She inserted the point—and the needle slipped seamlessly into the vein.

'Yay, us,' she breathed, but Hugo was already handing her some sticking plaster to tape the cannula. She was checking the track, but it was looking good. A minute later she had the bag attached and fluid was flowing. She just might have done the thing.

Hugo let her go. She swung out a little, clear of the truck. It was the sensible thing to do, but still…

She hadn't wanted to be…let go.

'Heart rate?' Her voice wasn't quite steady. She took a deep breath and tried again. 'How is it?'

'Holding.' Hugo had his stethoscope out. 'I think we might have made it.' He glanced into the bag. 'And we have adrenaline—and a defibrillator. How did you carry all this?'

'I tied it under my seat.'

'Where did you learn your knots?'

'I was a star Girl Guide.' She was, too, she thought, deciding maybe she needed to focus on anything but the way his hold had made her feel.

A star Girl Guide... She'd been a star at so many things—at anything, really, that would get her away from her parents' overriding concern. Riding lessons, piano lessons, judo, elocution, Girl Guides, holiday camps... She'd been taken to each of them by a continuous stream of nannies. Nannies who were chosen because they spoke French, had famous relatives or in some other way could be boasted about by her parents...

'*The current girl's a Churchill. She's au-pairing for six months, and she knows all the right people...*'

Yeah. Nannies, nannies and nannies. Knowing the right people or speaking five languages was never a sign of job permanence. Polly had mostly been glad to be delivered to piano or elocution or whatever. She'd done okay, too. She'd had to.

Her parents loved her, but oh, they loved to boast.

'ER Physician, anaesthetist and Girl Guide to boot.' Hugo sounded stunned. 'I don't suppose you brought a stretcher as well? Plus a qualification in mountain rescue.'

'A full examination table, complete with lights, sinks, sterilisers? Plus rope ladders and mountain goats? Damn, I knew I'd forgotten something.'

He chuckled but she didn't have time for further banter. She was swinging in a way that was making her a little dizzy. She had to catch the sapling.

Her feet were hitting the cliff. *Ouch.* Where was nice soft grass when you needed it?

Where was Hugo's hold when she needed it?

He was busy. It made sense that he take over Horace's care now, but...

She missed that hold.

'It's flowing well.' There was no mistaking the satisfaction in Hugo's voice and Polly, too, breathed again. If Horace's heart hadn't given way yet, there was every chance the fluids would make a difference.

In the truck, Hugo had the IV line set up and secure. He'd hung the saline bags from an umbrella he'd wedged behind the back seat. He'd injected morphine.

He'd like oxygen but Polly's culling of his bag had excluded it. *Fair enough*, he thought. *Oxygen or a defibrillator?* With massive blood loss, the defibrillator was likely to be the most important, and the oxygen cylinder was dead weight.

Even so... How had she managed to get all this down here? What she'd achieved was amazing, and finding a vein in these circumstances was nothing short of miraculous.

She was his locum, temporary relief.

How would it be if there was a doctor like Polly working beside him in the Valley all year round?

Right. As if that was going to happen. His new locum was swinging on her seat, as if flying free, and he thought that was exactly what she was. *Free*.

Not trapped, like he was.

And suddenly he wasn't thinking trapped in a truck down a cliff. He was thinking trapped in Wombat Valley, giving up his career, giving up...his life.

Once upon a time, if he'd met someone like Dr Polly Hargreaves he could have asked her out, had fun, tried friendship and maybe it could have led to...

No! It was no use even letting himself think down that road.

He was trapped in Wombat Valley. The skilful, intriguing Polly Hargreaves was rescuing him from one trap.

No one could rescue him from the bigger one.

Fifteen minutes later, help arrived. *About time too*, Polly thought. Mountains were for mountain goats. When the first yellow-jacketed figure appeared at the cliff top it was all she could do not to weep with relief.

She didn't. She was a doctor and doctors didn't weep.

Or not when yellow coats and big boots and serious equipment were on their way to save them.

'We have company,' she announced to Hugo, who couldn't see the cliff top from where he was stuck.

'More polka dots?'

She grinned and looked up at the man staring down at her. 'Hi,' she yelled. 'Dr Denver wants to know what you're wearing.'

The guy was on his stomach, looking down. 'A business suit,' he managed. 'With matching tie. How'd you get down there?'

'They fell,' she said. 'I came down all by myself. You wouldn't, by any chance, have a cushion?'

He chuckled and then got serious. The situation was assessed with reassuring efficiency. There was more than one yellow jacket up there, it seemed, but only one was venturing near the edge.

'We'll get you up, miss,' the guy called.

'Stabilise the truck first.'

'Will do.'

The Australian State Emergency Service was a truly awesome organisation, Polly decided. Manned mostly by volunteers, their skill set was amazing. The police sergeant had arrived, too, as well as two farmers with a tractor apiece. Someone had done some fast organising.

Two yellow-jacketed officers abseiled down, with much more efficiency and speed than Polly could have managed. They had the truck roped in minutes, anchoring it to the tractors above.

They disappeared again.

'You think they've knocked off for a cuppa?' Polly asked Hugo and he smiled, but absently. His smile was strained.

He had a kid, Polly thought. What was he about, putting himself in harm's way?

Did his wife know where he was? If she did, she'd be having kittens.

Just lucky no one gave a toss about her.

Ooh, there was a bitter thought, and it wasn't true. Her parents would be gutted. But then... If she died they could organise a truly grand funeral, she decided. If there was one thing her mother was good at, it was event management. There'd be a cathedral, massed choirs, requests to wear *'Polly's favourite colour'* which would be pink because her mother always told her pink was her favourite colour even though it wasn't. And she'd arrange a release of white doves and pink and white balloons and the balloons would contain a packet of seeds—zinnias, she thought because *'they're Polly's favourite flower'* and...

And there was the roar of tractors from above, the sound of sharp commands, and then a slow taking up of the slack of the attached ropes.

The truck moved, just a little—and settled again—and the man appeared over the edge and shouted, 'You okay down there?'

'Excellent,' Hugo called, but Polly didn't say anything at all.

'Truck's now secure,' the guy called. 'The paramedics want to know if Horace is okay to move. We can abseil down and bring Horace up on a cradle stretcher. How does that fit with you, Doc?'

'Is it safe for you guys?'

'Go teach your grandmother to suck eggs,' the guy retorted. 'But med report, Doc—the paramedics want to know.'

'He's safe to move as long as we can keep pressure off his chest,' Hugo called. 'I want a neck brace. There's no sign of spinal injury but let's not take any chances. Then Polly.'

'Then you, Doc.'

'Polly second,' Hugo said in a voice that brooked no argument.

And, for once, Polly wasn't arguing.

* * *

It must have been under the truck.

She'd been balancing in the harness, using her feet to stop herself from swinging.

The truck had done its jerk upward and she'd jerked backwards herself, maybe as an automatic reaction to tension. She'd pushed her feet hard against the cliff to steady herself.

The snake must have been caught under the truck in the initial fall. With the pressure off, it lurched forward to get away.

Polly's foot landed right on its spine.

It landed one fierce bite to her ankle—and then slithered away down the cliff.

She didn't move. She didn't cry out.

Two guys in bright yellow overalls were abseiling down towards the driver's side of the truck, holding an end of a cradle stretcher apiece. They looked competent, sure of themselves...fast?

Horace was still the priority. He was elderly, he'd suffered massive blood loss and he needed to be where he could be worked on if he went into cardiac arrest.

She was suffering a snake bite.

Tiger snake? She wasn't sure. She'd only ever seen one in the zoo and she hadn't looked all that closely then.

It had had stripes.

Tiger snakes were deadly.

But not immediately. Wombat Valley was a bush hospital and one thing bush hospitals were bound to have was antivenin, she told herself. She thought back to her training. No one ever died in screaming agony two minutes after they were bitten by a snake. They died hours later. If they didn't get antivenin.

Therefore, she just needed to stay still and the nice guys in the yellow suits would come and get her and they'd all live happily ever after.

'Polly?' It was Hugo, his voice suddenly sharp.

'I...what?' She let go her toehold—she was only using one foot now—and her rope swung.

She felt...a bit sick.

That must be her imagination. She shouldn't feel sick so fast.

'Polly, what's happening?'

The guys—no, on closer inspection, it was a guy and a woman—had reached Horace. Had Hugo fitted the neck brace to Horace, or had the abseilers? She hadn't noticed. They were steadying the stretcher against the cliff, then sliding it into the cab of the truck, but leaving its weight to be taken by the anchor point on the road. In another world she'd be fascinated.

Things were a bit...fuzzy.

'Polly?'

'Mmm?' She was having trouble getting her tongue to work. Her mouth felt thick and dry.

'What the hell...? I can't get out. Someone up there...priority's changed. We need a harness on Dr Hargreaves—fast.'

Did he think she was going to faint? She thought about that and decided he might be right.

So do something.

She had a seat—sort of. She looped her arms around the side cords and linked her hands, then put her head down as far as she could.

She could use some glucose.

'Get someone down here.' It was a roar. 'Fast. Move!'

'I'm not going to faint,' she managed but it sounded feeble, even to her.

'Damn right, you're not going to faint,' Hugo snapped. 'You faint and you're out of my employ. Pull yourself together, Dr Hargreaves. Put that head further down, take deep breaths and count between breathing. You know what to do. Do it.'

'I need...juice...' she managed but her voice trailed off. This was ridiculous. She couldn't...

She mustn't.

Breathe, two, three. Out, two, three. Breathe...

'Hold on, sweetheart—they're coming.'

What had he called her? *Sweetheart?* No one called Polly Hargreaves sweetheart unless they wanted her to do something. Or not do something. Not to cut her hair. Not to do medicine. To play socialite daughter for their friends.

To come home for Christmas...

She wasn't going home for Christmas. She was staying in Wombat Valley. The thought was enough to steady her.

If she fainted then she'd fall and they'd send her back to Sydney in a body bag and her mother would have her fabulous funeral...

Not. Not, not, not.

'I've been bitten by a snake,' she muttered, with as much strength and dignity as she could muster. *Which wasn't actually very much at all.* She still had her head between her knees and she daren't move. 'It was brown with stripes and it bit my ankle. And I know it's a hell of a time to tell you, but I need to say...I'm also a Type One diabetic. So I'm not sure whether this is a hypo or snake bite but, if I fall, don't let my mother bury me in pink. Promise.'

'I promise,' Hugo said and then a yellow-suited figure was beside her, and her only objection was that he was blocking her view of Hugo.

It sort of seemed important that she see Hugo.

'She has a snake bite on her ankle,' Hugo was saying urgently. 'And she needs glucose. Probable hypo. Get the cradle back down here as fast as you can, and bring glucagon. While we wait, I have a pressure bandage here in the cabin. If you can swing her closer we'll get her leg immobilised.'

'You're supposed to be on holiday,' Polly managed while Yellow Suit figured out how to manoeuvre her closer to Hugo.

'Like that's going to happen now,' Hugo said grimly. 'Let's get the hired help safe and worry about holidays later.'

CHAPTER FOUR

FROM THERE THINGS moved fast. The team on the road was reassuringly professional. Polly was strapped into the cradle, her leg firmly wrapped, then she was lifted up the cliff with an abseiler at either end of the cradle.

She was hardly bumped, but she felt shaky and sick. If she was in an emergency situation she'd be no help at all.

'I'm so sorry,' she managed, for Hugo had climbed up after her and he was leaning over the stretcher, his lean, strong face creased in concern. 'What a wuss. I didn't mean...'

'To be confronted by two guys about to fall down a cliff. To need to climb down and secure the truck and save them. To bring them lifesaving equipment and get bitten by a snake doing it. I don't blame you for apologising, Dr Hargreaves. Wuss doesn't begin to describe it.'

'I should...'

'Shut up,' he said, quite kindly. 'Polly, the snake...you said it had stripes.'

'Brown with faint stripes.'

'Great for noticing.'

'It bit me,' she said with dignity. 'I always take notice of things that bite me.'

'Excellent. Okay, sweetheart, we have a plan...'

'I'm not your sweetheart!' She said it with vehemence and she saw his brows rise in surprise—and also humour.

'No. Inappropriate. Sexist. Apologies. Okay, Dr Hargreaves, we have a plan. We're taking you to the Wombat Valley Hospital—it's only a mile down the road. There we'll fill you up with antivenin. The snake you describe is either a tiger or a brown…'

'Tiger's worse.'

'We have antivenin for both. You're reacting well with glucose. I think the faintness was a combination—the adrenaline went out of the situation just as the snake hit and the shock was enough to send you over the edge.'

'I did not go over the edge!'

'I do need to get my language right,' he said and grinned. 'No, Dr Hargreaves, you did not go over the edge, for which I'm profoundly grateful. And now we'll get the antivenin in…'

'Which one?'

'I have a test kit at the hospital and I've already taken a swab.'

'And if it's a rare…I don't know…zebra python with no known antivenin…?'

'Then I'll eat my hat.' And then he took her hand and held, and he smiled down at her and his smile…

It sort of did funny things to her. She'd been feeling woozy before. Now she was feeling even woozier.

'We need to move,' he said, still holding her hand strongly. 'We'll take you to the hospital now, but once we have the antivenin on board we'll transfer you to Sydney. We've already called in the medical transfer chopper. Horace has cracked ribs. Marg's demanding specialists. I'm more than happy that he be transferred, and I'm imagining that you'll be better in Sydney as well. You have cuts and bruises all over you, plus a load of snake venom. You can recover in Sydney and then spend Christmas with your family.'

Silence.

He was still holding her hand. She should let it go, she thought absently. She should push herself up to standing, put her hands on her hips and let him have it.

She was no more capable of doing such a thing than flying, but she gripped his hand so tightly her cuts screamed in protest. She'd bleed on him, she thought absently, but what was a little gore when what she had to say was so important?

'I am not going back to Sydney,' she hissed and she saw his brow snap down in surprise.

'Polly...'

'Don't Polly me. If you think I've come all this way...if you think I've crawled down cliffs and ruined a perfectly good dress and scratched my hands and hurt my bum and then been bitten by a vicious, lethal snake you don't even know the name of yet...if you think I'm going to go through all that and still get to spend Christmas in Sydney...'

'You don't want to?' he asked cautiously and she stared at him as if he had a kangaroo loose in his top paddock.

'In your dreams. I accepted a job in Wombat Valley and that's where I'm staying. You do have antivenin?'

'I...yes.'

'And competent staff to watch my vital signs for the next twenty-four hours?'

'Yes, but...'

'But nothing,' she snapped. 'You employed me, Dr Denver, and now you're stuck with me. Send Horace wherever you like, but I'm staying here.'

The transfer to the hospital was swift and efficient. Joe, his nurse administrator, was pre-warned and had the test kit and antivenin ready. Joe was more than capable of setting up an IV line. Wishing he was two doctors and not one, Hugo left Polly in Joe's care while he organised an X-ray of Horace's chest. He needed to make sure a rib wasn't about to pierce a lung.

The X-ray showed three cracked ribs, one that looked unstable. It hadn't punctured his lung, though, and Horace's breathing seemed secure. If he was kept immobile, he could be taken to Sydney.

'You're not sending Dr Hargreaves with him?' Mary, his

second-in-command nurse, demanded as he left Horace with the paramedics and headed for Polly.

He'd been torn... Polly, Horace, Polly, Horace...

Joe would have called him if there was a change. Still, his strides were lengthening.

'She won't go,' he told Mary. 'She wants to stay.'

'Oh, Hugo.' Mary was in her sixties, a grandma, and a bit weepy at the best of times. Now her kindly eyes filled with tears. 'You'll be looking after her instead of going to the beach. Of all the unfair things...'

'It's not unfair. It's just unfortunate. She can hardly take over my duties now. She'll need to be watched for twenty-four hours for reaction to the bite as well as reaction to the antivenin. The last thing we need is anaphylactic shock and it'll take days for the venom to clear her system completely. Meanwhile, have you seen her hands? Mary, she slid down a nylon cord to bring me equipment. She was scratched climbing to secure the truck. She was bitten because...'

'Because she didn't have sensible shoes on,' Mary said with asperity. The nurse was struggling to keep up but speed wasn't interfering with indignation. 'Did you see her shoes? Sergeant Myer picked them up on the roadside and brought them in. A more ridiculous pair of shoes for a country doctor to be wearing...'

'You think we should yell at her about her shoes?'

'I'm just saying...'

'She was driving here in her sports car. You don't need sensible clothes while driving.'

'Well, that's another thing,' Mary said darkly. 'Of all the silly cars for a country GP...'

'But she's not a country GP.' He turned and took a moment to focus on Mary's distress. Mary was genuinely upset on his behalf—heck, the whole of Wombat Valley would be upset on his behalf—but Polly wasn't to blame and suddenly it was important that the whole of Wombat Valley knew it.

He thought of Polly sitting on her makeshift swing, trying

to steady herself with her bare feet. He thought of her polka dot dress, the flounces, the determined smile... She must have been hurting more than he could imagine—those cords had really cut—but she'd still managed to give him cheek.

He thought of her sorting the medical equipment in his bag, expertly discarding what wasn't needed, determined to bring him what was. Courage didn't begin to describe what she'd done, he thought, so no, he wasn't about to lecture her for inappropriate footwear.

'Polly saved us,' he told Mary, gently but firmly. 'What happened was an accident and she did more than anyone could expect. She put her life on the line to save us and she even managed her own medical drama with skill. I owe her everything.'

'So you'll miss your Christmas at the beach.'

'There's no choice. We need to move on.'

Mary sniffed, sounding unconvinced, but Hugo swung open the door of the treatment room and Joe was chuckling and Polly was smiling up and he thought...

Who could possibly judge this woman and find her wanting? Who could criticise her?

This woman was amazing—and it seemed that she, also, was moving on.

'Doctor, we may have to rethink the hospital menu for Christmas if Dr Hargreaves is admitted,' Joe told him as he entered. 'She's telling me turkey, three veggies, commercial Christmas pudding and canned custard won't cut it. Not even if we add a bonbon on the side.'

He blinked.

Snake bite. Lacerations. Shock.

They were talking turkey?

Okay. He needed to focus on medical imperatives, even if his patient wasn't. Even if Polly didn't seem like his patient.

'The swab?' he asked and Joe nodded and held up the test kit.

'The brown snake showed up in seconds. The tiger segment showed positive about two minutes later but the kit says that's often the way—they're similar. It seems the brown snake venom's enough to eventually discolour the tiger snake pocket, so brown it is. And I reckon she's got a fair dose on board. Polly has a headache and nausea already. I'm betting she's been solidly bitten.'

Hugo checked the kit for himself and nodded. He'd seen the ankle—it'd be a miracle if the venom hadn't gone in. 'Brown's good,' he told Polly. 'You'll recover faster than from a tiger.'

'I'm feeling better already,' she told him and gave him another smile, albeit a wobbly one. 'But not my dress. It's ripped to pieces. That snake owes me...'

He had to smile. She even managed to sound indignant.

'But you're nauseous?'

'Don't you care about my dress?'

'I care about you more. Nausea?'

'A little. And,' she went on, as if she was making an enormous concession, 'I might be a little bit headachy.'

A little...

The venom would hardly be taking effect yet, he thought. She'd still be in the window period where victims ran for help, tried to pretend they hadn't been bitten, tried to search and identify the snake that had bitten them—and in the process spread the venom through their system and courted death.

Polly had been sensible, though. She'd stayed still. She'd told him straight away. She'd allowed the paramedics to bring her up on the rigid stretcher.

Okay, clambering down cliffs in bare feet in the Australian summer was hardly sensible but he couldn't argue with her reasons.

'Then let's keep it like that,' he told her. 'I want you to stay still while we get this antivenin on board.'

'I've been practically rigid since I got bit,' she said virtuously. 'Textbook patient. By the way, it's a textbook immobilisation bandage too. Excellent work, Dr Denver.'

He grinned at that, and she smiled back at him, and then he sort of paused.

That smile...

It was a magic smile. As sick and battered as she was, her smile twinkled. Her face was pallid and wan, but it was still alight with laughter.

This was a woman who would have played in the orchestra as the *Titanic* sank, he thought, and then he thought: *Nope*, she'd be too busy fashioning lifelines out of spare trombones.

But her smile was fading. Their gazes still held but all of a sudden she looked...doubtful?

Maybe unsure.

Maybe his smile was having the same effect on her as hers was on his?

That would be wishful thinking. Plus it would be unprofessional.

Move on.

Joe had already set up the drip. Hugo prepared the serum, double-checked everything with Joe, then carefully injected it. It'd start working almost immediately, he thought; hopefully, before Polly started feeling the full effects of the bite.

'How are you feeling everywhere else?' he asked, and she gave a wry smile that told him more than anything else that the humour was an act. Her freckles stood out from her pallid face, and her red hair seemed overbright.

'I'm...sore,' she admitted.

'I've started cleaning the worst of the grazes,' Joe told him. 'She could do with a full bed bath but you said immobile so immobile it is. There's a cut on her palm, though, that might need a stitch or two.'

He lifted her palm and turned it over. And winced.

Her hand was a mess. He could see the coil marks of the

rope. The marks ran along her palm, across her wrist and up her arm.

She'd come down that nylon cord…

He heard Mary's breath hiss in amazement. 'How…?'

'I told you,' he said, still staring at Polly's palm. 'She let herself down the cliff, carrying the bag with saline. Without it, Horace would probably be dead.'

'You did that for Horace?' Mary breathed, looking at the mess in horror, and Hugo thought he no longer had to defend her. Polly had suddenly transformed into a heroine.

'There's a lot to be said for elevators,' Polly said but her voice faltered a little as she looked at her palm and he realised shock was still a factor.

And there'd be bruises everywhere. He had to get that antivenin working, though, before they could clean her up properly. Joe had even left the remnants of her dress on. The polka dots made her look even more wan.

'Let's get you comfortable,' he said. 'How about a nice dose of morphine for the pain, some metoclopramide for the nausea and a wee shot of Valium on the side?'

'You want to knock me into the middle of next week?'

'I want you to sleep.'

She gazed up at him, those amazing eyes locked to his. He couldn't make out whether they were green or brown. They were…

Um…no. She was his patient. He didn't note the colour of his patient's eyes unless there was a medical issue. Bloodshot? Jaundiced? Fixed pupils? Polly's eyes showed none of those. He needed to ignore them.

How could he ignore them?

'You promise you won't transport me to Sydney while I'm sleeping?' she demanded, and he smiled and kept looking into those over-bright eyes.

'I promise.'

'That's in front of witnesses.'

'Joe, Mary, you heard me. The lady stays in Wombat Valley.'

'Very well, then,' Polly said, her voice wobbling again. Still, she looked straight up at him, as if reading reassurance in his gaze. 'Drugs, drugs and more drugs, and then Christmas in Wombat Valley. I can... I can handle that. But turkey with three veg has to go, Dr Denver.'

'You'll get a better Christmas dinner in Sydney.'

'No Sydney! Promise?'

'I already have,' he told her but suddenly she was no longer listening. The fight had gone out of her. She had the antivenin on board. Her future was sorted.

The flight-or-fight reflex relaxed. She sank back onto the pillows and sighed.

'Okay, Dr Denver, whatever you say,' she whispered. 'I'm in your hands.'

He had Horace sorted. He had Polly comfortable.

There was still the issue of Ruby.

How did you tell a seven-year-old she wasn't going to the beach for Christmas? She'd been counting down the days for months. He'd tried to figure it out all the way back to the house, but in the end he didn't need to.

Lois, his housekeeper, was before him. News got around fast in Wombat Valley and by the time he walked in the front door, Ruby was in tears and Lois was looking like a martyr who'd come to the end of her tether.

'I'm sorry, Dr Denver, but I can't stay,' she told him over the top of Ruby's head. 'I promised my son I'd spend Christmas in Melbourne with my grandchildren and that's where I'm going. I leave in half an hour, and I've told Ruby you're not going anywhere. You can see how upset she is, but is it my fault? You went and climbed into that truck. Was Horace worth it? He's a lazy wastrel and his wife's no better. Risking your life, losing your holiday, for such a loser...' She shook her head. 'I wash my hands of you, I really do.

Ruby, stop crying, sweetheart. I dare say your uncle will sort something out.'

And she picked up her handbag and headed out of the house before Hugo could possibly change her mind.

Hugo was left facing his niece.

Christmas. No beach. No housekeeper.

One fill-in doctor in his hospital instead of in his surgery.

He was trapped, but what was new? What was new was that Ruby felt as if she was trapped with him.

His niece looked as if she'd been trying not to cry, but fat tears were sliding down her face regardless. She stood silent, in her garden-stained shorts and T-shirt, her wispy blonde curls escaping every which way from their pigtails, and her wan little face blank with misery. She didn't complain, though, he thought bleakly. She never had.

He knelt down and hugged her. She held her stiff little body in his arms and he felt the effort she was making not to sob.

'We'll fix it somehow,' he murmured. 'Somehow…'

How?

Today was Monday. Christmas was Saturday.

He thought of the gifts he'd already packed, ready to be produced by Santa at their apartment by the beach. Bucket and spade. Water wings. A blow-up seahorse.

Lois had even made her a bikini.

He thought of his housekeeper marching off towards her Christmas and he thought he couldn't blame her. Lois was fond of Ruby, but he'd pushed her to the limit.

And there was another complication. It was school holidays and Ruby would need daytime care if he had to keep working. He'd need to call in favours, and he hated asking for favours.

Maybe he and Ruby should just walk away, he thought bleakly, as he'd thought many times this past year. But the complications flooded in, as they always did.

Wombat Valley was Ruby's home. It was all she knew. In

Sydney she had nothing and no one but him. His old job, the job he loved, thoracic surgery at Sydney Central, involved long hours and call backs. Here, his house was right next to the hospital. He could pop in and out at will, and he had an entire valley of people more than willing to help. They helped not just because it meant the Valley had a doctor but because so many of them genuinely cared for Ruby.

How could *he* stop caring, when the Valley had shown they cared so much? How could he turn his back on the Valley's needs and on Ruby's needs?

How could he ever return to the work he loved, to his friends, his social life, to his glorious bachelor freedom?

He couldn't. He couldn't even leave for two weeks. He had patients in hospital.

He had Dr Pollyanna Hargreaves in Ward One.

Polly...

Why was Polly so important? What was he doing, hugging Ruby and drying her eyes but thinking of Polly? But the image of Polly, hanging on her appalling handmade swing while every part of her hurt, wouldn't go away.

'Ruby, I need to tell you about one brave lady,' he told her and Ruby sniffed and swiped away her tears with the back of her hand and tilted her chin, ready to listen. In her own way, she was as brave as Polly, he thought.

But not as cute. No matter how much the Valley mums helped, Ruby always looked a waif. She was skinny and leggy, and nothing seemed to help her put on weight. She was tall for her seven years; her skimpy pigtails made her look taller and her eyes always seemed too big for her face. Her knees were constantly grubby—she'd have been mucking about in the garden, which was her favourite place. She had mud on her tear-stained face.

He loved her with all his heart.

'Is the lady why we can't go to the beach?' she quavered and he took her hand and led her out to the veranda. And there was another reminder of what they'd be missing. Hamster wasn't there.

Hamster was Ruby's Labrador, a great boofy friend. They hadn't been able to find a beach house where dogs were permitted so he'd taken Hamster back to the farmer who'd bred him, to be taken care of for two weeks.

Ruby had sobbed.

There was one bright thought—they could get Hamster back for Christmas.

Meanwhile, he had to say it like it was.

'Did Lois tell you about the truck accident?' he asked and Ruby nodded. She was a quiet kid but she listened. He'd learned early it was impossible to keep much from her.

'Well, the truck fell off the cliff, and the lady doctor—Dr Hargreaves—the doctor who was coming to work here while we were away—hurt herself by climbing down the cliff to save everyone.'

Ruby's pixie face creased as she sorted it out in her head. 'Everyone?'

'Yes.'

'Why didn't you save everyone?'

'I tried but I got stuck. She saved me, too. And then she got bitten by a snake.'

Ruby's eyes widened. 'What sort of a snake?'

'A brown.'

'That's better than a tiger. Didn't she know to make a noise? If you make lots of noise they slither away before you reach them.'

'The snake got stuck under the truck. I guess it got scared too, and it bit her.'

'Is she very sick?'

'She'll be sick for a couple of days.'

'So then can we go to the beach?'

He thought about it. *Don't make promises*, he told himself, but if Polly didn't react too badly to the antivenin it might be possible. If those cuts didn't stop her working.

She still wanted to stay in the Valley.

'I'm not sure,' he said weakly.

'Will she have to stay in hospital all over Christmas?'

That was a thought. And a problem?

Normally, snake bite victims stayed in hospital overnight for observation. She was a Type One diabetic. She might need to stay longer, but she was already having reservations about hospital food. How long could he keep her there?

He and Ruby had cleared out their best spare room. They'd made it look pretty. Ruby had even put fresh flowers in a vase on the chest of drawers. 'Girls like that.'

But he couldn't leave the moment she was released from hospital, he conceded. He and Polly would have to stay for a day or two.

He was counting in his head. Monday today. Bring Polly back here on Tuesday or Wednesday.

Leave on Thursday or Friday? Christmas Saturday.

It was cutting things fine.

Food... There was another problem. Sick and shocked as she was, Polly Hargreaves had already turned her nose up at bought pudding.

He had no food here. He'd assumed his locum could eat in the hospital kitchen.

He'd promised Ruby fish and chips on the beach for Christmas, and Ruby had glowed at the thought. Now... He might well have a recovering Polly for Christmas.

He didn't even have a Christmas tree.

And, as if on cue, there was the sound of a car horn from the road—a silly, tooting car horn that was nothing like the sensible farm vehicle horns used for clearing cattle off the road or warning of kangaroos. He looked up and a little yellow sports car was being driven through the gate, a police car following behind.

This was Polly's car. He'd seen it at the crash site but he'd been too distracted to do more than glance at it.

But here it was, being driven by one of the local farmers. Bill McCray was behind the wheel, twenty-five years old and grinning like the Cheshire cat.

'Hey, Doc, where do you want us to put the car?'

'What's the car?' Ruby breathed.

'I… It's Polly's car,' he managed.

'Polly…'

'Dr Hargreaves…'

'Is that her name? Polly, like *Polly put the kettle on*?'

'I…yes.'

'It's yellow.' Ruby was pie-eyed. 'And it hasn't got a top. And it's got a Christmas tree in the back. And suitcases and suitcases.'

There were indeed suitcases and suitcases. And a Christmas tree. Silver. Large.

Bill pulled up under the veranda. Both he and the policeman emerged from their respective vehicles, Bill looking decidedly sorry the ride had come to an end.

'She's a beauty,' he declared. 'I'd love to see how the cows reacted if I tried to drive that round the farm. And the guys say the lady doc's just as pretty. I reckon I can feel a headache coming on. Or six. When did you say you were leaving, Doc?'

'We're not leaving,' Ruby whispered but she no longer sounded desolate. She was staring in stupefaction at the tree. It was all silver sparkles and it stretched over the top of the luggage, from the front passenger seat to well behind the exhaust pipe.

Polly had tied a huge red tinsel bow at the rear—to warn traffic of the long load? It looked…amazing.

'We're staying here to look after the lady doctor,' Ruby said, still staring. 'I think she might be nice. Is she nice, Uncle Hugo?'

'Very nice,' he said weakly and headed down to unpack a Christmas tree.

CHAPTER FIVE

NIGHT ROUND. HE SHOULD be eating fish and chips on the beach right now, Hugo thought as he headed through the darkened wards to Ward One. He'd thought he had this Christmas beautifully organised.

Most of his long-termers had gone home for Christmas. He had three elderly patients in the nursing home section, all with local family and heaps of visitors. None needed his constant attendance.

Sarah Ferguson was still in Room Two. Sarah had rolled a tractor on herself a month ago. She'd spent three weeks in Sydney Central and had been transferred here for the last couple of weeks to be closer to her family. Her family had already organised to have Christmas in her room. She hardly needed him either.

But Polly needed him. He'd been back and forth during the afternoon, checking her. Anaphylactic shock was still a possibility. He still had her on fifteen minute obs. She was looking okay but with snake bites you took no chances.

Barb, the night nurse, greeted him happily and put down her knitting to accompany him.

'I'm fine,' he told her. 'I can do my round by myself.'

The scarf Barb was knitting, a weird mix of eclectic colours, was barely six feet long. Barb had told him it needed to be ten.

'Why my grandson had to tell me he wanted a Dr Who scarf a week before Christmas...' she'd muttered last night and he'd thought he'd made things easy for her by keeping the hospital almost empty.

But Barb did take her job seriously. She was knitting in front of the monitors attached to Ward One, which acted as the Intensive Care room. Any blip in Polly's heart rate and she'd be in there in seconds, and one glance at the chart in front of her told him Polly had been checked thoroughly and regularly.

'No change?'

'She's not sleeping. She's pretty sore. If you could maybe write her up for some stronger pain relief for the night...' She hesitated. 'And, Doc... She's not admitting it but I'm sure she's still pretty shaken. She's putting on a brave front but my daughter's her age. All bravado but jelly inside.'

He nodded and left her to her knitting.

Polly's ward was in near darkness, lit only by the floor light. He knocked lightly and went in.

Polly was a huddled mass under the bedclothes. She'd drawn her knees up to her middle, almost in a foetal position.

She's still pretty shaken...

Barb was right, he thought. This was the age-old position for those alone and scared.

He had a sudden urge to head to the bed, scoop her up and hold her. She'd had one hell of a day. What she needed was comfort.

Someone to hold...

Um...that wouldn't be him. There were professional boundaries, after all.

Instead, he tugged the visitor's chair across to the bed, sat down and reached for her hand.

Um... Her wrist. Not her hand. He was taking her pulse. That was professional.

'Hey,' he said, very softly. 'How's it going?'

'Great,' she managed and he smiled. Her *'great'* had been weak but it was sarcastic.

Still she had spirit.

'The venom will have kicked in but the antivenin will be doing its job,' he told her. 'Your obs are good.'

'Like I said—great.' She eased herself from the foetal position, casually, as if she didn't want him to notice how she'd been lying. 'Sorry. That sounds ungrateful. I am grateful. Mary and Joe gave me a good wash. I'm antivenined. I'm stitched, I'm disinfected and I'm in a safe place. But I've ruined your holiday. I'm so sorry.'

All this and she was concerned about his missed vacation?

'Right,' he said, almost as sarcastic as she'd been. 'You saved my life and you're sorry.'

'I didn't save your life.'

'You know what happened when they tugged the truck up the cliff? It swung and hit one of the saplings that had been holding it from falling further. The sapling lifted right out of the ground. It'd been holding by a thread.'

She shuddered and his hold on her hand tightened. Forget taking her pulse, he decided. She needed comfort and he was giving it any way he could.

'Polly, is there anyone we can ring? The nurses tell me you haven't contacted anyone. Your parents? A boyfriend? Any friend?'

'You let my family know what's happened and you'll have helicopters landing on the roof in ten minutes. And the press. You'll have my dad threatening to sue you, the hospital and the National Parks for letting the Gap exist in the first place. You don't know my family. Please, I'm fine as I am.'

She wasn't fine, though. She still had the shakes.

The press? Who was she?

She was alone. That was all he needed to focus on right now. 'Polly, you need someone...'

'I don't need anyone.' She hesitated. 'Though I am a bit shaky,' she admitted. 'I could use another dose of that nice woozy Valium. You think another dose would turn me into an addict?'

'I think we can risk it. And how about more pain relief, too? I have a background morphine dose running in the IV line but we can top it up. Pain level, one to ten?'

'Six,' she said and he winced.

'Ouch. Why didn't you tell Barb? She would have got me here sooner.'

'I'm not a whinger.'

'How did I already know that?' He shook his head, re-checked her obs, rang for Barb and organised the drugs. Barb did what was needed and then bustled back to her scarf. That meant Hugo could leave too.

But Polly was alone and she was still shaking.

He could ask Barb to bring her knitting in here.

Then who would look after the monitors for the other rooms?

It was okay him being here, he decided. His house was right next door to the hospital and they had an intercom set up in the nurses' station, next to the monitors. Ruby had been fast asleep for a couple of hours but, any whimper she made, Barb would know and send him home fast.

So he could sit here for a while.

Just until Polly was asleep, he told himself. He sat and almost unconsciously she reached out and took his hand again. As if it was her right. As if it was something she really needed, almost as important as breathing.

'I was scared,' she admitted.

'Which part scared you the most?' he asked. 'Sliding down the cliff? Hanging on that nylon cord swing? When Joe Blake did his thing...?'

'Joe Blake?'

'You really are city,' he teased. 'Joe Blake—Snake.'

'It was a bad moment,' she confessed. 'But the worst was when I saw the truck. When I realised there were people in it.'

'I guess it'd be like watching stretchers being wheeled into Emergency after a car crash,' he said. 'Before you know what you're facing.'

'Yeah.'

'But you broke it into manageable bits. You have excellent triage skills, Dr Hargreaves.'

'Maybe.'

She fell silent for a minute and then the hold on his hand grew tighter. But what she said was at odds with her obvious need. 'You shouldn't be here,' she told him. 'You should be home with your niece. Barb tells me she's your niece and not your daughter and her name's Ruby. Is she home alone?'

'Home's next door. Her bedroom's a hundred yards from the nurses' station. Her nightlight's on and whoever's monitoring the nurses' station can watch the glow and can listen on the intercom. If Ruby wakes up, all she has to do is hit the button and she can talk to the nurses or to me.'

'Good system,' she said sleepily and he thought the drugs were taking effect—or maybe it was simply the promise of the drugs.

Or maybe it was because she was holding his hand? It seemed an almost unconscious action, but she wasn't letting go.

'Tell me about Ruby,' she whispered and he sat and thought about his niece and felt the pressure of Polly's hand in his and the sensation was…

Was what?

Something he didn't let himself feel. Something he'd pushed away?

'And tell me about you too,' she murmured and he thought he didn't need to tell her anything. Doctors didn't tell personal stuff to patients.

But in the silence of the little ward, in the peacefulness of the night, he found himself thinking about a night almost a year ago. The phone call from the police. The night he'd realised life as he knew it had just slammed to an end.

He'd been born and raised in this place—Wombat Valley, where nothing ever happened. Wombat Valley, where you could sit on the veranda at night and hear nothing but the frogs and the hoot of the night owls.

Wombat Valley, where everyone depended on everyone else.

Grace, his sister, had hated it. She'd run away at sixteen and she'd kept on running. 'I feel trapped,' she'd shouted, over and over. Hugo had been twelve when she'd run and he hadn't understood.

But twelve months ago, the night his sister died, it was Hugo who'd been trapped. That night he'd felt like running as well.

He didn't. How could he? He'd returned to the Valley and it seemed as if he'd be here for ever.

'Tell me about Ruby?' Polly whispered again, and her question wasn't impatient. It was as if the night had thoughts of its own and she was content to wait.

'Ruby's my niece.'

'Yeah. Something I don't know?'

'She's adorable.'

'And you wouldn't be biased?'

He smiled. She sounded half asleep, but she was still clutching his hand and he wondered if the questions were a ruse to have him stay.

'She's seven years old,' he said. 'She's skinny, tough, fragile, smart. She spends her time in the garden, mucking round in the dirt, trying to make things grow, playing with a menagerie of snails, tadpoles, frogs, ladybirds.'

'Her parents?'

'We don't know who her father is,' Hugo told her. He was almost talking to himself but it didn't seem to matter. 'My sister suffered from depression, augmented by drug use. She was always…erratic. She ran away at sixteen and we hardly saw her. She contacted me when Ruby was born—until then we hadn't even known she was pregnant. She was in Darwin and she was in a mess. I flew up and my parents followed.

Mum and Dad brought them both back to Wombat Valley. Grace came and went, but Ruby stayed.'

'Why...why the Valley?'

'My father was the Valley doctor—our current house is where Grace and I were raised. Dad died when Ruby was three, but Mum stayed on. Mum cared for Ruby and she loved her. Then, late last year, Grace decided she wanted to leave for good and she wanted Ruby back. She was with... someone who scared my mother. Apparently there was an enormous row, which culminated in Mum having a stroke. The day after Mum's funeral, Grace drove her car off the Gap. Maybe it was an accident. Probably it wasn't.'

'Oh, no...'

'So that's that,' he said flatly. 'End of story. The Valley loves Ruby, Ruby loves the Valley and I'm home for good. I'm not doing a great job with Ruby, but I'm trying. She loved Mum. Grace confused her and at the end she frightened her. Now she's too quiet. She's a tomboy. I worry...'

'There's nothing wrong with being a tomboy,' Polly whispered, sounding closer and closer to sleep. 'You don't force her to wear pink?'

He smiled at that. 'She'd have it filthy in minutes. What I should do is buy camouflage cloth and find a dungaree maker.'

'She sounds my type of kid.'

'You do pretty.'

Where had that come from? He shouldn't comment on patients' appearances. *You do pretty*? What sort of line was that?

'I like clothes that make me smile,' she whispered. 'I have an amazing pair of crimson boots. One day I might show you.'

'I'll look forward to that.' Maybe he shouldn't have said that either. Was it inappropriate?

Did he care?

'So Ruby knows she's safe with you?' she whispered.

'She's as safe as I can make her. We had an interim doctor after Dad died but he left the moment I appeared on the scene. This valley could use three doctors, but for now I'm it. I've been advertising for twelve months but no one's applied. Meanwhile, Ruby understands the intercom system and she can see the hospital from her bedroom. If I can't be there in ten seconds someone else will be. That's the deal the hospital board employs me under. Ruby comes first.'

'So if there's drama...'

'This community backs me up. I'm here if, and only if, Wombat Valley helps me raise Ruby.' He shrugged. 'It's my job.'

Only it wasn't, or not his job of choice. He'd walked away from his job as a thoracic surgeon. Not being able to use the skills he'd fought to attain still left him feeling gutted, and now he couldn't even get Christmas off.

'But I've so messed with your Christmas,' she said weakly, echoing his thoughts, and he hauled himself together.

'I've told you—you've done no such thing.'

'Would it be better for you if I was transferred?'

'I...no.'

'But I'm supposed to be staying in your house. You won't want me now.'

At least he had this answer ready. He'd had the evening to think about it. Polly's tree was now set up in the living room. He was preparing to make the most of it.

'If you stay, you might still be able to help me,' he said diffidently, as if he was asking a favour. And maybe he was; it was just that his ideas about this woman were all over the place and he couldn't quite get them together. 'You'll need a few days to get over your snake bite and bruises. You could snuggle into one of our spare rooms—it's a big house—and Ruby could look after you. She'd enjoy that.'

'Ruby would look after me?'

'She loves to be needed. She's already fascinated by your

snake bite—you'll have to show her the fang marks, by the way. She's also in love with your Christmas tree.'

'My tree…'

'The boys brought your car to my house. Ruby insisted we unpack it. I'm sorry but it's in the living room and Ruby's already started decorating it.'

'You don't have a tree of your own?'

'We were going away for Christmas.'

'You still should have had a tree,' she murmured, but her voice was getting so weak he could hardly hear. She was slurring her words and finally the hold on his hand was weakening. The drugs were taking over.

He should tuck her hand under the covers, he thought, and finally he did, but as he released her fingers he felt an indefinable sense of loss.

And, as he did, she smiled up at him, and weirdly she shifted her hand back out of the covers. She reached up and touched his face. Just lightly. It was a feather-touch, tracing the bones of his cheek.

'I'm glad I saved you,' she whispered and it was all he could do to hear.

'I'm glad you saved me too.' And for the life of him he couldn't stop a shake entering his voice.

'And you didn't have a Christmas tree…'

'N…no.'

'And now I'm going to stay with you until Christmas?' What could he say? 'If you like.'

'Then it sounds like I need to be helpful,' she whispered, and it was as if she was summoning all the strength she had to say something. 'Sometimes I can be my mother's daughter. December the twentieth and you don't even have a tree. And you have a little girl who likes tadpoles and dungarees. And I just know you're a very nice man. What were you doing in that truck in the first place? The snake could just as easily have bitten you. You know what, Dr Denver? As

well as saving your skin, I'm going to save your Christmas.
How's that for a plan?'

But she got no further. Her hand fell away. Her lids closed,
and she was asleep.

He walked home feeling…disorientated. Or more. Discombobulated? There was no other word big enough to describe
it.

He could still feel the touch of Polly's fingers on his face
where she'd touched him.

He might just as well have been kissed…

There was a crazy idea. He hadn't been kissed. She'd been
doped to the eyeballs with painkillers and relaxants. She'd
had an appalling shock and she was injured. People did and
said weird things…

Still the trace of her fingers remained.

She was beautiful.

She was brave, funny, smart.

She was scared and she was alone.

But what had she said? He replayed her words in his head.

*'You let my family know what's happened and you'll have
helicopters landing on the roof ten minutes later. And the
press…'*

Who was she? He needed to do some research. He'd rung
her medical referees when she'd applied to do the locum. He'd
been given glowing reports on her medical skills but
there'd been a certain reticence…

He'd avoided the reticence. He'd been so relieved to find
a doctor with the skills to look after the Valley, he wouldn't
have minded if she'd had two heads. If she had the medical
qualifications, nothing else could matter.

Only of course it mattered and now he was stuck in the
same house as a woman who was brave, funny and smart.

And beautiful.

And alone.

He didn't need this, he told himself. The last thing he

needed in his life was complications caused by a beautiful woman. A love life was something he'd left very firmly in Sydney. No complications until he had his little niece settled…

Right. Regardless, he reached the veranda, sat on the steps and typed her name into his phone's Internet app.

It took time for anything to show. His phone connection was slow. He should go inside and use his computer, but inside the door were Polly's suitcases, and in the living room was Polly's tree. For some reason he felt as if he needed to know what he was letting himself in for before he stepped over the threshold.

And here it was. Pollyanna Hargreaves.

She had a whole Wikipedia entry of her own.

Good grief.

Only child of Charles and Olivia Hargreaves. Expected to inherit the giant small goods manufacturing business built up by her family over generations. Currently practising medicine. Aged twenty-nine. One broken relationship, recent…

He snapped his phone shut. He didn't want to read any more.

What was she doing here? What was she running from?

The broken relationship?

What was she doing being a doctor?

Why didn't she want to go back to Sydney?

He should insist she go back. She could no longer do the job he was paying her for. She deserved compensation—of course she did—but his medical insurance would cover it. He could discharge her from hospital tomorrow or the next day, organise a driver and send her home.

She didn't want to spend Christmas in Sydney.

He sat on the step and stared into the night. The decision should be easy, he thought. She couldn't do the job she'd come for. He and Ruby were still living in the house. She couldn't stay here, so he could send her home.

Her Christmas tree was already up in the living room. This was a big house. They had room.

What was he afraid of?

Of the way she made him feel?

For heaven's sake... He was a mature thirty-six-year-old doctor. He'd had girlfriends in Sydney, one of them long-term. He and Louise had even talked marriage, but she'd been appalled at the idea of Wombat Valley and Ruby. He couldn't blame her.

If he wanted to move on...

On to Polly?

He shook his head in disbelief. This was crazy. He'd known her for less than a day. She was an heiress and she was his patient.

She was funny and smart and brave.

And beautiful.

And he was nuts. He rose and gave himself a fast mental shake. He'd been thrown about too today, he reminded himself. He had the bruises to prove it. There'd been a moment when he'd thought there was a fair chance he could have left Ruby without any family and that moment was still with him.

He must have been hit on the head, he decided, or be suffering from delayed shock. Something was messing with his head.

Polly was a patient tonight, and tomorrow or the next day she'd be staying here as a guest and then hopefully she'd be a colleague. The jury was still out on whether she'd be well enough to take over so he and Ruby could spend a few days at the beach, but if he sent her back to Sydney he'd never know.

He could still feel the touch of her hand...

'So get over it,' he told himself. He needed Hamster. Ruby's big Labrador, given to her as a puppy in desperation on that last appalling Christmas, had turned into his confidante, someone to talk to in the small hours when life got bleak.

He'd fetch Hamster back tomorrow.

And Polly. Polly and Hamster and Christmas.

If she was still here… If he couldn't leave… He'd have to find a turkey.

He didn't know how to cook a turkey.

Turkey. Bonbons. Christmas pudding. Ruby was old enough to know what Christmas dinner should be. She'd been happy with her beach fish and chips substitute, but now…

'Maybe Dr Hargreaves will know how to cook a turkey,' he said morosely but then he glanced again at the information on his phone.

Heiress to a fortune…

'Maybe she has the funds to fly one in ready cooked from Sydney,' he told the absent Hamster.

Maybe pigs could fly.

Polly woke, some time in the small hours.

She hurt.

What was it with snake bite? she wondered. Why did it make everything ache?

Maybe she should write this up for her favourite medical journal—disseminated pain after accidental infusion of snake venom.

That sounded impressive. Her father would show that to his golf cronies.

Her mother, though…she could just hear her. 'Who are you trying to impress? You'll never get a husband if you keep trying to be clever.'

She winced. Her hand hurt.

Okay, maybe this wasn't disseminated pain from infusion of snake venom. Maybe this was disseminated pain from abseiling down a cliff with nylon cord and bare feet.

Her mother might like that better. It didn't sound clever at all.

Why did she feel like crying?

She should ring the bell. She would in a moment, she told herself. The nice night nurse would arrive and top up her medication and send her back into a nice dozy sleep. But for now...

For now she wanted to wallow.

She was missing...missing...

The doctor with the strong, sure hands. Hugo Denver, who'd sat with her until she'd slept. Whose voice was nice and deep and caring. Who looked a million dollars—tall, dark, strong.

Who made her feel safe.

And there was a nonsense. She was always safe. If she let them, her parents would have her cocooned in protective luxury, buffered from the world, safe in their gorgeous lifestyle for ever.

Marrying Marcus.

She winced and shifted in bed and hurt some more, but still she didn't call Barb. She felt as if she had things to sort, and now was as good a time as any to sort them.

She was staying here—for Christmas, at least. Hugo Denver owed her that. But afterwards... What then?

Overseas...

Maybe some volunteer organisation. Doctors were needed everywhere and heaven knew she didn't need money.

Her parents would have kittens.

Her parents were currently having kittens because she wasn't in Sydney. If they knew she was in trouble...

They'd come and she didn't want them to come. She did not want family.

Whereas if Hugo Denver walked in the door...

What was she thinking? She was falling for her boss? Or her doctor? Each was equally unethical.

So why did she want him to come back? When she'd woken, why had her gaze gone directly to the place where he'd been sitting?

Why could she still feel his hand?

Weakness, she told herself and had to fight back a sudden urge to burst into tears. Weakness and loneliness.

She had no reason to be lonely. She had her parents' world ready to enfold her, a world she'd had to fight to escape from.

It'd be so easy to give in. Her parents loved her. One phone call and they'd be here. She'd be whisked back to the family mansion in Sydney. She'd be surrounded by private nurses and her mother would be popping in every twenty minutes with so much love she couldn't handle it.

Love…

Why was she thinking of Hugo Denver?

'Because you're a weak wuss and he has a smile to die for,' she told herself. 'And you've been battered and cut and bitten and you're not yourself. Tomorrow you'll be back to your chirpy self, defences up, self-reliant, needing no one.'

But if Hugo came back…

'Dr Denver to you,' she said out loud. 'A bit of professionalism, if you please, Dr Hargreaves.' She wiggled again and things hurt even more and she got sensible.

She rang the bell for a top-up of morphine. She didn't need Hugo Denver. Morphine would have to do instead.

CHAPTER SIX

HUGO ARRIVED IN her room at eleven in the morning, with
Joe beside him. It was a professional visit: doctor doing
his rounds with nurse in attendance. That was what Hugo
looked—professional.

When she'd first seen him he'd been wearing casual
clothes—dressed to go on holiday. Jeans and open-necked
shirt. He'd been bloodied and filthy.

He'd come in last night but she couldn't remember much
about last night. She'd been woozy and in pain. If she had
to swear, she'd say he'd been wearing strength and a smile
that said she was safe.

This morning he was in tailored pants and a crisp white
shirt. The shirt was open-necked and short-sleeved. He
looked professional but underneath the professional there
was still the impression of strength.

Mary had helped her wash and Joe had brought one of
her cases in. She was therefore wearing a cute kimono over
silk pyjamas. She was ready to greet the world.

Sort of. This man had her unsettled.

The whole situation had her unsettled. She'd been employed to replace this man. What were the terms of her employment now?

'Hey,' he said, pausing at the door—giving her time to
catch her breath? 'Joe tells me you're feeling better. True?'

She was. Or she had been. Now she was just feeling…
disconcerted. Hormonal?

Interested.

Why? He wasn't her type, she thought. He looked…a bit

worn around the edges. He was tall, lean and tanned, all good, all interesting, but his black hair held a hint of silver and there were creases around his eyes. Life lines. Worry? Laughter? Who could tell?

He was smiling now, though, and the creases fitted, so maybe it was laughter.

He was caring for his niece single-handedly. He was also the face of medicine for the entire valley.

Her research told her the hospital had a huge feeder population. This was a popular area to retire and run a few head of cattle or grow a few vines. Retirees meant ageing. Ageing meant demand for doctor's services.

Hence the hint of silver?

Or had it been caused by tragedy? Responsibility?

Responsibility. *Family.*

He wasn't her type at all.

Meanwhile he seemed to be waiting for an answer. Joe had handed him her chart. He'd read it and was now looking at her expectantly. What had he asked? For some reason she had to fight to remember what the question had been.

Was she feeling better? She'd just answered herself. Now she had to answer him.

'I'm good,' she said, and then added a bit more truthfully, 'I guess I'm still a bit wobbly.'

'Pain?'

'Down to fell-over-in-the-playground levels.'

'You do a lot of falling over in the playground?'

'I ski,' she said and he winced.

'Ouch.'

'You don't?'

'There's not a lot of skiing in Wombat Valley.'

'But before?'

'I don't go back to before,' he said briskly. 'Moving on… Polly, what happens next is up to you. We have a guest room made up at home. Ruby's aching to play nurse, but if you're more settled here then we'll wait.'

Uh oh. She hadn't thought this through. She'd demanded she stay in Wombat Valley. She'd refused to be evacuated to Sydney, but now...

'I'm an imposition,' she said ruefully, and his grin flashed out again. Honestly, that grin was enough to make a girl's toes curl.

He wasn't her type. *He was not.*

'You're not an imposition,' he said gently. 'Without you I'd be down the bottom of the Gap, and Christmas would be well and truly over. As it is, my niece is currently making paper chains to hang on your truly amazing Christmas tree. I advertised for a locum. What seems to have arrived is a life-saver and a Santa. Ruby would love you to come home. We'll both understand if you put it off until tomorrow but the venom seems to have cleared. Joe tells me your temperature, pulse, all vital signs, are pretty much back to normal. You'll still ache but if you come home you get to spend the rest of the day in bed as well. We have a view over the valley to die for, and Ruby's waiting.'

His voice gentled as he said the last two words and she met his gaze and knew, suddenly, why his voice had changed. There was a look...

He loved his niece.

Unreservedly. Unconditionally.

Why did that make her eyes well up?

It was the drugs, she thought desperately, and swiped her face with the back of her hand, but Hugo reached over and snagged a couple of tissues and tugged her hand down and dried her face for her.

'You're too weak,' he said ruefully. 'This was a bad idea. Snuggle back to sleep for the day.'

But she didn't want to.

Doctors made the worst patients. That was true in more ways than one, she thought. Just like it'd kill a professional footballer to sit on the sidelines and watch, so it was for doctors. Plus she'd had a childhood of being an inpatient. Once her diabetes had been diagnosed, every time she sneezed her parents had insisted on admission. So now…all she wanted to do was grab her chart, fill it in herself, like the professional she was, and run.

Admittedly, she hadn't felt like that last night—with a load of snake venom on board, hospital had seemed a really safe option—but she did this morning.

'If you're happy to take me home, I'd be very grateful,' she murmured and he smiled as if he was truly pleased that he was getting a locum for Christmas, even if that locum had a bandaged hand and a bandaged foot and was useless for work for the foreseeable future.

'Excellent. Now?'

'I…yes.'

'Hugo, the wheelchairs are out of action for a couple of hours,' Joe volunteered, taking back the chart and hanging it on the bed. Looking from Hugo to Polly and back again with a certain amount of speculative interest. 'It's so quiet this week that Ted's taken them for a grease and oil change. They'll be back this afternoon but meanwhile Polly can't walk on that foot.'

'I can hop,' Polly volunteered and both men grinned.

'A pyjama-clad, kimono-wearing hoppity locum,' Joe said, chuckling. 'Wow, Hugo, you pick 'em.'

'I do, don't I?' Hugo agreed, chuckling as well and then smiling down at Polly. 'But no hoppiting. We don't need to wait. Polly, you're no longer a patient, or a locum. From now on, if you agree, you're our honoured guest, a colleague and a friend. And friends wearing battle scars won on our behalf get special treatment. Can I carry you?'

Could he…what?

Carry her. That was what the doctor had said.

She needed a wheelchair. She could wait.

That'd be surly.

Besides, she didn't want one. There was no way she

wanted to sit in a wheelchair and be pushed out feeling like a…patient.

She was a friend. Hugo had just said so.

But…but…

Those dark, smiling eyes had her mesmerised.

'I'll hurt your back,' she managed. 'I'm not looking after you in traction over Christmas.'

'I'm game if you are,' he said and his dark eyes gleamed. Daring her?

And all of a sudden she was in. Dare or not, he held her with his gaze, and suddenly, for this moment, Pollyanna Hargreaves wasn't a doctor. She wasn't a patient. She wasn't a daughter and actually…she wasn't a friend.

She was a woman, she thought, and she took a deep breath and smiled up into Hugo's gorgeous eyes.

He wanted to carry her?

'Yes, please.'

It was possibly not the wisest course to carry his new locum. His medical insurance company would have kittens if they could see him, he thought. He could drop her. He could fall. He could be sued for squillions. Joe, following bemusedly behind with Polly's suitcase, would act as witness to totally unethical behaviour.

But Polly was still shaky. He could hear it in her voice. Courageous as she'd been, yesterday had terrified her and the terror still lingered. She needed human contact. Warmth. Reassurance.

And Hugo… Well, if Hugo was honest, he wouldn't mind a bit of the same.

So he carried her and if the feel of her body cradled against him, warmth against warmth, if the sensation of her arms looped around his neck to make herself more secure, if both those things settled his own terrors from the day before then that was good. Wasn't it?

That was what this was all about, he told himself. Reassurance.

Except, as he strode out through the hospital entrance with his precious cargo, he felt…

As if he was carrying his bride over the threshold?

There was a crazy thought. Totally romantic. Nonsense.

'Where's your car?' she asked.

Polly's voice was still a bit shaky. He paused on the top of the ramp into Emergency and smiled down at her. The sun was on her face. Her flaming curls had been washed but they were tousled from a morning on her pillow. She had freckles. Cute freckles. Her face was a bit too pale and her green eyes a bit too large.

He'd really like to kiss her.

And that really was the way to get struck off any medical register he could care to name. Hire a locum, nearly kill her, carry her instead of using a wheelchair, then kiss her when she was stuck so tight in his arms she can't escape.

He needed a cold shower—fast.

'No car needed,' he said, and motioned towards a driveway along the side of the hospital.

At the end of the driveway there was a house, a big old weatherboard, looking slightly incongruous beside the newer brick hospital. It had an old-fashioned veranda with a kid's bike propped up by the door. A grapevine was growing under the roof, and a couple of Australia's gorgeous rosella parrots were searching through the leaves, looking for early grapes.

'This is home while you're in Wombat Valley,' he told her. 'But it won't be what you're used to. Speak now if you want to change your mind about staying. We can still organise transport out of here.'

'How do you know what I'm used to?' she asked and he grimaced and said nothing and she sighed. 'So I'm not incognito?'

'I don't think you could ever be incognito.'

She grimaced even more, and shifted in his arms. 'Hugo…'

'Mmm?'

'It's time to put me down. I can walk.'

'You're not walking.'

'Because I'm Pollyanna Hargreaves?'

'Because you have a snake-bitten ankle.'

'And you always carry snake-bite victims?'

'Oi!' It was Joe, standing patiently behind them, still holding the suitcase. 'In the time you've spent discussing it you could have taken her home, dumped her on the couch and got back here. I've work for you, Dr Denver.'

'What work?' Polly asked.

'Earache arriving in ten minutes,' Joe said darkly and glanced at his watch. 'No, make that in five.'

'Then dump me and run,' Polly said and he had no choice.

Like it or not, he had to dump her and run.

Ruby was waiting. Sort of.

He carried Polly over the threshold and Ruby was sitting on the couch in the front room, in her shorts and shirt, bare legs, tousled hair—she'd refused to let him braid it this morning—her face set in an expression he knew all too well. Misery.

He could hear Donna in the kitchen. Donna was a Wombat Valley mum. Donna's daughter, Talia, was Ruby's age, and Donna's family was just one of the emergency backstops Wombat Valley had put in place to make sure Hugo could stay here. He stood in the living room doorway, Polly in his arms, and looked helplessly down at his niece. When she looked like this he never knew what to say.

'We have a guest,' he said. 'Ruby, this is Dr Hargreaves.'

'Polly,' said Polly.

'Why are you carrying her?'

'She was bitten by a snake. I told you.'

'She's supposed to be working,' Ruby said in a small voice. 'And we're supposed to be at the beach.'

'Ruby...'

'It's the pits,' Polly interrupted. She was still cradled against him but she sounded ready to chat. 'Sorry, sorry, sorry,' she told the little girl. 'But we should blame the snake.'

'You should have been wearing shoes,' Ruby muttered, still in that little voice that spoke of the desolation of betrayal. Another broken promise.

'Yes,' Polly agreed. 'I should.'

'Why weren't you?'

'I didn't know I was planning to meet a snake, and it didn't warn me it was coming. They should wear bells, like cats.'

Ruby thought about that and found it wanting. 'Snakes don't have necks.'

'No.' Polly appeared thoughtful. 'We should do something about that. What if we made a rule that Australian snakes have to coil? If we had a law that every snake has to loop once so they have a circle where their neck should be, we could give them all bells. How are you at drawing? Maybe you could draw what we mean and we'll send a letter to Parliament this very day.'

Ruby stared at her as if she was a sandwich short of a picnic. 'A circle where their neck should be?' she said cautiously.

'If you have a skipping rope I'll show you. But we'd need to make it law, which means writing to Parliament. How about you do the drawing and I'll write the letter?'

Ruby stared at her in amazement. In stupefaction. The desolate expression on her face faded.

'"Dear Parliamentarians…",' Polly started. She was still ensconced in Hugo's arms, but she didn't appear to notice her unusual platform, or the fact that her secretary wasn't writing. 'It has come to our attention that snakes are slithering around the countryside bell-less. This situation is unsatisfactory, not only to people who wander about shoeless, but also to snakes who, we're sure, would be much happier with jewels. Imagine how much more Christmassy Australia would be if every snake wore a Christmas bell?'

And it was too much for Ruby.

She giggled.

It was the best sound in the world, Hugo thought. For twelve long months he'd longed to hear his niece giggle, and this woman had achieved it the moment she'd come through the door.

But the giggle was short-lived. Of course. He could see Ruby fight it, ordering her expression back to sad.

'You're still spoiling our Christmas,' she muttered.

'Not me personally,' Polly said blithely, refusing to sound offended. 'That was the snake. Put me down, Dr Denver. Ruby, can I share your couch? And thank you for putting up my Christmas tree. Do you like it?'

'Yes,' Ruby said reluctantly.

'Me too. Silver's my favourite.'

'I like real trees,' Hugo offered as he lowered Polly onto the couch beside his niece. 'Ones made out of pine needles.'

'Then why didn't you put one up?' Polly raised her brows in mock disapproval. She put her feet on the floor and he saw her wince. He pushed a padded ottoman forward; she put her foot on it and she smiled.

It was some smile.

'I know,' she said, carrying right on as if that smile meant nothing. 'You meant to be away for Christmas. That's no excuse, though. Trees are supposed to be decorated ages before Christmas. And you put all the presents for everyone from your teacher to the postman underneath, wrapped up mysteriously, and you get up every morning and poke and prod the presents and wonder if Santa's come early. It's half the fun.'

There was another fail. Add it to the list, Hugo thought morosely, but Polly had moved through accusatory and was now into fixing things.

'There's still time,' she said. 'Ruby, we can do some wrapping immediately. I'm stuck with this foot… Who's in the kitchen?'

'Mrs Connor,' Ruby muttered. 'She's cooking a Christmas cake 'cos she says if we're staying here we might need it.'

'Mrs Connor?' Polly queried.

'Talia's mum.'

'Talia's your friend?'

'Talia's at her grandma's place, making mince pies,' Ruby told her. 'She said I could come but I didn't want to. I don't have a grandma any more. My mum's dead too.'

But, despite the bleak words, Ruby was obviously fighting not to be drawn in by Polly's bounce. Hugo was fighting not to be drawn in, too. Polly was...magnetic. She was like a bright light and the moths were finding her irresistible.

What was he on about? He had work to do.

'I need to get on,' he said.

'I know. Earache.' Polly gave him a sympathetic smile. 'You could introduce me to Mrs Connor. Maybe she doesn't need to stay once her cake's cooked. Ruby and I can cope on our own. Do you have Christmas wrapping paper?'

He did get the occasional thing right. 'Yes.'

'Excellent. If you could find it for us...'

'We don't have anything to wrap,' Ruby said.

'Yes, we do. Have you ever heard of origami?'

'I...no,' she said cautiously.

'It's paper folding and I'm an expert.' Polly beamed. 'I can make birds and frogs that jump and little balls that practically float and tiny pretend lanterns. And I can make boxes to put them in. If you like I'll teach you and we can make presents for everyone in Wombat Valley. And then we'll wrap them in newspaper and make them really big and wrap them again in Christmas paper so no one will ever guess what's in them and then we'll stack them under the tree. Then we'll have presents for everyone who comes to the house or everyone in hospital or everyone in the main street of Wombat Valley if we make enough. Good idea or what, Ruby?'

'I...I'll watch,' Ruby said reluctantly and it was all Hugo

could do not to offer Polly a high five. *I'll watch*... Concession indeed.

'Then find us some wrapping paper and be off with you,' Polly told him. 'Ruby and I and Mrs Connor can manage without you.' And then she hesitated. 'Though…can you find me my jelly beans? They're in my holdall. And is there juice in the fridge?'

She was a diabetic. Of course. What was he thinking, not worrying about sources of instant sugar. Hell, why hadn't he left her in the hospital? And as for telling Donna to go home…

The weight of the last year settled back down hard. Two responsibilities…

But Polly was looking up at him and suddenly she was glaring. 'Do not look like that,' she snapped.

'Like what?'

'Like I'm needing help. I don't need help. I just need things to be in place.'

'If you have a hypo…'

'If I have my jelly beans and juice, I won't have a hypo.'

'How do you know? The snake bite…'

'Is your uncle a fusser?' Polly demanded, turning to Ruby. 'Does he fuss when you don't want him to?'

'He makes me have a bath every single day,' Ruby confessed. 'And I have to eat my vegetables.'

'I knew it. A fusser! Dr Denver, I will not be fussed over. A bath and vegetables for Ruby are the limit. I will not let you fuss further.'

'He'll get grumpy,' Ruby warned.

'Let him. I can cope with a grump.' And she tilted her chin and looked up at him, defiance oozing from every pore.

His lips twitched—and hers twitched in response.

'Jelly beans,' she repeated. 'Juice. Earache. Ruby—swans, lanterns, frogs?'

'Frogs,' Ruby said, watching her uncle's face.

He wasn't grumpy. He wasn't.

Maybe he had been a bit. Maybe this year had been enough to make anyone grumpy.

'Earth to Dr Denver,' Polly was saying. 'Are you reading? Jelly beans, juice, earache. Go.'

There was nothing else for it. A part of him really wanted to stay and watch...frogs?

Earache was waiting.

He had no choice. The demands on a lone family doctor were endless, and he couldn't knock patients back.

Back in Sydney he'd been at the cutting edge of thoracic surgery. Here, his life was so circumscribed he couldn't even watch frogs.

And he shouldn't even watch Polly.

CHAPTER SEVEN

THERE WAS A FROG, right underneath her window. Not the origami variety. The croaking sort.

She should be able to write to a Member of Parliament about that, she thought. *Dear Sir, I wish to report a breach of the peace. Surely environmental protection laws decree there shall be no noise after ten p.m....*

If she was honest, though, it wasn't the frog that was keeping her awake.

She'd given in an hour ago and taken a couple of the pills Hugo had left for her. Her aches were thus dulled. She couldn't blame her sleeplessness on them, either.

What?

This set-up. Lying in a bedroom with the window open, the smells of the bushland all around her. The total quiet—apart from the frog. Polly was a city girl. She was used to traffic, the low murmur of air conditioning and the background hum of a major metropolis.

There was no hum here. She really was in the back of beyond.

With Hugo and Ruby.

And they were both tugging at her heartstrings and she hadn't come here for her heartstrings to be tugged. She'd come here to give her heartstrings time out.

She'd had a surfeit of loving. Loving up to her eyebrows. And fuss. And emotional blackmail.

Why was it important to make a little girl happy?

Emotional blackmail?

'If I'm stuck here I might as well do my best,' she told herself. 'It's the least I can do and I always do the least I can do.'

Only she didn't. She'd been trained since birth to make people happy. This Christmas was all about getting away from that obligation.

Though she had enjoyed her origami frogs, she conceded. She had enjoyed giving Ruby pleasure.

Frogs... Origami frogs...

Real frogs...

Blurring...

Uh oh.

She was light-headed, she conceded. Just a little. Sometimes sleeplessness preceded a hypo. She should get some juice, just in case.

She padded through to the kitchen in her bare feet and the cute silk pyjamas her mum had brought her back from Paris last year.

They were a funny colour. The patterns seemed to be swirling.

That was an odd thought. Actually, all her thoughts were odd. She fetched a glass of juice and then, still acting on blurry impulse, she headed out to the veranda. If she couldn't sleep, maybe she could talk to the frog.

Hugo was sitting on the top step.

He was a dark shape against the moonlight. She would have backed away, but the screen door squeaked as she swung it open.

He turned and saw her and shifted sideways on the step, inviting her to join him.

'Problem?' he asked and she hesitated for a moment before deciding *What the heck*. She sat down. The moon was full, lighting the valley with an eerie glow. From this veranda you could see for ever.

She concentrated—very hard—on looking out over the valley rather than thinking about the man beside her.

She failed.

His body was warm beside her. Big and warm and solid. The rest of the night...not so solid.

'Blood sugar?' he asked and she remembered she was carrying juice. For some reason it seemed important not to make a big deal of it. She put it down carefully behind her.

A great blond shape shifted from the dog bed behind her. Hamster had been returned home this afternoon. Now he was headed for her juice. She went to grab it but Hugo was before her.

'Leave,' he ordered, in a voice that brooked no argument, and Hamster sighed and backed away. Hugo handed Polly back her juice—and their fingers touched.

It was a slight touch. Very slight. There was no reason why the touch should make her shiver.

She was...shivery.

It was warm. Why was she shivering?

'Polly?'

'Wh...what?'

'Blood sugar. You're carrying juice. I assume that's why you're up. Have you checked?'

'N...no.'

'Where's your glucose meter?'

'I'm okay.'

'Polly...'

'Don't fuss. I hate f...fussing.' But, even as she said it, she realised there was a reason. She was still fuzzy. Too fuzzy. Damn, she was good at predicting hypos. Where had this come from?

But Hugo was already raising her hand, propelling the glass up, holding the juice to her lips. 'Drink,' he ordered and he made sure she drank half the glass and then he swung himself off the step, disappeared inside and emerged a moment later with her glucometer.

Yeah, okay. He was right and she was wrong. She sighed and stuck out her finger. He flicked on the torch on his phone and did a quick finger prick test, then checked the result while she kept on stoically drinking. Or tried to.

As she tried for the last mouthful her hand slipped and he caught it—and the glass.

And he kept on holding.

'Why bring this out to the veranda?' he asked as he helped her with the last mouthful. She didn't bother to answer. 'Polly? You should have drunk it at the fridge if you were feeling...'

'I wasn't feeling,' she managed. 'And I know what I should have done.'

'So why didn't you do it?'

She glowered instead of answering. This was her business. Her diabetes. Her concern.

'The snake bite will have pushed you out of whack,' he said, and she thought about that for a while as the dizziness receded and the world started to right itself. In a minute she'd get up and make herself some toast, carbohydrates to back up the juice. But not yet. For now she was going nowhere.

'Out of whack,' she said cautiously, testing her voice and relieved to find the wobble had receded. 'That's a medical term?'

'Yep. Blood sugar level, two point one. You're not safe to be alone, Dr Hargreaves.'

'I am safe,' she said with cautious dignity. 'I woke up, I felt a bit odd; I fetched the juice.'

'You have glucose by the bed?'

'I...yes.'

'Why didn't you take it?'

'You sound like my mother.'

'I sound like your doctor.'

'You're not my doctor. I'm discharged. You're my friend.'

And why did that sound a loaded term? she wondered. Friend... It sounded okay. Sort of okay.

He was sitting beside her again. His body was big. Warm. Solid.

She always felt shaky after a hypo, she thought. That was all this was.

Um…post hypo lust?

Lust? She was out of her mind. She put her empty glass down on the step beside her. Hamster took an immediate interest but Hugo was no longer interested in Hamster.

'How the hell…?' he asked, quietly but she heard strength behind his voice. Strength and anger? 'How the hell did you think you'd manage in the country as a solo practitioner when you have unstable diabetes?'

'I don't have unstable diabetes. You said yourself, it was the snake.'

'So it was. And shock and stress. And this job's full of shock and stress.'

'I'd imagine every single one of your nursing staff knows how to deal with a hypo.'

'You intended telling them you were diabetic?'

'Of course. I'm not dumb.'

'And you'd accuse them of being like your mother, too?'

'Only if they fuss.' She sighed. 'I need some…'

'Complex carbohydrates to keep you stable. Of course you do. I'll get some toast.'

'I can…'

'Dr Hargreaves, you may not be my patient but I believe I'm still your boss. Keep still, shut up and conserve energy. Hamster, keep watch on the lady. Don't let her go anywhere.'

Hamster had just finished licking the inside of the juice glass, as far in as he could reach. He looked up, yawned and flopped sideways, as if he'd suddenly used up every bit of his energy.

That was a bit how she felt, Polly conceded. Having someone else make her toast was…well, it wasn't exactly standing on her own feet but it was okay.

Especially as it was Hugo.

There she was again, doing the lust thing, she thought.

The hypo must have been worse than she'd thought. She was feeling weird.

And Hugo seemed to sense it. He put a hand up and traced her cheekbone, an echo of the way she'd traced his cheek the night before. It was surely a gesture of concern, she thought, and why it had the power to make her want more...

'Sit,' he said. 'Stay. Toast.'

And she could do nothing but obey.

'Woof,' she ventured and he patted her head.

'Good girl. If you're really good I'll bring you a dog biscuit on the side.'

She ate her toast, sharing a crust or two with Hamster. Hugo made some for himself as well and they ate in silence. The silence wasn't uncomfortable, though. It was sort of...all right.

It was three in the morning. She should go back to bed. Instead, she was sitting on the veranda of a strange house in a strange place with a strange man...

He wasn't strange. He was Hugo.

Part of her—the dumb part—felt as if she'd known him all her life.

The sensible part knew nothing.

'So tell me more about you and Ruby,' she ventured into the stillness. The toast was gone. Hugo should be in bed too, she thought, but for now he seemed as content as she was just to sit. 'And you. Why are you here?'

'Do you remember me talking to you last night?'

'Yes.'

'Then you know I came back when my sister died.'

'So who was the doctor here before? After your Dad died?'

'Doc Farr. He retired here from Melbourne, thinking it was a quiet life. Ha. He intended to set up a vineyard, so he didn't want this house—my mother stayed living here. But Harry Farr felt trapped. When Mum and Grace died and I came home for good you couldn't see him for dust. I've never seen anyone leave so fast. His vineyard's still on the market but he was so inundated with work all he wanted was to get out of here.'

'You were working in Sydney. As a family doctor?'

'As a surgeon,' he said brusquely, as if it didn't matter.

'A surgeon.' She stared at him, stunned. 'Where?'

'Sydney Central.'

'Specialising?'

'Thoracic surgery. It doesn't matter now.'

'You left thoracic surgery to come here?' She was still staring. 'Your life... Your colleagues... Did you have a girl-friend?'

'Yes, but...'

'But she wouldn't come. Of course she wouldn't.'

'Polly, I don't need to tell...'

'You don't need to tell me anything,' she said hastily. 'I'm sorry. But Sydney... Friends? Surfing? Restaurants? The whole social scene of Sydney?'

'It doesn't matter!'

'I suspect it does matter. A lot. You had to leave every-thing to take care of Ruby. That's the pits.'

'It's no use thinking it's the pits. It's just...what it is. Ruby would know no one in Sydney, and if I stayed in my job she'd never see me. She needs me. She's my family.'

And there was nothing to say to that.

Family... The thing she most wanted to escape from.

She thought about it as the warmth and stillness envel-oped them. It was a weirdly intimate setting. A night for telling all?

Hugo had bared so much. There were things unspoken, things that didn't need to be spoken. He was trapped, more than she'd ever been trapped. By Ruby... A needy seven-year-old.

'Tell me about the Christmas thing,' she ventured, and he started, as if his mind had been a thousand miles away.

'Christmas?'

'Why is it so important?'

'I guess it's not,' he said heavily. 'Except I promised. Actually, Grace promised her last year. She said they'd go to the beach for Christmas and then...well, I told you what happened. This year Ruby came out and asked— "Can we have a beach Christmas?" What was I supposed to say? I booked an apartment at Bondi and then spent three months advertising for a locum.'

'And bombed out with me.'

'There's no bombed about it. You saved me.'

'And you saved me right back, so we're quits.' She took a deep breath. 'Right. Christmas at the beach is important. Hugo, you can still go. Today's only Wednesday. Christmas is Saturday. You haven't cancelled, have you?'

He gave a wry laugh. 'An apartment at Bondi Beach for Christmas? I prepaid. Non-refundable. Somewhere in Bondi there's a two-bedroom flat with our name on it.'

'So go.'

'And leave you here?'

'What's wrong with leaving me here?'

'Are you kidding? Look at you.'

'I'm twenty-four hours post snake bite. It's three days until Christmas. Two more days and I'll be perky as anything.'

'You're an unstable diabetic.'

'I'm a very stable, very sensible diabetic who just happens to have been bitten by a snake. You told me yourself that the venom will have messed with things and you're absolutely right. Usually my control's awesome.'

'Awesome?'

'Well, mostly awesome,' she confessed. 'After the third margarita it can get wobbly.'

'You have to be kidding. Margaritas!'

'One margarita contains alcohol, which tends to bring my levels down, and sugar, which brings them up. It's a fine line which I've taken years to calibrate. I'll admit after the third my calibration may get blurry, but you needn't worry. I only ever tackle a third when I have a responsible medical colleague on hand with margarita tackling equipment at the ready. So for now I've left my sombrero in Sydney. I'm anticipating a nice and sober Christmas, with not a margarita in sight.'

He was looking a bit…stunned. 'Yet you still brought your Christmas tree,' he managed.

'Christmas trees don't affect blood sugars. Don't they teach surgeons anything?'

He choked on a chuckle, and she grinned. He had the loveliest chuckle, she thought, and she felt a bit light-headed again and wondered if she could use a bit more juice but the light-headedness wasn't the variety she'd felt before. This was new. Strange…

Sitting beside this guy on the back step in the small hours was strange. Watching the moon over the valley…

The step was a bit too narrow. Hamster had wedged himself beside her—something about toast—and she'd had to edge a bit closer to Hugo.

Close enough to touch.

Definitely light-headed…

'So tell me why you're not in Sydney?' Hugo asked and she had to haul herself away from the slightly tipsy sensation of sensual pleasure and think of a nice sober answer.

'Smothering,' she said and she thought as she said it, *why?* She never talked of her background. She'd hardly confessed her claustrophobia to anyone.

He didn't push, at least not for a while. He really was the most restful person, she thought. He was just…solid. Nice.

Um…down, she told her hormones, and she edged a little way away. But not very far. An inch or more.

She could change steps. Move right away.

The idea was unthinkable.

'You want to elaborate?' he asked at last and she wondered if she did, but this night was built for intimacy and suddenly there seemed no reason not to tell him.

'My parents love me to bits,' she said. 'They married late,

I'm their only child and they adore me. To Mum, I'm like a doll, to be played with, dressed up, displayed.'

'Hence the Pollyanna…'

'You got it. Pollyanna was her favourite movie, her favourite doll and then, finally, her living, breathing version of the same. That's me. Dad's not quite so over the top, but he's pretty protective. They've always had nannies to do the hard work but there's no doubting they love me. I was diagnosed with diabetes when I was six and they were shattered. I'd been smothered with care before that. Afterwards it got out of control.'

'So don't tell me…you ran away to the circus?'

'I would have loved to,' she said simply. 'But there's a problem. I love them back.'

'That is a problem,' he said, softly now, as if speaking only to himself. 'The chains of loving…'

'They get you every which way,' she agreed. 'You and Ruby…I can see that. Anyway, I seem to have been fighting for all my life to be…me. They adore me, they want to show me off to their friends and, above all, they want to keep me safe. The fight I had to be allowed to do medicine… To them, medicine seems appallingly risky—all these nasty germs—but we're pretty much over that.'

'Good for you.'

She grimaced. 'Yeah, some things are worth fighting for, but you win one battle and there's always another. Two years ago, I started going out with the son of their best friends. Marcus was kind, eligible and incredibly socially acceptable. But…*kind* was the key word. He wanted to keep me safe, just as my parents did. I felt smothered but they were all so approving. I came within a hair's breadth of marrying him. He asked, and I might have said yes, but then I saw a video camera set up to the side and I recognised it. So, instead of falling into his arms, I found myself asking whether Dad had loaned him the camera and of course he had, and I pushed him further and he told me Mum had told him what kind of

ring I'd like, and his parents knew and they were all having
dinner together at that very moment and we could go tell
them straight away.'

'Whoa…'

'You get it,' she said approvingly. 'They didn't. But I
didn't just say "no" and run. Even then I had to let them down
slowly. I pretended to get a text on my phone, an urgent recall to the hospital, and Marcus offered to drive me and I
told him to go have dinner with the parents and then I went
to a bar and risked having a very bad hypo. That was when
I figured I needed to sort my life. I told them all kindly, in
my own way, but since then… I've fought to take control. I
need to back away.'

'Which is why you're here? Doing locums?'

'Exactly,' she said with satisfaction. 'It's five whole
hours' drive from my parents' Christmas. Oh, don't get
me wrong, I love Christmas, but they'll all be there, at the
most exclusive restaurant overlooking the harbour, all my
parents' friends, though not Marcus this year because he
had the decency to accept a posting to New York. He's now
going out with an artist who paints abstract nudes. He's
much happier than he was with me, and his parents are appalled. Hooray for Marcus. But the rest of them… Mum will
be trying to figure who I can marry now. She's indefatiga-
ble, my mum. Knock her back and she bounces back again,
bounce, bounce, bounce. The rest of them will be smiling
indulgently in the background, but feeling slightly sorry for
Mum because she has an imperfect daughter.'

'Imperfect…?'

'Perfection has perfect teeth and skin, a toned body and
designer clothes. Perfect doesn't argue, she moves in the
right circles, she marries the right man and never, ever has
diabetes. So here I am and I'm here to stay, so you and Ruby
might as well go to Bondi because I'm a very good doctor
and you've contracted me to work for two weeks and that's
just what I'll do.'

'Polly...'

'Go,' she said. 'Enough of this guilt stuff. If I have this right, you've left a perfectly good career, I suspect a perfectly satisfactory girlfriend, a perfectly acceptable lifestyle, all because you love Ruby. That's some chains of loving.'

'And you've left a perfectly good career, a perfectly satisfactory boyfriend, a perfectly luxurious lifestyle all because you want to cut the chains of loving?'

'Exactly,' she said.

'So why encourage me to break away?'

'Because if you stay I'll feel guilty and I'm over guilt. Go.'

'I don't think I can.'

'Hugo,' she said, figuring a girl had to make a stand some time and it might as well be now. She was full of toast. Her blood sugars had settled nicely. She was back in control again—sort of. 'This is nuts. You're a surgeon, and a thoracic surgeon at that. I'm trained in Emergency Medicine. If a kid comes in with whooping cough, who'd be most qualified to cope?'

'Whooping cough's lung...'

'Okay, bad example. Itch. In he comes, scratch, scratch, scratch. Is it an allergy or is it fleas? What's the differential appearance? Or could it be chickenpox? Some kids don't get immunised. And if it's chickenpox, what's the immunisation period? Then the next kid comes in, sixteen years old, cramps. How do you get information out of a sullen teenager? Do you suspect pregnancy?'

'Not if it's a boy. Is this an exam?'

'Do you know the answers?'

'I've been working as a family doctor for twelve months now.'

'And I've been training as an emergency doctor for five years. I win.'

'Did you know you look extraordinarily cute in those pyjamas?'

'Did you know you look extraordinarily sexy in those

jeans? Both of which comments are sexist, both beneath us as medical professionals and neither taking this argument forward. If you can't come up with a better medical rebuttal then I win.'

'You can't.'

'I just have. Give me one more day to get my bearings and you leave on Thursday.'

'Friday,' he said, sounding goaded. 'Tomorrow's another rest day and I spend Thursday watching you work.'

'That's ridiculous, plus it's discriminatory. I have diabetes, not gaps in my medical training. Tell you what, for the next two days we work side by side. That'll give you time with Ruby and it should set your mind at rest. If at the end of Thursday you can truthfully say I'm a bad doctor then I'll leave.'

'Go back to Sydney?'

'That's none of your business.'

'No,' he said. 'It's not. Polly, it's not safe.'

'Go jump. Ruby's Christmas is at stake. You're leaving, I'm staying, Dr Denver, and that's all there is to it. I have a nice little Christmas pudding for one in my suitcase, and I'm not sharing. Go away.'

'I can't.'

'You have no choice. Ruby needs you.'

'Everyone needs me,' he said, sounding even more goaded.

'I don't need you,' she retorted. 'I don't need you one bit. So get used to it, and while you're getting used to it, you might like to pack and leave.'

CHAPTER EIGHT

HIS STIPULATION WAS that Polly stayed in bed until noon. She agreed, but reluctantly. She also didn't like it that Hugo had pulled in yet more help.

His housekeeper was away. Ruby was on school holidays. He needed to care for Ruby, but Polly figured she could at least do that.

But she'd got tired of arguing last night. She'd fallen back into bed and when she woke it was nine o'clock. Okay, Hugo had a point. As a childminder she was currently less than efficient.

She snagged her glucose meter and took a reading. Six point three. *Nice.* 'I've won, Snake,' she said out loud and settled back on her pillows feeling smug.

Or sort of smug. She was still sore. She'd made origami gifts with Ruby the day before, but in truth it had been a struggle. Maybe Hugo was right with his two days of rest.

He looked like a man who was used to being right, she thought. Typical surgeon.

But the thought didn't quite come off in her head. It sounded a bit…lame.

Hugo wasn't typical anything, she thought.

There was a scratch on the door.

'Yes?'

Ruby's head poked around. Looking scared. She'd relaxed a little the day before when she'd been engrossed in origami frogs, but tension was never far from this little one.

'Hi.' Polly smiled, hoping for a smile in return.

'Are you awake?' she whispered.

'Yes.' She edged over on the bed. 'Want to come and visit?' The bedspread was pretty—patchwork. Had Ruby's grandma made it?

The house was cosy. A family house. Home of Hugo and Grace and their mum and dad.

She found herself hoping Grace had had a happy childhood and suddenly she thought she bet she had. Depression usually didn't strike until the teens. She looked out of the window at the valley beyond. A tyre swing was hanging from a huge gum nearer to the house.

Hugo would have used that swing...

She was still feeling odd. How bad had that hypo been last night? She shouldn't be feeling weird now.

Ruby was still by the door, still looking nervous, but she was obviously on a mission. 'I have to find out your blood sugar level before you get up,' Ruby quavered and Polly pulled herself back to the here and now.

Blood sugar level. It was six point three; she'd just taken it. She went to say it but then she paused. Something made her stop.

I have to find out your blood sugar level...

'Did your Uncle Hugo tell you to find out?'

'He says you're d...diabetic and your blood sugar has to be under ten and above four and if it's not I have to ring him and he says I have to make sure you still have juice on your bedside table.'

Polly glanced at her bedside table. There was a glass of juice there.

Hugo must have brought it in last night or early this morning. He must have come into her bedroom while she was asleep.

Creepy?

No. Caring.

But she didn't like caring. She didn't like fuss. She'd been swamped with fuss since childhood.

Ruby was patiently waiting for an answer.

'Can you help me with my glucose meter?' she asked and motioned to the small machine beside her.

'What does it do?'

'If you hold it out, I put my finger in it and it takes a tiny pinprick of blood. It tests the blood and gives a reading.'

'Does it hurt?'

'Not if you hold it still.'

Ruby looked fascinated. Still a bit scared, though. 'I don't want to hurt you.'

'I can do it myself,' Polly confessed. 'But I have to be brave, and now I have a sore hand. It would help if you do it for me.'

And Ruby tilted her chin and took a deep breath. 'Like doctors do?'

'Exactly.'

'My Uncle Hugo is a doctor.'

'Yes.'

'He could do it.'

'Yes, but he's not here. It's lucky I have you.'

'Yes,' Ruby said seriously and picked up the glucose meter and studied it. She turned it over and figured it out.

'That's the on switch?'

'Yes.'

'Then I think you have to put your finger in here.'

'Yes.'

'Do we have to wash your finger first?'

'You're practically a real doctor,' Polly said with admiration. 'Wow, how do you know that? Ruby, I would disinfect my finger if this wasn't my meter, but I'm the only person ever to use this. There are only my germs in there. I take a chance.'

Ruby raised one sceptical eyebrow. 'But it'd be safer if I did wash your finger,' she declared and who was Polly to argue?

'Yes,' she conceded, and Ruby gave a satisfied nod and

fetched a damp facecloth and a towel and a tube of disinfectant.

She proceeded to wipe Polly's finger, dry it and then apply disinfectant cream. A lot of disinfectant cream.

'Now it's done its job, maybe we need to use a tissue to wipe most of it off,' Polly offered. 'Otherwise, we'll be testing the disinfectant instead of my blood. You'd be able to tell your Uncle Hugo that your tube of disinfectant is safe, but not me.'

And Ruby stared down at the ooze of disinfectant, she looked at the meter—and she giggled.

It was a good giggle. A child's giggle, and Polly guessed, just by looking at her, that for this child giggles were few and far between. But the giggle died. Ruby was back in doctor mode. She fetched a tissue and wiped the finger with all the gravitas in the world.

'Put your finger in,' she ordered Polly, and Polly put her finger in and the machine clicked to register the prick and seconds later the reading came out.

'Six point eight,' Ruby said triumphantly. 'That's good.'

'That's excellent,' came a gruff voice behind them and Ruby whirled round and Polly looked up and Hugo was standing in the doorway.

How long had he been there? How much had he heard?

He was smiling. *Oh, that smile…*

'That's really good,' he reiterated and he crossed to the bed and ruffled Ruby's pigtailed hair. Which was easy to do because the pigtails looked very amateurish—blonde wisps were escaping every which way. 'Thank you, Ruby. How's our patient? Was she brave when you did the finger prick?'

'Yes,' Ruby said. 'She moved a little bit when it went in, but she didn't scream.'

'I didn't,' Polly said, adding a touch of smug to her voice. 'I'm very brave.'

'It's all about how you hold the meter.' Hugo was talking to Ruby, not her. 'You must have very steady hands.'

'Yes,' the little girl said, and smiled shyly up at her uncle but there was anxiety behind the smile. 'I did. Are we really still going to the beach for Christmas?'

'We're going to try,' Hugo told her. 'I told you this morning, and I mean it. If we can get Dr Hargreaves better…'

'I'm Polly,' Polly said fast, because it seemed important.

'If we can look after Polly,' Hugo corrected himself. 'If we can make her better, then she can be the doctor and we can still have our holiday.'

'She doesn't look like a doctor,' Ruby said dubiously.

'She doesn't, does she? Those are very pretty pyjamas she's wearing.'

'They are,' Ruby conceded. He and Ruby were examining her as if she were some sort of interesting bug. 'I'd like pyjamas like that.'

'I think I can find some like these on the Internet in your size,' Polly ventured. 'If it's okay with your uncle.'

'Doctors don't wear pyjamas.' Ruby seemed distracted by Polly's offer but not enough to be deflected from her main purpose, which was obviously to find out exactly how qualified Polly was to take over here and thus send Ruby to the beach.

'Does your uncle have a white coat?' Polly demanded, and Ruby nodded.

'He has lots. They're hanging in the airing cupboard.'

'If you put one of those on me, I'll look just like a doctor.'

'But your hair's too red,' Ruby told her. 'Doctors don't have red curly hair.'

'You've been moving with the wrong type of doctor. The best doctors all have red curly hair. If the medical board discovered your Uncle Hugo's hair was black and almost straight he'd be sent to the nearest hairdresser to buy a wig.'

'A wig…' Ruby's eyes widened.

'You can get wigs on the Internet too. You want to help me look?'

'No!' Hugo said, and both girls turned and stared at him.

At his hair. It was thick and short. It only just qualified as wavy—definitely not curly—and it was definitely black.

'A red wig would be perfect,' Polly decreed, and Ruby giggled and giggled some more and Hugo's face creased into a grin and Polly lay back on her pillows and smug didn't begin to describe how she was feeling.

She'd been in some tight situations before this. Lots of tight situations. As an emergency physician she'd even saved lives. It had felt great, but somehow this moment was right up there. Making Hugo and his niece smile.

'Ruby, Mrs Connor's just asked if you'd like to go to the pictures in Willaura,' Hugo said, almost nonchalantly. 'Three girls from your class will be there. Talia and Sasha and Julie. Mr Connor will pick you up in ten minutes if you want to go.'

And he picked up the glucose meter and studied it as if it was really interesting instead of something doctors saw all the time—and Polly realised that this was important.

How many times did Ruby accept this kind of invitation? She suspected seldom. Or never?

'Don't I have to look after Polly?' Ruby asked dubiously.

'She's awake now and she's been tested and her blood sugar's good. We'll give her breakfast and then she needs to go back to sleep. We can ask Hamster to snooze under her bed to look after her.'

'We could put a white coat on Hamster,' Ruby said and giggled again. 'He could be the doctor. And I could maybe teach the girls how to make frogs.'

'That's a grand plan,' Hugo told her and Ruby swooped off to get ready.

And Hugo was left with Polly and Polly was left with Hugo and suddenly there were no words.

What was it with this woman?

What was it that made him want to smile?

She should be just another patient, he told himself, or just another colleague.

She was both. She was neither.

She lay in the too big bed in her cute swirly pyjamas, pink and orange and crimson and purple. They should have clashed with her red hair but they didn't. She looked up at him and she was still smiling but her smile was tentative. A bit uncertain.

She looked...vulnerable, he thought, and suddenly he realised that was how he was feeling.

Vulnerable. As if this woman was somehow edging under his defences.

He didn't have defences. What sort of stupid thought was that?

'Lorna will bring you breakfast,' he told her.

'Lorna?'

'My housekeeper for this morning. Our usual housekeeper, Lois, has taken Christmas off.'

'And because of me you're having to find fill-ins.'

'I told you. Yes, because of you, Ruby and I are stuck here, but if it wasn't for you I wouldn't be here in the worst sense of the term. So lie back and get better without qualms. What would you like for breakfast?'

'Toast and marmalade,' she said, almost defiantly, and he raised an eyebrow in exactly the same way she'd just seen Ruby do it.

'Don't tell me.' The corner of his mouth quirked upward. 'Plus coffee with three sugars.'

'If you're about to lecture me...'

He held up his hands as if to ward off attack. 'You're a big girl, Dr Hargreaves. You manage your own diabetes. And we do have sourdough, which has a low...'

'Glycaemic index. I know.' She glowered. 'If you turn into my mother I'm out of here.'

'For the next two days I'm your doctor and I have a vested interest in getting your diabetes stable.'

'I like sugar.'

'You had enough last night to keep you going for a week.'

And she knew he was right, he thought. Her protests were almost instinctive—the cry of a kid who'd been protected since diagnosis, told what to eat and when, who'd not been given a chance to make her own choices.

'I'm not silly and I'm not a child,' she muttered, confirming what he'd thought.

'I know you're not. And of course you can have marmalade.'

'Your generosity overwhelms me.'

'Good,' he said cheerfully. 'Let me look at your hand.'

She held it out for inspection. He lifted a corner of the dressing and nodded.

'It's looking good. If you stay here and work you'll need to be extra careful. Glove up for everything.'

'Yes, Grandpa.'

'The correct term is *Doctor*. Say, "*Yes, Doctor*".'

'Won't,' she said and grinned, and he looked down into her face, that smattering of freckles, at those gorgeous auburn curls and...

And he had to get out of here.

She was messing with his equilibrium.

'Call Lorna if you need anything,' he said and she glowered.

'Why is Lorna staying? Ruby's going to her friends. Hamster and I are fine.'

'Humour me,' he told her. 'Lorna will stay until after lunch, just until I'm sure that you're...safe.'

'I don't like being safe,' she snapped and he grinned and patted her head as if he was patting Ruby's head.

Except it wasn't like that at all. It felt...different. Intimate. *Okay?*

'Says the woman who's just been playing with snakes,' he told her. 'You don't like being safe? You know, Dr Hargreaves, I'm very sure that you do.'

Polly slept on and off for the rest of the day. She woke late afternoon and looked at the time and nearly had kittens. Five o'clock? Where had the day gone? She must have been more shocked than she'd realised.

Lorna had brought in sandwiches around midday. She'd eaten two. The other plus her untouched mug of coffee still sat on her bedside table.

Two days' rest. 'That's enough,' she told herself and headed across to the bathroom and showered—just a little grateful for the hand rail—and then tugged on jeans and a T-shirt and pulled a comb through her curls.

Hamster was still under her bed. The rest of the house was in silence.

She ate her remaining sandwiches—yeah, she did have to be careful—checked her blood sugars and felt smug again and then headed to the kitchen.

No one.

There was a note from Lorna on the kitchen table.

I've had to go, Dr Hargreaves, but Dr Denver thinks you'll be okay. My number's on the pad by the phone if you need me. Ruby's staying at Talia's for a sleepover. Dr Denver has some emergency over at the hospital. He says help yourself to what you need and he'll see you as soon as he can. Fridge is full. Good luck.

She hardly needed good luck. She opened the fridge and stared in and thought it would take a small army to eat their way through this.

She meandered through the empty house feeling a bit intrusive, a bit weird. It was still very much Hugo's parents' home, she thought, furnished and decorated over years of raising a family. There were pictures of Hugo and a girl who was evidently Grace as babies, as they grew up. There were pictures of high school graduations, Hugo's medical graduation. Happy snaps.

Though Polly could see the telltale signs of early depression on Grace's face as soon as she reached her teens. Hugo smiled obediently at the camera. Some of his smiles said he was long-suffering but Grace's smiles seemed forced.

As were the smiles Grace produced in later photos, taken with Ruby.

Depression... *Aagh.* It was a grey fog, thick sludge, permeating everything and destroying lives.

And now it had destroyed Hugo's.

But had it been destroyed? He'd had to leave Sydney, commit himself to his family.

It'd be the same if Polly had to stay in Sydney, commit herself to her family.

'He has the bigger load to bear,' Polly said out loud, though then she thought of Hugo ruffling Ruby's hair and saw there would be compensations. And this did seem like an awesome place to live.

'But people probably think that about the six-star places my parents want to cocoon me in,' she muttered and thought: *enough.*

What she needed was work. Or at least an introduction to work.

She thought back to the note:

Dr Denver has some emergency over at the hospital...

Work. *Excellent.*

She found one of Hugo's white coats. It was a bit too big— okay, it was a lot too big, but with the sleeves rolled up she decided she looked almost professional.

'See you later,' she told Hamster but Hamster heaved himself to his feet and padded determinedly after her.

'Are you my minder?' she demanded and he wagged his tail and stuck close.

'Has he told you to bite me if I'm not sensible?'

Hamster wagged some more and she sighed and gave up and headed across to the hospital, her minder heading after her.

CHAPTER NINE

SURGEONS WEREN'T TRAINED to cope with human conflict. Surgeons operated.

Yes, surgeons consulted pre-operatively. Yes, they visited their patients at their bedsides, but consultations were done within the confines of appointments, and patient visits were made with a nurse hovering close by, ready to whisk away all but the closest of friends or family.

Death, however, observed no such restrictions. Max Hurley had passed away peacefully in his sleep, aged ninety-seven. He'd been in the nursing home section of the hospital for the last twelve months, during which time his daughter Isobel had been a constant visitor, having nursed him at home for years. His wife had died ten years back. Hugo had assumed there was little other family.

Two hours after his death, he'd learned how wrong he was. A vast extended family had descended on the place like a swarm of locusts. Isobel, seventy years old and frail herself, was jammed into a chair at the edge of the room while her family railed around her.

One of the older men in the group looked almost ready to have a medical incident himself. He was red in the face and the veins on his forehead were bulging. 'I can't believe it!' he was shouting. 'He's left her the whole blasted farm. She's seventy. A spinster. What the hell…? It's a family farm. It's hard up against my place. The old man always intended the farms to be joined. We'll be contesting…'

'There's no need!' another man snapped. 'Isobel will be reasonable, won't you, Isobel?' The men were standing over

her, obviously furious. 'But, as for your farms being joined…
We'll split, fair down the middle. You get half, Bert, and I'll
get the other half. Isobel, we can organise you a nice little
retirement unit in town…'

Isobel was surrounded by her family, but what a family!
She had a buxom woman sitting on either side of her. One
was even hugging her, but she looked…

Small. He could think of no better adjective. Her father's
death seemed to have shrunk her.

Any man's death diminishes me… It was a quote from
John Donne and, looking down at the helpless Isobel, he
thought, even though her dad had been almost a hundred,
that diminishment was just as powerful.

'Do you want everyone to leave?' he asked Isobel, thinking she needed time to be alone with her father, but she
shook her head.

'N…no. These are my family.'

Family. This was her call, but oh, he felt for her. Trapped
by loving…

But then, suddenly, standing at the door was Polly. Her
white coat reached her knees, with the sleeves rolled up two
or three times. Her freckles stood out in her still pale face,
accentuating the flame of her curls, but her green eyes were
flashing professionalism—and determination.

She was wearing a stethoscope around her neck. A red
one. It was inscribed, he thought, fascinated. *What the
heck…?*

Who had a personally inscribed stethoscope?

'I'm sorry but I need you all to leave,' she said and he
stopped thinking about personalised stethoscopes and stared
at her in amazement.

He'd thought of her as small, frail, ill.

She sounded like a boom box with the volume turned
up full.

'I'm Dr Hargreaves and I'm here to organise the death
certificate,' she said so loudly that she cut across arguments,

squashing the gathering that was threatening to become a riot. 'Dr Denver has asked me to confirm his diagnosis and I have limited time. I need the immediate next of kin. Who's that?'

After a moment's stunned silence Isobel put up a timid hand.

Polly nodded. 'You can stay. Everyone else must leave.'

'Why?' the oldest of the arguing men demanded. 'What the…?'

'If you wish to avoid a coroner's inquest and possible autopsy then this is what has to happen.' Polly glanced at her watch. 'My time is precious. Could you leave now?'

'You're the doc who got bitten by a snake.'

'Yes, which has pushed my workload to crazy limits before Dr Denver leaves on vacation. Go now, please, or I'll be forced to request an independent assessment from Sydney.'

'When can we come back?'

'When I've made my assessment and, since I've never treated this patient, it may be a while. I suggest…' She hesitated and looked at Isobel, and then at Hugo.

'This is Isobel,' Hugo told her, starting to enjoy himself.

'I suggest Isobel will tell you when it's possible,' Polly continued smoothly. 'Meanwhile, my apologies for the inconvenience but you have two minutes to say your goodbyes before I must start work.'

'We're family,' the closest guy muttered and Polly nodded.

'I can see that, and my condolences, but I'm afraid Isobel needs to face this alone.'

And then she stood back and crossed her arms and waited.

She was superb, Hugo thought. If he didn't know she was talking nonsense—in truth he'd already signed the death certificate—he'd have been totally taken in.

'Why do you need to worry about a death certificate?' one of the men demanded. 'He just died of old age.'

'That's nonsense,' Polly snapped. 'How old are you?'

'I…seventy-two.' There was something about Polly that said *Don't mess with me*, and the guy clearly got it.

'So you're older than your prescribed three score years and ten. If you drop dead now, surely you'd expect us to dignify your death with a diagnosis. Not just dismiss it as old age.'

'Yes, but…'

'But what? Do extra years mean fewer rights, less respect?'

'No, but…'

'Then please leave and let me get on with my work.' And, to Hugo's further astonishment, she stared at her watch and started toe tapping. Less than one minute later the room was clear and the door closed behind them.

As the door closed Isobel gave a muffled sob and crossed to the bed and hugged her father.

How had Polly understood this? Hugo thought, stunned. How had she figured so fast that Isobel desperately needed time alone? That sometimes family wasn't wanted.

'We'll come back in an hour,' he said gently and touched Isobel's shoulder. 'Or earlier, if you want. The bell's here. Just press it if you need it.'

Isobel's tear-stained face turned up to them. 'Thank you. I didn't think… When I got the call to say he was going I rang Henry to ask him to feed the dogs and suddenly they were all here. I didn't even know they knew the contents of the will. And…'

'And it doesn't matter,' Hugo said gently. 'All those things can be sorted later. I think it'd be a good idea if we got Ron Dawson—he's your dad's lawyer, isn't he?—to take responsibility for any questions. If anyone asks, just say Ron's in charge. No more questions, Isobel. No more worry. For now it's simply time to say goodbye to your dad.'

And he ushered Polly out of the room and closed the door behind them.

Wherever Isobel's obnoxious family were, they were no longer here. The silence after the din was almost tangible.

Joe came round the corner from the nurses' station, his arms above his head in a gesture of triumph. 'You're a champ, Doc Hargreaves,' he boomed. 'A clean knockout. You can come and work here any day.'

'Did you set that up?' Hugo asked faintly and Joe grinned.

'All I did was tell Polly that you and Isobel were surrounded by a rabid pack of mercenary relatives and she went off like a firecracker. I listened from out in the corridor. Did you ever hear anything like it? A couple of them asked how long before they could go back in and I said our Doc Hargreaves is known for thorough work. A detailed examination, pathology, maybe even scans. It could take until tomorrow.'

'Scans…' Hugo managed and Polly grinned happily up at Joe and Joe high-fived her with her good hand and suddenly Hugo was left feeling a bit…

Jealous? Jealous of his fifty-year-old head nurse high-fiving his colleague? He had to be kidding.

'Of course, scans,' Polly said happily. 'You have to scan a patient very thoroughly when you're looking for cause of death.' She tugged up her jeans and held up her still swollen foot. 'If you hadn't scanned me you might have missed the snake bite. See? Two little holes. Scans are vital and they can take as much time as Isobel needs.'

Hugo choked. Joe guffawed and high-fived Polly again then a bell rang down the corridor and Joe took himself off and Hugo was left with Polly.

She was amazing.

She was gorgeous!

'So,' she said, turning brisk again. 'Are you going to show me your hospital?' And she was back to being a colleague, purely professional, except her coat was too big and her hair was too red and her toenails were crimson and…

And she was a colleague.

'Sure,' he said and managed to do a decent professional

tour of his hospital without once—or maybe once but that was professional, as she bumped her leg on a trolley and he had to make sure the swollen ankle was still okay—looking at those amazing toenails.

And she was terrific. Any doubts he might have had about her ability to care for the medical needs of Wombat Valley were put to rest fast. She was just…right.

He now had four patients in his nursing home beds—yes, Max had just died, but over the last twenty-four hours he'd had two new admissions. Christmas often did that. The family was heading away for the holiday, Dad couldn't cope on his own and the easiest solution was respite care. Or a lonely senior citizen was suddenly overwhelmed with the memories of Christmases past and got chest pain or stopped eating, or even forgot normal care and fell…

Hazel Blacksmith was one such lady. She'd fallen chopping her firewood last night. Her hip had proven to be badly bruised rather than broken but she lay in bed, a ball of misery, refusing to be comforted.

But Polly didn't acknowledge misery. 'Hey, how lucky are you?' Polly demanded as Hugo introduced her and explained the diagnosis. 'Just a bruised hip? If someone made me chop wood I'd probably end up suffering from amputation from the knee down.'

'I've chopped wood all me life,' Hazel told her in a firmer voice than Hugo had heard since her neighbour had brought her in. 'I don't cut meself.'

'And you don't get bitten by snakes either, I'll bet,' Polly said. 'Wise woman. Look at this.' And she stuck her leg in the air for Hazel to see her snake bite.

'I heard you got bit,' Hazel said cautiously.

'It was Dr Denver's fault.' Polly cast a darkling look at Hugo. 'He trapped the snake with his shenanigans in the truck, so when I went to rescue them it was ready to attack.'

And Hazel's lips twitched. 'Shenanigans…'

'Men,' Polly said. 'You can't trust them to do anything

right. Holding snakes by the tail is the least of it. Would you mind if I had a look at your bruise? I've much gentler hands than Dr Denver.'

They were gentle. Hugo watched as Polly performed a careful examination of the old lady—a scan? She gently probed and teased and by the end of the examination the old lady was smitten and Hugo was getting close himself.

What a gem! He would be able to go away for Christmas and leave the hospital in her charge.

But…why did going away for Christmas suddenly not seem as desirable?

'Are you staying in for Christmas?' Polly asked cheerfully as she tucked Hazel's bedclothes back around her and Hazel looked brighter than she had since Hugo had admitted her.

'Dr Denver thinks I should.'

'Then I concur,' Polly said warmly. 'But I need to warn you, the Christmas dinner menu here is looking a bit dodgy. However, we have three more days. I'll see what I can do. I'll ring my mother's chef and get some advice.'

'Your mother has a chef?' Hazel sounded stunned.

And Hugo was stunned as well. Not only did this woman come from a privileged background, she was happily admitting it.

'Doesn't everyone's mother?' Polly said happily. 'Left to my own devices, I'm a beans on toast girl, but this is Christmas. We all have to make some sacrifices, and ringing Raoul might be the least of them. Just as long as he promises not to tell my mother where I am.'

She wasn't making sacrifices at all, Polly thought happily as she sat on the veranda that evening. She was about to have a very good time.

Her ankle still hurt. Her hand ached, but not so much as to mess with her equanimity. This was a beautiful little hospital, full of easy patients, and she was pretty sure she could cope.

Her silver tree was up in the living room, surrounded by origami gifts and a few real ones as well.

Hamster was lying by her side on the top step. He was due to head back to his temporary carer's but she intended to have a word with Hugo about that. She wouldn't mind Hamster staying here for Christmas as well.

She'd do a bit of online shopping, she decided. If she paid enough for express postage, she could get heaps of good stuff here. Lots of treats for her coterie of oldies in the hospital.

Would Isobel like to come too? Maybe she could take her tree over to the hospital and have Christmas dinner over there?

Maybe she could wear her little red alpine dress and the wig with the blonde pigtails. And her crimson boots and the Santa hat. She just happened to have packed them.

She grinned. Three suitcases… A girl could never be prepared enough.

The screen door opened behind her and Hugo emerged carrying two mugs of tea. She nudged over on her step, heaving Hamster to the side as well, and he sat down beside her.

Ma and Pa Kettle, she thought, and the feeling was sort of…okay.

More than okay. Good.

She liked this man.

Actually…

Um…don't go there. He'd be gone before Christmas. He'd come back in the New Year, she'd do a quick handover and then she'd have no reason to see him again.

Her bounce faded a little as she took the offered mug and she gave herself a swift inward kick. What was she thinking? Having fantasies about a man who was so steeped in domesticity he couldn't get out of this valley?

Falling for a man who was committed to love?

Love was what she was running from, she thought dryly. Love was why she'd packed her car and headed for the hills.

Love was chains, blackmail, guilt. Love was your mother

watching every mouthful you ate and mentally counting insulin dosages. Love was catching your boyfriend phoning in to report how you were— 'She's great, Mrs Hargreaves, and of course I'm looking after her. No, of course I won't let her get tired…'

Toerag. She glowered at the absent Marcus and took her tea and stared morosely out into the dark.

'Hamster been annoying you, then?' Hugo asked mildly and she caught herself and managed a rueful smile.

'Not so much.'

'Are you hurting? How's your…?'

'Don't you dare fuss!'

'Okay,' he said cautiously.

Silence.

It wasn't bad tea. Good and hot.

It was very hard to appreciate tea when Hugo was sitting beside her.

'Where would you be now?' she asked, suddenly needing to know. 'If it wasn't for Ruby.'

'Sydney.'

Of course. 'Working?'

'Possibly. If I wasn't on call, though, I'd be in a supper club around the corner from the hospital. It has a roof top bar that overlooks the harbour. Most of my friends use it.'

'And you miss it?'

'What do you think?'

'And your work? Your surgery?'

'Almost more than I can bear,' he said and she flinched at the sudden and honest sound of gut-wrenching loss.

'So why don't you take Ruby back to Sydney?'

'If I had Ruby in Sydney, do you believe for a moment that I'd be in the supper club?'

'You could get a housekeeper.'

'Yes, I could. The problem is that I love Ruby.'

'She's prickly.'

'Tough to love. She is. She lets me, though. Inch by inch.'

'Is it worth it?'

'What, hoping for Ruby's love in return?'

'I guess,' she said, doubtfully though, because she wasn't quite sure where she was going with this.

'I don't have a choice,' Hugo said gently. 'And I can't count its worth. I met Ruby when she was two days old. My sister was in a mess. I was called to a hospital up in Darwin because Grace was drug addicted and unable to cope. She went into rehab. I took four weeks off work, then my parents took over. But for those four weeks… I held Ruby in the palm of my hands—literally—and she's been there ever since.'

And what was there in that to make her tear up? Nothing, she thought, frantically sniffing, and Hugo handed her a tissue and she thought this was just the sort of man who walked round with spare tissues in his pocket because something about him made you…made her…

Back off. She needed to back off. She'd been here for less than three days and suddenly it seemed as if a fine gossamer web was closing around her. The web she'd run from.

A trap, every bit as claustrophobic as the one Hugo found himself in.

She stood up, so suddenly she splashed tea on Hamster, who looked up reproachfully and then started licking the tea from his paws.

Hugo looked up too, but not reproachfully. It was as if he understood where she was coming from.

And that was a scary thought all by itself.

'I should go to bed,' she said a bit shakily and he nodded.

'You should.'

And then his phone rang.

He answered it, listened, then clicked it closed and rose as well.

'Work?'

'What do you think?'

'Anything I can help with?'

'You're going to bed.'

'Is that an order?'

'Um…no.'

'So tell me.'

'Groin and knee injuries,' he said. 'Terry Oakshot. Local farmer and amateur footy player. Late twenties. This sounds like a party prank gone wrong. His mates are bringing him in now.'

'I'll stay up until I see what the problem is.'

'No need. If I can't handle it I'll send him out.'

'Evacuate when you have two doctors?'

'If I need to evacuate, I'll evacuate.'

'Of course you will,' she said warmly. 'But if it's not too complicated, don't forget I'm not just a pretty face.' She grinned and took his mug. 'Okay, Doc Denver, you go see what the problem is, but yell if you need me. I'll go put my feet up and garner strength for the onslaught to come. Ooh, I wouldn't mind a good onslaught. I'm a wee bit bored.'

CHAPTER TEN

ONE LOOK AT the mess that was Terry Oakshot's knee confirmed that he needed a surgeon skilled in reconstruction. The blood supply wasn't compromised, though. There was no need for immediate intervention for his knee. He needed decent pain relief and transport as soon as possible to the experts in Sydney.

Unfortunately, it wasn't his knee that was causing Terry to whimper. He was clutching his groin in agony.

It would be agony too, Hugo thought, as Joe helped examine him.

A fast conversation with the mates who'd brought him in had given him all the information he needed. The boys had been having a pre-Christmas party in the footy ground's stadium. After a few beers someone had shouted for Terry to come down to ground level to kick the footy. After a beer or six, Terry had decided there was a faster way than the stairs and he'd tried to slide down the banister.

It hadn't been a good idea. Terry had smashed groin first into the bottom post, then toppled onto the wooden stairs. The knee was bad. His groin was worse. One side of his scrotum was swollen and cut, and one testicle was higher than the other. The less injured side didn't look too good either, and Terry was retching with pain.

'What's going on?' he moaned as his wife arrived. Maree was in her early twenties and seemed terrified. She looked as if she'd been baking. Her face was streaked white with flour, and it was whiter still with shock.

'You seem to have given yourself a testicular torsion,' he

told him. 'Terry, your knee's broken and it'll need specialist surgery in Sydney, but what's happened to your groin is more urgent. The spermatic cord running to your testicles has been damaged. The cord's a blood vessel, so the blood supply's been cut. We need to work fast to get it sorted.'

'Fast'd be good, Doc,' Terry moaned. 'Fast like now?'

And, with that, Polly's presence came slamming back at him, bringing a wash of relief. He had an anaesthetist.

'You know I have another doctor working here?'

'The one that got bit by the snake?' Terry demanded.

'She's recovered.' Or almost recovered. She could still do with an early night but this needed to take precedence. 'Terry, you and Maree don't have any kids yet, do you?'

'No!' And Maree had understood the inference faster than Terry. 'But we want them. The spermatic cord… Doc, you're not saying…?'

'I'm thinking we need to operate fast,' Hugo told them both. 'I'll get Joe to ring Polly. She can do the anaesthetic.'

'Polly…' Maree managed. 'What sort of name is that for a doctor?'

'It's short for Pollyanna. It's a great name for a fine doctor,' he told her. 'Wait and see.'

Polly didn't see the wound until they were in Theatre. Terry declared he 'wasn't going to get looked at down there by a female'.

'You'll get looked at by anyone who can fix you,' Maree snapped and clutched Polly as soon as she saw her. 'We want kids,' she stammered. 'You get him right, no matter what.'

'We'll do our best,' Polly told her. She'd arrived at the hospital fast, she was heading to scrub, and she had no time to waste.

Once in Theatre she could focus, and she needed to. Terry was a big man, he was deeply shocked and he'd been drinking. In an ideal world she'd wait for him to sober up, but there wasn't time.

She ran through the options in her head, talked them through with Hugo. Then they went for it. With Terry safely asleep and intubated, Joe started disinfecting the injured area. For the first time she saw the extent of the damage.

'Ouch,' she said and Hugo cast her a look that could almost be amused.

'You might say that.'

But he was calm. She watched him assess the wound carefully. She watched as he started the procedure as if he'd done it a thousand times.

He was a thoracic surgeon. This was a job for a trained urologist.

He didn't look concerned. He looked…competent.

He's good, she thought, and then she relaxed a little, although not very much because her anaesthetic skills were basic, but they were good enough to spare her time to watch Hugo work.

No highly skilled urologist could do a better job than this, she thought. Repairing a damaged spermatic cord was tricky at the best of times, and that was in a large hospital with every piece of modern gadgetry. Large hospitals had magnification, monitors showing exactly what was happening. Large hospitals had skilled backup.

Hugo had a semi-trained anaesthetist, Joe and himself.

If she hadn't been here…

What then?

Hugo would have needed to send him to Sydney, she thought, and by the time Terry reached Sydney, he and his wife would be fated to be childless or needing a sperm donor.

What if this had happened when she was here by herself?

For the first time, her bold foray into bush medicine looked less than wise. She would have failed this couple.

How could Hugo work here by himself?

'If you hadn't been here I would have talked Joe through the anaesthesia. We've done it before,' Hugo said.

She glanced up at him in shock. 'How do you know what I'm thinking?'

'You have an entirely readable face. You were concentrating, concentrating, concentrating, and suddenly you looked petrified. I checked the monitors, saw you had nothing patient-wise to be petrified about and figured you had to be projecting yourself into the future.'

'He has eyes in the back of his head.' Joe was grinning. 'You'll get used to it.'

'She won't,' Hugo said. 'We'll work together tomorrow and then I'll be gone.'

But he'd be back, Polly thought as his skilled fingers continued their fight to repair the appalling damage. In the New Year he'd be back here being a solo doctor with his little niece. He'd be on his own and she'd be...

Where?

She hadn't figured that out yet. One locum at a time. Wandering...

She'd thought she'd quite like to do a stint for an aid agency, working overseas, getting right away from her parents.

Her diabetes was the killer there. No aid agency, working in Third World conditions, would accept a Type One diabetic.

Maybe that was one of the reasons she wanted it so much. Maybe the locum thing was part of it.

Locum to locum to locum? Never settling? Never doing family?

That was what she'd decided. No more fuss. She couldn't bear it.

Doing things despite her diabetes...

Was this another way her diabetes was controlling her?

'I'm thinking...' Hugo's voice was a lazy drawl but there was satisfaction behind it and it drew her attention back to where it should be. 'I'm thinking we might just have succeeded in repairing this mess. The left one's possible and the right one's looking certain. We'll transfer him to Sydney for his knee and get him checked by the urologist while he's there but I'm thinking we've done the thing.'

'Yes!' Joe said, but Polly didn't say anything at all.

Locum to locum to locum...

That was what she'd dreamed of. Why did it suddenly seem so bleak?

And why did what she'd thought of as a dream suddenly seem like running away?

There was no more time for introspection. Polly reversed the anaesthetic, Terry started to come round and Hugo sent her out to talk to Maree.

'She won't believe Joe. Something about the beard. Polly, go tell her Terry's okay.'

'So she'll believe a whippersnapper who came on the scene in polka dots with snake bite instead of a beard?' Joe demanded.

'Absolutely. If Polly, who's hung upside down with snakes, decrees someone's safe, then...'

'Then she'll think Polly has a weird definition of safe,' Joe retorted and he and Hugo chuckled and Polly looked from one to the other and thought that even though Hugo was trapped in this little hospital there were compensations.

It was like family...

Family... There was that word again.

'I have drips to adjust and you deserve to be the bearer of good tidings,' Hugo told her. 'How's the hand?'

She hadn't even noticed her hand. She'd double gloved because she couldn't scrub the dressing and then she'd forgotten about it.

Her ankle wasn't hurting. She couldn't feel a bruise.

She felt...a mile high.

Successful surgery... There was nothing like it.

She thought suddenly of her parents' recriminations when she'd decided on medicine and she knew, without doubt, that medicine at least wasn't running from her parents' world. Medicine was what she most wanted to do.

She met Hugo's gaze and he was smiling and once again she got that blast of knowledge that told her he understood what she was feeling.

'Good, isn't it?' he said softly and he smiled at her—and he might as well have kissed her.

It felt like a kiss. A caress from four feet apart.

And Joe was smiling at them, beaming from one ear to the other, and Polly stepped from the table a bit too fast and could have tripped, but she didn't. She wasn't that stupid.

She felt pretty stupid. She backed out of Theatre feeling totally discombobulated.

Terry's wife was waiting outside, sitting huddled on the room's big couch. There were people around her, two older couples who looked as if they'd come in a hurry. One of the women was wearing a crimson-smeared apron—very smeared. Her husband had matching crimson smears on his gingham shirt.

They all looked up at her as she emerged and Maree moaned and put her face in her hands.

'Hey, it's all right, love.' The bigger of the two men put a rough hand on her shoulder. He was watching Polly's face. 'The Doc's smiling. You're smiling, aren't you, Doc? You wouldn't do that if our Terry was bad.'

'I'm smiling,' Polly told them, smiling even more just to prove the point. 'Dr Denver's operated and everything went as smoothly as we could hope. Everything's been put back together. Terry's not quite recovered from the anaesthetic yet but as soon as Dr Denver's set up the drips—he'll be administering pain relief, fluids and antibiotics—you'll be able to see him.'

'Oh.' Maree put her face behind her hands and burst into tears. The crimson lady knelt down and gathered her into her arms.

'There, dear, what did I tell you? Terry always bounces

back.' And then she glared up at her husband. 'I told you. Now we have a pot full of burned toffee and a hundred un-coated toffee apples for nothing.'

There was uncertain laughter, the beginnings of relief, and then Maree put her head up again.

'And he will…we will be able to have babies?' she whispered.

Polly heard the door swing open behind her. She didn't have to turn to see it was Hugo—she was starting to sense this man.

Why? What was it between them?

He didn't say anything, though—it seemed this was her call.

'Maree, Dr Denver's done everything we can to make sure that can still happen. We think we've succeeded. I've just watched him operate and I don't think any city surgeon could have done better.'

'Excellent,' the toffee apple lady said. 'And will he be home for Christmas?'

'He won't be, Lexie.' And Hugo took over, putting a hand on Polly's arm as if to signal that he was about to impart medical advice from the team. It was a solid way to go, Polly thought, presenting a united front, and why it made her feel…

Um, no. She wasn't going there. Right now, she couldn't.

'Guys, we're going to send him on to Sydney,' Hugo said, firmly now. 'The operation I just performed was to his groin and, as far as I can tell, it's successful. But his knee needs a competent orthopaedic surgeon. I'd also like him checked by a specialist urologist. We'll send him on to Sydney Central as soon as possible. It'll take about an hour to get the chopper here for transfer. Maree, if you'd like to go with him, I'll tell the hospital you'll need accommodation—they have self-contained flats for just this purpose.'

The group had been starting to relax. Now, as one, they froze.

'But it's Christmas,' Maree whispered. 'We can't go to Sydney for Christmas.'

'You don't have a choice,' Hugo said, still gently, and Maree burst into tears again.

'Hey.' The toffee apple lady still had her in her arms. 'Hey, sweetheart, it's okay. We'll manage.'

'But what about Grandma?' Maree lifted a woebegone face to Hugo. 'What about you, Mum?'

'We'll manage.'

'You can't. Grandma's got Alzheimer's,' Maree explained, looking wildly up at Hugo. 'She's so confused and she gets angry with Mum, but if Terry and I are there she calms down and Mum relaxes and enjoys Christmas. If we're not there...'

'We'll take care of things.' The other woman spoke then, a woman who by her looks had to be Terry's mum. 'We'll look after everyone.'

'But we'll be by ourselves for Christmas.'

'With a recovering husband. Surely that's the most important thing?' It was Terry's dad, glancing back at the door into Theatre, but all three women turned and glared at him.

'Christmas with family...' Maree snapped. 'What's more important than that?'

'Now you know very well that health comes first,' her mum said. 'But you know what? Terry'll be recovering. And you know Aldi Baker? She moved to her son's big house in the centre of Sydney and now her son's gone to Paris for Christmas. She's gone with him and she said if ever we want a base in Sydney we can use that house. So why not now? Why not pack all of us up and we can go to Sydney?' She looked up at Terry's parents. 'You too. Aldi says there's six bedrooms—can you believe that? It's as if it's meant. We can pick up everything—except the toffee apples—they might be well and truly stuffed and they were just for the Christmas Eve fete at the school anyway. We can take everything down there tomorrow morning. If needs be, I bet we could have Christmas in Terry's hospital room.'

'The specialists might even let him out by then,' Hugo conceded, smiling as the despair in the room turned to tentative excitement. 'He'll still need tests but if he stays in Sydney... No promises, but it's possible...'

'There you go then,' Maree's mum said and before Hugo could protect himself she'd flung her arms around him and planted what was probably a very sticky kiss on his cheek. She hugged Polly for good measure and then headed back to hug each and every one of her family.

Family...

And Polly was suddenly staring at them all thinking... *family.*

She was running away.

Why was she running?

Enough. She was tired, she decided. She was overwrought. Her emotions were all over the place. What she needed right now was bed. Hugo was right—bed rest.

Somewhere away from Hugo.

Why did the presence of this man unsettle her so much? A week ago she'd never met him.

Why was the concept of family suddenly everywhere?

'I'll see you back at the house,' she mumbled and Hugo took her arm and led her to the door.

'I'll take you.'

'It's two minutes' walk.'

'I'll take you,' he said more firmly, and then he turned back to Terry's family. 'I'll be back in a few minutes. Joe's looking after Terry. He'll let me know the minute he's awake enough for you to see him. But, Maree, that chopper lands in an hour so it might be better to grab some clothes now...'

'We'll all be in Sydney by midday tomorrow,' her mum said. 'We can bring everything she needs.'

'And I don't need toffee apples, Mum,' Maree managed

and everyone laughed and Hugo's arm tightened around Polly's shoulders and he led her to the door.

'I do need to take Polly home,' he said. 'She's still suffering after-effects...'

'From the snake bite.' Terry's dad finished the sentence for him and came forward and took her hand—her bad hand—and gripped it and didn't even notice her wince. 'You're amazing. Thank God you came to the Valley, girl. If you'd like to stay for ever, you'd be very, very welcome.'

Her hand hurt. The grip had been hard.

Her ankle hurt.

Actually, all of her hurt. The aches and bruises that had been put on the backburner by adrenaline now started to make themselves known.

She really was wobbly. She really did need Hugo's arm around her as they headed across the path from hospital to house.

Or she told herself that. Because somehow it felt...okay.

It felt as if his hold was somehow linking her to...reality?

That was a nonsense thought, but then her head was producing a lot of nonsense at the moment.

It was his skill, she told herself. His surgeon's fingers had been amazing to watch. Skill was always a turn-on.

Skill had nothing to do with it.

Hugo was a turn-on.

She was so aware of him. She was behaving like a teenager with a crush, she decided, but the thought was fleeting because the sensation of being held, being cared for, was so infinitely sweet...

They reached the veranda steps. He took her arm and she let herself lean on him as she climbed.

She hated being cared for. Didn't she?

'I need to go back,' he said, and she heard a reluctance in his voice that matched hers. 'I need to organise transport.'

'Of course you do.'

'Polly...'

'Mmm?'

'Thank you.'

'There's no need to thank me,' she said, whispering suddenly although there was no need to whisper because there was no one to hear but Hamster, who'd wagged his tail once when they'd reached the top of the steps and then gone back to sleep. He was a dog obviously used to the comings and goings of his master. 'I believe I'm being paid.'

'Not enough,' he said and she turned and smiled. She knew her smile was shaky. She knew she was too close and she knew what she was doing was unwise—but she was doing it anyway.

'I'd do it for free,' she murmured and his smile suddenly faded and so did hers. And his hands came out to take hers and almost unconsciously—as if she had no say in what was happening at all—she tilted her chin in a gesture that meant only one thing.

That meant he had nothing to do but lower his mouth to hers.

That meant he had nothing to do but kiss her.

She'd never been kissed like this.

She must have been, she thought dazedly. She'd had boyfriends since her early teens. Her mum had been matchmaking for ever, and Polly wasn't exactly a shrinking violet. Boyfriends were fun. Kissing was nice.

This kissing wasn't nice. This kiss was...

Mind-blowing. There were no other words big enough, for from the moment his mouth met hers she seemed to be melting. It was as if his body was somehow merging into hers, supporting her, warming her, becoming part of her.

Her senses were exploding.

His mouth enveloped hers and all she could do was taste him, feel him, want him. She was kissing with a fierceness that almost frightened her.

She'd never been out of control with her boyfriends. She dated 'nice' boys.

This was no nice boy. This was a man who was as hungry as she was, as demanding, as committed...

Hungry? Demanding? Committed? That described her. She could be none of those things, yet right now she was all three. She surrendered herself to his kiss and she gloried in it. Her fingers entwined themselves in his hair, tugging him closer. She was standing on tiptoe but his arms were around her waist, pulling her up, so the kiss could sink deeper...

She was on fire.

Hugo... His name was a whisper, a shout, a declaration all by itself. Pollyanna Hargreaves was right out of her comfort zone. She was right out of control.

If he picked her up and carried her to his bed right now, would she submit?

There was no *submit* about it. If she had her way it'd be Polly who'd be doing the carrying. She wanted him!

She couldn't have him. Even as the crazy idea hit, the need to carry this straight through to the bedroom, he was putting her back.

It was a wrench like no other. Their mouths parted and she felt...lost.

'I need to go.' His voice was ragged. 'Terry needs...'

'Y...yes.'

He took a step back, turned away and then paused and turned back. 'That wasn't a casual kiss.'

'You could have fooled me,' she managed and he gave a twisted smile.

'Polly, what I'm feeling...'

And suddenly it was out there, this thing between them. Lust, love—whatever. Only it couldn't be love, Polly thought dazedly, because they'd only known each other for three days and no one fell in love that fast.

Lust, then. The way she was feeling...certainly it was lust.

'Yeah, I'm feeling it, too,' she managed. 'So it's just as

well you're going away soon because I'm just over a pos-
sessive boyfriend. And I don't do casual affairs, or family
either, for that matter, and you have a daughter...'

'A niece.'

'A niece.' She closed her eyes as she corrected herself.
A waif-like kid who Hugo loved. Why did that make him
seem more sexy, not less?

Why was Ruby suddenly in the equation?

'Hugo, I don't do family,' she said again and surprisingly
her voice sounded almost calm. 'That's why I'm here—to
get away from ties.'

'This isn't some kind of trap.' He said it fast.

Trap? How could she ever think of a kiss as a trap?

'Of course it's not,' she agreed. 'It was a kiss, simply that.
Excellent surgical skills always turn me on, Dr Denver.'

'So if I had warts on my nose, a sagging middle and a dis-
inclination to wash, but I removed an appendix with style,
you'd still turn into a puddle of molten passion?'

He was smiling, making things light, and she had to too.
'You'd better believe it.'

'So, on a scale of one to ten...speedy repair of ingrown
toenail?'

'Ooh, don't talk dirty,' she managed and scraped up a
grin. 'Next you'll be talking laparoscopic gallstone removal
and I have no defences.'

He chuckled but it sounded forced. He was as shaken as
she was, she thought.

But they were apart now. Work was waiting and they
both knew it.

'Bed,' he said and she blinked.

'Is that an order?'

'I guess it is.'

'You're not my doctor.' It suddenly seemed important—
incredibly important—to make that clear.

'I know.' He hesitated. 'And in two weeks I won't be your
colleague.'

'And I'll be on the other side of the world.'

'Really? Where?'

'Sudan, maybe. Ethiopia.'

'With Type One Diabetes?' He sounded incredulous.

'I can cope.'

'Polly…'

'Don't fuss.'

'I'm not fussing.' Except he was, she thought, and she also thought, with a modicum of self-knowledge, that she'd driven him to fuss. It was like someone with one leg declaring they intended to be a tightrope walker.

She could probably do it.

Her parents would worry.

This man might too, and by making such a declaration… it had been like a slap. *Fuss if you dare; it'll give me an excuse to run.*

It wasn't fair.

'Go,' she told him. 'Work's waiting. The chopper should be here soon.'

'Yes.' But still there was hesitation.

'The kiss was a mistake,' she said. 'An aberration.'

'We both know it was no such thing, but I can't push. I have no right. Polly…'

'Go,' she said. 'No such thing or not, I'm completely uninterested.'

Hugo headed back to the hospital feeling…empty. Gutted?

What had just happened?

He'd been knocked back. He'd kissed her. She'd responded with passion but that passion had given way to sense. She was fiercely independent and wanted to be more so. He had a commitment that would tie him here for life.

He was trapped here. How could he possibly ask a woman to share this trap?

Maybe he could move back to Sydney. Maybe he could

pick up the strings of the life he'd known before. He moved in the circles Polly moved in…

Except she wasn't going back to Sydney. She was escaping family and he had Ruby. The life he had in Sydney was over.

The thought of Sydney was like a siren song. He could go back to performing the surgery he'd trained for. He was picking up his family medicine skills here, but the surgical skills he'd fought to gain…to let them fade…

He had no choice but to let them go. Ruby had lost far more than he had. He could take Ruby back to Sydney—of course he could—but apartment life wouldn't suit her or Hamster. He'd be back working twelve-hour days. Ruby wouldn't be surrounded by people who cared about her.

His trap had firmly closed.

He sighed and squared his shoulders and headed up the ramp to the hospital entrance.

A wallaby was sitting by the door.

'Popped in for a check-up?' he asked the little creature. The wallaby seemed to be admiring her reflection in the glass door. 'Or is there anything more urgent I can help you with?'

The wallaby turned and gazed at him, almost thoughtfully. They stared at each other for a long moment and then the helicopter appeared, low and fast, from the east. The wallaby looked up at the sky, looked again at Hugo and then bounded off, back down the ramp and into the bush.

Back to freedom. No ties there.

'I'm not jealous,' Hugo muttered as he headed through the doors and made his way to the waiting Terry. 'I can make a life here.'

Without Polly?

'And that's a stupid thought,' he told himself. 'You made that decision well before Polly came on the scene. How one red-headed, flibbertigibbet doctor can mess with your equanimity…'

'A flibbertigibbet?' he demanded of himself and he must

have said the word too loud because Joe was waiting for him and he raised his brows in enquiry.

'The wallaby,' he explained. 'She was looking at her reflection in the glass door. She's headed back to the bush now. I thought she might have a medical issue, but she was probably just checking her mascara. Flibbertigibbet. Wallabies are like that.'

'Yes, Doctor,' Joe said cautiously. 'Mate, are you…okay?'

'Never better,' he murmured. 'One more day of work and then I'm off for Christmas holidays. Bring it on.'

'You can't wait to get out of here?'

'How can you doubt it?' he demanded, but he thought of Polly standing on the veranda looking after him and he knew that doubt was totally justified.

Polly stayed on the veranda for a very long time.

The kiss stayed with her.

She sank into one of the big cane chairs and Hamster licked her hand and put his big boofy head on her knee. It was almost as if he knew she needed comfort.

Why did she need comfort? What possible reason was there to feel bereft?

Just because someone had kissed her…

Just because someone was impossible.

She should leave now. That was what part of her felt like doing—packing her little sports car and driving away, fast.

That was fear talking—and why was she fearful?

Where was the new brave Polly now? The intrepid Polly who'd walked away from her family, who'd vowed to be independent, who'd hankered after a life free of the obligations of loving?

It had all seemed so simple back in Sydney. Toss in her hospital job. Declare her independence to her parents. Start treating herself as a grown-up.

She wasn't feeling grown-up now. She was feeling…just a little bit stupid.

'Which is stupid all by itself,' she told Hamster. 'Here I am, less than a week into my new life, and I'm questioning everything. I haven't given it a chance. And if I left here... where would I run to? Back to my parents? Not in a month of Sundays. Off to Ethiopia? We both know that's not going to happen. No, all I need to do is stay here, keep my feet firmly on the ground, keep lust solidly damped and get on with my work. And I'll work better if I sleep now.'

But the kiss was still with her, all around her, enveloping her in its sweetness.

'Hugo's back at work and he's probably forgotten all about it,' she told Hamster. 'Men are like that.'

Hamster whined and put a paw on her lap.

'With one exception,' she told him generously. 'And by the way, if Hugo thinks he's taking you back to that boarding place while he's away, he has another think coming. You're staying with me for Christmas.'

Because she didn't want to be alone?

The question was suddenly out there, insidious, even threatening.

She did want to be alone, she told herself. That was what this whole locum bit was about. She'd been cloistered since birth. She needed to find herself.

She didn't need Hugo.

'And he doesn't need me,' she told herself, rising and heading indoors, not because she wanted to but because it was sensible and a woman had to be sensible. She had the remnants of a snake bite and a cut hand to take care of. Medicine... That was what she was here for, and that was what she needed to focus on.

'And nothing else,' she told herself as she passed the tree in the living room with Ruby's stack of origami gifts.

She hoped Ruby was having a happy sleepover with her friend tonight.

'But that's nothing to do with me either,' she told Hamster and she took a couple of deep breaths and poured herself a glass of juice for her bedside, because a woman had to be sensible.

'That's the new me,' she told Hamster as she headed for her bedroom. 'Sensible R Us. I'm Dr Pollyanna Hargreaves, with the frivolous name, but there's nothing else frivolous about me. I'm here to focus on medicine and nothing else. I will not think about Hugo Denver. Not one bit.'

She lied.

She went to bed and lay in the dark and all she could think of was Hugo. All she could feel was Hugo. His kiss enveloped her dreams and she tossed and turned and decided that snake bite venom was insidious.

It had turned one sensible doctor into an idiot.

CHAPTER ELEVEN

POLLY WOKE AND rain was thundering on the roof. It wasn't a shower. This was a deluge.

In Sydney—in fact in any house or hotel she'd ever stayed in—she hardly heard the rain. At most it was a hushed background whisper. Here it was crashing so hard on the iron roof she figured she could sing Christmas carols out loud and no one would hear.

Why not? She did.

Ruby heard her. Two bars into 'Silent Night' there was a scratching on the door. She called, 'Come in,' and Ruby flew in to land on the bed beside her. Hamster arrived straight after. He was wet. Very wet. He leaped onto her bedcovers and shook and Polly yelped and Ruby gave a tentative giggle. A very tentative giggle.

'Is he...is he okay?' she stammered.

Polly surveyed the dog with disgust. He appeared to have taken a mud bath or six.

'He appears okay. Is there a problem?'

'He's scared of thunder. He was outside jumping in puddles when the last bit of thunder came. We got scared.'

'Where's your uncle?' Hamster's wetness was soaking her feet. So much for a nice invalidish sleep-in, she thought, and resigned herself.

'He's over at the hospital.'

'Why are you home?'

'There was thunder in the night. I got scared too, so Talia's mum rang Uncle Hugo and he came and got me.'

So even if they'd indulged in a night of molten passion

they would have been hit by kid-interruptus, Polly thought, and then snagged her errant thoughts and shoved them in the place in her brain marked 'Inappropriate'.

'It's raining a lot,' Ruby said, snuggling into Polly's bed as if she had every right to be there. 'Uncle Hugo says it's raining even in Sydney but it'll stop by Christmas so that's okay. And we're leaving first thing in the morning as long as you're better. But he says you're almost better anyway. He says I can stay here with you this morning. He says you have to stay in bed until at least ten o'clock. He says Hamster and I can make you toast but we can't make you coffee because I'm not allowed to use the kettle yet.'

'Your Uncle Hugo is bossy.'

'Yes,' Ruby said happily. 'I like it. My mum wasn't bossy. One day I had to make her a cup of tea and I burned myself. See my scar?' She held up a wrist, where a scar showed the burn had been small but significant. 'Uncle Hugo said Mum shouldn't have asked me but he said she only did 'cos she was sick. But he's not sick so he's allowed to be bossy.'

'And he's at the hospital?'

'Mr Millard's cow got bogged.' Ruby was right under the covers now, nudging Hamster's rear end with her feet. The dog was heaving up and down but grinning his dopey Labrador smile, thunder forgotten. 'And Mr Millard pulled it out with a rope but he fell over when it came out fast. He broke his arm and Uncle Hugo has to put plaster on it. But Polly, I've been looking at our presents and worrying. We won't have a Christmas tree at the beach. Uncle Hugo says it doesn't matter but I think we need one.'

'You definitely need one. You can take mine,' Polly offered.

'But what will you and Hamster have?'

'We'll chop down a gum tree.'

'With an axe?'

'Yes.'

'Uncle Hugo won't let you use an axe.'

'Uncle Hugo's not the boss of me.'

'He just doesn't want us to get burned,' Ruby said worriedly. 'You might hurt yourself.

'I can take care of myself. I'm a grown-up.'

'My mum was a grown-up and she didn't take care of herself. She died.'

There was no answer to that. Another clap of thunder rumbled across the valley. Hamster turned into a quivering mess; Polly and Ruby had to hug him and then the whole bed was pretty much a quivering and soggy mess and Polly decided convalescence had knobs on and she might as well get up.

'You would like to take my Christmas tree?'

Ruby looked through to the living room where the sparkling silver tree shimmered with its party lights on full. 'I don't want you not to have one,' she said longingly, 'but you aren't allowed to use the axe.'

'I'll let Uncle Hugo wield the axe,' Polly conceded. 'But we need more decorations. You're not going to leave me with nothing.'

'We could buy more tinsel.'

'Nonsense.' She was in her element here. Interior decorating had been bred into her—her mother had been making hotel rooms into Christmas-themed fantasies for ever. 'Let's leave the silver tree as it is—we'll pack it tonight for you to take. Then we'll concentrate on Tree Two. Plus making this house Christmassy for me and Hamster. Let's go.'

By two in the afternoon the inhabitants of Wombat Valley were mostly hunkered down. The weather forecast was dire. Leaving the house meant a soaking. Most minor ailments could be put in the worry-about-it-after-Christmas basket, so the population mostly stayed put.

Which meant Hugo didn't call on Polly for help.

Though maybe he should have, he thought as the day went on. The agreement was that she'd join him in the afternoon so she'd get used to the place and he could assess her work...

Except he had assessed her work and it was excellent. She'd given last night's anaesthetic with skill. On her tour of the place she'd moved seamlessly between patients, chatting happily, drawing them out without them realising it. Underneath the chat there were carefully planted medical queries, and skilled responses to the replies. She was good.

More, Polly's reputation had already spread through the Valley. She was the Doc-Who'd-Been-Bitten-Saving-Horace. Horace wasn't particularly popular but he was a local, and Wombat Valley looked after their own.

So she was already accepted. She already knew her way round the hospital. She could have another full day of rest.

Minding Ruby?

He did feel a bit guilty about that, but he'd assumed Ruby would stay at Talia's until midday so he hadn't worried about calling anyone in. And Ruby was quiet. She did her own thing. The monitor was on. He could be home in a heartbeat if he was needed.

He just sort of happened to wander past the monitor a lot.

'They sound like they're having a ball,' Joe told him. Joe was catching up on paperwork at the nurses' station. The whole hospital seemed as if it was snoozing, and in the silence Polly and Ruby's voices could be heard clearly.

He'd told Polly about the monitor. She'd know whatever she was saying could be overheard but it didn't seem to be cramping her style.

'The flour looks great. No, sprinkle some more on, Ruby, it looks like snow. Hamster, no! It's snow, you idiot, not flour. Oh, heck, it's on your nose—no, don't lick it, it'll turn to paste—no, Hamster, noooo...'

'Uh oh,' Joe said, grinning. 'When my kids sound like that I go in armed with a mop. You want to go home and check?'

'I should...'

'Should what?' Joe said, and eyed him speculatively. 'Think of something else to do? You've been thinking of other something elses to do for the past two hours. Don't you need to pack?'

'I've packed.'

'Then don't you need to go home and spread a little flour?' His brows went up. 'But Dr Hargreaves is there, isn't she? A woman in your living room.'

'With my niece,' he snapped.

'She's gorgeous,' Joe said.

'Ruby's cute.'

'I didn't mean Ruby and you know it. Polly's gorgeous. We're lucky to have her.'

'Yes.'

'But you're going away tomorrow.' His nurse administrator's eyebrows were still raised. 'Not having any second thoughts about going?'

'Only in as much as Polly needs care.'

'Care?'

'She's diabetic.'

'And I have a bung knee. We can commiserate.' Still the speculative look. 'So why don't you want to go home now?'

Because I might want to kiss her again.

Because I do want to kiss her.

Neither of those thoughts he could say aloud. Neither of those thoughts he should even admit to himself.

Polly...a wealthy socialite, a woman who was here for two weeks while he was away, a woman who...

Made Ruby chuckle.

A woman who made him want to pick her up and carry her to his bed.

A woman who he wouldn't mind protecting for the rest of her life.

Whoa... How to go on a hundred-mile journey in four days. He didn't know her. She was so far out of his league...

But he was there. He wanted her.

'Go home,' Joe said, watching his face, and Hugo wondered how much of what he'd been thinking was plain to see. 'Go and spend some time with her. Heaven knows, you could use a friend.'

'I have friends.'

'None like Polly,' Joe retorted. 'And isn't that just the problem? I'd go nuts without my Hannah, but for you... My Hannah's already taken and there's a limited dating field in the Valley. And now you have Pollyanna right in your living room.' He paused as Polly's infectious chuckle sounded through the monitor. 'Hannah or not, wow, Doc, I'm almost tempted to head over there myself.'

'I'll go when it stops raining.'

'Like that'll happen,' Joe said morosely. 'Forty days and forty nights... This is setting in bad. But it's not raining women, not on your parade...'

'Joe...'

'I know; it's none of my business.' Joe held up his hands as if in surrender. 'But she's there, she's gorgeous and you have no reason not to be there too. Go on, get out of here. Go.'

He went. Of course he went—there was no reason not to.

It was wet and it was windy. He opened the front door and was met by a squeal of protest.

'Uncle Hugo, nooooooooo!'

'Uh oh,' said another voice and he stared around in amazement. The other voice said, 'Maybe you could shut the door?'

The door opened straight into the living room. The living room was...white.

Very white.

'We may not have thought this through,' Polly said.

She was sitting on the floor threading popcorn onto string. Or she had been threading popcorn. She was now coated in a cloud of flour. It was all over her hair, over her face and nose, over the floor around her.

Over Hamster.

Ruby was closest to the door. She seemed to have escaped the worst of the dusting.

'You made it blow,' she said accusingly as he finally closed out the gale.

'Flour?' he said, and his niece sent him a look that put him right in the dunce's corner.

'It's snow. We made a nativity scene. See, we've made everything out of pods from the banksia tree, even the camels, and we got really wet looking for the right banksias, and then we spent ages getting everything dry so we could put them up along the mantelpiece and we put flour over the bottom to look like snow only Polly said I probably put too much on, but it looked *beeeyootiful* but now you've opened the door and you've ruined it.'

And her voice wobbled.

She really was fragile, Hugo thought, bending down to give her a hug. Last year had been tragedy for Ruby, and it still showed. She expected calamity.

'This isn't ruined,' he said gently. 'It's just flour.'

'It's snow to make Polly feel better when we're not here.'

'And Polly loves it,' Polly said and then she sneezed as if she needed to accentuate the point. 'Ruby, it's still great. Look what we've done, Dr Denver. All we need you to do is chop down a tree.'

'With an axe,' Ruby added. 'I wouldn't let Polly do it on her own.'

'Very wise,' Hugo said faintly, looking round his living room again.

At chaos.

His mother had kept this room perfect. 'The Queen could walk in unannounced and I'd be ready for her,' his mother used to say and she was right. His mother might even have made Her Majesty remove her shoes and leave the corgis outside.

'It was wet,' Ruby said, noticing his sweep of the room

and getting in first with her excuse. 'Polly needed something to do.'

'And now she has something else to do,' Polly decreed, using Hamster as a lever to push herself to her feet. 'In case you haven't noticed, Dr Denver, you seem to be dripping on our snow and our type of snow, when dripped upon, makes clag. So I suggest you stop dripping and start helping thread popcorn while I clean up your mess...'

'My mess?'

'Your mess,' she said and grinned. 'Walking in on artists at work...you should know better.'

'I'm glad I didn't,' he said faintly and he looked around at the mess and he thought for the first time in how long... this place looked like home.

What was better than this? he thought.

What was better than Polly?

He chopped down a Christmas...branch?...while the girls admired his axe technique. They all got wet, but what the heck; he was beyond caring. The branch dripped as he carried it inside but there was so much mess anyway that a little more wouldn't hurt. Then he cooked while they decorated.

He cooked spaghetti and meatballs because that was his speciality. Actually, he had three. Macaroni cheese was another. He could also do a mean risotto but Ruby didn't like it, so to say their menu was limited would be an understatement. But Ruby munched through raw veggies and fruit to stop him feeling guilty and Polly sat down in front of her meatballs and said, 'Yum,' as if she meant it.

They now had two Christmas trees. Ruby had declared Polly's silver tree was too pretty to take down until the last minute so there was a tree in each corner of the living room. There was 'snow' on every flat surface. There were strings of popcorn and paper chains and lanterns and Polly's amazing gift boxes, plus the weird decorations and nativity figures they'd fashioned out of banksia pods.

Polly ate her dinner but every now and then he caught her looking through to the sitting room and beaming.

She'd dressed for dinner. She was wearing another of her retro dresses. This one had splashes of crimson, yellow and blue, and was cinched at the waist with a shiny red belt. The dress had puffed sleeves and a white collar and cuff trim.

Her curls were shining. Her freckles were...freckling. She did not look like a doctor.

She looked adorable.

He didn't want to leave tomorrow.

How could he fall for a woman called Pollyanna?

How could he not?

'We've done good,' Polly was saying to Ruby and Ruby looked where Polly was looking and nodded her agreement.

'Yes. But you'll be here by yourself.' She sounded worried.

'Me and Hamster,' Polly reminded her. 'I'm glad your uncle agreed to let him stay. I might be lonely without him.'

'Won't you be lonely without your mum and dad?' Ruby asked and Polly's smile died.

'No.'

'Won't they be lonely without you?'

There was an uncomfortable silence. Polly ate another meatball but she suddenly didn't seem so hungry.

'They have lots of friends,' she said at last. 'They've booked a restaurant. They'll have a very good party.'

'It won't be much fun if you're not there.'

'They'll hardly miss me,' Polly said stoutly. 'Whereas if I wasn't here Hamster would miss me a lot. Plus Hazel Blacksmith's promised to teach me to tat.'

'Tat,' Hugo said faintly. 'What on earth is tat?'

'You come back after Christmas and I'll show you. Whatever it is, the house will be full of it.'

'That'll make a nice change from soggy flour.'

'Bah! Humbug!' she said cheerfully and got up to clear the dishes. Instead of getting up to help, he let himself sit for a moment, watching her, watching Ruby jump up to help, feeling himself...wanting.

It wasn't fair to want. He had no right.

To try and saddle her with Wombat Valley and a needy seven-year-old? And...

And what was he thinking?

He was trapped. He had no right to think of sharing.

At Ruby's request, Polly read her a bedtime story while Hugo did a last fast ward round. The hospital was quiet. The rain had stopped, the storm was over and what was left was peace. The night before Christmas? Not quite, but it might just as well be, he thought. The whole Valley seemed to be settling, waiting...

Waiting? There was nothing to wait for.

Of course there was, he told himself as he headed back to the house. He was heading to the beach tomorrow. Ten glorious days of freedom.

With Ruby.

He wouldn't have it any other way, he told himself, but he knew a part of him was lying. His sister's suicide had killed the part that enjoyed being a skilled surgeon in a tight-knit surgical team. It had killed the guy who could head to the bar after work and stay as late as he wanted. It had killed the guy who could date who he wanted...

And it was the last thing that was bugging him now.

Dating who he wanted...

Polly.

He wanted Polly.

And she was waiting for him. The light was fading. She was sitting on the old cane chair on the veranda, Hamster at her side. She smiled as he came up the steps and he had such a powerful sense of coming home...

He wanted to walk straight to her, gather her into his arms and claim her as his own. It was a primitive urge, totally inappropriate, totally without consideration, but the urge was so strong he held onto the veranda rail, just to ground himself.

Do not do anything stupid, he told himself. *This woman's ethereal, like a butterfly. You'll be gone tomorrow and when you return she'll flit on. Life will close in on you again. Accept it.*

'Ruby's asleep,' Polly said, leaning back in the rocker and rocking with satisfaction. 'I read her to sleep. Boring R Us.'

Nothing about this woman was boring, he thought, but he managed to make his voice almost normal. 'What did you read?'

'*The Night Before Christmas*, of course,' she told him. 'I just happen to have a copy in my luggage.'

'Of course you do.'

'My nannies read it to me every Christmas.' She sailed on serenely, oblivious to his dry interruption. 'I started asking for it to be read about mid-November every year. I can't believe you don't own it.'

'My mother didn't believe in fairy tales.'

And her eyes widened. 'Fairy tales? What's fairy tale about *The Night Before Christmas*? Next you'll be saying you don't believe in Santa.'

And Hugo thought back to the Christmases since his father died—the struggle to stay cheerful, Grace's depression—and he thought... *All we needed was a Pollyanna. A fairy tale...*

His parents had been down-to-earth, sensible people. He thought of his sister, crippled by depression. He thought of his father, terse, impatient, telling the teenage Grace to snap out of it.

Grace might still be alive, he thought suddenly, if she'd been permitted a fairy tale.

And... Life might be good for him if he could admit a fairy tale?

A fairy tale called Pollyanna?

'Polly...'

'I need your help,' she told him. 'You're leaving at crack of dawn and we need to pack the silver Christmas tree without making the living room look bereft. I don't intend to have a bereft Christmas, thank you very much.' She rocked her way forward out of the rocker and it was all he could do not to step forward and...

Not!

Somehow he managed to calmly follow her into the house and start the demolition process, following instructions as to which decorations would stay and which would go.

'I wonder if I could make a tatted angel for your tree next year,' she mused as she packed golden balls into a crimson box. It seemed even the crates she stored things in were a celebration. 'What do you reckon? If you get an angel in the post, will you know what to do with it? Will you value it as you ought?'

She was kneeling by the tree. The Christmas tree lights were still on, flickering multi-coloured patterns on her face. Her eyes were twinkling and a man wouldn't be human...

He didn't go to her. There was a mound of tinsel and a box of Christmas decorations between them. It had to act like Hadrian's Wall.

To stop himself scaring this butterfly into flight.

'Polly, I'd like to keep in touch,' he ventured and she went right on packing decorations as if what he'd said wasn't important.

'I'd like that too,' she said. 'But you're behind the times. Ruby and I already have it planned. We're going to be pen pals—real pen pals with letters with stamps because that's cooler than emails. Ruby will send pictures of herself, and of Hamster too, because I'm starting to think I'll miss him.'

Pen pals.

'That's good, as far as it goes,' he said cautiously. 'But it's not what I had in mind.'

'What did you have in mind?'

'The kiss,' he said and her head jerked up and the atmosphere in the room changed, just like that.

'The kiss…'

Stop now, the sensible part of him demanded, but there was a crazy part that kept putting words out there. 'It meant something,' he said. 'Polly, I'd like to keep seeing you.'

'That might be hard if you're in Wombat Valley and I'm in Ethiopia.'

'You're really thinking of Ethiopia?'

'No,' she said reluctantly. 'I can't.'

'Then how about an extension of your time in Wombat Valley?'

The question hung. It had been dumb to even ask, he thought, but he couldn't retract the words now.

'Stay here, you mean?' she said cautiously.

'We could…just see.'

'See what?' Her eyes didn't leave his face.

'If you and I…'

'I don't do family.' She stumbled to her feet and a crimson ball fell onto another and shattered. She didn't appear to notice.

'Polly, this isn't a proposal.' What had he done? He was appalled at the look of fear that had flashed across her face. 'I'm not asking for permanent. It's far too soon…'

'It's not only too soon,' she snapped. 'It's stupid.'

'Why is it stupid?' He knew, but he still found himself asking. Did she know what a trap his life was?

But it seemed she was worrying about a different kind of trap. 'Hugo, it's true, I kissed you and I felt…like I might be falling for you,' she managed. 'But it scared me. I don't want to go there. I can't. You worry about me, and Ruby hugs me, and even Hamster wriggles his way round my heart like a great hairy worm. But I came here to get away from family, not to find myself more.'

Her words cut, but they were no more than he'd expected.

To hope for more was stupid.

So now what? There was a strained silence while he tried to find a way forward. He'd thought he'd put away his love life when he'd left Sydney, but somehow Polly had hauled it front and centre. He wanted…a woman like Polly?

No. He wanted Polly herself, yet he had no right to haul her into his own personal drama. How could he possibly think of adding his constraints to hers? There was no way through this tangle to a happy ending.

So now? Now he had to get this situation back to a relationship that could go forward as it should. Employer and employee, nothing more.

'You don't think you might be propelling things forward just a tad too fast?' he ventured. 'I'm not asking you to commit to Wombat Valley for life.' He tried smiling, aching to ease her look of fear, but the fear stayed. It seemed she wasn't good at pretending. The employer, employee relationship was finished.

'Hugo, I know what I felt—when I kissed you.' She put her hands behind her and took a step back. 'When I'm with you I feel like someone else. It would be so easy to fall into this place, become your lover, become Ruby's best friend, become Hamster's third favourite cushion, but you'd tie me down. You'd fret—you already do—and before I know it you'd be watching what I eat and checking my long-term sugar levels and making sure I wear warm coats and boots when it's raining and not letting me do the hard medical cases because it might upset me. And I'm sick of cotton wool; I'm just…over it.'

'Polly, of all the things I'm offering, cotton wool isn't one of them.'

'You're saying you wouldn't fuss?'

'Warm coats, boots, the Hamster cushion thing…all those things are negotiable,' he said evenly. 'But if we ever tried it…maybe you couldn't stop me caring.' He had to be honest. 'I'd hope you could care back.'

'I don't do caring.'

'I've watched you for days now. You care and you care and you care.'

'Not with you.'

There was nothing to say to that. Nothing at all.

He'd been stupid to ask. This place—his life—had nothing a woman like Polly would wish to share. How could he ever have imagined otherwise?

He looked at her for a long moment and then, because he couldn't think of anything else to do, he started untangling tinsel. And Polly knelt again to put decorations into boxes.

'There's broken glass by your knee. Be careful.'

'I know,' she snapped, but she hadn't noticed—he knew she hadn't. She looked and saw the shattered Christmas bauble. 'Thank...thank you.'

'I'll get the dustpan.'

'I broke it. I'll fix it.'

'Fine,' he said and then his cellphone rang and he was almost relieved. He went outside to answer it because he needed space.

He felt like smacking himself over the head. For one brief moment he'd tried to prise open the doors that enclosed him. All he'd done was frighten her.

Where to take it from here?

Nowhere.

She was an idiot.

She gathered the shards of glass and then got the vacuum cleaner because you could never be too careful with glass on carpet and she wasn't stupid...

She was stupid, stupid, stupid.

For heaven's sake... He wasn't asking her to marry him, she told herself. He was simply asking her to extend her time here as a locum.

Ruby would love it. Hamster would love it.

Polly would love it?

Love... The word echoed round and round in her head. She hit the power switch to the vacuum cleaner so it faded to silence and she gazed round at the mess that was the living room.

Mess. Christmas.

Family.

She didn't do family. She hated Christmas.

But still she was staring around the room. One intact Christmas branch, gaily decorated. One lopsided silver tree, semi naked. Hugo saw this place as a trap, she thought. A prison. Oh, but if she let herself care…

If she cared, he'd care right back, and the cotton wool would enclose her.

'It's a mess,' she muttered to herself and suddenly she found herself thinking of her parents' Christmases. They were perfection in planning and execution. Exquisite. Her mother employed party planners.

There'd be no soggy flour on her mother's carpet. The only thing missing from her family's perfect Christmas this year would be her.

And, stupidly, she felt tears well behind her eyes. She dashed them away with an angry swipe. *What the heck*… She didn't cry. She never cried.

She'd walked away from her family Christmas without a second glance. She'd felt joyful to be escaping.

And here was Hugo offering her another family Christmas. Not yet, she thought, not this Christmas, but she knew his offer was like an insidious web—*'Come into my parlour,' said the spider to the fly*…

Only it wasn't like that. What fly had ever thought the spider doing the inviting was gorgeous? What spider was ever kind, skilled, gentle, loving, awesome…?

Stop it, stop it, stop it, she told her spinning head. *You've refused him and there's an end to it. You don't want to be caged. Get your head in order and get on with cleaning up this mess.*

And then Hugo walked back into the room and one look at his face told her cleaning had to be put onto the backburner.

CHAPTER TWELVE

'TROUBLE?' POLLY DIDN'T have to ask but she did anyway. Vacuum cleaning was forgotten.

'I need to go out.'

'Tell me.'

'If you could look after Ruby…'

'Tell me,' she snapped again and he paused at the door and looked at her—really looked—and she could almost see the struggle to transform her from a ditzy woman in a rainbow dress to someone who might just be a colleague.

She dropped the vacuum cleaner to help the transition. She thought about white coats but there was hardly time.

'There's been a landslide,' he said.

A landslide…

The rain had stopped now, but it had been torrential. With the steepness of this valley, landslides had to be an ever-present danger.

'I need to go…'

'Tell me,' she said for a third time and he got it then. She wasn't a ditzy redhead. She was an Emergency Medicine specialist and she was demanding facts.

And he switched, just like that. As unlikely a setting as this was, in that moment they joined forces.

A medical team.

'On the road to the south,' he told her. 'We already have trouble. The north road's still cut where Horace's truck went over. Everyone's been using the south road. But Ben Smart's cow got out and wandered down the road this morning in the rain. A petrol tanker came through and wiped the cow.

That wasn't a problem—apart from the cow. The tanker had bull bars. But Ben's cow was left dead on the side of the road and Iris and Gladys Freeman live right where it was hit and they don't want a dead cow smelling up their Christmas.'

He headed for his bedroom as he spoke, hauling on his jacket, speaking to her through the open door.

'Ben's not all that addicted to hard work,' he threw at her. 'But Iris and Gladys were insistent, so Ben got his brother and they looked at the dead cow and thought how hard it would be to bury her. They're Smart by name but not by nature. They looked at the nice soggy side of the cliff face and thought they could just dig a bit and shove her in.'

'Uh oh.' Polly was heading into her bedroom too. Jeans, she thought. Jacket. And shoes. Sensible shoes would be important.

Did snakes come out after rain?

'So…' she called out from the bedroom. 'Situation?'

'The whole side of the hill's come down. Ben's brother, Doug, seems to have a broken leg but he got himself out. Ben was completely buried for a bit. Amy and Max Fraser were there first—they're sensible farmers. Amy's an ex-nurse. She says Ben's in a bad way. Oh, and Iris and Gladys are there too, but Iris has fallen over and Gladys has hurt her back. I might be a while.' And then she emerged from her bedroom and he was in the living room and he looked at her jeans and jacket and boots. 'What the…?'

'I'm coming too. Incident with multiple casualties. Why question it?'

'Ruby?'

'Excuse me? Am I here as a childminder?'

'No, but…'

'Isn't Ruby asleep?'

'Yes…'

'And isn't your normal child care system working?'

'Polly, you can't. You're three days post-snake-bite.'

'Yeah and you'll be post-kick-on-the-shins if you fuss for

no reason,' she snapped. 'Do what you must to let the hospital know Ruby needs monitoring. Then let's go.'

What confronted them could have been a tragedy. It was bad, but by the time they got there Ben was sitting up, retching mud and wheezing. He was still gasping but at least he was conscious.

Iris and Gladys, two very elderly ladies, were fussing over him and berating him at the same time.

'We had to do CPR for ages.' Iris, an indomitable lady who looked to be in her nineties, was sitting back on her heels, glaring as if she wanted to punch Ben again. 'I hit him so hard to get him breathing before Amy and Max arrived that I've hurt my wrists, and then he threw up on my dressing gown. And I'll never get it dry in this weather.'

All this and she was complaining about the weather? Polly and Hugo shared a grin as they set to work.

Ben was indeed all right. He'd been momentarily buried in the mud. Luckily, Amy and Max had had a shovel on their truck and had done some fast digging. Amy was now tending to Doug, who lay beside his brother, moaning in pain.

Doug's leg was fractured. His patience with his brother had snapped completely.

'That's the last time I'm gonna agree to one of his harebrained schemes. "It'll be easy," he said. "Just dig a bit into the cliff and shove her in and we won't even have to move her".'

The cow, thankfully, was now buried, but at what a cost?

'You've succeeded, you idiots,' Max said dourly. 'You've also succeeded in cutting the road. The north road's still impassable so we're stuck. The town'll have your guts for garters, guys. Just saying.'

But while he was talking, Hugo and Polly had moved into triage mode, figuring what needed to be done and doing it with the ease of a team that had worked together for years. Polly was wiping the mud from Ben's face, checking his mouth, his nose, his neck. She was preparing an oxygen mask. Ben was breathing but his colour was poor. Assuming his breathing had stopped, even for a moment, it was important to get his oxygen levels up.

Hugo was administering morphine to Doug, then slitting his pants leg to expose the leg break. Polly glanced over and saw no exposed bone, no break in the skin.

They might be lucky, she thought. Doug looked well into his seventies, maybe early eighties. Even a simple fracture would take time to heal but a compound fracture could be disastrous.

'I think you've been lucky,' Hugo told him, confirming what she was thinking. 'Okay, without moving anything—head, neck, arms or legs—let's do a bit of wiggle checking.'

She did the same for Ben, carefully checking each limb. She fitted a neck brace as a precaution—if the dirt had come down on his head she wanted an X-ray before she let him move.

'We'll need to get everyone to hospital,' Hugo told her. 'I want a proper examination.' He turned to Gladys who looked, if anything, even older and more withered than her sister. 'Max said you hurt your back.'

'It's a twinge,' Gladys said with dignity. 'We had to pull to try and get this idiot's head out. Iris fell over—look at her first.'

Iris had indeed fallen over. She had a long graze, the length of her shin.

There was another exchanged glance between Hugo and Polly. Iris's skin was old-age-dry, scarred from years of bumps and bruises and varicose veins. It'd be a miracle if her leg didn't ulcerate. And Gladys's hands were surreptitiously going to the small of her back. Pain was obvious and both she and Hugo could see it.

'Right,' Hugo said. 'Let's get you all into the hospital where we can look at you properly. We need to do it carefully. Amy, Max, are you happy to help? Great. Can you take Iris and Gladys—they're both good to go sitting up, but drive slowly. Try not to bump. Ben and Doug, though, need to be transported flat. I have matting in the back of my van. Polly, can we do a three-way shift? Max, can you help?'

'But we're not going to the hospital,' Gladys said, astounded, and Hugo put a hand on her shoulder and met her frightened gaze with compassion.

'Gladys, how long did Iris's leg ulcer take to heal? Let's try and prevent one forming. And Iris, you can see that Gladys has hurt her back. Do you really not want me to see what the damage is? Won't you let me see if I can stop it hurting for Christmas?'

And, put like that, heading to the hospital for each other, there was no choice.

'We need to ring a couple of local farmers.' Hugo had been carrying lanterns in his truck. So had Amy and Max, so the scene they were working in was lit, but to the north there was a sea of mud where the road should be. 'We'll need to set up road blocks and warning lamps.'

'Can't we get the ambulance?' Polly asked. 'Surely it'd be better to wait.' The ambulance had proper stretchers—a much safer way of carrying patients with potential spinal injuries. To put them in Hugo's van…

'We can't do it,' Hugo said grimly. 'We share the ambulance service with Willaura. They're fifteen miles down the road, on the far side of the land slip. Given that the south road's cut and now the north road… Sorry, guys, the truck it is.'

They worked solidly for the next few hours. Each of the four, although not dangerously injured, had their own urgent needs. Ben had swallowed—and inhaled—dirty water and mud. He needed intravenous antibiotics. Doug's leg needed setting. Luckily, it was a simple tibial break but he was a pack a day smoker. He coughed and wheezed and the decision was admission, oxygen and observation.

They admitted Gladys and Iris, too. Gladys's back showed little damage apart from osteoarthritic change but she was more shaken than she'd admit. Iris's leg needed scrupulous cleaning and dressing, and once they'd got over their first protests the elderly ladies seemed content to be fussed over.

'And you do need to let us fuss over you,' Polly declared as she tucked them in for the night. 'You're both heroes.'

'I agree.' Hugo must have finished at the same time as she did. He was suddenly standing at the ward door, smiling warmly at the two old ladies. 'Heroes, both of you. Max tells me even though you didn't have a spade, by the time he got there you'd already got Ben's head clear.'

'We're gardeners,' Iris said as if that explained everything.

'But we're tired gardeners,' Gladys whispered and snuggled down a bit further on her pillows. Polly had given them both pain relief and they seemed dozily content. 'Thank you, dear.'

And Hugo grinned and crossed to each of them and planted a kiss on each elderly cheek.

'No. Thank you. You've saved Ben's life.'

'Well, we're much happier being kissed by you than by Ben,' Gladys said and she giggled, and Hugo and Polly slipped out of the ward and left them to sleep.

Drama over. They could go home.

They walked in silence across the small distance that separated house from hospital. The silence between them was strained. Almost as soon as the hospital doors closed behind them they seemed no longer colleagues.

What then? Friends?

Ha.

But that was how they had to act, Polly thought, at least until tomorrow.

And with thought came another...

'Hugo... If the roads are cut in both directions... You won't be able to leave.'

Hugo didn't break stride. 'You think I don't know that?'

The surge of anger in his voice was almost shocking. 'That road can't be made safe until it dries out, and the engineers have already assessed the other road. They need to blast further into the cliff to make it safe.'

'So that would be...after Christmas?' She could hardly make herself say it but it had to be said. 'Ruby will break her heart.'

'She'll understand.' But the anger was still in his voice. 'I'll show her the roads.'

'And she'll be stoic,' Polly whispered. 'I don't think I can bear it.'

'So how the hell do you think it makes me feel?' His words were an explosion. He stopped and closed his eyes and she could see the pain, the fury that fate had once again messed with his plans for his little niece's Christmas. 'How am I going to tell her?'

'Oh, Hugo...'

'I meant the Valley to be her base, her one sense of continuity. Now it's like a trap.'

'A trap for you both?' she ventured and he stared at her for one long baffled moment and then dug his hands deep in his pockets and started walking again.

Polly didn't move on. She stood and watched his retreating back.

She couldn't help him. Not without...

No. She couldn't help him.

Or could she?

Her parents' money... Her parents' power and resources...

They could get a chopper here first thing tomorrow, she thought. Hugo and Ruby could be at the beach long before they could ever have driven.

But how could she ask that of her parents? She thought of the look on her parents' faces as she'd told them she wouldn't spend this Christmas with them. They'd been gutted. So now...

How could she tell them where she was, ask them for such a favour and then tell them to leave her alone?

Family... Love...

She stood stock-still in the darkness while her thoughts headed off in so many tangents she felt dizzy.

She should be home for Christmas.

She wasn't home. She was here. And so was Hugo because he'd chosen this place—because of love.

'Polly? What's wrong?' Hugo had reached the gate into the house yard and had turned back to see what was keeping her.

'Nothing,' she said in a small voice. 'Just...recalibrating. I guess this means...Christmas together.'

'Can we keep our hands off each other until the roads clear?' He tried to say it with humour but she heard the strain.

'I'll do my best.' She walked towards him in the darkness, but there was a part of her that said she should retreat.

She was as trapped as he was. But...define trap? Some traps you had to walk right into.

'Polly...' She was too close now, she thought, but she couldn't retreat. She was close enough to...close enough to ask for what she wanted?

'If you kiss me,' she managed, 'I think I might crack.'

'I've already cracked,' he said roughly, still with that edge of anger. 'Because all I want to do is kiss you.'

'And where will that leave us?'

'Together until after Christmas? Time for one mad passionate affair?' He snapped the words as if she'd been taunting him. 'Crazy.'

But what if it's not so crazy? It was her heart doing the thinking, not her head. *What if I want to stay? What if I don't think this is a trap at all?*

The thought was almost terrifying. How could she think of staying? She'd railed around the confines of her parents' loving. How much more would she hate the confines of being here?

Of being loved by Hugo?

'You're looking scared,' he said, suddenly gentle, and she wished he wouldn't say things gently because it was almost her undoing. His voice made things twist inside—things she seemed to be unable to untwist.

She wanted him.

They were between house and hospital—no man's land. Medicine and home.

She'd used her career to escape from home, Polly thought with sudden clarity. Maybe that was driving her nuts now. In her world of medicine, she could forget the confines of her parents' worry, her parents' overwhelming adoration. She could be Dr Hargreaves, known for her over-the-top dress sense but respected for her medical skills.

Here, between hospital and home, nothing seemed clear.

Hugo was standing beside her. He was her colleague, except he wasn't a colleague. He was just… Hugo.

How could a heart be so twisted?

How could he be so near and not reach for her?

And in the end, because the silence was stretching and she didn't know how to step away and it seemed that he didn't either, it was Polly who reached for Hugo.

She put her hands up to his face and she cupped his bristled jaw.

'You are the nicest man, Dr Denver…'

'Polly, I can't…'

'One kiss before bedtime,' she whispered and she raised herself on tiptoe. She tugged his head down, her lips met his and she kissed him.

She kissed him, hard and sure and true. She kissed him as she'd never kissed a man before and doubted if she could ever kiss a man again. It was a kiss of aching want. This was a kiss that came from a part of her she hadn't known existed.

But he didn't respond. His arms didn't come around her. He didn't kiss back.

He didn't push her away, but the heat she'd felt before

was now under rigid control. She could feel his tension, his strength, the power of his boundaries. She sank down to stand on firm ground again, feeling the first sharp shards of loss.

'Whatever I said...Polly, a short affair over Christmas is never going to work,' he managed. 'We both know that. Bad idea.'

'It is a bad idea,' she conceded.

'So we need to figure the ground rules now. No touching.'

'None?'

'Don't push me, Polly.'

And it was all there in his voice. He wanted her as much as she wanted him, but this man had already learned what it was to give up what he loved. How much had he hated to give up his surgical career, his friends, his lifestyle? He'd done it for love.

How could she ask him to give up more? An affair and then walk away? It'd hurt her. How much more would it hurt Hugo, who had no power to follow?

She had to be very sure...

'Okay, no touching,' she managed. 'I might...I might as well go to bed, then.'

'That's a good idea.' He touched her cheek—which was breaking the rules but maybe they didn't start until morning. He traced the line of her face with a gentleness she found unbearably erotic. But then, 'Sleep well, Polly,' he told her. 'Tomorrow's Christmas Eve, the night Santa comes. Maybe the old gentleman will bring sense to the pair of us.'

He didn't follow her inside. Instead, he stood where she'd left him, staring into the darkness.

He wanted her so badly it was a physical pain. She'd kissed him and the control it had taken not to sweep her into his arms and claim her had left him dizzy.

Hell, he wanted her.

'Yeah, and Ruby wants Christmas at the beach,' he told

himself. 'And I want my career back. We can't all have what we want—you're old enough to know that.'

He knew it but it didn't stop him wanting.

He wanted Polly.

Sleep was a long time coming, and when it did it was full of dreams she had no hope of understanding.

She woke to the dawn chorus. Stupid birds, she thought, lying in her too-big bed listening to the cacophony of parrots, kookaburras and bellbirds. She wouldn't have had to put up with this in Sydney.

Christmas Eve. Her mother would be up by now, doing the flowers—a task undertaken with care for every important occasion. Then there'd be the hair salon, nails, a massage, lunch with her friends, then a nap…

Then there'd be the final gift-wrapping, followed by drinks with more friends and dinner.

And, at every step of the way, her mother would miss her.

Polly lay in bed and listened to the birds and thought about her parents' demands. Why was she suddenly feeling guilty? Her parents smothered her with love and they were constantly disappointed. Last year she'd managed to juggle leave so she could join them in Monaco on Christmas Eve, but her mother had been gutted that Polly hadn't arrived early enough to get her nails done.

'And when did you last get your hair done?' she'd demanded. 'Polly, how can you bear it?'

She smiled then, remembering her father rolling his eyes, and then she thought of her father demanding she tell them the results of her last long-term blood sugar test and telling her he'd researched a new diabetic regime being tested by a clinic in Sweden and he'd fly her there in the new year…

She was right to get away. She knew she was.

It was just…they were her parents. And somehow, looking at Hugo and Ruby, she thought…she thought…

Maybe behaviour had boundaries but love was different? Maybe running away couldn't lessen that.

She sighed and rolled over and tried to sleep a bit more and she must have succeeded because the next thing she knew there was a scratch on her bedroom door. The door flew open and Hamster landed with a flying thud, right across her stomach.

He'd left the door open and from the living room she could hear every word Hugo was saying.

'Ruby, I'm so sorry.' She could almost see Hugo. He'd be crouched in front of his little niece, she thought. Ruby would have flown up as soon as she woke, letting Hamster inside and then bounding to find her uncle. The beach. They were supposed to be leaving right now.

'There's been another accident,' Hugo was telling her. 'Ruby, the roads out of here have been cut. The storm's caused a landslide. We're just going to have to put the silver tree up again and have a two-Christmas-tree Christmas.'

There was no sound. She could have borne it better if Ruby sobbed, Polly thought, but Ruby didn't cry.

If enough was taken away from you, you expected nothing.

Like Hugo... So much had been taken away from him.

How could he expect her to love him?

Would he want her to love him?

She'd only known him for four days. Ridiculous. How could she feel this way about a man after four days?

How could she fall in love with Ruby after four days?

She could still hear Hugo's muffled voice. Maybe he was hugging. Maybe he was holding, trying to comfort...

Beach for Christmas... It was a little thing. A minor promise. Kids got over things.

Last Christmas Ruby had lost her grandmother and then her mother.

Beach for Christmas...

She heard one sob, just the one, and somehow she knew that'd be it. This kid didn't rail against fate.

Polly did, though. She put her pillow over her head and railed.

There had to be a way.

She could still ring her father, ask him to send a chopper to get them to the beach. The idea was still there but she knew it wouldn't work, or not like she hoped. Her father would be incapable of carting away Wombat Valley's permanent doctor and leaving his daughter on her own.

What would he do? Cart her away by force? Not quite, but he wouldn't leave her here.

And with that thought came another. It was a thought so ridiculous... So over the top...

She was trying to escape her parents. She was trying to escape loving.

But if she let loving have its way...

The more she thought about it, the more she started to smile. And then to chuckle.

It was crazy. It'd never work. Would it?

It might.

Hamster wriggled down beside her, trying to nose his way under the covers. 'Don't you dare,' she told him. 'You're needed in the living room. Your mistress needs all the hugs she can get, and you're just the Hamster to give them to her.'

And Hugo? How would he take to hugs?

Ridiculous, ridiculous, ridiculous.

But a girl had to try. She reached for her phone.

'Nothing ventured...' she whispered and then she took a deep breath and finished the thought with force. 'Nothing gained. Okay, Hamster, listen in. My parents have spent their lives wanting to do things for me that I've thought unreasonable. In return I'm about to ask them to do something that is the most unreasonable thing I can think of. Watch this space, Hamster. We're about to push the limits of loving to outer space.'

CHAPTER THIRTEEN

CHRISTMAS EVE AND Wombat Valley Hospital was almost full. None of last night's injured were ill enough to require evacuation but each needed care, pain relief and reassurance.

They also needed sympathy; indeed, with the road closure, sympathetic ears were required everywhere. Many of the Valley residents had been expecting guests for Christmas or had intended going elsewhere. Now everyone was stuck.

However, most accepted the situation with resignation. The Valley had been cut off before, by fire or by flood. The population moved into planning mode. Those who'd been expecting guests shared provisions with those who'd been going away, and some of them swapped Christmas plans, so by mid-afternoon it seemed to Hugo that everyone seemed to have planned an alternative.

As the day went on and he heard more and more rearranged plans he felt…

On the outer?

He and Ruby could be included in any Christmas in the Valley—he knew that. He only had to say the word. But the Valley assumed that he and Ruby could have a very merry Christmas with Polly. There'd been offerings of food but no offers of hospitality. The Valley was collectively stunned by Pollyanna Hargreaves and the assumption was that he was a lucky man.

'Make the most of it, Doc,' Joe growled. 'There's mistletoe growing over by the church—you want me to cut you a trailer-load? You could string it up in every room. By Christmas night…hmm. Do you have brandy sauce? I could get my girls to make some for you. Add a bit more brandy, like…'

'Joe…'

'Just saying,' Joe said placidly. 'You gotta enjoy Christmas.'

But how could he enjoy Christmas when Ruby was simply…flattened? Her life had been full of broken promises. She'd almost expected this, he thought, and it broke his heart.

And Polly… How could he spend Christmas not thinking about kissing her?

How to spend Christmas avoiding her?

Polly, however, was almost infuriatingly cheerful. She was wearing another of her amazing dresses—hadn't anyone advised her on appropriate dress for a working doctor? She'd appeared this morning in crimson stilettoes, for heaven's sake, and had only abandoned them when Joe pointed out the age of the hospital linoleum.

'Not that I don't love 'em,' he'd said, looking wistfully at her patent leather beauties. 'They're an artwork all by themselves.'

So the compromise was that a pair of crimson stilettoes brightened up the desk of reception, while Polly padded round the wards in her harlequin dress, her reindeer earrings with flashing lights and a pair of theatre slippers.

There wasn't one disapproving comment. She went from ward to ward, she helped in his routine clinic and, wherever she went, chuckles followed.

She'd offered to take over his morning clinic and, the moment people knew, it was booked out. 'Where's she come from?' a normally dour old farmer demanded as he emerged after consulting her for an allergy he'd had a while but had suddenly deemed urgent this morning. 'No matter. Wherever she came from, let's keep the road blocked. She's a keeper.'

A keeper. Right. As if that was going to happen.

Polly headed back to the house at lunch time. By mid-afternoon there was nothing else to do. It was time for Hugo to go home.

He wasn't looking forward to it.

Ruby had spent the morning at Talia's, but she was home again too. She was sitting on the veranda with Hamster on one side and Polly on the other. She looked despondent and didn't manage a smile as Hugo reached them.

Polly might have cheered the Valley up, but she was having less luck with Ruby. The promise of the beach had held the little girl in thrall for months.

'Hey.' Polly smiled, rising to greet him. 'All finished?'

'I…yes.' He was watching Ruby, thinking how impossible this was. Polly had cheered her up for a while with her laughter and her origami and her crazy flour snow, but that was surface stuff. What really mattered was trust.

Hell, he was giving up so much by being here and he couldn't even get this right. No logic in the world could get through this kid's sense of betrayal.

'So everyone's tucked up for Christmas?' Polly was still smiling, but he thought suddenly her smile seemed a bit nervous.

'Yes.'

'Then…' She took a deep breath. 'Hugo, I know this is an impertinence, and I really hope you don't mind, but I've invited guests for Christmas.'

Guests…?

He thought of all the Valley's oldies. The Valley had its share of lonely people but he'd thought they'd all been catered for. Who'd been left out? Polly was just the sort of woman who brought home strays, he thought. Which particular strays had she chosen?

'For Christmas dinner?' he asked, his mind heading straight to practicalities. 'Polly, our turkey's tiny.' It was the turkey Polly had brought—or rather a turkey breast, cryopacked, enough for a couple at most.

'Our turkey's rubbish,' she told him. 'A minnow. I gave him to Edith and Harry Banks.'

'You gave away our turkey?'

'It was actually my turkey,' she reminded him. 'I bought it from home when I thought I'd be alone here, but now a bigger one's coming.' She tried to beam but there was uncertainty behind it. 'I... If it's okay with you... It's not too late to call it off, but...'

'But what?' he said and if he sounded goaded he couldn't help it. Ruby was on the sidelines, looking just as confused as he was. He didn't need any more confusion.

This woman had blasted her way into their lives and knocked them both off-kilter, he thought, but then...maybe they'd been off-kilter since Grace died. Maybe their foundations had been blasted away and the force of Polly's enthusiasms was simply making them topple.

That was pretty much how he was feeling now. As if there was no solid ground under his feet.

'My parents...' she said. 'I've invited my parents.'

The ground didn't get any more solid. Confusion, if anything, escalated.

'You don't get on with your parents. Isn't that why you're here?'

'I ran away from home.' She looked down at Ruby and smiled. 'How dumb was that? I didn't figure it out until I saw how much your Uncle Hugo loves you that running away was crazy. And cruel. But it seems too late to run back now, so I thought I'd bring them here.'

'You ran away?' Ruby asked and Polly nodded.

'My mum and dad treat me like a little girl and I was trying to make them see I was a grown-up. But grown-ups don't run away.' She took a deep breath and looked directly at Hugo. 'They stay with those they love.'

'Do you love us?' Ruby asked, still puzzled, and Polly gave a wavery smile.

'I might. I don't know yet. But I do know I love my mum

and dad, so this morning I rang them and invited them for Christmas.'

'Didn't you say they've booked out a Harbour restaurant?' Hugo demanded.

'That's just the thing,' she told him, still trying to keep her smile in place. 'Yes, they've booked out the restaurant. They have fifty of their closest friends coming, but most of those friends have been moving in the same social circles for years so if Mum and Dad aren't there they'll hardly be missed. We were in Monaco last year and our Australian friends seemed to get on fine without us. It's me who they will miss. So I thought...'

'You'd invite them here? I thought...they don't even know you're here.'

'They do now,' she confessed. 'Wow, you should have heard the screech on the phone. And I even had to confess about the snake bite. I figured, seeing I'm referred round here as The Doc the Snake Bit, it'd be about two minutes before they found out.' She sighed. 'But I can handle it. I'll just square my chest, tuck in my tummy and face them down.'

There was a moment's stunned silence. He wanted to smile at the vision of Polly with her chest out and tummy in, but he was too...what? Hornswoggled?

Focus on her parents, he thought, because focusing on Polly was far too discombobulating. Her parents, cancelling their amazing Christmas. The best restaurant in Sydney...

'Won't your parents be paying for the restaurant?'

Polly nodded, and then her smile faded.

'They will, but they won't mind, and that's something I need to talk to you about. My parents are over-the-top generous and also over-the-top extravagant. They have the money behind them to back that up. Hugo, if that's likely to be a thing between us...if you mind...then maybe you'd better say so now.'

What was she saying? There were undercurrents everywhere. The question from Ruby, and Polly's answer, kept reverberating in his head.

Do you love us?

I might. I don't know yet.

And now…

If her parents' wealth was likely to be a problem, say so now? Was she thinking future?

'Polly…'

'Because they're coming and they're bringing Christmas with them,' she said, more urgently now. 'I rang them and said I'd love to have them here, but we have a few specific requirements. So Mum's taken it on as a personal challenge and she's loading the choppers as we speak…'

'Choppers?' he said faintly.

'A truck would be better but if the residents of Wombat Valley insist on destroying all roads, you leave us with no choice. So, are my parents welcome or not?'

'Yes,' he said, even more faintly because there was no choice.

'Great.' She gave him a wobbly smile and then she turned to Ruby. 'Ruby, if you really want—if you really, really want—then my mum and dad can put you and your Uncle Hugo into one of their helicopters and take you to the beach. That'll be fine with me. But can I tell you… My mum and dad organise some of the most exciting Christmases I know. One year I even woke up and there was a snowman in my bedroom.'

'A snowman…' Ruby breathed and Polly grinned.

'I know. Ridiculous. Ruby, I don't know what they'll do this year but I know it'll be a Christmas to remember. And it'll be a family Christmas. It'll be you and your Uncle Hugo, and me and Hamster, and my mum and dad. And presents and lovely things to eat and more presents and Christmas carols and fun. And family. You and your Uncle Hugo can go to the beach after Christmas because I'll stay on until you can, but I'd love you to stay at least until tomorrow. I'd love you to share my Christmas.'

And then there was silence.

The whole world seemed to hold its breath—and Hugo held his breath even more.

The generosity of this woman...

She'd come here to escape. She'd been bruised and battered and bitten and yet she was staying. More, she'd now invited the very people she was running away from.

She was doing this for him, he thought. The helicopters could be an escape for him and for Ruby—or they could mean something more. So much more.

A family Christmas...

'How did they put a snowman in your bedroom?' Ruby sounded as shell-shocked as he was but the fact that she required more information was encouraging.

'It was made with packed ice. We were in Switzerland. Christmas was stormy so we couldn't get out, but that didn't stop Mum getting me the Christmas snowman she'd promised me. It sat in a little paddling pool so it could melt without damaging the hotel's carpet. It had a carrot for a nose and chocolates for eyes and it was wearing my dad's best hat and scarf. Dad got crabby because they got soggy. But there won't be a snowman this year. Mum never repeats herself. There'll be something just as exciting, though. But you don't need to be here, Ruby. You can still have fish and chips on the beach with your Uncle Hugo—if you want.'

And Ruby looked at Hugo. 'What do you want to do?' she whispered and there was only one answer to that.

'I want to stay with Polly.'

'Then so do I,' Ruby whispered and then she smiled, a great beaming smile that almost split her face. 'As long as it's exciting.'

'If Polly's here, I think we can guarantee excitement,' Hugo said gravely, although there was nothing grave about the way he was feeling. He was feeling like a kid in a toyshop—or better. 'Christmas with Polly can't be anything else but excitement plus.'

The Hargreaves senior arrived two hours later, two helicopters flying in low and fast from the east. They landed on the football oval and it seemed half the town came out to see. The Christmas Eve service had just come to an end in the Valley's little church. The locals were wandering home and they stopped to look.

They saw Polly being enveloped.

Polly's mother was out of the chopper before the blades stopped spinning. Olivia was wearing a bright, crimson caftan with gold embroidery. She had Polly's auburn hair—possibly a more vivid version. Her hair was piled in a mass of curls on top of her head, and her huge gold earrings swung crazily as she ran.

Charles Hargreaves was small and dapper and he didn't run, but he still covered the distance to his daughter with speed.

Polly simply disappeared, enveloped in a sandwich hug which looked capable of smothering her.

Hugo and Ruby stood on the sidelines, hand in hand, waiting to see if she'd emerge still breathing.

For Hugo, whose parents had been...restrained, to say the least, this display of affection was stunning.

Ruby's jaw had dropped and was staying dropped. The combination of helicopters, Polly's over-the-top parents and the effusiveness of the greeting left them both awed.

But eventually Polly did break free, wriggling from her parents' combined embrace with a skill that spoke of years of practice. She grabbed a parent by each hand and drew them forward.

'Mum, Dad, this is Dr Denver. And Ruby.'

Charles Hargreaves reached forward to grasp Hugo's hand but Olivia was before him. She surged forward and enveloped him in a hug that matched the one she'd given her daughter.

'You're the dear, dear man who saved our daughter. Snake bite. Snake bite! And us not even knowing. Of all the places... And you saved her. Putting herself at such risk... We knew she shouldn't leave Sydney. Never again, that's what we said, Charles, isn't it? Never again. And what about her blood sugars? What if she'd died out here? I don't know how we can ever...'

Enough. He was enveloped in silk and gold and crimson and he had a feeling if he didn't take a stand now he'd stay enveloped for Christmas. He put his hands on her silk shoulders and put her firmly away from him.

'Mrs Hargreaves, I'm not sure what Polly's told you, but your daughter's made a very good job of saving herself.' He said it strongly, forcibly, because a glance at Polly said that this was important. Her face had sort of...crumpled?

Never again, her mother had said. What sort of strength had it taken to tear herself from these two? But she'd voluntarily brought them back—so he and Ruby could have Christmas.

'Polly's the strongest woman I know,' he continued, and he reached out and took Polly's hand. It seemed natural. It also seemed important and Polly's hand clung to his and he thought: he was right. These two were like bulldozers, and their daughter stood a good chance of being crushed by their force.

'But don't accept my word for it,' he continued. 'The whole Valley agrees. Polly came to this town as the fill-in doctor. She saved two lives the day she arrived. She looks after her own health as well as everyone else's, and she spreads laughter and light wherever she goes. You must have brought her up to be a fiercely independent woman. Her strength is awesome and the whole of Wombat Valley is grateful for it.'

They were taken aback. They stared at him, nonplussed,

and then they stared at Polly. Really stared. As if they were seeing her for the first time?

'She has diabetes,' Olivia faltered and Hugo nodded.

'We have three kids with Type One diabetes in the Valley. Polly's already met one of them. Susy's a rebellious thirteen-year-old and Polly knows just what to say. If Susy can get the same control Polly has, if she can make it an aside to her life as Polly has…well, I'm thinking Susy's parents will be as content and as proud as you must be.'

And it sucked the wind right out of their sails. It seemed they'd come to rescue and protect their daughter, but their daughter was standing hand in hand with Hugo and she was smiling. She had no need of rescue and her armour was re-forming while he watched.

'Polly said…Polly said you might bring a snowman.' Until now, Ruby had been silent. She was on the far side of Hugo, quietly listening. Quietly gathering the courage to speak. 'Polly says you make Christmas exciting.'

And it was exactly the right thing to say. Hugo's arm came around Polly. She leaned into him as her parents shifted focus.

From Polly to Ruby. From Polly to Christmas. He felt Polly sag a little, and he knew it was relief. Somehow energy had been channelled from saving Polly to saving Christmas.

Olivia looked down at the little girl for a long minute, and then she beamed.

'So you're Ruby.'

'Yes,' Ruby said shyly.

'Pollyanna said you wanted to go to the beach for Christmas.'

'We did,' Ruby told her. 'But now… Uncle Hugo and I want to stay with Polly.'

There was a sharp glance at that, a fast reassessment. Hugo expected Polly to tug away, but she didn't. Which was a statement all by itself?

'That's lovely,' Olivia said after a moment's pause. 'Can we stay too?'

'Yes,' Ruby said and smiled and Polly smiled too.

'We have spare bedrooms,' Polly said and Hugo thought *we?*

Better and better.

'Then I guess we need to get these choppers unloaded so the pilots can get back to Sydney for their own Christmas,' Polly's father said, moving into organisational mode. 'Can we organise a truck, Dr Denver?'

'A truck?'

'For the Christmas equipment my wife thought necessary.' Charles gave an apologetic smile. 'My wife never travels light.'

'Excellent,' Polly said and moved to hug her parents. 'Mum, Dad, I love you guys. Ruby, welcome to my parents. My parents are awesome.'

At two in the morning Hugo finally had time to sink onto the veranda steps and assess what had happened over the last few hours.

Polly's parents were overwhelming, overbearing, and they loved Polly to distraction. He could see why she'd run from them. They were generous to the point of absurdity and he could see why she loved them back.

They were also used to servants.

Right now he'd never been more physically exhausted in his life. Polly, on the other hand, didn't seem the least exhausted. She was happily arranging potted palms around a cabana.

There was now a beach where his yard used to be.

The centrepiece was a prefabricated pool it had taken them the night to construct. They'd started the moment Ruby had gone to bed. That had been six hours ago—six hours of sheer physical work. Because it wasn't just a pool. The packaging described it as *A Beach In Your Backyard*, and it was designed to be just that.

A motor came with the pool, with baffles that made waves run from one side to another. Hugo had shovelled a pile of sand—almost a truckload had emerged from the chopper—to lie beside it. A ramp ran up the side—it could be removed to keep the pool child-proof and safe. A lifebuoy hung to the side. Seashells were strewn artistically around. Polly had done the strewing, making him pause to admire her handiwork. There were also sun umbrellas, deckchairs and a tiny palm-covered cabana.

'Because Christmas isn't just for children,' Olivia had decreed as she'd handed over a sheaf of instructions and headed to bed herself. 'There needs to be somewhere to store the makings of martinis. And margaritas. Polly loves margaritas but she's only allowed to have one.'

His eyes had met Polly's at that and laughter had flashed between them, silent but so strong it was like a physical link.

'Don't say a word,' Polly had said direfully and he hadn't.

Charles had helped for the first hour but at the first sign of a blister he, too, had retired. Since then Hugo and Polly had laboured non-stop.

For Ruby's joy was in front of them. In the hope of Ruby's joy he'd even allowed Polly to override his own concerns.

'I want to play Santa as much as you do,' she'd decreed when he'd tried to send her to bed. 'If you fuss, Hugo Denver, I'll throw a tantrum big enough to be heard in Sydney.'

So they'd worked side by side, by torchlight and by the help of a fortuitous full moon. It was hard. It was fun. It was…wonderful.

Six hours of working with Polly was somehow settling things. There were promises being made, unspoken yet—it was much too soon—but working side by side felt right.

It was a promise of things to come? The disintegration of the walls of two different traps?

Whatever it was, now he had a beach in his front garden.

'We've taken over.' Polly had arranged her last palm to her satisfaction. Now she settled onto the step beside him and gazed at the scene before them in satisfaction. 'Goodness, Hugo, are you sure you want us here?'

For answer he reached out and took her grimy and blistered hand. It matched his grimy and blistered hand. He didn't reply. He simply held and the silence settled around them with peace and with love.

They didn't need to say a thing.

'They didn't bring buckets and spades and surfboards,' Hugo said at last, and Polly cracked a guilty grin.

'I checked the back of your wardrobe,' she admitted. 'Hugo, it pains me to admit it but I'm a Christmas snooper from way back. Let me tell you that you're very bad at hiding. The shapes of buckets and spades and surfboards take skill to be hidden and the back of your wardrobe is chicken feed in the hiding stakes.'

'So you told your parents what not to bring?'

'I told them what I thought the bumpy presents were. Mum might be over the top, but she never tries to outshine anyone.'

'Really?'

She giggled. 'Well, she never tries but sometimes she's very, very trying.' She hesitated. 'Hugo, I try not to,' she confessed, 'but I love them.'

'They're hard not to love.'

'You wait until they decide to decorate your bedroom to look like a Manhattan chic hotel...'

'They wouldn't.'

'Only if they love you.' She sighed. 'And they'll probably make you do the painting. Mum'll drink martinis and boss you as you paint. Love doesn't get boundaries.'

'It doesn't, does it?' he said softly and his hold on her hand tightened. 'Polly...'

'Hey, I didn't mean anything by that,' she said hurriedly, as if it was important that she said it. 'I wasn't hinting...'

'You don't need to hint.' He hesitated a moment more, but why not say it? It was all around them anyway.

'Polly, I'm falling in love with you,' he said softly. 'I may have already mentioned it but I'll mention it again now. I have so much baggage I'm practically drowning in it but…'

'By baggage do you mean Ruby?' She sounded incensed.

'I can't leave her.'

'I'd never expect you to. But you think you have baggage! I have Mum and Dad and I've already figured there's no use hiding from them. Wherever I am, they'll be hovering. The term "helicopter parents" takes on a whole new meaning when you're talking about my parents.'

'They love you. They worry.'

'Which infuriates me. It makes me claustrophobic.'

'Are you feeling claustrophobic now?'

'I guess I'm not.' She smiled tentatively. 'You seem to have set new boundaries. They're recalibrating their position but they won't stop worrying.'

'Maybe it's natural.' His hand held hers, gently massaging her fingers. He wanted her so much, and yet he had to say it. There was no space here for anything but truth. 'Polly, I'd worry too.'

She turned and looked at him, square-on. 'When would you worry?'

'If you let me close. As close as I want to be. And Polly, this Valley constricts your life.'

'Like my diabetes.'

'I guess…'

There was another long silence. The night seemed to be holding its breath. There was so much behind the silence, so much it was too soon to say or even think, and yet it was undeniably there.

'If you worried,' she said at last, 'then I might react with anger. I've had enough worry to last me a lifetime.'

'So you might never worry about me?'

He'd been running the hose into the pool. It was now almost full. The moonlight was glimmering on its surface. A wombat had been snuffling in the undergrowth as they worked. Now it made its way stealthily up the ramp and stared at the water in astonishment. It bent its head and tentatively tasted.

'Happy Christmas, Wombat,' Hugo whispered and Polly's hand tightened in his and she smiled.

'It is a happy Christmas. And Hugo, okay, maybe I would worry. Maybe I already do worry. You're a surgeon with amazing skills. You've uprooted yourself, buried yourself...'

'Is this what this is? Burying myself?'

She looked out again, at the pool, at the wombat, at the lights of the little hospital and at the moon hanging low over the valley. 'Maybe not,' she whispered. 'But I would still worry. And you'd have the right to tell me it's none of my business.'

'We're moving forward,' he said gently. 'Into places I hardly dare hope...'

'Me too,' she whispered. 'But maybe we're allowed to hope? Maybe we even have grounds for hoping?'

'Maybe we're stretching our boundaries,' he said softly. 'Figuring they can be stretched. Figuring how to see them as challenges and not chains.'

'I thought I was trapped by family,' she whispered. 'And you're trapped with family too. Maybe the way not to feel trapped is...to combine?'

'Polly...'

'Hush for now,' she whispered. 'Think about it. Just know that I'm thinking about it all the time.'

And it was enough, for now. They sat on, in silence, the stillness of the night enveloping them. It was too soon, too fast, there were too many things ahead of them to even think this could be a beginning, but somehow hope was all around them.

'It's almost full,' Polly ventured at last, almost inconsequentially. 'The pool...'

'That's why I'll stay sitting out here. To turn the hose off.'

'Really? I thought you were sitting because you're too exhausted to move?'

He grinned, and then he kissed her because it seemed okay. No, it seemed more than okay. No touching? *Ha!* Rules were made to be broken. The kiss was long and lingering, insidious in its sweetness and an affirmation of the future all by itself.

And then the first splash of water hit the ground and if a flooded garden was to be avoided they had to pull apart. So Hugo went to turn off the tap while Polly looked at the water, and looked up at the stars and made a decision.

'You should always trial Christmas gifts before the day,' she said as he returned to her. 'What if it's faulty?'

'The wombat already tried it.'

'And then he waddled away. What if he thought there was something wrong? He could hardly have reported it.'

'So you're suggesting…what?'

'A swim,' she said promptly. 'Just to make sure.'

'Me?'

'Both of us. It'd be kind of cool.'

'This water comes straight from the creek. It hasn't had any warmth from the sun yet. You can bet it'll be cool.'

'Chicken.' She rose. 'I'm putting on my bikini.'

'You have a bikini?'

'With polka dots. You want to see?'

'Yes,' he said fervently.

'Only if I get to see you in boxers.'

'How do you know I don't wear budgie smugglers?'

She grinned. 'You're not that type of man. I know it.'

'How do you know?'

'Intuition,' she said happily, heading up the steps to the front door. 'But it's not infallible. Will I still love you if you turn out to be a man who wears budgie smugglers? Watch this space, Dr Denver. In the fullness of time, all will be revealed.'

But he didn't follow. 'Polly, wait.' He hesitated, not because he wanted to, but because things were suddenly moving with a speed that made him dizzy. Boundaries seemed about to be crossed, and if he was to ask Polly to step over them then honesty was required. She needed to see the things he'd railed against for the last twelve months for what they were.

She turned and smiled back at him, but her smile faded as she saw his face. 'What? Are you about to tell me you've two wives and nineteen children in Outer Mongolia?'

'Only Ruby.'

'Then what's the problem?'

'Polly, there's no ER here. We have no specialists on call. There's no three hat restaurant or even a decent curry takeaway. Everyone knows everyone and everyone knows everyone else's business. If you dive into the pool in a polka dot bikini it'll be all over the town by morning.'

'Really?'

'The wombat's reporting it to the grapevine this very minute.'

She didn't smile. 'Do you hate it?' she asked and the question caught him off guard.

Did he hate it?

There'd been times in the past year when he had. There were still times when he longed for his old life, his old job, his friends. But now...

He'd learned to love this little hospital, he thought. Joe and his teasing. Barb and her incessant knitting. Mary and her worries. And his patients... He was becoming part of the lives of the Valley and he was finally starting to see why his father had worked here for so long.

But would he still escape if he could?

Not if Polly was here.

And suddenly he thought that even if she wasn't, things had changed. Polly had brought him laughter. She'd brought smiles to his little niece. She'd brought him Christmas.

But more. She'd brought him courage and, no matter what happened now, something of her would stay.

Did he hate Wombat Valley? Suddenly it was like asking: Did he hate life?

'I did hate it,' he said slowly. 'But I hadn't figured that all it needed was a dusting of polka dots.'

'And flour,' she said and grinned. 'Flour's important. And tatted angels. I'm learning fast. By next Christmas you could have tatted angels from one end of the house to the other.'

'That sounds okay to me,' he said, and it felt okay.

Actually, it felt more than okay. It felt excellent.

'But you?' he asked, because he had to be fair. He had to know. 'Polly, I will not trap you.'

And in answer she walked back down the steps and she took his hands. 'I'm not walking from one trap into another,' she said softly. 'Eyes wide open, I'm stepping into magic.'

Christmas *was* magic, he thought, as finally they broke away and he headed inside for his board shorts. Kiss or not, decision or not, Polly was still insisting on a swim and Polly was bossy and he had the gravest forebodings of bossiness to come.

He couldn't wait.

But for now they were heading for a swim and maybe it wouldn't even be cold.

For magic happened. It was the night before Christmas and the night was full of promise of magic to come.

CHAPTER FOURTEEN

HUGO HAD SLEPT for three hours or maybe a bit less before a squeal broke the stillness of dawn.

Polly had tied a balloon to the end of Ruby's bed, with a red ribbon stretching across the floor and out of the open window. Ruby had obviously found the ribbon.

There was another squeal, longer than the first, and then a yell of pure joy.

'Uncle Hugo! Polly! Hamster! Everyone! Santa's been and he's left a…a pool! There's sand and umbrellas and it's just like the beach. And there's presents piled up beside it and *ohhhhhh*…'

They heard a thud as she jumped out of her window and then hysterical barking as Hamster discovered the enormous intruder in his yard.

'I'd better sneak back to my bedroom before she finds me,' Polly murmured, laughing, and he rolled over and smiled down into her dancing eyes.

'Why would she come and find you when she has a beach?'

'Uncle Hugo!' The yell from outside was imperative. 'Come and see!'

He had to come and see. He had no choice, he thought, as he hauled on his pants and headed for the door, giving Polly time to work out a decorous strategy for her appearance.

He had no choice at all, he thought, as he walked through the front door and was hit by the world's biggest hug from the world's most excited seven-year-old.

'How wonderful!' He emerged from the hug to find that

somehow Polly had made it back to her bedroom and was leaning out of her window, smiling and smiling as she called to them both, 'Happy Christmas, Hugo. Happy Christmas, Ruby. Yay for Santa.'

He had no choice at all, Hugo thought as Ruby dragged him forward to inspect every aspect of this amazing transformation of his yard.

He hadn't had a choice twelve months ago and he didn't have a choice now.

And the strange thing was, no choice at all seemed wonderful.

Polly lay on her sunbed beside the swimming pool and thought about dozing but the world was too big, too wonderful, too full of magic.

Around her was the litter of Christmas. Ruby had woken to little-girl magic, to gifts she loved, to excitement, to fun. She was now asleep on a daybed, cuddled between Olivia and Hamster. Charles was asleep on the next bed.

Weird, wonderful, somehow fitting together...

Family.

She wouldn't run again, Polly decided. She didn't need to.

For Hugo was coming towards her, striding up the slope from the hospital. He'd gone across to check Bert Blyth for chest pain. It'd be indigestion, Polly thought. Hospitals the world over would be filling with indigestion after Christmas dinner.

'All clear?' she asked as he reached her. She stretched languorously, deliciously, and he sat down beside her and tugged her into his arms.

'All done.' He kissed her nose. 'If you stay out in the sun you'll get more freckles.'

'I have cream on.'

'I'm not complaining. I like freckles. Polly, I don't have a gift for you.' He hesitated and then kissed her again, more deeply this time. And when he put her away his smile had faded.

'It's okay,' she told him. 'I don't have a gift for you either.'

'We could take a raincheck until the roads are open. We could buy each other socks. Socks are good.'

'I don't have a lot of time for socks.'

'Really?' He was holding her shoulders, looking down into her eyes. 'Then I have another suggestion.'

'Wh... What?'

'What about a partnership?'

Her eyes never left his face. 'A partnership?'

'Polly, you know the partnership I'm thinking of,' he said, and he smiled, his best doctor-reassuring-patient smile. And it worked a treat. She loved that smile.

'But I know that's too soon,' he told her. 'So I thought... what's not too soon is a professional partnership. Wombat Valley has only one doctor and that leaves me on call twenty-four seven. That's more than enough to keep me busy. The Valley could easily cope with a doctor and a half.'

'A half,' she said dubiously. 'So you're offering...'

'Three-quarters.' He was smiling again but there was anxiety in his smile. He wasn't sure, she thought, but then, neither was she. 'Three-quarters each,' he said softly. 'A medical practice where we have time to care for our patients but we also have time to care for ourselves.'

'If this is about my diabetes...'

'It's nothing to do with your diabetes. It's everything to do with Ruby and Hamster and swimming and enjoying the Valley and making origami frogs and maybe even, in time, making a baby or two...'

'A...what?'

'Given time,' he said hastily. 'If things work out. I don't want to propel things too fast.'

'Babies! That's propelling like anything.'

'I'm sorry,' he said hastily, but he kissed her again, lightly at first and then more deeply, making a liar of himself in the process. 'No propelling,' he repeated as the kiss came to a reluctant end. 'A professional partnership first and then, if things go well…maybe more?'

'Wow,' she breathed. 'Just…wow.'

'What do you think?'

What did she think? 'If we're not propelling…I'd need somewhere to live.'

'So you would. There are a few Valley folk who could be persuaded to take in a boarder. Or,' he suggested, even more tentatively, 'we might be able to split this house. We could put a brick wall or six between us.'

'It wouldn't work.'

'No?'

'Not now I've seen you in boxers.' And without boxers, she thought, and she felt her face colour. She looked up at him and she couldn't help but blush, but she managed to smile and he smiled back.

She loved him so much. How could she love someone so fast?

How could she not?

'So you think it's too soon?' he asked.

Define too soon, she thought. Too soon to love this kind, gentle man who'd given up his world for his little niece? This skilled and caring surgeon who had the capacity to twist her heart?

This gorgeous, sexy man who had the capacity to make her toes curl just by smiling?

Too soon?

She forced herself to look away, around at her parents, at Ruby, at Hamster, then at the little hospital and the valley surrounding them.

Too soon?

'It's Christmas,' she whispered. 'Christmas is magic. Christmas is when you wave a wand and start again, a new beginning, the start of the rest of your life.'

'Isn't that New Year?'

'Maybe it is,' she said as the last lingering doubts dissipated to nothing. She tugged him back into her arms and felt him fold her to him. If home was where the heart was, then home was here. 'So we have New Year to come.'

'What could possibly happen in the New Year that could be better than right now?' he murmured into her hair, and she smiled and smiled.

'Well,' she whispered, 'if we sign for a professional partnership on Christmas Day, what's to stop another type of partnership occurring in the New Year?'

And it did.

EPILOGUE

Christmas, one year on. Dawn...

POLLY STRETCHED LANGUOROUSLY in her enormous bed, and Hugo's arm came out to tug her close. Skin against skin was the best feeling in the world, she decided. She closed her eyes to savour the moment. The dawn chorus would soon wake the house. Ruby and Hamster would burst in at any minute, but for now she could just *be*...

With Hugo.

'Happy Christmas, my love,' he murmured, and she snuggled closer.

'Happy Christmas to you too.' But as his hold tightened and she felt the familiar rush of heat and joy, she tugged back. 'Oi,' she said in warning. 'Ruby and Hamster will arrive at any second.'

'So let me announce number one of my Christmas gifts,' he told her. 'One lock, installed last night. Eight years old is old enough to knock.'

'Really?'

'Really.' His arms tightened and he rolled her above him so she was looking down into his eyes. 'So it's Happy Christmas, my love, for as long as we want.'

'Hooray!'

But the house was stirring. There were thumps and rushing footsteps and then whoops as one small girl spotted what was under the Christmas tree. And then they heard Polly's mum's voice...

'We've hidden a gift for Hamster in the backyard,' Olivia

called. 'Let's go help him find it. We'll give those sleepy-heads a few more minutes' rest.'

'Sleepyheads?' Polly murmured. 'Who's she calling a sleepyhead?'

'That would be you.' And it was true. For the last few weeks Polly had seemed to doze any time she had to herself.

The first trimester often did that. She must have fallen pregnant on the first week of their honeymoon.

It had been…that sort of honeymoon.

'But I'll defend you,' Hugo offered. 'If I can just hold you first…'

And who could resist a bargain like that?

It was good to hold. No, it was truly excellent, Polly decided some time later. She was curved against her husband's body, feeling cat-got-the-cream smug, nowhere near sleep.

Thinking *Christmas.*

Thinking *family.*

How had she ever thought family could be a trap? It had freed them all.

It had even given Hugo back his career.

For two doctors in Wombat Valley had transformed the medical scene. No doctor had wanted to practice here, knowing it meant isolation and overwork. But, with two doctors already committed, more followed.

A couple wanting to escape the rat race of Sydney had looked at Wombat Valley six months ago with fresh eyes. Doctors Meg and Alan Cartwright had bought Doc Farr's vineyard, but the vineyard was a hobby and they needed income to support it.

That meant the Valley now had four doctors, which meant there was cover for holidays. They could go to the beach. What was more, the locals no longer had to go to Sydney for thoracic surgery. A new, stable road meant Hugo could operate twice a week at Willaura. Meg's specialty was urology so she spent a couple of days in Willaura too. The rotation of surgical medical students through Willaura had increased. Hugo could even teach.

It was all Hugo wanted.

No. It wasn't all he wanted.

He wanted Polly and Ruby and Hamster. He even wanted Polly's parents, which was just as well, as Charles and Olivia were constant visitors.

They'd backed off, though. From that first day when Hugo had set the boundaries, they'd accepted them. There was even talk of them building a 'small granny flat', though Polly and Hugo had almost choked when Olivia had explained what she meant by 'small'.

That was for the future, though. For now, for this Christmas, Charles and Olivia were once again staying in their house. 'For how can we not be there on Christmas morning to share the joy?' they'd asked and who could say no? Definitely not Hugo. Definitely not Polly.

For joy was here in abundance. This morning they'd tell them about the baby. They'd already told Ruby. 'It's a secret,' they'd told her, and Ruby was almost bursting with excitement.

'Happy?' Hugo asked. They could hear Olivia and Charles, Hamster and Ruby, heading back to the house. Lock or no lock, their peace was about to be blasted.

'Can you doubt it?'

'I don't doubt it,' he murmured. 'Not for a moment.' He kissed her deeply and then swung out of bed—and paused. Polly's Christmas outfit was hanging by the window, ready for her to slip on. Red and white polka dots. A sash with a huge crimson bow. Crimson stilettoes.

'Wow,' he breathed. 'I thought we'd lost the polka dots for ever.'

'Mum had this made for me,' Polly told him. 'Seeing the snake got the last one.'

'And stilettoes...' He looked at the gorgeous dress with its tiny waist and then he looked at the high stilettoes. He grinned. 'You know, Dr Hargreaves, you may need to consider slightly more staid dressing as our baby grows.'

'Bah! Humbug!' Polly said and chuckled up at him. 'Our baby will love polka dots. Polka dots are delicious, life's delicious and so are you.'

'Package deal?'

'You got it,' she said serenely. 'I have polka dots, life and you, all tied up in one delicious Christmas package. Happy Christmas, Dr Denver. Who could ask for more?'

* * * * *

LET'S TALK
Romance

For exclusive extracts, competitions
and special offers, find us online:

- facebook.com/millsandboon
- @MillsandBoon
- @MillsandBoonUK

Get in touch on 01413 063232